Randall

or

The Painted Grape

16.06.2014

Randall

or
The Painted Grape

Jonathan Gibbs

GALLEY BEGGAR BRITAIN

First published in 2014 by Galley Beggar Press
37 Dover Street, Norwich, NR2 3LG

Typeset by Ben Cracknell Studios
Printed in the UK by
TJ International, Padstow

A CIP record for this book is available
from the British Library

ISBN 978-0-9571853-6-4

For Sarah

UNTITLED (VINCENT)

Once through customs Vincent gave the cabbie the address in Tribeca and sat back, tense and exhilarated, for the drive in. He'd never liked air travel particularly, but the journey on from the airport – that was different. The way it dropped you slap-bang into the kick and swell of life, after the enforced quiescence of the flight, and brought your heart rate up to the correct speed for wherever it was you'd arrived. Berlin, Jo'burg, Tokyo or New York.

He soon found himself sitting forward though, picking out sights as they went. The familiar clapboard houses, the awful, dull, desperate concrete-ness of it all. He barked out short laughs, where appropriate, at the cabbie's lazy, practised monologue. Saw the empty shell and spindly concrete mushrooms of the State Pavilion. The Cinemascope ad screens on either side of the Long Island Expressway, lounging like poolside movie stars against the vertical spikes and slabs of Manhattan. The canals and waterways flashing with the last flat light of the dipping sun. The skyscrapers, as they approached and overtook him, changed from the stacked microchips they seemed from a distance to some other, more confusing *trompe l'oeil* constructions: patterned motorways leading to the heavens.

His hand on the bag on the seat beside him.

Through the tunnel, and they emerged into a magic land. Every-where, people steaming along, or standing alert, as if somehow unconscious of the fact of being New Yorkers, but caught up in the workaday drama of it nevertheless. The late-shift delivery vans and street cleaners, home-going workers, breezy cyclists. He glimpsed the Empire State as they went left onto Bowery, craned ahead for a sight of the Woolworth Building.

It was six years since he'd last seen the apartment; two years at least since he'd last seen Justine; seven since Randall's death. It was a sad, paper-thin irony that, after everything they had been through, in whatever configurations, it should have taken Randall's death to put Vincent's name next to Justine's on an official document, as trustees of his estate, along with his London and New York dealers. How like him, Vincent thought, to create such an intricate cat's cradle of obligations and tensions, and then step deftly out of it, leaving them all dumbly roped together, held in place around that central, sparkling absence.

Art is the occult practice of omnipresence, of getting in people's faces when you're not there to do it. A Randallism.

She had something to show him, Justine had said.

Well, he had something for her, too.

She hadn't said what it was, and he had respected her reticence. It was something to do with Randall, that much was obvious, and something big, but he couldn't guess what, hadn't wanted to know, hadn't pressed her on the phone, lest she relent and tell him what it was after all, dissolving at a stroke the need for him to even make the trip.

Now, though, he was here, and armed. He'd been torn as to whether he should do this, how she'd react, what he meant by it at all; it was abandoned, more or less, after all, and largely forgotten. But then the call, and the desire to see her; and the moment he had taken the pages from the printer it had felt right, appropriate to the matter in hand. To the historical past, and the artefacts that attest to it. To the physical fact of the work of art, stuck there in the world.

4

At the building he paid the cabbie and let the doorman take his case. He was expected, no need to phone ahead. He followed him along to the lift. The last in a line of four, it went straight up to the penthouse.

Vincent took his stand in the middle of its mirrored quadrangle, bag over his shoulder, the hard-shell case at his side, and stared out his own reflection as the machine took him up.

When he stepped out into the lobby she was there.

'Vincent,' she said.

'Justine.'

He abandoned the case, leaving it to rock on its wheels as he stepped into her embrace. There was a split second – he could feel it, even as their bodies came together – when it could have been a brief, token hug. But it held, and lengthened, as if some mechanism had stalled, a cog slipped, or as if the muscle memory had taken over, overriding the social niceties and laying them void.

He shunted his chin minutely on her shoulder, until it found its place. He didn't want to even breathe. His nose in her hair; his arms spanning her back, one over her shoulder, the other under her arm. Her breasts pressed between them, a barrier, or the opposite of a barrier. It was incredible to have her against him again. The fit of them, even after all these years; the unchanged drop of the nape of her neck; the electric scent of her hair, as it fell over her ears; the way that, after a long moment, that he would have had still longer, she moved her hands to his arms, just above his elbows, and gave him two brief squeezes there, the signal to disengage: all these things moved him.

He stood back and took her in anew. Their eyes flicked across each other's features, scanning and assessing, logging the sly depredations of age. He was aware of being hugely affected by the lessening of her beauty. It had not gone so much as tilted in the light, lengthening like a shadow at evening. There was this thing about the light of autumn, for Randall – and, ever after, for

5

Vincent, too – the way it came low over the landscape, strafing it, throwing every blade of grass into relief. Well, now it was happening to them.

He smiled, and she smiled too, each letting their own, particular version of happiness play out across their face.

'It's good to see you,' she said.

'You know, that's just what *I* was thinking. It is *so* good to see you. You're looking wonderful, by the way.'

She said, 'Thank you,' in that strange, impossibly knowing way she had, that he'd never got to the bottom of, as if she was responding to what he'd meant to say, rather than to the words he actually managed to get out.

'Come on in. How was the flight?'

'The flight was fine.'

'And thank you for coming so quickly.'

Vincent made a hopeless gesture, that did little more than betray the obvious fact that thanks were beside the point, that he'd have rowed across the Atlantic in a kayak if she'd only asked, but thankfully she'd already turned and was leading him through into the entrance hall that opened on to the great lightbox of the apartment.

Apartment: it was too small a word. Justine and Randall's loft was a modernist cathedral that had settled atop a brownstone, a world-class gallery that someone had happened to roll a few pieces of furniture into, as if for an art installation. He'd been here before, of course, and chanced across it plenty of times in magazine spreads and books, but even then, in reproduction, it never failed to astonish, to *gladden* him. Not that he could have lived somewhere quite so dramatically, forbiddingly perfect himself, but he was pleased that someone he knew did, and that he could be persuaded to feel at home there.

He walked towards the nearest window, those massive floor-to-ceiling sheets of glass that made of the city just another work, another piece in the curatorial scheme. Manhattan: rising from the ground like a manifold shout, an endlessly complex, endlessly extended chord. The myriad lights. The hollowing dark of the Hudson. The sky, purpling to night.

He turned back to the room. Yes, it had changed, a little, from how he remembered it. Yes, it was still the same. Still Randall's, full of his presence. There, dominating one side of the space was his *Mental Mickey*, the huge angry cartoon mouse bursting out of the wall, manfully huddling a swaddled baby the size of a golf bag in its bright yellow arms.

Justine was at the kitchen counter, making them both drinks. Vincent looked to her, as if asking for permission – and she nodded, as if permission were needed – and he headed over, letting down his shoulder bag onto a sofa as he passed.

He stood under the mouse and looked up at it. It was just a maquette, a third of the size of the final piece, but still it was immense, incredible. The bodywork was just as vivid as he remembered it, as if it had been resprayed, which made no sense. He went up on tiptoes and reached to brush his fingers along the creature's fibreglass leg, raised for its leap through the wall.

Justine came over with the drinks and he struck a pose under the sculpture, making like a tourist.

'Good to see it again?'

'Very good.'

He took his drink, they clinked glasses, a little awkwardly, and he drank, watching her over the rim. She had become, he decided, more glamorous than ever. There were wrinkles under the powder, but each wrinkle was, like the sparrows to god, known, cared for, indulged.

The drink went down well, vodka-tonic with lime, all the better for being remembered. He had his hand up on the leg above his head and he knocked his fist on it, for the low hollow sound of it.

'Like an old friend,' he said.

'Nothing wrong with old friends. Plenty of them around.'

'Splendid.'

'We can do the tour if you want.'

So, whatever it was that he'd been summoned here to see, he noted with pleasure, it wasn't so urgent that it ruled out the observance of a certain patient decorum, a decorum that played out somewhat like flirtatiousness.

She gestured for him to walk with her, and they went at gallery pace, taking in the wall-hung pieces, the floor-standing sculptures, the vitrines and display cases. It was an awe-inspiring collection, if not quite in the top fifty private collections in the US, then certainly the country's best collection of British contemporary art. There was a Kevin, of course, a Crag-Martin, a Gary Hume. He spotted one of Tanya's pieces from the boat show, for the Great Day of Art, a threaded pillar of multi-coloured fabric winding up seven feet from the ground like an Indian rope trick, complete with its crucial, vicious splatters of paint.

'Ah yes,' he said, mock-earnestly. 'A historic piece.'

'I quite like it, actually.'

She was serious, he saw.

'Well,' she said. 'It wouldn't be here if I didn't, would it? Despite everything.'

'Quite.'

She linked her arm through his, and they moved on.

'Seriously though, I do worry sometimes that I'm gradually erasing him from the place. The last thing I want is to end up living in a mausoleum.'

'Of course.'

He nodded at the trio of canvases set dramatically in the centre of the far wall, that they'd been heading towards all along, that dominated the room from this end as the mouse did from the other. A Bacon pope, a Warhol electric chair, a Koons.

'Aha,' he said. 'The competition.'

'Indeed. You know they're the only things that have stayed put, right from the word Go. Everything else was just: schoom-schoom-schoom. You'd just get used to something, then, bam! There he'd be, with his Oompa-Loompas, manhandling a dozen more bubble-wrapped monsters out into the middle of the room.'

They stood in front of the three paintings. Justine laughed, a soft breath of remembrance. 'Lining them up and then walking up and down in front of them, like some, I don't know...'

'Like a sergeant major on the parade ground, inspecting the new recruits.'

'Yes, exactly. Or a merchant in an Egyptian slave market, choosing girls for his harem. Lifting their chins, checking their teeth. Matt, bring over the Kippenberger. Go there, next to Nuala. Now, both of you, go and stand over there by the Goldins.'

She was doing his voice, the gruff yowl of it, with the hint of a Brummie burr that he'd managed, by the end, to erase completely. He spoke, trying to match it.

'The *cataclysmic juxtaposition*.'

'Yes.'

'You thought he wanted them to climb down off the wall and have it out with each other, right there in the middle of the floor. Warhol versus Koons. Sargent versus, I don't know, Hockney. Ding-ding, round one.'

'Or like wrestling, American TV wrestling, when the referee wades in and starts bashing the contestants.'

He leaned in to look at the paintings more closely and she let him, their arms still linked at the elbow. He enjoyed pulling forward, feeling her resistance, enough not to get dragged along with him, not enough to break the connection.

'And you're still buying new stuff?'

'Hardly ever. Carl gives me the nod ever so often, some bright young thing he insists would go in the collection *just so*, but my heart's not in it.' She shrugged. 'Really he just wants the name on the chit.'

'I had to put a stop to it. I was just buying up old stuff. Like some old sod trying to complete his vintage Hornby collection.'

They passed a bronze torso he couldn't place, with feathers and what looked like drinking straws protruding from its sides; a pair of stacked breeze-block plinths each displaying a Sarah Lucas *Nud*, as grotesquely erotic as ever; a photograph of someone's foot, stuck directly on to a wide column with pins – a Tillmans?

They had worked their way back towards the entrance, to where the apartment extended beyond it, to the south. There, only now coming into view, on one of the interior walls, and positioned so that you wouldn't see it unless you'd been led there, Vincent saw something that stopped him dead.

It was a *Sunshines*. He moved without thought, going straight towards it, saying 'Oh my' as he went. It was, he knew instinctively and immediately, from the size of it, and the palette, one of the originals, the absolute originals: a self-portrait from Gina's studio, that first time. And just not one of. *The* original. Randall's own.

'Good God, Justine. Where did you get this?' He turned towards her. 'Is this what you wanted to show me?'

'No. No, it's not.'

He looked at her and she shrugged.

'Turns out we had it all along,' she said. 'He found it I guess a year before he died, wrapped up in one of the warehouses, but I didn't get around to hanging it until recently. You recognise it?'

'Do I? God, Justine. I haven't seen this in, what, twenty-five years.'

Its smallness was what struck him at first. Four by three, at most. Its delicacy, too. *Mental Mickey* shone as bright as it ever did, but this, for all its exuberant slamming together of colours, seemed unassuming, almost drab. Properly lit, the lurid lime green splodge, smeared across its orange background, would be acutely, eye-grabbingly unpleasant. Leaving it like this allowed the colour to hedge into the background.

The patina of the ink, up close, was what set it apart from the obvious Warhol comparisons. There was something almost visible, being dragged along under the surface. He thought of sand at low tide, how it lay in ripples and ridges, dragged grain by grain into a particular arrangement by the departing sea.

He shook his head, as if in disbelief.

'What are you thinking?'

She was right next to him, and he had to suppress the impulse to take hold of her, to squeeze her arm, or drag her against him, or into him; to butt his head into her body, her shoulder, her breasts: anything to get across that what he was *thinking* wasn't the half of it. He contented himself with blinking and pulling a face, an attempt to fit all of this into his expression – or the sense of the scale of it, of the inexpressibility of it: of seeing it, and her, and this place.

She stayed silent, letting him look. Then, eventually, she said:

'Have you seen *you*, then, recently?'

'How do you mean? His one of me?'

'Yes.'

'Not in ages. There's Jan's one in Amsterdam, of course. But that's been years. And the other one of me, that went to Sheikh Hamad, I guess that's still in Qatar. I should have bought it when I could. No way I'll ever be able to afford it now.' The thought jumped in his mind and he looked at her. 'You haven't found another one, have you? Of me? That's not what this is?'

She smiled, shook her head.

'Sorry, no.'

'Ah well.' He realised he was blushing.

They ate at the large glass table by the kitchen, with its vases of delicate, dipping red flowers and oriental lilies. The conversation stuck to safe topics, careful questions answered in considered, uncomplicated terms. He asked about Joshua, and she told him he was well; better, really, than he'd ever been, both health-wise and happiness-wise. Living in Brooklyn, and in his first year at the New York Film Academy, though he still had his room here and usually spent a night or two with her every week or so. Very much fallen in with the art crowd, quite funny really. All Dumbo and Williamsburg and beyond. No doubt he'd drop by at some point. She talked a little about the consultancy, the time she spent in Japan, less each year, the work she did for the Zen Temple here.

When he talked of his life, he didn't mention the manuscript, instead evoking a quiet existence of gym, golf, the villa outside Montalcino, the uninvolving day or so a week his directorships demanded, a bland roll-call of unengaging social engagements.

Afterward, she made coffee and carried it to the set of sofas by the north-facing windows. He sat down, with his bag beside him, and took out the leather wallet. He waited until she looked up from pouring the coffee, then he said, 'I've brought something for you. Something that I want you to see.'

'What's this, then?' she said, passing him a cup.

He took the cup and wondered, as he held out the wallet in return, if he couldn't discern the first glancing edge of falseness in her voice.

She took it and turned it in her hands, looking up at him enquiringly. It occurred to him: she already knows what it is.

'It's just something I've been working on,' he said, 'In my spare time.' He was aware suddenly of how fast he was talking. 'Spare time, being, obviously, something of an asset right now. I should have had it wrapped for you, or found a box or something for it, some tissue paper.'

She smiled, then opened the flap and edged out the block of paper.

He cleared his throat. 'I've been trying to write about Randall. Just, you know, what happened. What it was like, the whole mad thing.'

This time she didn't look at him, but took up the first page. He craned his neck to follow her eyes. The text on the cover sheet seemed awfully big: 'Everywhere I Look: A Memoir of Randall' it read, and, underneath, 'By Vincent Cartwright.' In fact, he had been in two minds as to whether to include a title like that at all, but it seemed wrong not to have anything, to just thrust your words without warning into someone's face.

'It's not very... I mean, it's not finished or anything. It's a bit weird, I suppose.'

'Wow. How long have you been doing this? Have you got a publisher, or an agent or something?'

'God, no. It's not at that stage, nowhere near. I don't even know why I'm doing it, really. But, well, I wanted you to see it.'

She looked at him, then looked at the next page. He could read, or recognise, the words, upside down. 'The first time I laid eyes on Ian Randall Timkins, better known to the world as simply Randall, the most celebrated and reviled artist of the 90s and 00s...'

He felt his confidence wash from him. Whenever he had thought about this moment, even just hours ago, on the flight over, it had always been the handing over that he imagined. The gift of it, the revelation. As if two hundred pages of prose could be taken in at a glance, like you take in a piece of art in a gallery. The thought of her actually reading it was, he realised, agonising. She might even want to read some of it right now. Or, worse still, feel obliged to do so.

She skimmed a moment, then flicked on a page, then ten, then opened the sheaf at halfway – the soft sound of paper falling against itself – and scanned what she found there. Then she replaced the top half of the stack.

'Vincent, thank you. I'm going to have to read this properly.'

She rested her palm on the top sheet, a gesture of benediction, or containment, then sat herself upright, stretching her back, and looked straight at him.

'But maybe I'd better show you first what it was I wanted *you* to see.'

'Okay,' he said. He said it slowly, dragging the word out. He didn't want to appear too casual, but nor did he want to leave himself exposed. It might not be that important at all. Or else it might.

'Right then.'

She put the manuscript down on the table, then got up. He followed her across the main living area of the apartment into a corridor on the opposite side from the entrance, that led to a large office. There were computer desks and high shelves stacked with books and box files and other random objects. In the middle of the room stood a large architect's cabinet with six drawers and, for its top, a square lightbox, its surface cloudy and opaque.

She unlocked the cabinet, then took from the top drawer a portfolio, four or five feet long on its longest side, which she placed on top of the cabinet.

She undid the zip which ran along three of its sides, then paused and looked at him. He gave her a look of bemused encouragement, and put on his glasses, to show he was ready. Her smile back was short and tight, like the smile of someone struggling with a key in a lock. It said that what was coming was important, after all, and probably not a thing to smile about. He went on smiling, to show that he understood, that that was fine.

But still, he thought, he wanted this to be over, whatever it was. He wanted to go back and find the ambiguous, fuzzily significant mood of the evening so far, that seemed to have vanished all of a sudden. He wanted to tell her that, whatever it was, it didn't matter – that it was her he had come to see, not this thing of Randall's. That, much as he loved his friend, and honoured him, nothing to do with him could mean as much to him, now, as he felt that she did, or might again.

She laid the portfolio open. In it was paper – works on paper, big sheets, a number of them, covered with a gauzy protective sheet. She turned the whole thing on the light box so it was facing him, then lifted away the top sheet.

It was a watercolour, barely smaller than the portfolio, rough at the edges and curling slightly along one axis. It was a portrait, a nude: it was a woman sitting on a bed, hands between her legs, holding apart the folds of her cunt.

Vincent looked up at Justine, giving himself only enough time to see if she was looking at him. She was. He looked back down, and felt the familiar, creeping sensation of vertigo, of being put on the spot. He forced himself to look harder, to *see* the painting. It could have been Schiele, could have been Freud, a sicker, more morbid Freud. The aggressive, angular style that chipped away at her flesh. The dark, deliberate lines of what was probably pen ink following the edges of her limbs, that bled slightly into the pale wash of the paint.

He reached out and held a finger so it wobbled just merely above the surface of the painting.

'What is this?' he said, sounding almost angry. 'You're not telling me this is him, are you?'

Justine did not answer his question, but shifted the painting sideways onto the open lid of the portfolio, then the next protective sheet, to expose the next piece. It was her – it was Justine – on her knees on a bed, the same anonymous rumpled bed as the first one; he noticed the sheets, the dishwater grey for the material and dark inked cracks for their creases. Randall couldn't have done it, he thought, it was too good. Could he?

She was leaning on her elbows with her face resting on her fists, eyes bulging and tongue lolling like a dog's. The artist had lingered on the face, working the paint to blend the red of the cheeks into the other features. It was grotesque. A plump, happy Justine, as doughy and plain as the first woman was squeezed and twisted. Behind her, barely filled out by comparison, a cartoon, was Randall, one foot up on the bed, hands pressing down on her arse, neck tendons straining and face uplifted in the agony of release. A third figure stood watching, sketched in pencil only.

'Justine, you're going to have to help me out here.'

She held his gaze and shifted the second picture, to show the third.

'Bloody hell,' he said, catching the edge of a laugh.

He was looking at a pen and ink drawing of himself. Himself, fucking Randall. Randall standing with one foot up on a chair, while he – Vincent – worked and pushed at him from behind, hands tight around his waist, forcing him up on his toes. The Randall figure was arching away from him, his fingers splayed in stiff bony bridges against a wall not shown, as if they could conduct along them and discharge the pain explicit in his face and his posture. The look on his own face was, horribly, one of eager surprise. He was twisting to look around from the back, his face aglow like a child at Christmas, for the sight of the presents heaped up under the tree.

Vincent put his hand to the sheet again, and shifted it, hearing the sound it made against the sheet underneath.

'How many of these are there?' he said.

'Here? I've got about ten of them here.'

'*Here*? There are more?'

'Oh yes, Vincent. There's more.'

He closed his eyes, and spoke, clearly and deliberately.

'Look, just to be a fucking idiot for a moment. Are you seriously telling me these are his?'

And he opened his eyes.

'As far as I can tell, yes, they're his. That's why I wanted you to see them. I wasn't about to trot off down to Christie's with them, was I?'

16

'Sure. But did you *know* he was doing these?'

'Of course I didn't know he was doing them,' she said, evenly. 'I only found out they existed four days ago. And well, look, do you know who she is?' She shifted the pictures to point to the first one, the woman on the bed.

'No. Should I?'

'It's Con Eckhart.'

'Con Eckhart at *Sotheby's*?'

'Yes.'

'Shit.'

'Yes, well. Let's see who else we have here.' Justine covered up Con Eckhart with herself and Randall, then Randall and him. Underneath was a naked man standing, one hand resting on the hilt of a huge medieval broadsword that he was holding point down next to him, while two women knelt before him, mouths open to accept his cock. The man was Albi Reinger, one of Randall's most loyal European collectors. One of the women was Raissa Hansel. The other was Maria Bergqvist from the Serpentine. The next picture showed a three-way arrangement between Robert Rauschenberg, Fi McKenna and Carl, Randall's US dealer, each with a hand inserted to the wrist into one of the others' mouth, anus or vagina.

What he was looking at, if it was by Randall, was incredible. It was a million things, but the thing that it was before it was anything else was incredible. This isn't what he did. Or rather, this is exactly what he did, but not like this.

The paper shifted, and he was looking at a most strange composition, with Loretta Reis, who'd dedicated so many *New York Times* column inches to castigating him – squatting over a recumbent Randall like an imp out of Goya, one hand around his erect penis, the other holding back her hair so she could look out at the viewer, while she pissed in a soft sputtering stream into Randall's open mouth. Looking on, wearing a shirt and tie but naked from the waist down, and masturbating with characteristic reserve, was Jan de Vries.

No one would believe it. Except that belief didn't come into it. This was him, it was him through and through.

He looked up at her.

'Has Carl seen these?'

'Vincent, please. He's the *last* person I'd show them to.' She leaned towards him, over the portfolio, spacing the words. 'The only people who have seen these paintings are you and me.'

He turned back to the remaining pictures. They showed similar couplings and combinations, and though he didn't allow himself to linger he gradually began to accept how good they were: the colouring, and the line. *Were* they Randall? Or could he have got someone else to do them, to his instructions? He put his hand to the face of Florian Duerr, from Art Basel, thrown back in wavering ecstasy as Randall and Tom Nasmith each bit down on one of his nipples. It wasn't just that they were so grossly, venomously offensive, but that they were so embarrassingly intimate. They had none of the too-good-to-be-true verisimilitude of photo-realism, that let you doubt it because it seemed so real. This was rough, and immediate, and it was impossible to believe they weren't from life.

He slid Duerr over, and there – it was the last one in the pile, or the next to last – was Randall, alone, masturbating, his right leg raised and his left arm arced over his head, like he was doing some demonic monkey dance. He thought of Hindu deities, Shiva or Kali. Kali, for the gargoyle face, similar to the one Randall had given Justine in the other picture, deliberately making himself look foul and ridiculous.

He laughed, and slid that one aside.

Under it was a painting of Vincent himself and Justine.

He felt the skin on his temples tighten, a rush of something leaving or passing though his head.

They were fucking against a wall, she flopped forward onto it, torso and belly pressed flat, and arms stretched out above her head. She looked fat, the round weight of her near-most arm half hiding her face. He was behind her, his arms reaching around her body, hands cupping her breasts, even as she used her breasts to squash his hands against the wall. His bent knees pushing into the backs of her calves, forcing up her buttocks towards him. His face on her back, skin against skin, turned sideways towards the viewer, the painter. Both of them with their eyes closed and their mouths open and trying, at least, for happiness.

She came around the table to stand next to him.

'Beautiful, isn't it,' she said.

He laughed again, from relief. 'Yes, I suppose it is.'

He touched the painting, then went to realign the last one, of Randall, so he could look at them together. The sound of the grain of the paper as it slid, sifting, across the one beneath.

'Well, Justine. I don't know what to say. They're quite extraordinary.'

'Vincent.'

'Yes.'

'These are sketches.'

'Sketches? How do you mean?'

'The real ones are in oils.'

'The real ones?'

'Oils and acrylics. There are over forty of them.'

'Fuck me. Where?'

He caught the smile as it twisted itself in the corner of her mouth. She looked down and began sorting the watercolours back into one pile. 'Well, yes. Not here. I'll show you tomorrow. Sixty watercolours, hundreds of drawings, thirty or forty *major works*, some of them six by ten.'

'Christ. I don't know what to say. And they're all...'

'Yes. They're all like that.'

'Fuck me, has he left anybody *out*?'

'No. I think it's fair to say that anybody who could possibly be offended by them, by what they show, and what they seem to say, is in there. Now then.' She closed the folder and put it back in its drawer, then locked it and pocketed the key. 'Would you like another drink? *I'd* like another drink.'

He got halfway to the door, then stopped.

'Are they good though?' he said, and he heard the husk in his voice, how it nearly gave way to something else. 'I mean, these are good, but could he paint? Really?'

'Oh, he could paint alright.' Then, quietly, 'Some of them are quite magnificent.'

She switched off the light and stood, holding the door open for him.

'Justine,' he said, and she tipped her head on one side, to show he had her attention. 'You know that thing I gave you to read?' She nodded. 'You're not going to read it, are you?'

'Not if you don't want me to.'

'No, I don't. I don't want you to. Don't read it.'

'Okay, I won't.'

'Thank you.'

PERFECT CIRCLE

The first time I laid eyes on Ian Randall Timkins, better known to the world as simply Randall, the most celebrated and reviled artist of the 90s and 00s, was at the opening of his degree show at Goldsmiths, in the summer of 1989. I went to the show not because I had any interest in up-and-coming artists – I was a trader at LIFFE in the City and the only art on my bedroom wall was a framed and signed poster of supermodel Cindy Crawford – but because of a woman I knew. She was called Emily and she worked in marketing, specialising in 'guerrilla marketing', the seeding of products among taste-setters and early adopters. One of her clients was a brewer that wanted to get a buzz going for a new brand of imported beer, and part of how she did this was by identifying groups of hip young things in the worlds of music, art and fashion, and offering to supply their events and parties with cases of the stuff, often hundreds and hundreds of bottles. Despite what you might think this was often a thankless task – those hip young things tended to show their gratitude for all this free booze by being at best condescending, at worst dismissive or actually quite vilely nasty – and I sometimes used to go along with her as moral support.

Randall's degree show came the year after the Freeze warehouse show, organised by a young Goldsmiths artist called Damien Hirst, which featured a swathe of his contemporaries from that college, some of whom (Mat Collishaw, Sarah Lucas) went on to huge success. Hirst himself was hit by a train and killed, apparently when drunk, not far from his childhood home in Leeds, in February 1989. He remains an ambiguous figure in the myth and history of recent British art, seen by some as a tragic lost figurehead. There are even those who say that Randall only ever finished what Hirst had started, stepping into his shoes and taking the credit for heading up what would come to be called the Young British Artists. While there may be a grain of truth in this – Randall did know and admire Hirst, who was two years ahead of him at Goldsmiths – the truth is that Hirst was untested as an artist. His contribution to Freeze was by all accounts uninspiring, consisting of a pile of painted cardboard boxes, and a pattern of coloured dots painted directly on to the wall. Neither has survived. The show, however, was a seminal event, for the sense it gave that, despite the recession, London was ready to challenge New York and Cologne as a centre of the art world. This sense of excitement was something that Emily thought she could use, which is why we found ourselves that hot July evening in this particularly dingy corner of south-east London, so far from our usual stomping grounds.

We were late arriving, and when we got out of our cab, there were people streaming out of the main college building. When I asked someone where the private view was, they laughed and told us not to bother. The free booze had run out and everyone had gone to the pub. Fair enough, we said, and followed along.

The Duke of Devonshire was the pub of choice among Goldsmiths art students at the time. It was a traditional boozer, the sort of place that doesn't exist anymore, with cheap, bad beer and worse wine, its comprehensively ruined furnishings skulking within a fug of cigarette smoke. I hated it then, but of course now I look back on it with unalloyed nostalgia.

The clientele of the Devonshire was a volatile mix of art students and locals – proper drinkers, as permanent and raddled as the furniture. They regarded the students with absolute disdain, while at the same time tolerating them as an unending source of moans, bitching and letching. Randall, of course, they loved. It was always fun to watch him wade into the thick of their tables, pint in hand and fag in gob, shaking hands and exchanging greetings left and right. The old sods would welcome him among them like one of their own, pulling out a chair and slapping it on the seat to get him to sit, asking him how the bloody hell he was doing. We could only watch from the margins. Occasionally someone would try to follow him into this hostile territory, usually a girl who was trying to mark some kind of claim on him, and we'd happily hang back and watch as she got glared down, or dismissed with a gruff, unanswerable 'Alright, love. Can I help you?' Randall would tell us to go on up, he'd be along in a minute, and we'd go and sit there, in the top room, waiting for him to come – and taking the piss out of him for being such a working-class hero.

'How are the old folk, then?' we'd say, when he joined us, laying on the Cockney accent. 'How's old Bert? How's old Martha?' And he'd reply, 'Fine and dandy, people, fine and dandy.' Then he'd tap the side of his nose and say, 'Got a sure thing from Eric, in fact. Tomorrow at Aintree. Can't lose,' and we'd laugh and get back to our drinking, but I don't suppose we could have said any longer who we were laughing at: them, or Randall, or ourselves.

The top room was where we went that night. I remember standing in the scrum of the downstairs bar, dressed in what would probably have been an Armani suit, and looking at the stairs, which were practically impassable from the bodies squeezed onto them, sitting and standing and leaning, all gabbing furiously, deafeningly away. My heart sank. We could have been at Harry's Bar with everyone else, or moving on somewhere for food. I wondered how easy it would be to find another cab out here.

'Are you sure you want to do this?' I said to Emily.

She did, so I got us drinks and we made our way up the stairs, stepping over and around the legs and elbows. The room was rammed. Everyone was jostled together in one thick morass, drinks pressed up against chests. The noise was relentless, a battle between the music, coming from a DJ set up at the far end of the room, and the barrage of human voices, all of them raised to levels of hysterical, drunken excitement. I looked with dismay out over the bad hair and ludicrous clothes – as if the 80s had never happened. We inched our way through the jam of bodies towards the DJ, asking for sightings of Randall as we went. We repeated our request to the nodding, bobbing figure at the decks, headphones clamped to one ear in that self-absorbed, cooler-than-thou pose these people always had. He bent down to talk to someone behind his table and the someone stood up to see who it was.

The someone was Randall, holding a screwdriver and a length of speaker cable, jack plug dangling comically.

'Hi, you're Randall, right?' I shouted, leaning right across the table to him.

'Yeah,' he shouted back, grinning wildly as he looked from me to Emily and back again.

'I'm Vincent. This is Emily. She's from Second Sight PR.'

'Hang on,' he said. 'I'm coming round.'

He came round the table and shook our hands. He was taller than me, and wider, and he pumped my hand hard, embarrassingly so, as if we were his oldest pals and he was particularly glad that we of all people had come. I got that heart-sinking feeling you get when you realise you're trapped at a party with the king of uncool.

'So, did you see the show?' he asked.

Emily shook her head. 'No. We ended up coming straight here, I'm afraid. We should really pop our heads in, shouldn't we?' This looking over at me. I nodded thoughtfully, as if actively considering it.

But Randall just laughed. 'Sod that. If you're that keen you can come back and see it another time. We're here all week.' He did a little sweep of the arms, like a bad comedian. 'In fact,' he said, 'I wouldn't be surprised if we *were* here all week. Come on, there's some people I want you to meet.'

I assumed this was some kind of low tactic, and we were about to be off-loaded onto the saddest and geekiest sub-set of this crowd of basically, as far as I was concerned at the time, Grade A geeks and saddoes. But no, as it turned out, they were his friends, his friends among this crowd of his friends: the inner circle. Present on that first occasion were Kevin Nicholson-Banks, Tanya Spence, Frank Greene, Gina Holland. There must have been a dozen other names of that stature in the room (Matthew Collings says in his memoirs that he was there), but those were the ones that I remember. They were the ones that we broke into the college with that night.

Randall led us over to the huddled group off to the side of the DJ's table and shouted a round of introductions that no one could hear. They seemed happy enough to let us join them. We tried to show interest, and ask them about the show, but they waved the questions down. They seemed happier just being loud and joking and dancing, or doing the closest possible approximation of it. All hands in the air, eyes closed and lips caught between teeth. I assumed they were all on ecstasy. You'd have to be, would have been my thought, to be actually enjoying yourself in a hole like this. (Though the last time I set foot in The Duke of Devonshire, which must be ten years ago now, I was served a café macchiato better than any you could have had in London in 1989, outside of Soho.)

Fine, I thought, so long as we're here, there's no point in acting like a ponce. I counted heads in our little group, excused myself and went to the bar to get in a round of tequilas. You will occasionally find someone in life who doesn't like champagne, but no one – no one under thirty – ever turns down tequila. People warmed to us considerably after that. Randall seemed – not pleased as such, but gratified, as if the tequila was a genuine and considered gesture.

Which had the strange effect of making me think that maybe it had been.

What were my first impressions of him?

Well, as before, my very first thought was: what a dork.

Pen portrait of the unknown, pre-fame Randall: a tall, frizzy-haired, lumpen idiot of a man, too sparky and genial to be the brute you might have taken him for across the room. The hair pulled back in a pony-tail, one stud earring in the left ear. Mouth always hung slightly open, to give you a sight of the far from perfect teeth within it. Huge, grabbable nose. Oblong face with the mottled colouring of cheap meat, spam maybe. Dry skin, shaving rash and dandruff.

Maybe I'm laying it on a big thick, but no one ever accused Randall of being one of the beautiful people, inside or out. The hair was particularly unpleasant, the hangover from teenage years spent as a committed metal-head. When he arrived at Goldsmiths, aged twenty, he was by all accounts still sporting his studded denim jacket, with Eddie, Iron Maiden's skeletal zombie, leering out at you from its back. It was acid house and ecstasy that cured him of that inclination, just as it was the rave scene, rather than any image consultant or ultra-fashionable hairdresser, that eventually lost him the ponytail.

You might say that, in repose, it was a horrible, even an unforgivable face. But it never *was* in repose. The eyes never stopped looking, flicking this way and that, but always returning to dig into you, as if he was expecting you to do something extraordinary – or extraordinarily stupid – at any moment. The mouth, with its shark-like incisors, always showing the first millimetre of the next smile, the next goofish aphorism or point-blank put-down or ranting, reeling proclamation.

As for clothes, it's a fair guess to say he was wearing a plaid shirt, or similar, jeans or combat trousers, and that perennial item: his leather jacket. If there's one thing that somehow *stands* for Randall, in those early years, it's the jacket. Blazer-cut, rather than biker-style, crinkled and split in a hundred places, it must have come from the sickliest animal in the herd. It survives in a hundred photos, but the article itself went onto the Millennium Eve bonfire at Peploe, the house in Cornwall belonging to Gina Holland's family. I remember coming across its half-burned carcass lying in the ashes of the fire on the morning – or, more likely, the afternoon – of New Year's Day, 2000, a pitiful, stillborn phoenix. That event, too, will get its moment in this story: the Millennium, which everybody – not just us, *everybody* – thought was the beginning of something. Of course it wasn't. It wasn't the beginning of anything. It was the end of something.

When the pub kicked out, we headed back to someone's house. (Emily decided to call it a night, and I put her in a cab home.) What happened then is the perfect opportunity to show how the reality of being around Randall differed from the myths and tall tales that have tended to grow up around him. I don't want to suggest that everything you might have read or heard about him is wrong, or hopelessly exaggerated. It's more complicated than that. And, over the years, I've been as guilty as anyone of adding to that atmosphere of hype, of accentuating the exotic and the outrageous for the journalists, and the collectors, and just the ordinary people who asked, when they found out that I knew Randall, what he was *like*. Perhaps the simple fact is that an event or moment such as those I experienced with Randall has to be embellished or inflated when you tell it to someone who wasn't there, just to give a sense of the scale and the thrill that you would have got, to be there, inside that moment. So, to set the record straight (if such a thing is even possible) we didn't actually 'break in' to Goldsmiths. Randall didn't vandalise his own show, or try to set it on fire. Nor did he climb in through a window, although he, and the rest of us, did climb out of one.

What happened was that, as the party downshifted from dancing to sitting, people did get around to talking about art, discussing the different works: the good, the bad and the wonderfully, peerlessly awful. It was the end of their time at the college, so they were keen to look both back and forward, to pass final judgment and extend fantastical prophesies.

At one point I turned to Randall and asked him what it was he'd done.

'It's called *Perfect Circle*,' he said.

He took a final, squint-eyed draw on a joint, and passed it to me.

'*Perfect Circle*,' I said.

'Yeah. There's this famous story about the Renaissance painter Giotto, who lived in Florence in the thirteenth century. He's got this great painting of Judas giving Jesus the traitor's kiss.'

'A fresco.' This was Kevin Nicholson-Banks, sat on the floor, head tipped back on the sofa, where someone, possibly a girl, was stroking his hair. 'Early fourteenth century. The Scrovegni chapel in Padua.'

'Early fourteenth. Gotcha.' Randall gave Kevin an ironical salute, and went on. 'Anyway, Judas looks really creepy, he's shorter than Jesus and kind of ugly and bulky and he's got his arm up on Jesus's shoulder, like he's going to wrap him in his cloak and drag him down to hell.'

'He looks like a fucking monkey. That's what he looks like.'

'Thank you, Kevin. Anyway, that's not the point. The point is, one day the Pope sent a messenger to Giotto because he was thinking of commissioning some work from him, some frescos or whatever. The messenger asked him for a sample of his work. Presumably he was expecting Giotto to give him a few nice Biblical scenes to take back, but Giotto just took a piece of paper and painted a perfect circle in the middle of it, and gave him that.'

I laughed. 'Good man. Did he get the job?'

'He did. I guess the Pope knew his shit. And so, all I've done is copy Giotto. He had to convince God's representative on earth he had the shit. I've got to convince a bunch of professors and external examiners. Obviously, I'm not putting myself up there with Giotto, but I thought, if I can produce a decent circle, then how can they not pass me?'

'And? How do you think you've done?'

'Not bad. I guess I've done about four thousand circles. I reckon there are six or seven really good ones.'

'How about now?' I asked. 'Could you do one now?'

I think this was the point at which Randall really noticed me. Perhaps this was even when the possibility of our friendship was born. For myself, I'd only known him a few hours, but still I knew, or perhaps I didn't know, but it was true nonetheless, that I wanted to know him better. He had something I wanted, though what it was I couldn't have said.

'I think we could do that. Yes.'

Someone passed him a piece of paper and a pen and he kneeled on the carpet and cleared a space on the coffee table. He settled himself – there was a lovely touch of the maestro in the way he shot his sleeves, rolled his shoulders and coughed – then he tucked his elbow into his side, gave a couple of quick ghost arcs above the white and calmly, not fast at all, drew the pen round, barely touching the paper, it seemed, but leaving a line behind it. One movement, and it was done.

It was indeed a very good circle, and I clapped and whooped along with everyone else, though I couldn't help looking round to check for tell-tale smirks or other evidence of conspiracy. I was enjoying myself tremendously – I'd turned down the offer of half an E, but was carried along on the general tide of positive vibes, a high by association – but I wasn't yet comfortable enough in their company, let alone in my understanding of art, not to worry that I was being taken for a ride.

31

Randall raised his hand, acknowledging the general applause, and waved the piece of paper towards me.

'There you go,' he said.

I grinned, and reached out to take it. It felt, that moment too, like a connection being made. But, just as I was about to take hold of it, he whipped the sheet back out of my grasp.

'No,' he said. 'I've got a better idea. Let's put it with the rest.'

His eyes were fixed on me, but I could tell it was the reaction of the others he was waiting on.

'Come on. Vincent hasn't seen the show. What better time?'

In the end it was about eight or nine of us that made the trip out of the house and up the road to the college. Some of us may have been apprehensive about the plan, or dubious as to its chances of success, but we all, drunkenly, or druggedly, but anyway obediently, trooped along behind him as Randall strode up to the entrance.

He leaned close to the doors to look through them, then rapped on the glass. After a moment the security guard appeared; of course, he knew Randall. He opened the door and listened while Randall sweet-talked him into letting us in. The degree show at this time was held in the Richard Hoggart building, the Georgian red brick building that is still the college's public face. (In 2005 Randall and I, together with Justine and various other luminaries, attended the opening of the Ben Pimlott building, just around the corner. Designed by Will Alsop, with its eye-catching 'squiggle' sculpture, this is where the degree shows are held these days, along with – amusingly enough – the old swimming baths on Laurie Grove. I remember standing with Randall out on the roof terrace, underneath the sculpture, on a blustery and rainy January evening, and marvelling at the view of London – New Cross being, no less than Primrose Hill, somewhere that gives you a *perspective* on the place. Specifically, it shows the way these twin eruptions of finance, the City and Docklands, old money and new, dominate the skyline. Goldsmiths seemed like the third point of a triangle, part of an exercise designed to chart the invisible flow of money and influence around the capital.)

The guard accepted our promises to behave, and not to take too long, then Randall stood holding the door and smiling maniacally at us as we filed in. It was my first time inside the building, obviously, and the long corridors and marble floors looked far more impressive in that severe, mechanical light, devoid of people, than they ever did during the daytime. We went through a couple of sets of double doors to the gallery rooms, and I was given a tour of the other students' work. There was some photography and the odd weird painting (Frank Greene's early 'acid cloud' pieces were there) but most of it, it seemed to me, was made up of installations (Gina Holland's betting shop, complete with shop dummies, Aya Inouye's rugs made from unstitched canvas sneakers). I observed these solemnly enough, but I had no way of getting a handle on them whatsoever. They looked to me like nothing more than poorly executed parodies of what sculptures are supposed to be like, done by someone who'd never actually seen one, and that had been stood squarely in the middle of the big, white-painted rooms as if to shame them.

Then we came to Randall's space.

There was a long table in the middle of it, covered in pieces of paper, some of them messily collected into piles, some spread out, as if at random. Pots with pens, brushes and other bits and pieces, a basic office chair on wheels. There were more sheets on the floor: a carpet of rejects, scuffed and torn. And on the wall, pinned or taped, more again: these the chosen, the miraculous few that approached perfection. Each sheet blank but for its circle: some thin of line, some thick, some monochrome, some coloured. The walls made for a gallery of empty targets, a hundred zeros without a one to put in front of them.

'They're all the same,' I remember thinking, as I strolled around the room, can of beer in hand, looking at them all and trying to look like I was thinking the kind of thoughts I guessed the rest of them would be thinking; trying to *think* the thoughts. 'All circles are the same. There aren't any other kinds.' That was the limit of what I my hazed, untutored brain could produce.

Taken as a whole, it was certainly impressive. At that time of night, with our words and footfalls echoing off the white-painted plywood flats that divided the room into individual spaces, but without diminishing the sense of Georgian grandeur, it was certainly spooky. Drunk, and a bit stoned, and otherwise intellectually high on my sudden ingress into this strange new world, I was perfectly willing to accept that it was art.

Randall wanted to decide where 'my' circle should go – he had a scoring system, with different bits of wall given over to the different grades – so we amused ourselves for a time by debating its merits and deficiencies, sharing round the beers, smoking more cigarettes and joints out of a back window.

Then things got a little silly.

Someone made a paper aeroplane from one of the circle drawings on the floor, and aimed it across the room. Someone else responded, and soon we were in the midst of a full-on paper ball fight, that quickly spread out into the other rooms. For five, maybe ten minutes we charged around the suite of rooms, ducking and lunging and hiding and hurling our ineffectual missiles, swearing and joking and reeling off quotes from films. As well as each other, we used other art works, installations and paintings and photographs, as targets. The artists made yelping reference to liminal trajectories and the necessity of reconfiguring the canon as they hurled around their scrunched-up balls of paper.

Interestingly, although we used the sheets on the table and the floor, no one touched any of the ones on the wall – I say interestingly because, looking back on the show, and with a degree more knowledge about how to read these things than I had then, it is clear that the quality of the best circles was not what the show was about. Randall constantly railed against what he called 'the tyranny of technique'. Anyone who thought art had to be skilfully executed, or look good, was in thrall to outmoded ideas. Randall must have found it ironical to the point of quaintness that we – even the most advanced, theoretically-minded of his peers – left the most 'perfect' circles alone.

The game came to a close when someone nearly fell into a tall, thin sculpture made out of umbrella frames, and it was decided we'd better stop before something actually got damaged. Randall went and opened a window to smoke out of, his chest heaving with laughter and exertion. He put a cigarette in his mouth, picked up a ditched plane from the floor, twisted it into a spill and put his lighter to it, then used the burning sheet to light his cigarette. I stood next to him, took an offered fag and leant in, but it burned out before I could get the cigarette going. Randall lit another sheet, and that one did the job. We'd got three or four sheets in flames, passing from person to person, before the fire alarm went off, together with the water sprinklers.

We rushed around under the fine spray, laughing and choking, trying to gather together as many of the sheets as possible and shelter them under the table.

'The guard's coming,' someone shouted, and, giddy with delight, we exited, one after the other, though the window and onto the sloping, moon-green back lawn, which, together with the distinguished, ivy-covered rear façade of the building, gave me the impression we had stepped through some kind of magic portal into the grounds of a country house somewhere far away from London.

The guard appeared at the window, and told us to clear out, which we did.

Things wound down pretty quickly after that. Most of us went back to the house, where I was allocated a sofa and found a sleeping bag, and I crashed out.

The next day was a Saturday, and I came round to find a slow, hung-over routine of sorts taking shape about me. Breakfast was cooking in the kitchen, and people were drinking tea and coffee and smoking and reading the papers. They were piled up on the table, all of them: the ones I read, the ones my parents read, and the ones my bosses read. How insanely bored, or brainy, you'd have to be, I remember thinking, to want to read *all* the newspapers.

The house was a dump. It was, I suppose, just your average student digs, but this was a corner of the property market I was hardly familiar with. Part of me thought I'd be best making a move as soon as possible – get home, get into the shower and into some clean clothes – but my body, huddled inside its grub-like bag, was in no hurry, and nor did anyone else seem to be. Someone brought me tea and a pint glass of orange juice, someone else pushed a packet of painkillers across the table, and a packet of fags, and a couple of sections of newspaper. It was a series of gestures that suggested unquestioned acceptance and I found it, in my vulnerable state, quite affecting.

'Where's Randall?' I asked, eventually, immediately feeling silly for asking.

'Oh, he's not here,' I was told. 'He went back with Evelyn. I'm sure he'll put in an appearance at some point, though.' The person – it could have been Kevin, I'm imagining his rolling, refined Scottish accent as I type the words – looked up and yelled, into the air, 'What are we doing today? Does anybody know?'

At the time I would have been trying to work out who Evelyn was – there had been no sense, the previous evening, of Randall being part of a couple – but writing those words, I'm remembering how this became our catchphrase, or rallying cry, over the long months, and brief years, that followed.

'What are we doing?'

Bellowed by Kevin, or Randall, or me, or any one of us, in any one of a number of houses, or pubs, or clubs, or galleries. It was a call-sign, a way of gathering the troops when they had become too widely dispersed in the crowd.

'I don't know,' would come the reply, in a ragged chorus.

'Doesn't *anyone* know what the hell we're doing?'

'No!'

Kevin was the only person from the circle who could be said to be Randall's equal. He was certainly the superior intellect, and no less forceful a personality. While Randall was well read, he couldn't construct an argument like Kevin could, and tended to fall back on the explosive – even nuclear – maxim or slogan.

Kevin was a leaner-in, a finger-on-the-table jabber, a counter-off-of-points on his fingers. Those long, intricate fingers. 'You could've been a pianist. Or a *painter,*' was a line of Randall's.

Randall, by contrast, was a looker-away, a virtuoso of the vague, condescending smile. Or perhaps that's not quite true. That makes him sound aloof. He wasn't aloof, there was nothing he loved more than getting right into the nitty-gritty of an issue. It's just, he wasn't ever coming at you from a stable, thought-through position. He was like a caustic, sardonic Socrates, if that's not putting it too strongly, less interested in forming his own argument than in spotting the weak link at the heart of yours, and then, once he'd found it, egging you on to lean on it, push it and expand it until it collapsed under the weight of your logic.

Randall and Kevin resented one another, but, to start with at least, that resentment took the form of an intimate rivalry. This worked to both of their advantages, as if they knew that if they kept pushing each other, goading each other on, they would eventually reach a level where it could be established, in full view of everyone, exactly which of them was the winner. (I'd hate to have seen Randall's reaction to Kevin getting the Tate Modern Turbine Hall.) Kevin with his insistent good looks –

give him a moustache and he'd have passed muster as a Second World War flying ace, though at six foot four he would have been rather cramped in a Spitfire cockpit – versus Randall, with his infuriating ability to triumph in any conceivable social situation, despite his extremes of behaviour. His pissing in pot plants at social functions, his leading the Groucho Club in a raucous 'Time Warp' from atop a table, before windmilling off the end of it into a miniature palm tree, his sneezing beer down the front of a blouse of a journalist from *Vanity Fair* at an opening at Victoria Miro Gallery, then taking off his shirt for her to wear, the journalist obliging his sense of occasion by stripping off and putting it on, then and there. Kevin hated playing second fiddle to all of this. And why wouldn't he? He was, for many people, the better artist. Snapped up by Maureen Paley more than a year before anyone else had a gallery, with sell-out shows in Cologne and Los Angeles while the rest of us were still dancing the night away in Dingwalls, or some Hoxton squat party, and yet all anyone wanted to know about was Randall, Randall, Randall.

There was no shortage of talent in the circle, but there was a sense that the potential was pooled. Everyone was *good*, but not everyone would make it. Except those two. It was almost as if the rest of them knew their place, and their job. They were like the boosters on a space rocket; there to give the velocity needed to escape the pull of gravity, but destined to fall away once their fuel was spent. They would disengage and fall back to earth. They would not see the planet framed in a porthole, would not step down from the capsule, would not plant the flag.

In a way this makes them more interesting than Randall, or interesting in a different way. What is it like to be ambitious, and talented, but to know that you are not touched by genius? And to know it precisely because you have sat at the feet of genius, sat in illegal drinking bars with genius, and the bar at St Martin's Lane, staggered erratically down the Embankment with genius, arms around each others' shoulders and bellowing filthy songs to the moon and tramps and lampposts?

From that year at the college, were, as I said, Kevin Nicholson-Banks, Frank Greene, Aya Inouye and Tanya Spence, all of whom went on to significant success in the art world. Others from that year were certainly part of the gang, but never really made it big, for perhaps equally pertinent reasons: Gina Holland, Malcolm Donner, Debbie Reid and Mikhail Krenz. Some weren't artists at all, but were just students or ex-students at the college, like Evelyn Betts or Tara Lewis. And then there were the rest of them, the random individuals who had found themselves caught in this strange orbit. The character actors and the bit parts, the one-line extras sat around the fire at Peploe, or making up the numbers at an opening, or generating the noise and crush at the party for 'Everywhere I Look'. Those on the edge of the circle, that meshed it to the world at large. The posh girls who liked artists and private views because they'd maybe had a bad experience with musicians; the trust fund kids who liked sitting around doing coke and talking about Situationism and Deleuze; the non-aligned intellectuals and journalists who moved with ease between artistic and literary circles, picking up titbits in one and trading them on in the next. They're the ones that I want to celebrate, in part, with this book. Randall was self-created, in many ways, but they created the conditions for him.

What about me? I must have seemed an unusual addition to the group; I seemed it to myself. What did I know about art? Nothing. What intellectual grounding did I have? None. I'd gone straight from school to the City, where I worked at LIFFE, first in the back office of a medium-sized investment bank, then as a floor runner, then as a trader. I was twenty-two years old, two years younger than Randall.

Equally, you might ask: what makes me think I can write a book about this immensely important, and immensely complex, cultural figure, about whom everyone from the Prime Minister to the last London cabbie has an opinion, not to mention every journalist, every art critic? When there have been hundreds of thousands of newspaper and magazine column inches puffing him up, knocking him down and generally picking him apart, both before and especially after his death, hundreds of hours' worth of television, and three biographies, one of them, *Randall: Young British Artist*, by Ed Hitchcock, at least credible, if not always reliable.

Why me? What have I, a former investment banker and 'wealth consultant' with too much time on his hands, got to add?

Well, I could point out that I know more about art – the theory and practice of making it, the confidence trick of looking at it, and the strange, holographic game of buying and selling it – than I did then.

And for that I have Randall to thank, Randall who once said, 'There's only two things you can do with art: make it, and buy it. Everything else – talking about it, thinking about it, selling it, looking at it – either comes under one of those two, or doesn't count.'

But that's not what leads me to put pen to paper, or rather fingers to keyboard. I was there, not as a participant, but as a witness. I am a pair of eyes. Beyond the fact that they were *my* eyes, nothing about me – not my job, not my background, not my personal life, my wishes and desires and achievements and regrets – has any bearing on what I am intending to write here.

I got to see how a group of people manoeuvred themselves to a position of dominance within the capital's art world, and how a nation, charmed and titillated by their antics and self-belief, took them and placed them at the apex of its culture, of its vision of itself, and all this at a moment when the world looked to London and declared that it was, once again, swinging. I saw all this – and what followed – from the inside, but from the outside edge of the inside, if you see what I mean. I wasn't an artist, I wasn't a critic, I had nothing to gain from my proximity. Nothing but Randall's friendship.

That is why I am sat here, stabbing hesitantly at my laptop in the shuttered midday shade of the kitchen of a villa in Tuscany, with its tiles cold to my feet and the slow, Mogadon cooing of the doves from the trees in the still, bleached-glare garden. Typing and deleting and retyping and staring blankly at the screen. Randall was my friend – the best friend I have had in this life, or am likely to have – and if his work and to a certain extent his life are to continue to resonate with people after he is dead, then I want to ensure that the man I knew is a part of what people remember of him.

Or, to be self-obsessed about it for a moment, the debt that this book is trying to repay is the one I owe Randall for making me the person I am. Not that I have him to thank for the villa in Tuscany. I earned that. And maybe I would have ended up with the same or some equally good paintings on the wall without him. But I wouldn't be sitting here in the kitchen, trying to write about him, trying to weigh out a lifetime's debt in words and sentences – if he hadn't shaped my view of the world. He shaped *me*. There, if you were looking for one, is my definition of friendship. If knowing someone doesn't change you as a person, then they're not a friend, they're an acquaintance.

A small amount of context, then: as short as I can keep it. I was born in 1967 in Sleaford in Lincolnshire, and my family moved to Buckhurst Hill in Essex when I was ten. My parents divorced when I was sixteen and I, like Randall an only child, stayed on in the house with my mother. With Randall it was the other way round: it was the mother who left, emigrating to South Africa with a sports physiotherapist, and it was his father who guided him through the rest of his teenage years in a council house in Moseley.

My own father was a financial analyst, and thanks to his contacts I spent a fortnight's work experience at an investment bank when I was fourteen – licking envelopes and running out for coffee and bacon sarnies – but I was hooked, and went back to work during the school holidays. I did try staying at school for A levels, but the thought of actual wages sitting there ready to be earned while I sat thumbing through text books was too much (and the thought of going to university and delaying my earning potential another three years made me positively sick with anxiety) and I quit halfway through my first year.

In 1989 I was making £40,000 a year, plus bonus. I drove a Porsche 944, had a rack of designer suits and took two long-haul holidays a year, plus plenty of weekend breaks to Prague, Amsterdam and Barcelona. I had two pensions, and played the market on my own account, though I wasn't into casinos or the horses. Like many of my peers I had a retirement target – for me, of retirement at thirty-five with £10 million – and like most of them I hit the target, but didn't stick to the deal. I discovered, like we all did, that making money is more fun than having money. Despite all this I still lived at home, sleeping in the same room I had when I was ten. The situation suited both me and my mother. The house would have been big for her on her own, and the money I handed over every month for living expenses was generous, to say the least. Me, I got my food cooked and my washing done. I fully expected to move out, to buy somewhere, at some point, but I would never have guessed, in a million years, where it was I would move out to.

The impact on my life of meeting Randall and the others was immediate and total. I felt like I'd been given a window into a life, and I didn't know if I wanted to join it, or visit it, or watch it from outside, but I did know that I wanted in. After that first night at Goldsmiths I left two or three messages on Randall's home number before I got a call back, an invitation to head on over to the Devonshire that evening.

I was nervous going back. Walking into the pub's upstairs room, dressed this time in jeans and Chelsea boots and – a new purchase, this – a distressed leather jacket, I couldn't hold back a grin. Randall waved me over and moved up his chair to make space for me at the table.

'Vincent. Good man. How's tricks?'

'Tricks are good, Randall.'

'The Footsie holding up? Money still circulating?'

'Just about, just about.'

This genial piss-taking about my occupation was, I quickly learned, compulsory: the price of my admission. I was unsure – and remained unsure for some weeks, or months, or forever, really – why I had been welcomed into the group, but in retrospect it's easy to say that Randall treated me like some kind of manifestation, or symbol, of financial success. I stood for money. I showed how money could enter their lives, as it had entered mine. I was a mascot, perhaps.

I went back that night expecting to talk more about the degree show – I had a few lines and opinions rehearsed – but that, it quickly became apparent, was old news. Their talk was of the next show, the one that they would put on themselves. Something to take up the gauntlet thrown down by Freeze: who was going to be in it, and where it would be held. It had to be somewhere big, somewhere unexpected, somewhere *fun*. Someone wanted a disused power station, someone else one of the military-use tunnels that apparently ran in a clandestine network all around the underside of the capital, or a squat in Camberwell, or a drained swimming pool.

I sat, drinking, content to listen in as their plans drifted higher and higher into the realms of fantasy, until Randall turned to me, brow dipped and showing a sharkish tooth, and said, 'Come on, Vincent. Mister City. Your lot must have some nice empty office somewhere we can have for a few weeks.'

'God, I don't know,' I said, both thrilled and flustered to find myself put on the spot, not wondering until later if that had been the only reason I'd been invited back. 'An investment bank doesn't take up much space. We've only two locations in London as it is.' Randall narrowed his eyes, an encouragement to do better. 'But, I mean, our clients. There's bound to be someone with something, especially at the moment. There are a fair few over-extended portfolios around just now.'

They nodded sagely, as if what I'd said was an important insight, instead of a wry, self-deprecatory dig.

Randall just said, 'Excellent work,' and turned back to the others.

As it happened, I didn't have long to wait for an opportunity to play my part. Two or three weeks later I got an invitation to the bank's box at Lord's, for a Test match.

I pitched it to Randall and Kevin the following evening. We were at Kevin's house, getting ready to go out to a club. I warned them that it was far from being a sure thing, but that there were bound to be some potentially very useful contacts there.

'Vincent, I fucking love you,' Randall said, putting his arm around my shoulder. 'You're absolutely the *richest* person I know.'

'For the moment,' said Kevin, stooping to inspect his face and hair in the mirror. 'For the moment.'

The match was the next weekend. On the day itself I was a mess of conflicting anxieties. I wanted the plan to work, of course, but I was worried, too, that Randall would find the whole affair pathetic, and would end up lumping me in with my colleagues, who could be quite offensively shallow, if you didn't know how to take them. I was aware, too, that Randall had the potential to embarrass me quite severely, possibly even harm my career.

When I met him, outside the Tube, I was relieved to see that he had made an effort with his clothes. He was in a cream suit, albeit one that could have done with a press, a natty blue-and-white striped shirt and a somewhat battered panama hat. The outfit may have been an ironic statement on his part, but – to bounce the irony right back at him – he fitted in perfectly. This was Lord's, after all, not Ascot.

There were twenty or so people already in the box, which was one of an interconnecting pair. It was mostly men – traders, clients – with the odd wife or girlfriend. Everyone was decked out in the weekend uniform of light summer suits, or slacks and a blazer. I'd been to a fair few of these things, but I still took a tie, folded up in a pocket, just in case.

Barry was there, my boss and mentor at the bank – the man in fact who had nudged the invite in my direction – together with a few other board members. They had a group of clients with them, carefully corralled off from the rest of us behind an invisible velvet rope. He gave me a wave of acknowledgement, mimed putting a glass to his lips and pointed at his watch.

We took drinks from one of the staff and went to join some other junior traders down at the front of the box. I did some quick introductions, and Randall sat, crossing his legs and hitching his trousers over his knee. He took off his hat and fanned himself with a programme as we gazed out at the men in white on the pitch.

It was a good hot August day, with one of those curdled-milk skies, the clouds all shrunken gobbets, as if there's something toxic in the sunlight. Waves of applause lifted up to us from the stands. The commentary fizzing from a transistor radio in the next box. The *thock* of another cork exiting the neck of a bottle, sounding in fact rather like a stroke being played. Whistles, shouts, the odd far cry of an appeal, as strange, abstract and archaic as that of a newspaper seller. I couldn't tell you what the match was, but I was surprised at Randall, knowledgably discussing the players' form with the people sat around us.

We didn't see Barry properly until a good few hours later, after lunch, by which time we had made absolutely no progress with our mission, other than getting royally sloshed. Champagne tended to flow like water at these events, as if no one had the imagination to drink anything else.

We were sat at the back of the box, knocking back coffees to sober ourselves up, when Barry landed himself with a grunt in a chair at our table, and clunked down an ice bucket with a new bottle in it. The man was a hero to all the young traders and workers in the firm, but to me was something more. We were very different – he was private school and university-educated – but still there was something rough around the edges about him, that gave me something to aspire to.

I made the introductions, calling Randall 'an up-and-coming artist'.

Barry clearly found the idea of me hanging out with artists a funny one. He peered over the top of his sunglasses at me – if Randall hadn't been there he would have made some insinuating and doubtless homophobic remark – and then turned to Randall.

'Enjoying the game then?' he said.

'Absolutely. I mean, what's not to like?' Randall gestured with his glass, a brief circling movement that took in the surroundings, the weather, the cricket, the free booze. This seemed acceptable to Barry. He took his bottle out of the bucket and untwisted the foil, waving off the offer of help from a hovering waitress. He popped the cork and refilled our glasses, with that waiter's trick of holding the base of the bottle in his palm and tipping the whole thing.

'So, Randall,' he said. 'You're, what, a painter? A sculptor? Or one of these new...' A wave of the bottle stood in for the word. He was half watching the game even as he spoke.

'Yes,' said Randall, and he copied the gesture, somewhat more camply. 'I'd say that about sums it up.'

'So,' Barry said, once he'd taken a drink. 'Painting's dead, is that it?'

Randall gave a moue of his lips that was something like a shrug. 'I think no one should have any more reason to lay paint on a canvas today than they would to dig up and fuck the corpse of their favourite dead grand... father.'

Barry laughed at this. His eyes were hidden by his sunglasses, but I could tell from the way he shifted himself in his chair that he approved. He fished out his cigarettes, plugged one into his mouth, then offered them around.

'Go on, then,' Barry said. 'Let's have it.'

'Well, in a nutshell, what's done cannot be redone. The history of art is a history of dead forms. You've got to find some new way to say the same old things.'

I sat there, shitting myself, hoping against hope that Randall wouldn't be too much a prick, wouldn't think Barry wanted him to gas on about art theory as if this was the Devonshire. In fact, he did know how to keep things brief when necessary. And, also, this was the first time I'd heard him express his theory of artistic development, like this, in plain terms. There are plenty of quoted examples of it, but I can pinpoint one exactly. An interview with Lynn Barber in *The Observer* in 1998:

Once something's been done, you can't do it again. Painting, sculpture, drawing, conceptualism, it's all a search for new means of expression. An art gallery or museum is nothing more than a catalogue of interdictions made concrete. For an artist, the ultimate vanity is to think that you might have found the last remaining form, closed off the last avenue of experimentation. Bang! Art is dead, finally. That's what we're all aiming for, in the end. When we get there – and it might take an apocalypse to do it – it will be like Year Zero. All bets off, all restrictions repealed. We'll be back at the cave wall, at Lascaux, scratching away with sticks and charcoal. And I'll be there, at the front of the queue. Until then, though, painting's... not dead, exactly, but cryogenically suspended, let's say.'

There was a roar from the crowd. Someone's century. We added our diffident applause to the rest of the ground's.

'So, for instance, you couldn't do a portrait of me, then?' Barry said. He blew out smoke, as if to neutralise the question, but there was an edge to his voice that I recognised. 'Just a sketch, nothing fancy. What'd your rate be for that? Fifty? A ton?'

Randall grinned at me – that same grin he'd given me the night of the degree show, when I asked him to draw the circle. Don't draw a fucking circle now, for Christ's sake, I thought to myself.

'A hundred quid,' he said. 'I think we can do that.'

They shook on it, then Barry signalled to a waitress.

'Excuse me, love. Do you have some paper and pencils or something?' His voice, just that bit louder than was needed, turned heads momentarily in our direction. There was all at once a subtle tension in the air, as if someone had tightened a cord around us, inched us closer in towards each other. In fact, this was just the sort of thing we loved, that the office thrived on. Contests, bets, anything that put people on the spot, or in conflict with each other. It was like an off-duty version of that critical moment on the floor – watching the numbers climb, totter or drop into a spin, waiting for the one perfect second to make a move, to sell or buy. Getting in first, or toughing it out, to see who could make the best, closest call.

48

Barry extracted two fifties from his wallet, holding them slightly crimped, his thumb running down their middle. The appearance of cold hard cash hadn't gone unnoticed, and a few people had come over to see what was going on. Barry brandished the notes at them, as if they were witnesses to something, before sliding them under an ashtray. He had just started arranging himself in his chair, when he stopped.

'Now there's a thought,' he said. 'Andy, you wouldn't pop next door and see if Jan's still there, would you? Drag him over, if he is.'

Jan, I guessed, was Jan de Vries, chief operating officer of a large institutional investor that put a lot of work our way. I gave Randall a significant look, as if to say, this could be someone *very* interesting.

Andrew came back with de Vries, a tall, extremely well-dressed man, as slim as his suit. He had one of those severe, northern European faces, that seem to say: you're enjoying yourselves now, but soon it will be winter. De Vries, for all his philanthropic work, and his pre-eminence in his field, was not what you'd call an approachable man.

'Jan,' said Barry. 'Excellent. You'll like this. I'm about to sit for my portrait.'

He spread his arms wide, but de Vries hardly seemed impressed. He stood there, like someone in a receiving line at a funeral, hands crossed loosely in front of him, and said, 'Oh?'

'This is my portraitist, Randall. And that's Vincent Cartwright, one of our hungry young traders. Randall, this is Jan de Vries.'

I'd pushed back my chair to get up, but Randall was ahead of me. The bottle and glasses rattled on the table, from the jolt he gave it as he stood. His voice, when it came, was cracked and breathless.

'Mr de Vries? Mr Jan de Vries?' De Vries nodded yes. He took Randall's offered hand.

'Pleased to meet you. How are the de Koonings, Mr de Vries?'

De Vries put his head on one side, retaining Randall's hand in his grasp. A smile threaded itself along the line of his lips. 'They're very well, thank you,' he said. 'You are a fan?'

'Oh, absolutely. And it's so good to have them back in Europe, don't you think?'

'Well, I agree, of course. Randall…?'

He left the word hanging, an interrogation.

'Just Randall, actually. I was at Goldsmiths.'

'And you're about to do Barry's portrait?'

'Something like that, yes.'

'Well, please don't let me stop you.'

De Vries stepped back from the table, refusing the chair I pulled out for him, and took up a stance at the rail that marked off the hospitality section from the viewing area, allowing him to keep half an eye on the game.

Randall and Barry went back to their places, Randall shooting me a loaded glance. What he couldn't tell me then, but did later, was that de Vries was a legendary collector of modern and contemporary art, most noted for his championing of young European artists, at that stage largely Dutch and German ones.

Barry set about selecting his desired pose. 'I'm hoping for something I can hang in the boardroom,' he said, for the benefit of his onlookers. People laughed, more came by, heads were poked over shoulders. We were a focus of attention.

Meanwhile, Randall sifted through the pens and paper that had been provided for him, then he steepled his fingers and looked over them at his subject, sizing him up.

After a moment he stood and made his way round the table – 'Excuse me, thanks, excuse me' – to the cloth-covered trestle tables right at the back of the box. We watched as he collected an ice bucket, then another, then scooped the ice from these two into a third. Barry, though, held his pose, gazing doggedly out over the ground, as if to have turned and looked would have been a sign of weakness.

Randall brought his bucket back over and transferred the ice from it into the bucket already on the table. Then, still standing, he took up our bottle of champagne and topped up our glasses, mine and his and Barry's, before putting it to his mouth and draining the last of it.

Then he reversed it and pushed it down into the bucket, neck first.

The table wobbled as he leaned his weight on to the bottle, forcing it in, the ice cracking and shifting. He packed the ice cubes around it to keep it in place, then, slowly, took his hands away.

The bottle stood, stable, tipped at a slight angle.

Very carefully Randall moved the bucket to the middle of the table, then made a little gesture with his hands, like a magician revealing his trick.

There were a few bewildered laughs, but the general sense was of terrible anticlimax.

'Is that it?' Barry said. I could tell from his face that he was angrier than he would allow himself to show. He looked around the table, working his disbelief to get the response he wanted.

'You asked for a portrait,' said Randall, calm as you like.

'Fuck sake,' Barry said. I could tell he was struggling to keep on top of his sarcasm, presumably for the benefit of De Vries. What had begun as a fun diversion had fallen dramatically flat. I was appalled. I could see my career imploding in front of me in slow motion, breaking apart like a crashing Formula One car.

'You going to pay him then, Barry?' someone said.

'Of course, of course, why wouldn't I?' Barry said. He slipped the money out from under the ashtray and tossed it on to the table. 'Though for a hundred quid a full bottle might have been nice.'

I watched Randall, willing him not to take the money.

Don't take the money, I was thinking.

He took the money.

'I think you've got yourself a bargain, actually,' he said. 'Though obviously it will cost you a certain amount in maintenance. You don't want the ice to freeze together completely. There's got to be some give in it, as if the bottle might go over at any moment.'

Barry's laugh would have sounded almost indulgent, if it hadn't been dismissive. 'You actually expect me to take this home and keep it in my freezer?'

'Well, it's yours. Give it ten years. I shouldn't be surprised if you'll be looking at ten, twenty, thirty grand.'

'Ten years?' Barry leaned forward. 'You think I want assets that take a *decade* to mature? I don't think you know very much about how money works, do you?' He was playing to the room again now, holding up his glass for someone to refill. 'Anyone want to go long on a bottle in a bucket?'

More laughter, but I watched as Randall reached for the bucket again. He'd torn a shape out of one of the fifty pound notes to make of it a strange, off-kilter oblong, like a thick, curved banana. He wiped it carefully through the condensation on the outside of the bucket, to dampen it, then pressed it to the glass of the bottle. It lay slanted across like a ragged second label. Like a mouth. A wide, ugly mouth. It was crude, but it was spot on. He turned the bucket back.

'There we go,' he said. 'Barry, by Randall.'

Barry sat there, frozen, glass in hand – almost, in fact, like a sculpture of himself. 'For fuck sake,' he said again, but it went unnoticed under the general reaction to the new, improved portrait. There were a few whoops, laughter, some still cagey, some more gleeful. Someone clapped, a loud empty sound.

'Nice one.'

'Got you there, Barry.'

'Look. It's Barry – waah!'

There was, indeed, something about the note stuck on the glass of the bottle, something about its shape, its blocky oval-ness, that seemed to conjure Barry. The Barry whose roar you could always hear above the migraine-inducing cacophony of the pit, who stalked the office like a slave driver in a Roman galley, who juggled phones at his desk, barking instructions at people stood five feet away. The wailing, childish gape of it, with the queen's face mooning lugubriously out from the side. Her smile, so wan, and so sure in its wan-ness; it must be the second most famous smile in any portrait, after the *Mona Lisa*.

Compare those two ladies to the mouth on Randall's Barry – an angry, complaining mouth, verging on the hateful. In my memory it takes on something, too, of a Bacon Screaming Pope – the raw, skinned pain, the scream beneath the skin.

'The thing is ...'

We all looked up. It was Jan de Vries.

He had left his place at the rail and was standing above us. 'The thing is, Barry,' he said, and I see him, hand in trouser pocket, as he speaks, the other hand hanging limp at his side, 'art doesn't behave like that, not in the long run. It's not a bond. Bonds don't notice who it is that's bought them.'

Everyone had shushed. De Vries's expression was open and relaxed, but there was something about his eyes, something that reminded me of Randall. That spark of distant veiled intention that was always burning away at the back of them.

'I'll give you a thousand for it,' he said.

Barry looked up at him. 'Jan, come on. You're not being serious.' He indicated the bucket. 'Don't tell me you actually think this is worth something?'

De Vries made a moue with his lips. 'I give you a grand for it now. It'll be worth ten in two, three years, I should think.' He turned, for the first time, towards Randall. 'Is this your thing, then?'

'My thing?'

He gestured. 'Is it representative?'

53

'No. I mean, yes. I suppose so. In fact, I've got a show coming up. A group show, that I'm curating. You're certainly more than welcome to take a look at that, when it happens.'

'When it happens.'

'Or before, I mean. In fact, we're looking for involvement right now. Sponsorship and so on. There are some very exciting artists on board. I'd gladly talk you through it.'

De Vries turned back to Barry and spread his hands.

'There, you see. Art is not the same thing at all. That conversation, for instance, would be illegal, would it not, if it had been about stocks?'

Barry looked up, hand shading his eyes against the afternoon sun. He looked again at the bucket, then back to Jan.

'Well, Jan. Now I think about it, perhaps I'll hang on to my portrait after all.'

Jan took out a pen and a business card and wrote something on the back of it. 'Don't be silly, Barry,' he said, 'It won't do anything if you keep it. Only if I buy it. Surely you see that.' He passed the card to Randall. 'There you go. Give Henrik a call. He's my buyer. Barry, good to see you. Thanks so much for the invite and sorry I can't stay longer. I'm expected elsewhere, alas. You'll have the money in the week.' He looked his watch, and sighed. 'Right, I'd better get someone to come and pick this thing up before it goes off.'

And with that, Jan De Vries moved his gaze once around the table, without it alighting on any one of us, and then made his way to the exit, leaving what can only be called a stunned silence in his wake.

I hustled Randall out of there as soon as was humanly possibly. We progressed, in triumph, across town to New Cross, first to Kevin's house, and then on to the pub. It was a good, drunken, celebratory evening. I was a marvel, a networking maestro, and newly crowned Marketing Consultant to the still un-named but now actually-likely-to-exist show, and Randall had a work in the collection of Jan de Vries.

It's strange how acceptance into a group works. You might not see how it happens from the outside. It's in the way someone slides up on a bench, or the willingness with which they move their chair up to give you space at the table. It's in the offering of a packet of cigarettes, or in the manner of its offering, the sense of whether it's being counted. It's in whether your name sticks, your jokes carry, your comments are allowed to matter. It's in the way that, at closing time, with jackets being pulled on and pints downed, someone invites you back to someone's house, or – more than that – doesn't have to, because your inclusion is assumed: 'You coming then?'

I've been there to see people get squeezed out, allowed along for a certain time before being dropped. Not 'You coming?' but 'See you later.'

Yes, I had money. I bought rounds. (The tequila became something of a signature purchase.) I tried not to flash it around – though, in later years, when they had more of it themselves, I saw how they had learned how to do just that from me.

Of course they mocked me for being a City boy, for knowing sod all about art, and of course I played up to the caricature, but then everyone was mocked for something: Kevin for his obsessiveness and his politics, Tanya for her fake dyke-ishness, Gina for never being able to finish anything. Randall, too, for his god complex, his tendency to sit on top of things and watch us all, with an infuriating Zen calmness, when he was the least Zen person on the planet.

As it was, Randall and Kevin went along to meet Jan's art buyer, Henrik Klass, with a portfolio of work from the artists in the circle.

The upshot was that the property development arm of de Vries's company agreed to sponsor the show, which was soon named 'Everywhere I Look I See Death, Death In Everything I See' (after a huge black and white painting by Louis Burnham of a baby crying, an image he'd copied from a poster he'd bought from the new defunct high street store Athena). The company picked up the cost of the necessary permits and licences, and printing the catalogues – which meant they could be done properly, with full colour images and a catalogue essay by Claude Jacobs, then a Philosophy of Art PhD student at Goldsmiths.

Henrik and Jan visited Kevin's studio soon after, while the show was still in preparation, and bought two of his pieces for £12,000 the pair. This was by far the biggest sale any of us had ever achieved at that time, and Kevin diverted a fair amount of it to paying for the show. This is worth remembering when people talk about Randall as the prime mover of the YBA group; Kevin was the first artist to achieve real commercial and critical success, if not cultural notoriety, and indeed it was Jan de Vries's interest in him, or at least Klass's interest, that guaranteed the success of 'Everywhere I Look'. Indeed, Klass hadn't thought much of Randall's work, passing over his pages in the group portfolio almost without comment.

Things moved quickly, then slowly, as print deadlines for the catalogue came and went, venues became available, then not. In the end it dragged over to the new year, but in January the disused Shandy Street pools near Mile End was fixed as the site, for a two week show in March, and everyone set about trying to accumulate enough decent work to submit. Kevin, encouraged by his sales to de Vries, wasted no time in making bigger and more impressive pieces in what would become his trademark style: abstract and sometimes semi-figurative sculptures in iron and high-carbon steel and featuring often dangerously sharp edges – like 'an Anthony Caro fashioned from lethal Japanese kitchen knives', as Jacobs put it. Tanya Spence had her knitted genitalia, which for 'Everywhere I Look' she displayed under a set of glass cloches that had once belonged to her great-great-uncle, who had been a noted horticulturalist, under the title *Schwert and Scheide*; Malcolm Donner had his tediously brilliant hyper-realist paintings of food (de Vries bought a particularly unsavoury one of fried eggs afloat in a sea of baked beans); Frank Greene more of his acid clouds. There were mannequin assemblages from Gina, humorous photos of dogs from Andrew Selden, Aya Inouye's road-work installation.

Randall, though, was blocked.

At weekends I went round to the Deptford studio he shared with Aya and listened, for what seemed like hours, to him rant, invent and expostulate. Trashing his old ideas, angrily throwing up new ones, only to bring them straight back down again. De Vries's purchase of the portrait of Barry had thrown him. Like *Perfect Circle*, it had been a brilliant improvisation: a marker of talent, rather than an expression of it. It wasn't, in the collector's word, 'representative'. More pertinently, it wasn't *repeatable* and, if there's one thing they'd had drummed into them at college, Randall said, it was that 'you have to have your thing'.

A Randallism: 'A monkey who sits down at a typewriter and comes up with *Hamlet* is a marvel of nature. But the one who comes up with the *Complete Works* has a *career*.'

During his years at Goldsmiths, where tutors such as Michael Craig-Martin very much encouraged students to experiment across the available forms, Randall had largely worked on installations, usually involving television sets. These were still the old cathode ray design, with its weird, curving, staticky screen and huge bulging back. Though they hadn't yet been replaced by the slimmer LCD and plasma versions, they were getting cheaper to buy, and you could find obsolete sets quite easily, at council tips or in skips – we used to spend whole nights driving round London, scavenging. Randall piled them up, left them in corners, facing the wall, made totem poles out of them. What with Aya working on her installations at the other end, their studio would have looked to most people like a junk yard. It was beyond me to tell what among the mass of sets and parts was a completed 'piece', what a half-finished one, what an abandoned one.

Now that the opportunity for genuine exposure loomed, though, he decided they simply weren't good enough. They were derivative, 'junk', overly reminiscent of Nam Juine Paik without properly making that reminiscence do any real work. 'Nothing *surprising*,' he'd say, stood in a rage of impotence in the middle of his clutter. 'Nothing *untoward*. Really, television. Who gives a shit?'

The breakthrough came one Sunday afternoon, during the slow comedown at the end of a long weekend's clubbing. There weren't any true hardcore ravers in the group, but clubbing was one of the mainstays of our social life, the other, of course, being sitting in the pub and talking.

During the week, drinking and talking; at the weekend, dancing and getting off your tits.

It would be difficult to state exactly how rave *inspired* the YBAs' art, other than the fact that they saw in the whole scene something absolutely new and distinct from what had come before, and that they felt something similar was possible in art. Of course, in retrospect, acid house looks far less unprecedented than it did at the time – you can trace its musical heritage back through techno to Kraftwerk, and its social one back through Northern Soul and, in a way, punk. It was the drug, ecstasy, that was new. Similarly, the YBAs owed plenty to Warhol, Koons, Fluxus, Duchamp and Dada: take your pick. The lines of influence are always easier to draw backwards, either because posterity offers a more secure perspective, or because what survives is defined by grand, historical tendencies that are invisible in the moment of their operation. And, of course, as they grew, and grew apart, the artistic links between them became more tenuous.

So, just as the new drug amplified and facilitated the music of the late 80s and early 90s, it was the fervid reception, the attendant pulse-quickening thrill – the hype – that made the art of that time seem newer, fresher, more exciting than it maybe actually was.

Sundays, then, were traditionally a day of chilling out, and coming down from whatever we'd taken the night before. I balked at the more adventurous pharmaceutical intake of the others – not least because I had to be at work on Monday – so I would have been struggling against the time-honoured physical symptoms of a hangover, while they would have been navigating the more recherché psychological ones of this chemical revolution. There was lots of smoking, lots of drinking orange juice and coffee, lots of watching videos – Švankmajer, Tarkovsky, John Hughes. That Sunday, as on many of them, we were at Gina Holland's house – me, Gina, Randall and Kevin.

It was a big house, in one of the nice streets of Bethnal Green, and, most importantly, centrally heated. Gina was a generous host, as she was generous with much else. In fact, this made her position in the group problematic. Although she did her best to hide it, she came from money – just as Kevin came from culture, me from suburbia and Randall from the council estates. The Hollands were farmers and landowners in Somerset back as far as the druids, and Gina's father owned a food processing company that produced, she said, half the cheddar in the country.

So, while some of the circle were living the traditionally penurious existence of artists down the ages – Randall and Aya both slept in their barely heated studio for long stretches of time, and they weren't the only ones – Gina had a large studio on the ground floor of her house, kitted out with all manner of equipment and materials. Although she was not without talent, she struggled to settle on a medium, flitting from painting to printing to sculpture to photography and so on. Crucially for everyone else, for whom kit and material represented a significant outlay, she was always happy to pass along stuff she no longer needed. So there was some quiet disappointment, if not outright resentment, when Gina eventually settled on performance art as her chosen medium – an art form that called for the absolute bare minimum of expensive, borrowable or inheritable kit.

That Sunday, then, in Bethnal Green, late January, the last possible deadline for the catalogue just days away.

Randall had sloped off to the toilet. It would be hard to say if he had been gone a long time, but when he came back it was in a state of some agitation. He cleared a space on the coffee table – shifting glasses and plates, spent cans and ashtrays – and started laying something out on it. Nobody paid much attention, until he said, 'There we go. What do you think?'

Laid out in a row on the low table were three pieces of toilet paper, each smeared with a patch of brown, where it had been applied to Randall's arse.

'Oh, for fuck's sake.'

'That's gross.'

'Randall. Get those off my table *now*.'

So, yes, you could say that the original response of Randall's peers to this zeitgeist-defining work, as it came to be, was largely identical to that of the great British public, when they were brought before one another. Or no, I'm being glib. The great British public *wanted* to be appalled, but found it couldn't be, or not for long.

'No, no,' said Randall, waving his hands. 'Don't worry.'

'Don't worry? You're showing us your shit? It's disgusting.'

Kevin had returned to his supine position on the sofa. 'Disgusting?' he said. 'It's not even original.'

'I know, I know,' said Randall. 'But this is different. Bear with me.' He adjusted the sheets, spacing them to his liking. 'Which do you think is the best one?'

'The *best one*?' I said.

'Can we ask where you're going with this?'

He said nothing, but sat back on his haunches. He waited for us to look at him, then held up his hands in front of him, measuring an imaginary frame.

'Screen prints. Big as we can get. Warhol colours. *Big*. Gina, you've got some ink lying around, haven't you?'

She nodded.

Kevin swung his long legs down from the sofa and looked again at the three sheets, touching one at the corner to set it straight on the table. What a moment ago had been a poor joke was, somehow, suddenly a serious proposition.

You often get people saying, 'I don't understand conceptual art.' Well, here, if you want it, is a perfect working example of conceptual art.

'Conceptual art – art you don't have to see to get.'

Another Randallism, to go alongside the more famous 'Modern art – art you don't have to like to buy.'

Imagine a square of toilet paper with your shit smeared on it. Now take that shape and imagine it printed up in lurid clashing colours – pink and turquoise, lime green and purple – and hung on a wall in a gallery. It's not difficult. After all, once you've got over your natural squeamishness as to what it depicts – or whence it derives – it's not an unpleasant shape: random and abstract, but also earthy, mysterious and suggestive. 'A Rorschach blot of the soul,' as Claude Jacobs had it in his catalogue essay. Certainly, a *Sunshines* canvas is capable of bringing to mind many things beyond the bare fact of its origins.

And that's what they did, Randall, Gina and Kevin, that day: analyse it, deconstruct it, work it up. Beyond the obvious references, that it looks like a Warhol screen print – 'Warhol doing Rothko' – they talked about Piero Manzoni, an Italian artist who sold tins packed with his own excrement as 'Merda d'Artista'. (This in 1961, incidentally, the year before Warhol showed his first Marilyn and Campbell's Soup paintings.) They also dropped in references to the Hubble Telescope images of distant nebulae, and at the other end of the scale, electron microscope images of chromosomes and viruses. They talked about how these types of advanced scientific imagery used what's called *false-colour*: bright, non-naturalistic tones, intended to make the image as clear as possible, though it can't have hurt the Public Understanding of Science that they also make it look fucking good. When did that start to happen, Kevin wanted to know. Could it be that the scientists, in their desire to get their discoveries across to the wider public, were themselves influenced by Pop Art?

This, I was coming to understand, was how you made art: hypothetically, discursively, hungeroverly. You come up with the idea, then you test it, turn it as you'd turn an object in your hands, interrogate it until it gives up its underpinnings and allusions, its theory and significance. And of course its degree of originality.

'Everything's derivative,' Randall said to me once. 'It's just a question of whether anyone else has ripped off what you're ripping off.'

'But what if you're copying their copy? Doesn't that count?' I said, somewhat belligerently.

He clapped a hand on my shoulder.

'Vincent, my boy, we'll make an artist of you yet.'

'So if I just photocopied the *Mona Lisa* and stuck it in a frame, that'd do, would it?'

'Ah, that's been done.'

'Of *course* it has.'

'Duchamp.'

'Okay, so I'm copying Duchamp.'

'Not if you didn't know he'd done it.'

'So how am I supposed to show who it is I'm ripping off?'

His hand, still on my shoulder, contracted, a brief, conciliatory squeeze.

'That, Vincent, is where the true art lies.'

A professional wine taster, he said another time, can tell what you've been drinking by sipping at a glassful of your piss.

Aya had turned up by now and the four of them took positions for and against – rather how I imagine lawyers discuss patents – but it wasn't long before we moved downstairs to Gina's studio.

Gina and Randall scurried around getting the kit together: the polyester mesh, the wooden frames to hold it, drawing fluid and screen filler to make the stencil, a random collection of half-full pots of ink. Kevin was bent to the construction of one of his clever little cigarettes, carrying on the critical discourse with Aya – dry as it was to me, this abstruse, jargon-heavy idiom was, for them, a medium perfectly suited to flirtation. I took photos, excited at the prospect of seeing this art work, which I had just had elucidated and explained to me for half an hour, actually become real.

It's worth pointing out that, whereas most of the *Sunshines* canvases you see in galleries around the world were produced on the massive industrial machines at Randall's Kent studio, the first few dozen were made by hand. Randall, with Gina's help, copied the shape of the chosen shit stain, enlarged ten or so times, on to a piece of fine-meshed polyester screen, and filled it in with soluble drawing fluid. Once that was dried they applied a screen filler to the frame and then sprayed down the whole thing in the sink, washing away the drawing fluid to leave the solidified filler stuck to the screen in a negative of the original shape.

We produced ten prints that first day, squeegeeing ink through the mesh screen on to the canvas, all of us helping out with pouring and inking, holding and handling sheets of canvas, cleaning frames. It was great, messy fun. Randall experimented with different ink weights, and often took a brush to the ink before it was dry, to give it texture, add in the little darker spots made by flecks of semi-digested food, or a stray hair.

Once the five best prints were taped up side by side on the wall, we stood and looked at them. Randall's own faeces, blotted and smeared onto absorbent paper, were transformed into this bright, discordant explosion, sliding off on brusque topographic tangents, as fleetingly figurative as cloud forms seen in the sky on a summer's day. There were bold, knife-edged triangles cutting into the mass, and cute little rows of wrinkles, where the paper had been folded and pushed between his arse cheeks.

It was Gina who, as we stood there in her house, on that winter's day, pointed out another link to Warhol, how the forms' more divergent extremities recalled the way Andy's fright wig stuck out in all kinds of mad directions in the famous 1986 self-portrait. She pulled a monograph off the shelf and found the image.

'That's it,' said Kevin, and he clicked his fingers at the prints on the wall. He looked at Randall. 'They're self-portraits.'

Randall put his head on one side and smiled, nodding with an air of restrained, or deferred, condescension, as if Kevin had only just clocked on to what he'd intended all along. 'Exactly,' he said.

Kevin laughed. That was the thing about Kevin, he never let himself be taken in by Randall. He saw through him every time – or until the time that it counted most of all.

Randall asked me what I thought, and I made some anodyne comment about the colours. He waved me down.

'The colours don't matter,' he said. 'We muck about with the colours until we get it right, or just do them at random.'

Gina, becoming more animated now: 'The more colours, the better. Ten of them in a row, all different. Different tones, different combinations, different shapes.'

Randall shook his head, grinning. 'Even better,' he said, and again there was that pause, as he waited for the attention to swing back to him.

'Kevin's right,' he said. 'It's a self-portrait. Well, that's it, isn't it? Portraits – all of us. Each person's shit on a sheet of loo roll. Wipe it, copy it, print it up. An intimate portrait.'

And that was it, the critical moment in which the work acquired a genuinely transformative concept and, as such, made the leap from puerile art school prank to the high point of British late Twentieth Century Pop Art. They were portraits: repellent, but decorative. A dirty joke, but also a mosquito-sharp satirical jibe at the swaggering mythology of Abstract Expressionism. Above all, they were also a stunning reversal of the art-historical idea of portraiture. Yes, they were deeply intimate – they brought to light an aspect of the subject's life that no one, not even their nearest and dearest, had ever seen; but they were also absolutely universal – everyone wipes their arse, and, of course, you couldn't tell one person's 'portrait' from another's.

Nonetheless Randall insisted that everyone – all the great and good and rich and famous that queued to up to 'have a Randall done' – produce their own 'holograph', as he called it, in situ, in the studio. You wanted a Randall portrait, you had to *sit* for it. And, even today, I – and, I assume, most people – can't look at any of those iconic works – his Bowie, his Abramovich, his Moss – without thinking of the sitter emerging from the loo in Gina's house or his later studios, piece of toilet paper held daintily in hand, by the corner, like a just-exposed Polaroid photograph.

And so the four of us – me, Gina, Kevin and Aya – dutifully trooped off to the toilet, as the opportunity availed itself, over the remaining hours of that Sunday, and most of the rest of the circle, over the following days, to provide Randall with the raw material he needed for his contribution to the show. Individually, they were titled according to the sitter's name, as in a traditional portrait, but it wasn't until I saw the dummies of the catalogue that I saw what Randall had called them as a whole.

'*Sunshines?*' I said, and looked at him.

'*Sunshines,*' he replied, and spread his arms wide, in a gesture of magnificence. 'Isn't it obvious?'

Kevin was on hand to deliver the punch line. 'Yeah, Vincent. It's because the sun shines out of his fucking arse.'

You could hear in his voice at once the desire to puncture his friend's ego, and his resignation to the fact that Randall was already immune from any such damage, protected both by his sense of irony, and the strength of that ego. This was, in a way, his greatest weapon. He was so forthright, so *vocal* with regards to his own absurdity that any external criticism came across, even as it was being said, as limp and facile, and irrelevant. Any attempt to undermine this – to get him to admit to his strategy – was doomed to failure, because he unhesitatingly agreed with whatever you said to or about him; every attack was effortlessly assimilated into that amorphous, grinning energy field. It drove people mad. Artists and curators, and critics and journalists – I've seen them go incandescent with rage in the face of it. For one or two of them incandescent is barely even a figure of speech. They *hated* him, some of them, and not just for what he stood for, but for *how* he stood for it. In Randall, self-deprecation could become a radical form of arrogance.

I can remember – or can convince myself that I remember – sitting there in the toilet that day, trousers round my ankles and hands on knees, waiting to make my holograph. The heat of embarrassment, of being passive subject to one's own body, and, more than that, the feeling of foolishness, of putting my dignity entirely at the disposal of this man; and, yet again, as so often when I analyse my friendship with Randall, I flip one feeling to find its opposite, equally present: in this case, the desire to make it good, my holograph, make myself worthy of his approbation.

The memory – if that's what it is – is tainted by a sense of bitterness regarding 'my' *Sunshines* portrait. The fact is, I never owned a copy of my portrait during Randall's lifetime, nor do I now. As the series grew, following that first show, he produced them as multiple editions, with a fiendish pricing scheme partly of my devising, but the original thirteen were unique. Some of the others he remade – in some cases, as in Kevin and Tanya, very much against the subject's wishes – but mine he did only one more of. It was something he used to dangle in front of me – 'I'm trying something new with the *Sunshines* idea, using yours actually, you'll be *astounded* when you see it' – sometimes refusing outright to countenance any new version. The original, along with its siblings, is there for all to visit in the collection of the Stedelijk Museum in Amsterdam, as part of the de Vries bequest, made after his death in 2002. A second is in a private collection.

At the time, though, I took the work to be a very public gesture of acceptance into the circle. Mine was the only portrait of someone who wasn't an artist showing in the exhibition. Even this sense of pride, though, was shadowed by a darker emotion, a background hum of paranoia. I was genuinely afraid, as the show approached, that word would get back to my friends and colleagues in the City that you could see a sheet of my used toilet paper, done up in puce and yellow and stuck on the wall in an art gallery, plain as day. Would Jan de Vries see it, and tell Barry? Barry, I was sure, wouldn't let pass the opportunity to take some kind of local revenge on me for that day at Lord's.

And, beyond that, even up to the day of the opening, there was the great, deep fear, still and silent and never to be broached, that it was all a trap: that I would walk into the gallery and see, not twelve prints in a row, but just mine, side by side, over and over. Look: Vincent Cartwright's shit. He thinks it's art. Everybody turning towards me, Barry and Randall and everyone else from the bank, my mother and father and friends from school, all pointing at me and laughing.

The show opened on 15 March 1990 and was, if not the overnight sensation that posterity seems to want to paint it as, then at least a major and unprecedented explosion of energy, and of attention.

The private view was huge – 'immense' was the word that, for a while, was on everybody's lips. It was the sort of night that seemed to tumble straight into a glorious, self-regulating chaos, to have you permanently in three different places and times: evening, middle-of-the-night and morning. There was the official viewing, with its cheap plastic cups of white wine that set your teeth buzzing, and the bottles of beer – I remember the endless ripping open of new boxes, my arms glowing cold from dunking bottles in and out of the huge bin of ice water.

We rigged up a sound system and disco lights in the gallery space for the evening, and for an hour at the end we set up the strobes and speakers to blast their noise and colour off and between the art. People were sort of encouraged to dance – but also not really. They bopped about like audience members from some pop music TV show from the 60s, awkwardly self-conscious and careful not to go too near any of the works. The chaos of the Goldsmiths night was a salutary memory, and nobody wanted *anything* to happen to any of the pieces on show here. There was a sense – entirely justifiable – that Randall was as ready to bring this thing crashing down as he had been with that. It's strange, he was incredibly serious about the art – both his and his friends' – but there was something flagrant about his attitude at the same time, that verged on the immoral.

He was in his element, though, and even briefly joined in with the dancing, doing that strange elemental frug he rolled out when absolutely called on to participate. There was a sort of group hug at one point involving all the twelve showing artists; they formed a circle with their arms around each others' shoulders and bounced up and down around the main space, growling and whooping. I remember seeing Tanya Spence and her boyfriend Griff Dolis, who was exhibiting some paintings of beer bottle labels, wheeling away in a spinning, dancing embrace, and Randall actually had to grab hold of them to stop them careening straight into one of Gina's posed dummies, bent seductively over an old twin tub washing machine.

But – and this is really what gave us the sense, from the start, that it was going to be big – the art never got left behind. The thrill of walking around the room, through this throng of half-known and unknown people, hearing shreds of conversation after conversation about the art *my friends* had made. Art, in one case, that I had helped make. Andrew's dogs gazing lugubriously out at the dancers; Frank's acid clouds pulsing in time with their movements; the antique glass cloches warping their faces as they danced up to them, waving their arms in a kind of idolatrous veneration of the knitted cocks and cunts sat under them; the reflective strips on Aya's cones and barriers sliding through the colour spectrum as the racks of coloured lights looped through their combinations. I remember seeing, among the crowd packed into the dark of the main space, individuals stood stock still in front of the *Sunshines*. No doubt off their heads, but gawping nonetheless like schoolchildren in front of a pornographic window display. They would be knocked and buffeted as they stood, looking, watching, taking it in, but still they stood. 'That's mine,' I wanted to say, standing alongside them and nodding at the canvas. In a world governed by individual success – where our bonuses were awarded in private, and our rank in the hierarchy adjusted only ever tacitly and impersonally – this was an unusual feeling for me, one of communal pride, and belonging.

They made it, and people came. It wasn't just dealers and gallery owners that Randall sent the high-gloss invitations and catalogues and press releases to, it was magazine and newspaper editors, and not just the broadsheets. And not just them, but people on the hipper fringes of the creative-celebrity circuit, actors and musicians and fashion designers and models. The very first newspaper clipping in my collection is from the diary column of *The Times*: 'Musician couple Siobhan Fahey (ex-Bananarama) and Eurythmic Dave Stewart were seen grooving at the private viewing of an art exhibition earlier this week. The show, which would seem to have been as much about exhibitionism as art, is taking place in a disused swimming pool in the East End. It goes under the title "Everywhere I Look I See Death, Death In Everything I See", which one could in fact imagine gracing the tracklisting of the next Shakespears Sister album. Not so sure about the art, which included some large colourful prints based on used pieces of one artist's toilet tissue.'

But it was a news item in the ever-dependable *Sun* that really did the trick, under the headline 'Official: Modern art is total cr★p!' and, more importantly, featuring full colour reproductions of both a *Sunshines* self-portrait and a *Schwert and Scheide* cloche. Once that was out, the others all trooped along, with their entirely predictable variations on the original headline: 'Modern art finally disappears up its own backside'; 'Contemporary artists let it all hang out'.

Inevitably somewhere in the copy alongside the pictures would be a quote from Randall. 'Naturally it's art. I've never seen a skid-mark I didn't find beautiful.' 'Painting's not dead. That's the glory of it, it just won't give up. It's like the Black Knight in Monty Python. Chop off its arms, chop off its legs, and still it wants more. "It's just a flesh wound!" That's painting for you. You've got to love it.'

By the weekend following the *Sun*'s news piece, the show was everywhere. All of London was talking about us. (By which I mean, of course, that it was all that *we* talked about, and all that everyone we *knew* talked about, at least when they were talking to us.) I was still in work, and enjoyed the strange echoes between my two lives. By day, the boisterous, foot-to-the-floor whirl of LIFFE, with its leaf litter of trading slips, and the furniture of flickering screens, and our crooked necks from craning at them. By evening, the under-the-radar hum of the gallery, so different from the cavernous murmur of the big galleries most people see art in – the Nationals and Tates, with their toddlers and tourists and drifting Sargasso seas of Italian schoolkids. A contemporary art show, Randall always said, is so much more exciting than a blockbuster exhibition, because of the risk that everything in it might just be the most pointless, vacuous, unforgivable and irredeemable shite. Not that those places don't have their fair share of shite, but here no one else has decided if what you're seeing is any good, so it's up to you.

The trading floor began to look to me like a massive art installation, and one on a far grander scale than anything Randall or the others had ever even considered. The gallery, with its patches of whispered conversation and furtive body language, and the gradual presence of more important, better connected people, leading to the continual second-guessing of every new arrival, felt like a strange, underwater trading floor.

It was like being caught under a magnifying glass, in that it amplified our every word, thought and act to giant size, but also that it concentrated the incoming rays of the outside world's attention exactingly upon us. You'd turn up at six, seven o'clock, and there'd be a hundred people in the gallery, dozens of them ranged in front of Randall's images. They'd look at them, then walk away, making some asinine comment, but five minutes later they'd be back, taking a second look.

We decided to hold a second party on the last night of the show. We had originally intended to go to the pub as usual, and then dancing, but people were suddenly falling over themselves to sponsor us, give us money and coverage, and it somehow seemed incumbent upon us to entertain all these wonderful new people who had deigned to drag themselves across town to attend our show. It seemed like half the people who had come through the doors during its two-week run came back to honour their good taste in making it such a hit, not to mention the people who turned up just because it was *the* party to be at that night. London's Poll Tax Riots had happened during the fortnight the show was on, and there was growing anger about the speed with which the police were stamping down on raves and warehouse parties. As such, it seemed like people wanted to come and take a stand – to 'fight for their right to party' as the Beastie Boys had it. So, things felt celebratory, but at the same time rather impersonal. It was like we were attending the party incognito: a good proportion of the attendees had no idea who we were, let alone vice versa. (People who have claimed or otherwise told me they were there that night: Graham Coxon, Justine Frischmann, Ekow Eshun, Tara Palmer-Tomkinson, Sadie Frost, Adrian Searle, Nicky Haslam.) We stuck together in a happy cluster, fielding the well-wishers who made it through the crowds, everyone trying above all to make sure they didn't miss anyone they shouldn't.

As well as more and better drink, and a proper laser light show borrowed from some club or other, there was a proper sound system, and it did get quite loud. So when Tanya came cutting through the scrum looking for Randall and Kevin, with Griff loping along behind her, we had to press in to hear what she had to say.

'You'll never believe it.'

'No. What?'

She paused and put her hand across her mouth, as if she couldn't bring herself to say what she had to say, but more properly to accentuate her twinkling, resolutely elfin eyes. She took the hand down, and flapped it.

'Randall, you're a fucking genius. I love you.'

'Well, I love you too, darling. Tell me what's occurring.'

'I've only just had a call from Charles fucking *Saatchi*. He wants to buy it. *Schwert and Scheide*. The whole thing. He wants to buy the lot of it.'

I looked at Randall. He looked at Kevin. There was a smile on Randall's face, but it was cagey, evasive. Kevin put his head back and emitted an inaudible groan.

'What?' Tanya's eyes flicked between them. 'What's going on? You could at least *pretend* to be happy for me.'

'Well, Tanya,' Randall began, and he put an arm around her shoulder and turned her into our corner, away from the noise. 'You can't just *sell* them to Saatchi. Not just like that. Or anyone. Jan's got first dibs.'

'First *dibs*. What are you talking about?'

Randall shrugged. 'It's in the contract. He put the money up for the show, he gets first choice of what he wants to buy. He was supposed to be here yesterday, but he's stuck in Tokyo. Ask Vincent.' And he nodded towards me – as if the whole thing was my idea.

'I suppose that's right,' I said. 'It's like a call option in the futures market.'

'What?' She leaned in towards me, narrowing her eyes to concentrate, but signifying, too, I suppose, her complete lack of any respect for me or what I might have to say. She was petite, Tanya, but a forceful personality, then as now, if you ever come across her in her guise as elegant, ageless principal boy of many an arts committee, prize jury and gallery board. That self-delightedly mischievous face, framed by the oversized necklaces below and the neat, tucked grey hair above. Then, she signified her bolshiness through her hokey, farmhand clothes – corduroy trousers, thickly woven men's shirts and Arran sweaters. She didn't have much time for me, I suppose, and the feeling was reciprocated.

I repeated myself: 'A call option. The initial payment, for the catalogue and fliers and so on, is called a premium...'

But she had already turned back from me to Randall and Kevin.

'That is so much bollocks. You can't stop me selling my own work to who I want to.'

This time Randall made a face and spread his hands, hitching up his shoulders – an apology that was at the same time an apology for that apology. A gag, and entirely the wrong move to have made with Tanya.

'It's right there in the contract,' he said.

'Fuck the contract. *I* didn't sign any contract. Anyway, he's had two fucking weeks to say if he wants to buy anything. Time's up.'

'But he has the option.'

'No he fucking well doesn't.'

Randall laughed. 'I'm sorry, Tanya. But he fucking well does.'

She turned to Kevin.

'Did you know about this?'

Kevin didn't reply.

'But, for fuck sake, he's bought your stuff?' she said, putting a finger on Kevin's shirt front. Looming over her shoulder was the fuzzy-haired figure of Griff, her boyfriend. He was always so gaunt and dour, Griff, but somehow soft, too, like a puppy dog version of the heroin-chic look that was such a feature of the decade. I may not ever have seen eye to eye with Tanya, but I came to become quite fond of Griff, despite his profound, almost congenital class hatred of me. He was true, old Left, Griff. The beer labels he painted were intended as a celebration of traditional English working man's culture, though I very much doubt the people who bought them saw them that way.

'Well,' said Tanya, to Kevin. 'Come on, has he bought your new things?'

'One of them, yes.'

'And what about you?' Turning to Randall. 'He's bought yours?'

'Well, actually, yes.'

She laughed at him, stood there with her hands on her hips, and gave a sort of derisive whooping jeer. She must have been a foot shorter than him, or more, but she made him, for a moment, look cowed.

'Fuck you, Randall. You really are just out for yourself, aren't you? But you,' jabbing her finger once more at Kevin, 'You should be ashamed of yourself.'

With that, she turned and started to make her way away from us into the busily dancing crowd, all those bare arms lifting, shoulders twirling.

Randall called after them, 'Tanya, don't worry. We'll sort it out.' Getting, for his trouble, a raised finger.

I didn't actually ever see a copy of the contract, if there even was one, so I don't entirely know who was in the right. Nevertheless it's true that the money for the show and the catalogue and the glossy fliers and invitations wasn't coming from de Vries's own pocket, it was coming from the marketing and promotion budget of Vries Heffer Holdings – and it wasn't Vries Heffer that was in the market for buying Tanya's knitted lingams and vaginas (as he predictably said he wanted to, once he heard that Saatchi wanted them), it was de Vries. Compound this legal murkiness with the sense of incipient rivalry between the two collectors – de Vries had largely stuck to continental artists before this, and Saatchi felt he was trespassing on his patch – and you had the beginnings of quite a spat on your hands. Saatchi, of course, held a grudge against Randall for years, although he and Kevin eventually patched things up, once Kevin had put some clear blue water between himself and Randall.

With Tanya, though, things came to a head almost right away.

It was at about one o'clock, just when the party was finally untethering itself from any remaining sense of occasion, and really starting to take off, that we saw, rather than heard, a commotion at the far end of the main room. Or saw the turning of heads that gave notice of it. Coming through the room, towards the exit, with people stopping dancing to watch, pressing backwards to let it pass, was a procession. Tanya at its front. A line of people, eight of so of them, each carefully carrying before him or herself a glass cloche on its sturdy wooden base and, caught under it, one of Tanya's knitted genitalia. It was like a Saint's Day parade from some remote Umbrian village, those faces heavy with concentration stepping solemnly through the massed ranks. There was laughing, and cheering. Someone kneeled, as if in reverence. Tanya had to stop and sidestep as someone stumbled, or was pushed, and nearly knocked into her, then she moved on again.

Randall started elbowing his way through the crowd at an angle to them, aiming to cut them off before the main door. I followed, picking my way by the patches of coloured light among the dark, finding the gaps in people's movements.

When I caught up with him they were facing each other, a few feet apart, a space cleared in the crowd, like something in a school playground. I took up a position next to Randall, Griff was opposite me, hugging carefully to him an erect blue penis caught in its glass dome. Randall was talking to her, but I couldn't hear what he was saying. She was shaking her head and shouting at him, still holding her own precious load, flinging her chin up with every word.

I looked up as I saw more movement further back in the crowd, where they'd come from. It was a more powerful wave, and a more random one, that seemed to grip and shake the whole room until eventually it reached Tanya and nudged her a step further into our makeshift arena. I could see panicked little currents and whips of movement, heads turning, words passing, someone pressing down on the DJ behind his tables.

I don't know whether I saw them, or heard someone say they were here, but somehow it became clear that the police were on the premises. I grabbed at Randall's elbow, but he and Tanya were caught up in their tussle, shouting at each other more angrily now, so you'd catch the occasional outline or underbelly of a word, he making angry, dismissive gestures, she tightening up her face, her jaw locking, twisting her cloche in her arms as she spat out her words.

Then the music stopped.

'You ridiculous cock-hungry *peasant!*'

The words jumped into the sudden vacuum of the room and hung there, glowing amid the incipient tinnitus thrum. And then there was a policeman, and a second, coming through the room towards us. They knew, I suppose, like people always knew, that Randall was the person to go to. The lead policeman gave a glance down at Tanya's cloche. If it awoke any thoughts, aesthetic or otherwise, he kept them to himself. He looked at Randall.

'Right, this shindig got a license?'

'Absolutely. Yes.'

'No matter. It's too loud. I'm closing you down.'

Randall patted down the air between them. 'I'm sure that won't be necessary. Officer.' (Did he really say 'Officer'? I wouldn't put it past him.) 'Bit loud. No problem. No harm done.'

'No harm done? Don't think so, pal. I could hear you from halfway to the station. It's going off and it's staying off.'

The policeman's shoulder radio crackled, and he turned from us, scanning the crowd as he brought it up and listened, then spoke into it. The crowd stood its ground, not ready to retreat or remonstrate, but on edge. Voices and shoving from the back told us there were more police present. There were a few shouts of 'Pig' and the like – some of them even sounding genuinely heartfelt – but there was also a trickle of people edging towards the door. The policeman nodded at them.

'That's right, run along. Let's get this place cleared.' Then, as they began to move more quickly, 'Don't worry. No one needs to turn out their pockets. We just want to let your neighbours get some kip.' He turned back to Randall. 'Right, do I have to take any details, or can we wrap this up nice and quick?'

Tanya and Griff took the opportunity of Randall's indisposition to move past us, and they lost themselves in the exodus. I half followed them, half hanging back for Randall. Once the policeman was done he pitched in past me, elbowing his way through the guests. We followed them along a corridor that ended in an exit onto a side street. Once out on the pavement, we broke into a run and caught up with the two of them in no time, burdened as they were by their cargo.

Griff turned and tried to block our way, launching into some righteous outburst, but Randall shoved him aside – 'Excuse *me*' – and went after Tanya.

'Tanya, wait up,' he called. 'Don't let's be silly about this.' But as he reached her she turned, spitting further invective, then tripped, took a couple of steps backwards, her face caught in the delicious drift of uncertainty, then she went over, twisting back the way she was heading, so that she landed with the cloche part beneath her.

The glass of the thing was so delicate that we didn't even hear it break, but when she sat up, her hand held in front of her face, the other hand gripping it by the wrist, it was clear that it had. And not like modern, shatterproof glass, as you'd get in a car window or phone booth, but like the old, dangerous Victorian kind it was.

'Fuck.'

'Are you alright?'

'Does she look like she's alright?' said Griff, who'd caught up with us. 'You arsehole.' He gave Randall a shove that had him staggering.

You could see the blood coming from the cut, which was deep and circular, curling under Tanya's thumb from the heel of her hand to the below her index finger. An inch lower and it would have hit the vein of her wrist, and things would have taken a very different turn. The blood was coming out in a thin sheet, viscous, like paint poured from a tin.

She held her hand up at him.

'You stupid *fucker*,' she said, leaning into the word.

'Hey,' Randall replied. 'How is it my fault?'

'It might as well be,' she said, brushing off Griff's assistance with little flaps of her other hand. And she glared up at Randall, putting her hurt hand to her mouth and sucking at the cut. Then she looked down at the shards of glass – just two shards really, it had split itself apart cleanly, decisively, like some terrible Asian martial arts weapon, as if to cut the most vicious line possible through the volume of air it had previously enclosed. She put back her head and moaned.

It might as well be his fault, she'd said, and I think that's how Randall saw it. She was angry at him for the way he'd organised the show, and the price he had to pay for that was acceptance of responsibility for her hurt. It was bad enough that she had to have stitches, and it did leave a scar once it had healed, a scimitar smile under her thumb that she liked to display to Randall, incorporating it into the simple gesture of waving hello or goodbye. It was her way of marking the event, alluding to it, fixing and refixing Randall's guilt.

For, despite the anger of that night, and despite the lurid symbolism of Tanya's cut hand, the circle around Randall, or of which Randall was the apex, and of which I was now an orbiting piece of space debris, was not broken. No longer perfect, perhaps – even I could see that – but not yet dissolved or dispersed. The two of them patched up their differences. They had known each other, after all, as long as anyone in the circle. They went way, way back. Tanya found a replacement cloche from somewhere and sold the whole of *Schwert and Scheide* to Saatchi. De Vries seethed, but Randall won him over with the *Sunshines*, which he loved. He bought them all and put them up straight away in his company's headquarters in Bonn, though there were new ones to be seen in London not long after. And he bought one more of Kevin's pieces, and pieces by Andrew Selden, Don Fievre and Aya, even one by Gina. The catalogues were soon changing hands for thirty pounds each, then a hundred. Today it would be ten times that.

London had taken notice. That we knew, for sure. But it was the fact that, quietly, or unbeknownst to any of us, or perhaps just to Randall and Kevin, or perhaps to all of them, the European art world was taking notice, too. Jan de Vries had anointed our little circle, our little scene, and people outside our ken would look to us, from now on, for what we would do next.

I think what Tanya knew, as much as anyone, sat there on the pavement with her hand weeping red, was that they had to stick together, for the moment, or stick to Randall, just as Randall, for the moment, had to stick with them.

But every time that Tanya waved goodbye to Randall – just to Randall: I never saw her use the gesture to anyone else – she did so by folding her fingers down to her palm and up again, so that her middle finger just touched the scar. It was a childish, overtly little-girlish way of doing it, like a kind of secret handshake. And every time I saw her do it, with the sense that she was teasing Randall with the power she had over him, that bond formed of blood and art and commerce, I thought: this will end.

UNTITLED (NEW YORK CITY)

The next morning Vincent was awake early, dry-lipped and scratch-eyed and alert to his own precocity. It was just the time zones, he knew, and he'd known it before, but it felt special, nonetheless: something gifted him, a head start on New York City. He stood at the windows with his coffee, looking out at the buildings and the streets cut between them. It wasn't so much that the city was still sleeping as that it hadn't arrived yet: was still out over the Atlantic, incoming.

He took his coffee cup and padded around the main room of the apartment in sock feet, going slowly but not pausing to take in anything in particular. The vitrines and display stands were especially spooky at this early hour, lit from inside the glass by their tiny angled spots, while the rest of the room got by on the grey light brought in through the windows.

There was some pottery, some netsuke, some Japanese dolls – so it wasn't all Randall's. Justine had a hand in some of this, too. This gave Vincent an obscure feeling of disappointment. He liked the sense of Randall as a presence in the apartment that had been parcelled out and distributed among the objects, by Justine, presumably; was imprisoned in them, almost: stored, safe. While she, Justine, was here purely, solely, in physical form, embodied only in herself, asleep still in her bed. He didn't want to be reminded of her by anything except herself.

He enjoyed the internal loop of the thought, like feedback.

Tiredness giving itself to suggestibility, like being mildly wasted. For even this idea – that he could see Randall, quivering inside every canvas, photo, object... even this was his, was part of him. He was there with him in the room, trailing at his shoulder, big hands shoved in pockets of an awful silk kimono dressing gown, not saying anything, but seeing every glance and hearing every thought of Vincent's. *What do you think about my paintings, Vincent?*, he was thinking.

You can't outthink a painting, you can only stare it down.

There's only two things you can do with a work of art: make it, and buy it.

This was why, in the end, it was a little perverse, even obscene, for Justine to have the *Sunshines* on display. This was another rule: have nothing of your own in your house. To do so is like incest, or masturbating in the mirror: a vicious and unholy activity. No, you get rid of it, kick it out into the world, like you send out your children, get them as far from yourself as possible. Vincent thought of the ink sketch last night, the solo self-portrait, and the thought unnerved him. If paintings weren't finished until they were gone from the studio, slipping from white-gloved hand to white-gloved hand till they found a room in which to rest, then those drawings and paintings, laid flat in the drawer of the cabinet in the room in this apartment, and the others, wherever they were, were still vibrating with urgent, dangerous energy. They were a hex, or a bomb, or a mine, primed and ready and designed to do damage, and until they did that damage or were safely defused, they would not be still, would not degrade or die.

Eventually, he made his way to the *Sunshines* self-portrait. In the wash of dawn, it looked especially ominous, like some dour modernist museum piece, something from the far end of the last century, a mustard gas cloud unfolding across the fields of the Somme. He sat, watching it, while the dark of the room retreated into light and air, was split open and spread against the walls by the slow-moving spears of brightness.

At seven o'clock he went and showered, and was sat again at the breakfast bar, eating a piece of toast, when Justine emerged, still in her gown, hair caught up precariously with a clip. They said their good mornings and he pushed her a coffee along the counter. Her face without makeup was pale and doughy. She looked like the whole world had looked two hours ago, untouched by daylight. But it was a gift, he told himself, or a gesture of some kind, that she came out to him like this, naked, and unselfconscious of her nakedness. There was an intimacy to it.

'You're raring to go, I take it,' she said.

'No hurry,' he replied, but couldn't stop himself grinning, stupidly – grinning at his own stupidity.

'I'll shower, then we can go.'

'How are we getting there?'

'Well, I was going to take a cab. What, you want to walk?'

'I'd like to walk. Just to, you know. I mean, if it's not too far.'

'It's a fair way, like forty-five minutes. But we can walk, if you want. There's no hurry. We can pick up some decent coffee on the way.'

She took them right out of the entrance, Vincent nodding to the doorman in a way that made him feel distinctly odd, coming out of the lift with her, at this time of day, as if they'd been caught by his parents slipping out of his bedroom. They got to Broadway and turned left, heading north. He had his phone out, following their route, but she clearly had no need for directions.

It was a clear day, the sky remote, flung up high beyond the planes. A winter's day, only warmer, until a snatch of wind whipped around the corner and caught you under the collar or up the sleeves. Justine walked quickly, and Vincent had to work to keep up, skipping and sidestepping the commuters and schoolchildren, going down into the gutter when he needed to, like a klutzy Gene Kelly.

They took Grand Street east into Little Italy, the shops and restaurants mostly still dark, but the cafés busy, a constant exchange of people stepping in and out, being sucked in and ejected. They weren't really talking, the two of them, it was too brisk and hectic for that. He was happy to look about him, taking it all in.

The business-like awnings and stacked, mismatched facades above. The scaffolding, and the hoardings and protective netting, and the cones and hoses in the road, where there was work, and only the trees not yet in leaf to keep the picture this side of perfection – they were needed, he thought, to give the streets the breath of humanity that was lacking.

And, everywhere, the geometric graffiti of the fire escapes, stitched down the fronts of the buildings in zigs and horizontal zags.

Soon they had moved out of the neighbourhoods that were familiar to him, and he had only a vague sense of where they were heading: not towards the Williamsburg Bridge, for they followed Roosevelt Park north, but more or less in the direction of Katz's, or Alphabet City. The streets widened, the buildings stepping back from them and from each other, becoming taller and less interesting.

They slowed up a little, able now to walk alongside each other, and talk. It was the same talk as last night, the same easy, careful to-and-fro: other people, other places, London and New York and Italy and Japan, but not Randall, not the paintings, not themselves and each other.

While they were waiting to cross East Houston she got out her phone and thumbed it on.

'I'll just text Joshua,' she said. 'Let him know you're here.'

'He shan't be able to contain his delight, no doubt.'

She said nothing, but frowned at her screen, and he felt a sharp twist of annoyance at himself. The two of them had never seen particularly eye to eye. Well, Joshua was a kid, so it was hardly fair to apportion the blame equally between them. He'd always found it hard to deal with him – he found it hard to deal with children, in general, they made him self-conscious, he didn't know how to enter into their world, and had no sense that any part of his own life would be interesting to them. And while he'd had no problem with the realignment that came with Justine and Randall's relationship, and had been able to deal with Randall's giant steps up into global success and celebrity, the arrival of Joshua had changed things. Easy to say he represented something he wanted himself, back then. Easier still to say he resented his very existence now: the precious, breakable boy, that made of a woman a mother.

He just made him nervous, he thought, as he followed her across the crosswalk. The misfiring electricity dancing around his body, the lack of control: all reasonable symptoms, and in fact Vincent had known people with more developed cerebral palsy, who had not half the control of Joshua. In fact that was it: it was the uncertainty of Joshua's level of self-control, as a teenager, and a young adult, that unsettled him. He was reckless, and let the recklessness get mixed up with his innate lack of motor control, so you never knew what was real and what feigned, or rather what genetic and what temperamental.

They were five minutes up dull, rosy-red Avenue A when Justine's phone rang, and she retrieved it from her bag, its trill leaping to a shout as it emerged. She stopped and put it to her ear.

'Hello darling,' she said. 'You okay? You got my text?'

Vincent peered in through the window of a restaurant. There was a young man wearing an apron, taking down chairs from the dark wood tables and setting them out.

'Yes, he's here,' she said.

He could see her reflected in the window. She was having to talk quite loud; a truck was reversing in the side-street.

'He's just in town for a few days. At the apartment. Well,' she said, after a while, 'We might do something at the weekend. You could join us. Sure.'

Then her head came up and she said, her voice starting deep and rising, with a teasing lift, '*We?* Who's we?'

Vincent turned to see her laugh. She raised her eyebrows at him in a dumb show of gossip and shared intrigue.

'Well, yes. I might be. Most likely. Come out, do. Saturday or Sunday, either. Okay, great. Of course, will do.'

She ended the call.

'Sorry about that,' she said.

'Josh?'

'Yes. He sends his love.'

'Fine. Look, sorry. I didn't mean to be rude, earlier.'

'Oh, you're probably right. He has his spiky moments, like anyone.'

'It would be nice to see him. I'd like to feel like I know him a bit better.'

'Well,' she said, and she hitched her bag up on her shoulder. 'As his mother, I'd have to say I'd like the same thing.'

He didn't know what to say to that.

'Are we nearly there?' he said.

She looked at him – she gave him a look – and he blushed.

They crossed, and kept going. Justine was quiet, which made him think they were probably getting close. The streets were getting more interesting again, more neighbourhoody, and Vincent concentrated again on the things they passed: these were the things that Randall saw, he thought, when he came here, if he came this way. Here was a shop selling antique sewing machines, there a tree with twisting branches painted up the side of a tenement block, here what appeared to be a Mexican gay bar, there a costume hire agency, its store-front mannequins dressed up as a burglar and a housemaid.

Then Justine turned them off onto East 12th Street, a quiet and personable stretch of road with five- and six-storey brownstones and red-brick buildings, colourful stoops and columns and messily tagged grills over ground floor windows. Pots on the sidewalks with crocuses and an elegant thin-leaved bamboo-like shrub.

There was a little café with benches outside and a chalk board, where they went in for take-out coffees and pastries. When she went to pay she fished out of her bag a large bunch of keys and kept them in her hand, ready.

And, sure enough, four doors along, they were there, tucked in next to a Chinese dry cleaner's. An ugly turquoise ironwork gate over a red door. Five storeys, as romantic and non-descript as any other villagey New York block. Clean red brick. Clothes and a sheet hung over the fire escape railing, plants on another above that, shadows of pigeons.

Justine tried a key in the lock, wiggled it, then took it out and tried another one. They were both silent, while she tried a second, then a third. The third worked, then they were in, in a dim hallway, with notes tacked on a cork noticeboard, and scuffed takeout menus and circulars kicked against the skirting. Vincent pulled the gate closed behind them, it rattled like a cage in its frame, then the door.

'How many floors?' he said.

'All the way.'

'Of course.'

He followed her up. The last door, too, at the top of the stairs, took her two tries, before she got the right key. He could sense her tensing as she flicked the keys around on their ring, her lips pushed tight together. He was breathing at her back, two steps down. Then she had it, and she pushed the door open, then pressed herself back against the wall, arm stretched out along the door to invite him in ahead of her.

He took a step up and faced the door.

'Bloody hell,' he said, on the threshold.

He stepped through.

'Bloody hell,' he said again, slower, and more considered.

Holding out the coffee shop bag away from his body he bowed his head and widened his eyes, bringing his free hand up to hover, quivering in mid-air before him, then his head lifted and came down again, violently, a crashing, magisterial sneeze.

'Shit.'

'It's a bit dusty,' she said. 'Sorry, I should have warned you.'

'No, don't worry,' he said. 'Excuse me.' And immediately sneezed again.

ANGRY PUPPETS

The three or four years after that first show, 'Everywhere I Look', are the ones that I think of when I think of Randall, and London, and the time we spent there together. They are the years that took us from kebabs on the Mile End Road to rich men's yachts off Skiathos; from getting high on paint fumes whitewashing Shoreditch basements for jump-up shows to watching the three-hundredth *Sunshines* canvas roll off the LAC-6000 digital screen-printing machine in the studio outside Faversham; from crashing afterparties to having our own afterparties crashed in turn.

Naturally I look back on that time, the first half of the 1990s, through a revisionist haze. It is easy to think forgiving thoughts about the hard times when you know they led somewhere. Each individual goal – Randall getting a dealer and moving to the Haggerston studio; the two of us setting up IRT Enterprises, and employing our first assistants, employing a secretary and then an accountant, me taking his share portfolio over the 8% hurdle – each becomes a minor step on a grander ascent. I don't doubt that, though I saw each one as a real achievement in itself, Randall always had the shape of the larger game in mind.

I had no such notion. My experience was practical, short term, myopic, even. Two, three evenings a week I'd be out with them, at openings, at the pub, at someone's house or studio. I'd listen, and laugh, and put in my opinion when it seemed appropriate, or called for, happy in my role as mascot, goad, bogeyman, the essential toxin in the bloodstream. I had found my place. They liked it to the point of a fetish that I dressed well, or at least expensively. Andrew Selden was always fingering my lapels, giving out a crabby impression of a Jewish tailor. 'The weave,' he'd say, his voice quivering with emotion. 'The cut. The weave.'

They liked it when I talked about my and my colleagues' spending sprees and trips, the places we'd flown to and what we'd gone there for – the more frivolous the better, the easier to splutter into their beers over. They liked it when I bought champagne for everyone, or tequila, or tossed a bag of cocaine on to the table, or put a meal on my card, especially when it was somewhere particularly naff and unsuited to the entertainment of the sort of clients I was supposed to be using my expense account for. They appreciated all these things – and the cabs I got us across town, paying for two or three if two or three were needed – as much for the symbolic power of the gesture, as for the money saved. It wasn't as if I was paying their rent for them, or buying them their groceries.

'My shout,' I'd say, and Randall would wag his finger at me.

'I hope you're keeping a tally, Vincent, of all of this,' he'd say. 'Because, you know, we're going have to pay you back one day.'

And I'd say, 'Don't be silly. My treat.'

'No,' he'd say, and he'd lean in and squeeze my shoulder in his pinch-grip, working his fingers until he got at the muscle. 'It's a true and unavoidable fact. One day all of this shit that you buy for us will flood back into your life when you least expect it. Every last pint. Every last cab ride. Every last red cent.'

But I didn't care. I was getting my money's worth. The things I bought were baubles; they served as payment for my education at the gutter academy that was Randall and his circle. It was more than him simply taking me under his wing. He moulded me, and instructed me. Crucially, it wasn't that he was trying to make me more like him. What I think he was trying to do was to turn me into the ideal buyer of his work. And not in the sense that he actually wanted *me* to buy his work. There was an unspoken agreement – or at least I understood there to be one – that our relationship functioned on levels other than that of the artist and patron. What he wanted was to see what a clever but essentially ignorant rich young financial whiz-kid would look like if he *got art*, and I was his Pygmalion, his plasticine model, to achieve that end.

It's not something I mind, or minded. And, if that's what the plan was, then it worked. By the turn of the millennium, there were plenty of people like me: young, rich opinionated offspring of Thatcher and Blair, lolling around like pigs in shit in the pot of gold at the end of the credit rainbow, yet sufficiently culturally adept to be able to discuss Randall and his work, and, increasingly, to buy it.

It was a consummate education.

We went to the cinema. The deeply mourned independent cinemas of London, where you could see Godard, Hitchcock and Eisenstein, on flickering racketing pre-digital film, any night of the week. The Lumière, the Scala, the Everyman, as was.

Never the theatre, mind; never music, of any kind, unless you counted clubbing. Occasionally a lecture – philosophy, critical theory – or an artist's talk. But art, yes, and books, yes.

Lots of books. Randall was a great lender and borrower of books. Invite him into your house and you were essentially giving him the run of your shelves. 'Oh, I've never read this!' or 'Oh, look!' or 'Hm, what's this?' were all unavoidable preludes to the borrowing of a book. To my shame I have in my head to this day a list of the books of mine that I lent him and never got back, but then there are far more books of his on my shelves, not that they were necessarily all his to lend. In a sense, all the books on my shelves, give or take the odd John le Carré and Who Moved My Cheese-type self-help bromide, are his.

He lent me books, gave me lists, took me to Compendium or Foyles or the secondhand bookstores on Charing Cross Road and picked out titles for me, half a dozen at a time: Baudrillard, Sontag, Debord, Artaud, Clement Greenberg, John Berger, Van Gogh's letters, Arthur Danto, David Sylvester's book of interviews with Francis Bacon, Vasari.

Now when I take up my copies of those books I come across underlined passages, and I read them and feel that I am reading something actually written about my friend.

Here, for instance, is Baudelaire, from his essay 'The Painter of Modern Life':

> When at last I found him, I saw straightaway that what I was dealing with was not exactly an 'artist', but rather a 'man of the world'. Please take the word 'artist', here, in a very narrow sense, and the term 'man of the world' very broadly indeed. By 'man of world' I mean a man of the *whole* world, a man who *understands* the world and the mysterious and legitimate reasoning behind its every custom. By artist I mean a specialist, a man tied to his palette like a serf to the soil.

'Tied to his palette like a serf to the soil.' A brilliant line, and absolutely not something you could ever apply to Randall. If ever there was an artist who was an artist by virtue of being a 'man of the world', then it was he.

And, by God, here is a line that could have gone on his tombstone: *he understood the mysterious and legitimate reasoning behind the customs of the world.*

As for art, he was eclectic, to the point of arbitrariness. We went to everything: small hip shows and middlebrow nonsense shows and *critically important* shows and blockbuster shows at the National Gallery and the Tate, as it then was.

Weekday openings I'd go to straight from work. Weekends I spent at the New Cross house. Strictly speaking this was shared between Kevin, Andrew, Griff and a law student, Winston

Morrison, who went on to be a judge, but really it was an open house and designated centre of operations. At end of play on Friday, after a couple of drinks with the work lot (not entirely for the sake of form: these were my friends too) I'd show up there with a change of clothes stuffed into a rucksack, dropping off my suit and shirt at the dry cleaner's on Saturday morning, and picking up last week's to hang on the back of a door.

Then, for two days we careered around east London in Kevin's Volvo, or crammed into Gina's VW Beetle, or Tubed and cabbed it, sticking to a variable but thematically limited itinerary of pubs, clubs and galleries, like animals patrolling their territory, and marking it as they went. Sunday mornings featured a monumental fry-up prepared with as much care and planning as your average roast dinner.

Then there was Peploe, Gina's parents' house near Porth Navas in Cornwall. If there's a part of my life, of our shared life together, that I want to do justice to, in writing these pages, beyond the figure of Randall himself, then it's Peploe. More than London, more than Miami or New York or Venice, it is the place that I associate with us all, where all my best memories converge and prosper.

From the very first time I went there, it has been a place that I have navigated by. By which I mean, things that happened there have a stronger, fuller, deeper resonance than if they had happened elsewhere. Or perhaps it's that big things, important things, were more likely to happen there, because of the sort of place it is, or simply because of the importance we chose to place on it. So much of what happened in the circle happened there, or found its meaning there. It's where we were most ourselves, individually and as a group.

Peploe Hall is a seven-bedroom manor house, dating in parts back to the sixteenth century, that sits in a wooded valley high above its own tributary of the Helford River, Scott's Creek. It has a boathouse, a tennis court, and woods enough to lose yourself and fifty other people in. You come at it down a long gravel road through oak and beech trees, jagged lightning bolts of silver birch thrust into the ground here and there between them. When the weather is fine, the foliage acts on the sunlight like a kaleidoscope, spinning a hundred different shades of green, light and dark, onto your car bonnet and windscreen. You drive down that road, slowly – painfully slowly, because of the gravel – after caning it down the M3, and you drop your shoulders and breathe out, finally.

Your first view of the house is sideways on, its façade laid at a slant. It's the gaping openings of the converted stables that welcome you as you enter the wide gravel forecourt. There is no sense of your height above sea level, or the precipitousness of the descent to it. It is only once you go through the house, or around it, that you see how quickly the ground drops away, the terraced formal gardens giving way quickly to a strip of rhododendrons and, below them, untrammelled nature.

You can't see the river from the back of the house, it's tucked in too tight below you, but its presence is betrayed by the gap in the greenery, from here to the other side of the valley: you'd think you could throw a stone right across, but to get there by car would take half an hour, at least.

It is a warm, wet place, the climate benefiting from the gulf stream, and the shelter offered by the woods. Palm trees grow happily alongside the red-beamed Scots pines in the upper gardens, while the woods below are close and dense. Here, the world becomes quiet, poised, anticipatory. Bark comes away in your hand. Tread on a twig and there will be not a loud dry snap, but a muted complaint. The ground is slippy with leaf litter, and ferns grow from under every rock, moss in every crevice. Eventually – it's a ten minute walk, a reckless five-minute race down the quickest, steepest way, grabbing at whip-springy branches to guide and steady you as you go – you come to the river.

The stretch of beach on offer when you get there is hardly picture postcard stuff; just a scattering of shingle across grey, silty sand, or sandy silt, whichever, but it is the house's own. There is just enough flat ground above the high tide mark, and in the lee of the first trees, to accommodate the fire circle: half a dozen felled trunks, grey and barkless with age and laid in an irregular hexagon around the blackened centre, permanently decorated with the charred remnants of the last offering. It is here we congregated, summer and winter alike, not every evening, but always at least once, properly, every visit, to drink and talk and gaze with childish awe into the fire.

Fire by water, it's such a primal thing. On the one hand, the hypnotic effect of the flames, that grab at your attention every second, and again every second, with their fleeting, momentary dance, like a striptease that reveals nothing, living and dying and living again. On the other side, the deeper, quieter, but no less insistent drag of the sea, that gets you not in the eyes, but in your guts.

Look at me, I'm here, say the flames, I'm here now, and now, and now.

And the sea shrugs and says, I'm *always* here.

Peploe is a place that, even just thinking about it, as I write, here, perhaps a thousand miles away, under the Mediterranean sun, gives me the heebie-jeebies, the shiver up the spine – perhaps at the thought of people being there, merely alive, while I am elsewhere.

The first time I visited was the summer of 1990, in the high following the success of the first group show. There were maybe ten people invited, all of us the London circle, and not counting Gina. Gina's parents, Matthew and Hem (for Wilhelmina), were there, that time, for the duration of our stay. In later years, as Hem's and then Matthew's health deteriorated, they were there less often, or less in evidence, though the house remained thick with their personalities.

There was some art in Peploe, but not much, and certainly nothing to hold the metropolitan guest's attention. The library actually had portraits of various Holland ancestors glowering down at you from its walls, and a bronze bust and allegorical figure or two, but most of the other paintings around the place – in the entrance hall, in the drawing room – were of dogs or boats, upstaged by their heavy gilt frames. The house was fitted out for entertaining, but entertaining of a particular, rather dated kind. The central room of the ground floor was the dining room, dominated by a great long banquet table in forbiddingly dark wood, with glass-doored cabinets standing sentry around the walls. I never saw it used as intended, to feast twenty people on peacock and suckling pig, though occasionally you'd look in and catch someone perched at the corner of the table, quietly scoffing a bowl of cereal. The kitchen table sat twenty, too, at a pinch, and that's where we ate, pushing and shoving and passing great plates of food this way and that. Likewise, there was a casual sitting room and a formal drawing room, where Matthew liked to have us gather at cocktail hour – for sherry, by preference, though he also mixed a mean Tom Collins. Asking for a simple gin and tonic was considered impolite.

While we spent the evenings there together, as a group, days tended to be more loosely organised. Dinner apart, there were no fixed meal times, and people split off into small groups, or couples, or on their own, out on day trips, or to go with Gina in the house's motor launch to explore the Helford and the coast down towards the Lizard, if the weather was good, or take walks or bike rides, or just hide somewhere with a book. Or sleep in. We read a lot at Peploe, strange as it is to say. For all their cautiousness as regards art, the Hollands had a well-stocked library. (Hem had studied at the University of Heidelberg and there was a lot of Continental philosophy, in English as well as the original languages.) You'd often find a couple of people in there, reading in silence, as if completely unaware of the other person, or unwilling to talk to them. Randall, perhaps, more likely than most: pushed deep in one of the red leather armchairs, thick-socked feet up on a side table, an invisible 'do not disturb' sign swinging above his head. Camera click. Move on.

The tennis court was in pretty bad repair, but we played a lot of ping-pong. The table was in a sort of outhouse, dingy from the clematis that covered most of the windows, and heated by a two bar electric fire in winter. People perched on workbenches or slumped in prolapsed canvas-backed chairs, cradling cans of beer and calling out random comments. We played Clocks, mostly, where all the players go round and round the table, until they miss a shot and are knocked out. The fewer people still in, the more frenetic the circling.

My educational schedule didn't stop for the holidays, and Randall would make use of the ancient photocopier in Matthew's home office to produce reading material for me. I can see Justine, having got out of bed one morning to venture downstairs and make us cups of tea, laughing as she pulls on a jumper over her night clothes. She has found a set of carefully stapled pages slid under the bedroom door. She brings it back over to me, yawning and smiling and mussing her hair as she scans the text. 'Here you go, darling. Schiller on selfhood. You make a start on that and I'll bring you up a nice cup of tea.' But I'm getting ahead of myself.

We're in London, in the time between the first group show and the explosion of *Sunshines* into London's febrile consciousness. We're in the time when the young men and women of the 'circle' were already Young British Artists, though not known as such. We're in a time when what I saw from them was not work so much as *activity.* Everything seemed to be permanently building towards something, but that something seemed to permanently regress, to slip around the next corner.

Talking about what you were actually doing was seen as bad form. It showed up those who weren't getting anything done, anything 'worthwhile', anything 'proper', anything 'real'. I wonder about Kevin, in retrospect. He was the one who was producing significant work during this time. Did he talk the talk, too, or did he sit there, basking in his own secret productivity and listening to the rest of them spout? Probably the latter.

And if they talked, rather than acted – or talked as a form of action – what did it matter to me? I watched them work, on occasion, but really how interesting is it to watch an artist at work? Randall gutting television sets. Aya dismantling ironing boards and welding them back together in weird configurations. Andrew spending the day moving in and out of the dark room. Griff or Keith painting – at least there was something to look at in that, the weird slow accretion of paint on canvas, though you had to be careful not to get caught up in the mystique of it. There was no alchemy to their technique: that's not where the meaning lay.

Perhaps I just thought that an artist was someone who talked about art.

Oh, we talked. And we looked. We saw so much art. Randall took me to so much art. There was a patience about him, and a generosity – a generosity to me, and to the art he introduced me to – that his critics just wouldn't believe. Sometimes we went on our own, just me and him, first thing on a Sunday or last thing on a Friday, when they started doing late openings.

In the gallery, he'd tell me to close my eyes and take me by the elbow and guide me through the rooms to a particular work, then stand himself next to it, so that he blocked the information label on the wall, and it would be: 'Open your eyes. Now don't say anything. Stare it down. Embarrass it into meaning.' Then, minutes later. 'Okay, now. Tell me what you see. And make it good, or those nice American tourists there will think you're a right spanner.' He liked to leave me sat in front of a painting while he went off to the café have a cup of tea, or make a phone call, or chase up someone he knew who worked there.

Once he left me in the Rothko room at the Tate for three hours straight. 'Sit there. Don't move,' he said, and went. I did as he said, and sat, slowly, conscientiously, in the spot he'd picked out for me. I allowed myself to acclimatise to the room, to the stutter and flow of the other visitors as they moved around it, in and out of it. I observed how they approached the huge paintings, directly, or sidling up to them, how they arranged themselves in front of them, accessed and considered them, then how they dropped them, detached themselves and moved on. How they stood, shifting their weight, jutting a hip as if to flag the precise degree or particular quality of their impressionability at that given moment.

'Body language can speak art criticism just as well as the verbal kind.'

I sat as still as possible, hands on knees, feeling smug and entirely self-contained. I forced myself to focus exclusively on the painting in front of me, letting the others fizz and pulse in my peripheral vision. I defocused my eyes, tried to make them blurrier than they already were, as if there was some fuzzy secret heart to them that could only be accessed through physical distance, or some other form of disconnection. I harvested thoughts as they occurred to me, counted them out on my fingers, and then constructed mnemonics around them, so that I would be able to retrieve them when needed.

Was there really a spiritual dimension to these drab red and maroon blooms? They looked so uncomfortable, hanging there on the wall like rugs brought back from some exotic souk, that should by rights have been down on the floor, being honourably walked over. Was the room different for having them in it? If you took them away would it change?

I picked an individual and tracked them from the corner of my eye. Tried to gauge their opinions and intentions regarding the painter and his work, to get at their reasons for being here. Tried to read their readings – and to read how they would read me. Was I just a sad banker in a suit, consoling himself with abstraction? Had I been sacked, or stood up? How did my thoughts measure up to theirs?

The fantasy of the gallery as levelling ground or pick-up joint lives on. Is it the art, or the building? Did it happen in churches, when churches were where we went for this? I felt certain Randall could walk into this room and walk out, ten minutes later, accompanied by whomsoever he chose.

Or was I hoping for a moment of grace, for the room to suddenly slow and cool, for the people in it to dissolve and the maroon curtains to part for something terrible and ineffable to step down from inside them, come towards me and take me up, lift and crush me into an annihilating embrace? Would the other visitors come back to themselves to find me sprawled on the floor, unconscious, or dead, or delirious with enlightenment?

I had, I noticed, been clocked by the gallery attendants. For a while two of them seemed to be in conversation about me, but even after the second one had gone I felt the eyes of the other on me, from there on her stool by the doorway, a thirty-something Eastern European-looking woman. Did she love art, I wondered? Was this a vocation? Perhaps she was as bored as I was, and passed her time making up stories about the gallery visitors. Or was I merely something to rest her eyes on other than the paintings? The finger running down the rota of a morning: Rothko, *fuck*.

Or perhaps I was a potential threat, simply by virtue of having sat in the Rothko room, without moving, for over an hour. Perhaps I had inadvertently triggered some clause in a security protocol, and the other guard had gone to fetch more and bulkier attendants, who were at this very moment waiting in the next room, with a white-jacketed doctor, syringe held discreetly behind his back? Perhaps I was on the point of leaping up to attack the paintings, of hurling myself bodily at their bland tumourous womb-worlds, or stabbing and slashing at them with… what? My fingernails? My fountain pen? My Amex card? The thought made me laugh, and the laugh made the possibility more real.

As if in an actor's exercise, I tried to make myself seem more like a psycho. I petrified myself, tensing my neck and shoulder muscles until you could have bounced a coin off them. I set my jaw, and drilled my eyes into the depths of that one picture, felt the red of it pound in my vision like the rising blood-blindness of a madman. I imagined myself as a psycho killer in a movie, moved by art to raging obscenity.

No dice.

No one pounced.

Not the staff, and not me.

Clearly, I was not mad, or no madder than any person who sits in an art gallery for hours on end at the behest of a so-called friend, for no apparent reason beyond their own spurious edification.

Look at me, in the art gallery! Look at me, looking at all the art!

I began to need to pee, and the warm fist of my bladder bolstered me in my resolution. I would sit and look at the Rothkos until Randall came back, or until I pissed myself.

What Randall liked about the Rothkos above all was their backstory. He painted them, in his fifties, as part of a commission for the restaurant in the Seagram building in New York – absolutely the most exclusive dining venue in the city – only to withdraw them before they were unveiled, in a fit of self-doubt, and disgust at the use to which his work would be put. Food and art. One of Randall's beloved juxtapositions. For him, the story was a flag to smack into the ground at the far end of the continuum that started with the French *modernes* handing over sketches in lieu of payment at La Rotonde.

As if in deference to this historical association, he occasionally tried to pay for food with art, too, but with less success. I once saw him, staggeringly drunk in Venice, during the Biennale, trying to repeat the upturned champagne bottle in a bucket trick, to settle a bill at De Pisis. That was a wrench. Other times, it was more controlled, though perhaps never entirely so. 'Times have changed,' he would say, unlit fag wobbling just out of sync with his shaking head, as the barman or waiter stood by, variously amused or pissed-off, looking at the piece of paper, covered with some inane scribble, that was being held out to them, or that rested on their little silver tray. Randall would take the paper, crumple it in his big, careless hand, and toss it over his shoulder. He had the comic timing down, you can't fault him that. A wave of the arm, a raising of a finger. 'Times indeed have changed.' And he'd reach, with a shake of the head, for his wallet. Or look to me, head on one side, as if I might perchance have a drawing about my person that would pass muster. Or, failing that…

That trick didn't work, or rarely, but for a year or so, from about 2000, you could eat your seared scallops and milk-fed veal in the Dorchester surrounded by *Sunshines*.

Two years later you'd have been eating at Fugu, Randall's sushi chain, with Malcolm's photos on the walls, the cutlery designed by Kevin.

The other thing he liked about Rothko was the line, I can't remember where he heard it, that Rothko killed himself because he met the people who bought his paintings.

It was a joke that Randall liked to tell to the people who bought *his* work.

Clapping them on the shoulder and shaking them until they, too, laughed.

But there's me, sat in the Rothko room, legs tightly crossed in my Armani and Churches, gently humping myself in the hope of keeping my bladder under the cosh. I passed through boredom, fatigue, frustration and fury, and eventually, I suppose, achieved some kind of distracted serenity. Of course I couldn't leave the room – if he should come back when I was gone! – but I did get up and walk around a bit. I placed myself right in front of each of the six paintings, as close as was permitted, shins brushing the low black cable, to see if they gave up anything more to intimate inspection than they did to formal, detached appraisal. They did not. They were still dull, drab daubs, the pitiful work of the secular spiritualist equally afraid of death and of faith, of nothing and something.

I imagined unzipping my fly and actually pissing on them, tried to guess how far up them I could get the arcing stream of my disgust. It made me laugh, at the pity of it, and the laugh jerked out a warning drop of urine into my fabric of my underwear. I really was about to piss myself. I turned from the painting and walked, then jogged out of the gallery, gifting the attendant a dagger look as I passed. She watched me go, unimpressed… *the Rothko-bladder equation, proven once again.*

I pissed, hurriedly, carelessly, then splashed water on my face and ran back through the galleries, throwing myself clumsily between visitors – 'Excuse me, sorry, excuse me' – like I was late for a meeting. I heaved a shoulder against the heavy doors of the Rothko room, pushed it open and went inside.

There he was.

He was stood at the far end of the room, just in front of where he'd left me sitting, gazing at the painting, my painting. With his legs spread, his arms crossed, and his broad back and shoulders, he looked like Nero facing down an arena full of gladiators. I slowed my pace as I crossed the room, regulating my breathing, trying to order my thoughts, retrieve my aperçus.

'Randall, hi.'

He turned.

'There you are. I wondered where you were.'

'I had to go to the toilet.'

'Fine. Look.' He looked at his watch. 'Let's make tracks. There's someone I want you to meet.'

I don't remember where we went, or what it was that was so important, but I do remember spending the rest of the day struggling to suppress my fury that he hadn't asked me a single question or made a single comment about my total-immersion Rothko session; didn't so much as acknowledge the fact that I'd sat there, as instructed, for three whole hours, thinking deep thoughts, or otherwise inventing them, and getting nothing more for my trouble than a righteously numb backside.

But that was Randall. Always ready to push people to extremes, to stretch their patience and their tolerance to breaking point. But he was always ready, too, to go to those extremes himself, to force himself down meaningless avenues just to see how his response altered the further he travelled from any rational purpose.

'Failure is a species of achievement,' he said.

And, 'Success is largely a case of knowing when to stop. And I'm glad to say I've never known when to stop.'

Which is something of a gag. For most of his creative life, Randall's biggest problem was working out where to start.

During the spring and summer that followed 'Everywhere I Look' he returned to the studio he shared with Aya, and to his television sets, sometimes removing the screens to construct little theatre sets inside them, complete with dolls, sometimes going so far as to actually show moving images on them, mostly video loops of an undistinguished banality.

Meanwhile, behind his back, the *Sunshines* series was acquiring a life of its own. It was getting seen. The thirteen that de Vries owned were hung prominently, first, in his company's Bonn offices, then in Paris, Amsterdam and London. Which is how, one evening, I found myself collared by a fund manager by the name of Jed Cousins at a charity event at the Guildhall.

It was towards the end of the evening, after we had weathered the various speeches and presentations, and bid, some of us, for signed guitars and weeks in villas in Zermat and on Mustique, when a man manoeuvred himself into the seat next to me.

'You're Vincent Cartwright, right?'

'That's right,' I said.

'Jed Cousins.' And he held out his hand, and we shook, both of us trying to gauge how drunk we both were. 'I'm with Merrill.'

'Of course.'

'So, you're a pal of this Randall, then.'

Amused and disoriented by my friend's intrusion into this most un-Randall-like environment, I pushed myself up in my chair.

'Randall. Yes. Yes, I am.'

'*Sunshines* Randall.'

'*Sunshines* Randall. Yes.'

'Good.' He nodded, and waved at a passing waitress. He ordered us drinks, then went back to his previous posture, chin on chest. 'I'm quite the admirer, you know,' he said.

It turned out Cousins was, or held himself to be, something of a collector – 'in a minor sort of way, you understand' – and had indeed seen the *Sunshines* pictures at Vries Heffer in Paris. Jan was here; we had shaken hands briefly and exchanged pleasantries, but in this situation, and without Randall, I had no business associating with him; and it was he who'd pointed me out to Cousins.

'I was very taken with them,' he said. 'They are stunning pieces, don't you think?'

'I do. They are.' I nodded, then frowned.

He was right, after all. I didn't want him to think I thought he wasn't right.

'Now, Jan tells me Randall doesn't have a dealer as such, and that you're my best chance of getting in touch with him. So I wanted to ask. Do you know if he's still making them?'

'The *Sunshines*?'

'Yes, the *Sunshines*.'

'Well, I don't know. It's not something I feel able to speak for him on. But I can certainly make enquiries.'

'Splendid. I'm very interested.'

'Of course,' I said.

He sat a moment longer in his chair, looking at me in that blank drunk way that people fall into at the end of such evenings. It was as if he couldn't get over his disappointment that I wasn't Randall, or couldn't produce him then and there, from inside my hat or up my sleeve. Then he downed his cognac or whatever it was, and stood. He faced out into the room, and held himself abruptly still, like someone suppressing a belch.

'I had a Matisse once, you know,' he said. 'Not a big one, but a good one.'

The ornate ceiling of the Guildhall jellyfished in place behind him.

'Did you,' I said.

'Yes.' He removed a hand from his trouser pocket and affected a gesture of indifference. 'The Peter Blake I've still got, and one or two Bridget Rileys, but the Matisse I had to give up, I'm afraid. You know how these things are.'

I tried to give the impression I did.

He patted his jacket pockets, found a card and gave it to me, suddenly bored of me, bored of Randall, and of the picture he hadn't even bought yet, that hadn't even been made. 'I wouldn't have wanted it anyway, by that point,' he went on. 'It felt tainted. But still. *Woman With Blue Flower*. A characteristic work. There was a man who really *got* women, wouldn't you say?'

The news, when I passed it on, with precisely the flourish I had failed to provide at the Guildhall, that Jed Cousins, senior fund manger at Merrill Lynch and one-time owner of a small but characteristic Matisse, wanted to buy a *Sunshines* painting, was greeted in the Randall camp with a predictable display of hilarity and exuberance.

That evening turned into a sort of war council, as Randall canvassed opinions as to how he should proceed. He knew exactly what he was going to do, of course; he just wanted the talk, wanted to coax out any and all opposing arguments, warm them in his hands, take one of them and turn it, like an expert turns a vase on a television antiques show, or, it occurs to me, like Ai Weiwei with one of his Han Dynasty vases, then look up, into the camera – oops! – and let it drop.

The two main options seemed to be, either to turn down the commission, and let the baker's dozen *Sunshines* portraits stand as a complete, finished project; or to really go for it. Randall would set himself up as a portrait painter, a contemporary Sargent, holding up a mirror of intellectual flattery to London's great and good, even as he moved breezily amongst it. He would be a society painter. A Randall in the hallway of every house; in Randall's hallway an invitation to every house.

The goofiness and excitability with which the debate was conducted didn't entirely mask a certain amount of unease. Kevin, in particular, was beginning not to find the joke as funny as he once had. Was it simply because he was on the verge of success – acclaim, sales, a measure of financial and artistic security, *being taken seriously* was the phrase everyone used, not without irony, like they later said *major work* and *international reach* – and he felt that he had got where he was purely on the merits of his art, rather than the performance that went along with it? There was that, but I think he was worried for Randall, sincerely so. He thought that his friend's act would, sooner or later, backfire on him.

'Just be aware of how far you are going to them, and how far they are coming to meet you,' he said. 'What you don't want to do is take up a position that, if they suddenly retreat, if they stop finding the joke quite so funny, you find yourself exposed.'

Taking up a position, exposure, how far you are going. He wouldn't have thanked me for saying it, but Kevin was so nearly talking City-speak.

'I respect money, Vincent,' he said to me once, 'and I respect people who handle it with respect. But I don't love it, and I have absolutely no respect for people who do.' This was more recently, after Randall's death, certainly, and after the financial meltdown of 2008, when it was easier to talk in such terms, but then that was Kevin's take on things all along. He never became caught up in the idiocy of those years when art and money were booming upwards, alongside each other, bouncing off each other and gaining energy and velocity with each collision, racing up the screen towards unsustainability.

If Randall had worries about going back to *Sunshines*, and 'rolling it out', as they said (*floating* it, would have been my phrase), then it wasn't along these lines, but rather that he wanted to be absolutely sure that it was the right work, and the right time, for him to put himself out there.

'The way it works is that you're only going to be remembered for four things.'

We're still in the pub, the Devonshire – where we went when we wanted to reassure ourselves of our authenticity.

He held up four fingers, and moved his hand to show them to the others around the table, like someone playing charades. 'Four things. Or pieces, phases, whatever. Four. Any more than that doesn't fit into people's narratives of creativity, of the artist's life and work. Three is too pat, five too complicated. Posterity may have a long memory, but it has a fuck of a short attention span. No, really. Look.' He counted on his fingers. 'Warhol: Brillo

112

Boxes, Marilyn, *Empire*… I don't know – the *Car Crashes*, maybe. Duchamp: *Fountain, Large Glass, Étant Donnés*. Four, or three. Or, I don't know, *Nude Descending A Staircase*, if you really must.'

'What about Koons?' someone said.

'Koons? Easy. *Equilibrium. Rabbit. Made in Heaven*.' Beat. 'And some shit he hasn't made yet?'

'Bacon?'

'*Three Studies. Pope. George Dyer*. Um…'

'*Crucifixion*. The '33 one.'

'Yes. Thank you, Kevin.'

'What about Picasso,' someone said, perhaps a hanger-on, a clinger-on. Someone, at any rate, unaware of the protocol. Someone surprised at the sudden drop in the temperature in the room, the icy hush. 'What?' they said, or maybe didn't even say, just said it with their face, looking around himself or herself, blankly, uncomprehending, waiting for the punch line.

It would have been Kevin or myself, or Tanya, who leaned across to stage-whisper the warning: 'Best not talk about Picasso.' And then, when they tried to smile, to earn the laugh, 'Honestly. Don't go there.'

Picasso: another joke in which the humour resided purely in the degree to which it was taken seriously. Either Randall pretended to be genuinely afraid of Picasso, because he was so monstrously prolific and unassimilable, or else he *was* genuinely afraid of him. Which it was, I don't know, but certainly the façade never dropped in my presence, and there's more than one journalist, and one television presenter, who found their interview cut unexpectedly short when they dropped that particular name. Was he for real? Go figure. There were no Picasso monographs or catalogues or biographies on his shelves. We never went to the museum in Paris or Barcelona, always walked straight past his paintings in galleries when we came across them. And I happen to know he was particularly anxious about Chicago buying his huge *Chrome*

Bionic Duck piece for the city. Was he worried it wouldn't stand up against the Daley Plaza sculpture?

Randall, flustered, went on. 'Four. That's it, four. So, Vincent, *Sunshines* could be huge, if I go for it. It would be, no question. I just need to be absolutely sure that that's the one I want as that first piece. It's not enough for *Sunshines* to bring me fame and money and adulation and a queue of beautiful, willing women leading out of my bedroom door and down the street. It's got to stand for me when I'm dead.'

And he moved his head, just a touch, towards me, fixing his eyes more firmly on mine, or mine on his, and bringing all the pressure of his available seriousness to bear, and the air between us seemed to slow and vibrate, his hand held there, the four fingers, upright, vibrating, them too, just a touch. It was a performance all right.

Not that it made any difference to his thinking, but I encouraged him to go ahead and take the commission, perhaps for no better reason than it kept me in the loop, as the contact man, the go-between. And it seemed like the fun thing to do: fun being, for me, if not synonymous with art, then a fair approximation of it. It was me, after all, who got to phone Jed Cousins and arrange the sitting, who got to not only negotiate the price, but also explain to Jed, as delicately as possible, what a sitting would entail.

In the end the first *Sunshines* commission was produced in December 1990, a marker of sorts for the new decade, for in retrospect it seems like the 90s only really started in 1991 – the year of *Nevermind*, of *Generation X*, of Richard Linklater's film *Slacker* – a Randall favourite. Cousins was followed by Harvey St. John Hall, and then Robert Emery and Cindy Bryce-Elliot. We soon had the routine down pat: the commission of a *Sunshines* portrait bought you breakfast at Gina's house, which Randall effectively moved into until he found the studio in Stean Street, Haggerston. Breakfast was cooked, when we could persuade him to come, by Ken Maltese, who at that time was sous-chef at Marco Pierre-White's Harvey's restaurant, to a menu of your choosing, in consultation with Randall's personal dietician (sometimes me, sometimes Aya), who could even offer suggestions of what to eat the night before. We usually recommended the full bacon, eggs and beans, on wholemeal bread, with perhaps muesli or Weetabix or Shredded Wheat beforehand. There was always plenty of coffee and fresh fruit to hand. Prunes, for the anxious. A half of Guinness, if allowed, worked wonders.

Anthony Burridge and Elton John – though this was later, when we were more firmly established – brought their own personal chefs. David Bowie had this yoga position which he said did it for him. One now ennobled business leader, whose name I probably shouldn't mention, turned up unannounced and in something of a rush, and bolted along the corridor, his legs half bent beneath him, while his car waited outside and Randall stood holding the door, doing a slow, dazed double-take, like the straight man in a farce.

Then there was Alexei Leonov, the Georgian aluminium oligarch, who brought along the ingredients for his breakfast and had one of his two drivers (he came in two cars) stand over Ken as he prepared it. The drivers were huge and hugely frightening men who looked like they'd had their suits welded on to them. The other one spent the entire time stood by the front door with his hands held crossed in front of his crotch.

Once Leonov had eaten his breakfast – smoked salmon and scrambled egg with chives on very thin slices of incredibly heavy bread, together with several cups of milky coffee – he sat and talked art prices with Randall for ten minutes, quite knowledgeably. Then he excused himself and nodded to the other driver, who was waiting by the window, with a Gucci holdall at his feet. He opened it and took out a roll of no doubt very special toilet paper and followed his boss out of the room.

'He's actually going to wipe his arse for him,' I said to Randall, eyes boggling.

Randall tried to get me to go and tell them they couldn't use their own toilet paper.

'Tell him it's got to be ours. Say it's something to do with the absorbency.'

'Fuck off. You tell him. He's probably armed.'

'Get away.'

It was Ken who told us, after they'd gone, that he almost certainly was carrying. 'Leonov has got his fat fingers in all kinds of dodgy pies,' he said. 'He's been trying to get a British passport for years, but we won't have him.'

'Should we even be selling to him, then?'

Ken looked at us like we were mad. 'Fuck, yeah. Get his money while you can.'

Leonov was eventually convicted in the Russian courts in 1995, for tax evasion, although that seems to have been a standard trumped-up charge. He was killed in prison, presumably in revenge for reneging on some deal. I have no idea where his portrait is now. I don't doubt but that it will reappear, along some marvellous or dubious route. For the moment, however, it presumably hangs on a wall in some dacha or secure Moscow apartment, like a scalp, the shrunken head of a vanquished rival.

But I'm getting ahead of myself. We had made maybe a dozen bespoke *Sunshines* when Tom Nasmith called and invited Randall to visit him at his office.

He had first approached Randall after the group show, and they had talked, but he hadn't pushed himself forward. 'Honestly,' he'd told him, coming on like some benevolent uncle, 'the last thing you need right now is a gallery. You need to work out what you want to do.' He'd given him his card, and said, 'Just promise me this, don't sign with anyone else until you've heard my pitch.'

I went along with Randall to Nasmith's gallery near Hoxton

Square, in my semi-official role as his 'financial advisor'.

The gallery rooms themselves were par for the minimalist course, scrubbed and whitewashed to give the work on show that sterile 'serious art' vibe, though the high ceilings had been left untouched, blackened concrete slabs showing through the confusion of ventilation ducts and lengths of bundled cable.

Once through the passcard-locked door, however, the backrooms buzzed with a giggly, caffeinated energy, like a fashion show an hour from curtain up. People strode about with important-looking pieces of paper in their hands, greeting each other in Mockney patois, the yowling fairground ride vowels of the age. There were cardboard boxes piled everywhere, and whiteboards scrawled with lists and flow charts in coloured pen.

Nasmith himself was – and remains – a strange mixture of the refined and the risible. His suits were sharp enough, but he styled his hair with a Brideshead flop, and he had a fondness for brocaded waistcoats that Randall – and not just Randall – ribbed him mercilessly about. 'You're not fat enough to wear a waistcoat, Tom,' was his opinion. 'Wait till you're fifty.'

Nasmith waved us into a pair of chairs and sat himself at his desk, while we accepted cups of coffee from an attractive young assistant. He lifted a pile of correspondence and magazines placed in front of him and dumped them unceremoniously off to one side. Then he leaned his arms in front of him and fixed us, one after the other, with his gaze. I got the impression he was sizing me up, in particular, as if he'd *got* Randall, already, but he didn't know quite where I fitted in, or to what extent he would have to accommodate or displace me in order to operate on Randall as he wanted to.

'Right, guys,' he said, eventually, still leaning on his desk. 'The *Sunshines* are good. They're great. You've done well.' And he proceeded to reel off, rather to our surprise, a list of the people we had sold them too. 'Now most of those are acceptable, but there are a few there that you really don't want. With care, something like this could be a major concern, a long-running concern, but you don't want to spread yourselves too thin. At the moment, frankly, that's where it looks like you're heading.'

And then he counted off on his hands another half dozen people who, he said, were in the market for a *Sunshines* portrait. Names that were, without exception, of a significantly higher calibre than those we'd sold to.

'Look,' he went on, focusing now on Randall alone. 'I'm not saying I can make you rich. Any fool could do that.'

Randall barked out a gruff laugh of pleasure.

'No really, let's not kid ourselves.' Now Nasmith looked at me. 'He's going to be rich, right? Right. But, Randall, I can make you rich in the most fun, and stylish, and' – he leaned further over the desk, his fingers spread out before him – 'basically *fuckable* way.'

'How so?' Randall said. 'How fuckable, Tom?'

Nasmith pushed himself back in his chair and braced his arms on the desk. Randall was concentrating on his words, I could tell, but it was his behaviour that had me entranced. He was masterful. His body language seemed to be saying this was a done deal. Not just that we would sign up, but that everything he said would come to pass.

'Well,' said Nasmith. 'By selling your work to the very best people. The people who, if *they* were artists and *you* were rich, you'd want *their* work on *your* walls. Honestly, guys, you've got to be way, way more picky about who you give your work to.'

'It's not like we're *giving* them anything,' Randall said.

'You are, though, the prices you're charging. Remember, it's not just your picture you're selling them, to hang on their wall. It's the *ownership* of that picture. You're selling them the right to profit from your art in the future, and potentially far more than you've been making from them.' He tipped his chair back, and

118

balanced it, on its back legs, letting his hands lift and almost hover over the desk.

'I promise, if you come on board with me,' he said, 'that we will sell only to the very classiest of buyer. And, if we are, on occasion, forced to sell to some fucking rich cunt, then I guarantee that I'll be right there alongside you, having a good old fucking laugh.'

Fucking rich cunts.

I've no idea if it's a phrase that Nasmith made up on the spot – I've never heard him say it to anyone else – but it became the catchphrase, the catechism, the central tenet of his relationship with Randall.

Certainly, you could say it sealed the deal then and there.

'That sounds like a plan to me,' Randall said, and stood up. He held out his hand across the desk and Nasmith took it, then mine, a tiny hint of a bow in his posture, a signal that he intended to defer to me in precisely nothing.

He called for champagne and the assistant came straight in with it, in its bucket, as if she'd waiting right outside the door for her cue.

Nasmith popped the cork and poured out three glasses, humming a little tune to himself as he did so. We raised our glasses, but it was Randall who proposed the toast.

'To the fucking rich cunts,' he said.

Nasmith's smile stretched, for a moment, then he killed it and frowned, puckering his eyebrows and letting his fringe bob menacingly over his eyes.

'The fucking rich cunts,' he said, sober as you like.

'Fucking rich cunts,' I said, too.

Nasmith lifted his glass, then drank, downing the champagne with professional ease. 'Right,' he said. 'I'd say this calls for a proper celebration. What would you say to lunch?' Lunch turned into an afternoon at the Groucho Club, with mine and Nasmith's cards behind the bar, and a gradual accretion, hour by hour, of additional celebrants. There is documentary evidence available suggesting how the day ended, but I'm not in a position to personally corroborate very much of it.

Fucking rich cunts. Even when we were all indisputably rich, ourselves, and sometimes (for Randall at any rate) richer than the people he sold work too, we went on saying it.

Another thing that Nasmith said, that stayed with me, this whispered across a restaurant table to Randall, six months or a year later, when he had successfully increased the price of a *Sunshines* portrait by a factor of five, and lined up a couple of absolutely top-notch collectors for sittings: 'I'm going to make you rich enough that one day you'll even be able to afford one of your own paintings.' Which, when you think about it, was kind of an admission vis-a-vis the stonking commission he suggested, and we stupidly, ignorantly agreed to.

The way he went about turning Randall from a *succès de scandale* into a stable, saleable name, was an object lesson in the workings of the market. What Randall loved about Nasmith, at this point in their relationship, was precisely what I loved about Randall: the sense he gave of being his ticket into a secret world.

He used *Sunshines* portraits as bait to lure in art ingénues, whom he then worked hard, to build them into serious spenders on his other, more established artists. For some buyers, a *Sunshines* portrait was no more than the equivalent of a bumper sticker. 'I was in London in the 90s, and I made a killing.' They weren't all overpaid, Flaming Ferrari numbskulls, however. More and more people were coming to London from Russia and the Middle and Far East to make money, and to spend it. London wasn't just a market, it was a bazaar. First they bought the paintings, then they bought the galleries. Eventually they bought the auction houses, and the banks.

Of course, Nasmith had to hide from the serious collectors quite how many *Sunshines* Randall was making (and the price he was selling them at). They were understandably suspicious, partly because of Randall's overt, perhaps temporary fashionability – this was the time in which he began to start making an appearance in the diary pages of the tabloids – but more importantly because Randall was untested on the secondary market.

The problem with the *Sunshines*, for Nasmith, was that they were individual commissions. Which was good for him, as a dealer, in the short term – if someone wanted a *Sunshines*, they had to come through him – but the paintings had a distinct, though as yet untested lack of viability on the secondary market (who wanted a picture of someone else's shit on their wall?) and that meant Randall had only limited potential as a long-term client. What Nasmith wanted was a show for the gallery, a collection to take Randall up a step in his career, and that he could place with his top-flight collectors.

Which is where Randall didn't deliver for quite a while.

Perhaps he was just having too much fun being profiled and photographed, going to and throwing parties, and being flown around the world at the invitation of his various collectors, for some of whom having an artist on their yacht was almost as important as having the work of art. Some of them, Randall said, wanted him pretty much to stand next to the portrait, there where it was hung, to be pointed out as they passed by, giving a tour to some other, more important guests. It was, he said, like racehorse owners: the horse gets the adulation; the jockey gets a pat on the head.

Of course, the parties were fun. It was fun, certainly, to feel that strange butterfly feeling you get in your stomach in a lift, ascending, as the parties we went to started to move up into the next-level-up of parties. At some of these, Randall was the only person there from the circle, but not always. As intended, the group was moving up, not in concert as such, but in increments, as if giving each other the sly, occasional leg-up. You would look around the room at an opening to see who was there, and you'd see Tanya or Kevin, Gina or Andrew. A short nod of recognition, that the rules remained intact: stay clear when needed, allow in and make an introduction when wanted.

I went along when I could. An entourage, of a certain size, was often expected. Turning up alone was somehow an insult. An invite to a weekend house party might come with a request scrawled across the bottom or dropped in at the end of the conversation to 'just let us know how many you will be'. The air tickets might be taken care of, or a car sent. The etiquette was fluid and intuitive, and it presented, for Randall at least, a steep learning curve. I think it reassured him to have me there beside him. I was more at ease in this kind of life, even if I didn't quite yet take it for granted.

Put Randall in a Cork Street vernissage, on a hot London night, and he's in his element. Put him on a yacht off the Côte d'Azur, caught between the white of the limestone cliffs and the whiter August sun, ply him with cocktails and surround him with a crowd that contained, say, a smattering of catwalk models, some fabulous and not-so-fabulous movie types, plus businessmen and their wives and girlfriends, and you would see a less assured figure.

An early example was a long weekend with television comedy producer Dominic Baxter, in his villa in the hills above Marseilles, with his yacht on hand in the harbour to drift east along the coast to the *calanques*, the remote, steep-cliffed bays that loop towards Cassis.

It was easy to see how bewildering Randall found it. He just didn't get the idea that the same rich people who were quite happy to listen to him pontificate about Koons and Deleuze back in London, didn't necessarily choose, when relaxing on their boats, to talk of such things, and while they were happy to have him along and include us in their bubble of luxury, when he started to talk about art, they tended to blink their eyes and look a little startled, and seemed, as he soldiered on, not to be paying quite the same level of attention as they had at Maureen Paley only a month or so ago. Small talk didn't always come easily to Randall, who depended so often on saying the opposite of what people expected him to say.

Another stumbling point was dress. Knackered black jeans and a faded Nirvana t-shirt under a donkey jacket was fine in London, fine even, at a push, at a Mayfair opening, but people looked rather shocked to see you coming up on deck in them on the Côte. People assumed they were an outfit, when in fact they were a uniform. In packing to go to Baxter's villa I had to force Randall to bring along his one pair of shorts, a pair of these terrible baggy skate shorts. When I saw him in them, the cups of his knees glowing with ominous pallor in the Mediterranean sun, surrounded by stunningly beautiful women in up-to-the-minutely revealing swimwear, I rather wished I hadn't.

I wasn't the only one to be dismayed by his wardrobe. I caught a couple of young actresses, or actor's girlfriends, I don't recall, giggling over him. 'Who *is* that? Why is he dressed like that?' But the high point of the visit, for me, was Yana, Dominic's gorgeous though rather imperious wife – no mean collector in her own right, and the owner/subject of two different *Sunshines* portraits – commandeering Randall and taking him shopping in town. They returned three hours later, she gaily triumphant, he sheepish, and between them some several thousand euros poorer, with an impressive collection of bags and what he explained to me was 'a whole new look'.

In fact, I did try to help Randall with clothes. After all, this was one area in which *I* was qualified to instruct *him*. But there are only so many quiet suggestions you can make, before you start to sound like a nag. I set him on the road to – if not elegance, then at least a better appointed dishevellement. It would take Justine, as always, to tame, or turn, him entirely. That is the thing about really expensive clothes, for men at least. With a few startling exceptions, you have to try very hard indeed to look bad in them.

They may all have started out as scruffs, but not all the circle adapted so badly to their new surroundings. I remember one party, at a pair of villas on Ibiza owned by Irish record label head Mike Buck, to which Gina, Tanya and Kevin were also invited. Three days spent largely in and out of the pool, the evening piling into taxis to head down to the quayside restaurants. To see Gina, and even Tanya, swan around in bikini tops and ripped denim hotpants, for all the world as if this was their usual get-up, was dazzlingly strange and, I think for Randall, unnerving. (Kevin, by contrast, had a decent physique, and was happy to show it.) The worst thing was – and I'm not saying this simply to denigrate Gina and Tanya – they did seem to come back from weekends such as this with their artistic reputations enhanced. As if lounging by a pool in a two-piece swimsuit, sipping a mojito, could make you a better artist. They were tan, they were beautiful – even Tanya, who seemed to step out of her fusty mannish London clothes into an entirely new persona. In fact, it was amusing to see Griff and Randall almost corralled together under the parasols, in their bad clothes, while the women prostrated themselves in the sun, and swam lazy lengths of the pool, and flirted with (or *flirted with* flirting with) the money and money men that surrounded them.

There is success, and there is success. To have your art displayed, and bought, and collected, and written about and appreciated by the critics and tastemakers around you is a form of success to which every artist must aspire, but once achieved, it begins to pall. Success, like the profits of a limited company, must increase;

shareholders don't want the same profits next year as this year, they want more. It can be easier, however, for a company to expand, than for an artist to improve, and precisely where the comparison breaks down is that, for an artist, the shareholders – those you must appease – are people who, actually, have no vested interest in you at all. They are external, and indifferent.

The danger of success is that you fail to grow as an artist in proportion to it. You must get better, as you get bigger. While you're alive, you've got to keep the primary and secondary markets in some kind of alignment: the secondary, resell market for your old work and the primary market for your new. There's nothing worse than seeing an artist going for astronomical figures in the auction houses, while his or her new works sit in the gallery unsold. It's a feature of the art market that has never been seen before the last thirty years. And the thing about contemporary art, as opposed to, say, being a film director or a novelist or a musician, is that there is no natural and generally understood creative cycle to hide behind. If you make a great film, people want your next film to be bigger and better, but they will have the good grace to wait – for a certain amount of time – for you to make it. The same with a novel or an album. You've got to go away and do the damn thing. The problem with art is that you don't make one big thing, you make lots of little things, and people don't see any real reason why they should have to wait for their own little thing. Especially with conceptual art, or the quasi-conceptual version of Pop Art the YBAs made. After all, it's not as if you're actually going to paint it *yourself*, is it?

By 1993 the *Sunshines* series had given Randall a platform from which to mount his next project. They were part of the landscape, and there certainly was no apparent let-up in the numbers of people willing to sit for them.

Randall at this point was experimenting with the television-head sculptures that would eventually make up his 1995 Nagoya show, but Tom Nasmith had no affection for them, and refused, then at least, to show any of them in his gallery.

What he and Randall came up with, as a first full solo UK show at Nasmith's gallery in late 1993, was a brilliant extension of the *Sunshines* work, entitled *Sunshines and Nightskies*.

What Nasmith needed was a selection of works that he could sell to those major players who didn't fancy the process of sitting for a *Sunshines*, but also, and more importantly, to public collections (museums) and corporate ones (companies) who had no collective anus to wipe.

Their solution was to do a series of portraits of anonymous sitters. The canvases were given titles according to their professions – 'Unknown Soldier', 'Unknown Banker', 'Unknown Pop Star', 'Unknown Doctor' and so on. The other innovation of the series was that they were diptychs: on the left you had a standard *Sunshine* picture, and on the right, a *Nightsky,* based on a CAT scan image of the sitter's brain.

The metaphysical connotations of the pairing were obvious, but the critical thing about the *Nightsky* pictures was the jaw-dropping cost of producing them. A brain imaging machine cost well over a million pounds in the mid-1990s, and we had to pay a private hospital nearly ten thousand pounds for the use of their machine. Naturally, this expense was not an afterthought or by-product of the work, but integral to it. Nasmith was able to price the diptychs far higher than the individual commissioned single portraits, and was also able to offer diptych portraits as commission – again, at greatly increased price.

Sunshines and Nightskies, held in October 1993, needed to be a success, and it was. The papers jumped at the chance to re-engage with Randall's work, now that he was properly famous in his own right. The critical response was mixed – Tom Sutcliffe in *The Independent* called it 'a collection of quite remarkable fatuousness' – but others warmed to the deeply compelling concept at the heart of the show. It was simple, but not throwaway; easy to grasp, but easy, too, to lose yourself in contemplation of it.

Randall, whose cousin was a demolition expert in the Royal Engineers, was particularly proud that 'Unknown Soldier' – modelled in fact by an infantryman from the Black Watch regiment wounded in the first Iraq war – was bought by the Ministry of Defence, and was for a long time displayed at one of their rehabilitation centres in East Sussex. (And no, I'm not going to tell you who the Unknown Pop Star was. That secret dies with me.) But all the works sold, and Nasmith was gratified with their spread – including the Kunsthaus in Stuttgart and the Getty Foundation. He made repeats of the show three times during '94 and '95, in Chicago and Dusseldorf and Edinburgh.

It was a natural consequence of Randall's success that I began to see him less during these years, and the years that followed. He began to travel widely, and if he and Nasmith flew to Dusseldorf – or Miami – to organise a show, they might stay a week, and I might fly out for a day or two, for the opening. I wasn't there for the preparation, with the attendant gaps in the schedule, the precious downtime, the hanging out and kicking of heels that was the most fun part of all, because I got to be alone with him, or him and Tom. I missed it, but I was busy myself, building up my portfolio of clients as a private wealth manager, and I did have a social life of my own, too. I was in the beginnings of a relationship with Justine Giovanni, the woman who would later – to everyone's surprise, including, I think, their own – marry Randall, and start a family with him, though at this point I was carefully – some might say paranoiacally – keeping the two sections of my life apart.

In 1994 and 1995 Randall re-organised his working and living arrangements, retaining the Haggerston studio, moving into a house in Stoke Newington, and then establishing a larger studio outside Faversham on the then highly unfashionable north Kent coast, where most of his work for the market was produced. I ran my private wealth management business from an office in One Canada Square, the Canary Wharf tower, so it was easy for me to take the DLR to see him in East London, either at home or at work.

We tended to meet – like this, formally, at his office – once every couple of weeks, supposedly to talk about financial matters, though largely he left that in my hands, and that of his accountants. Usually he took me down to his studio on Stean Street (no longer there, if you are in the mood for some heritage tourism), a much smaller set-up than in Kent. This was where he did his experimental work – the work that would become *Angry Puppets* – and as such it was much closer to how I remember the space he had shared with Aya, though now he had assistants, usually ten or so in attendance here, with the same again – and, later, many more – in Kent.

There were two huge workbenches running down the length of the room, usually strewn with various tools: saws and drills, paint spray guns, steel rules and soldering irons. One wall was covered in warehouse-style shelving, in which were stored his raw materials – television sets in various states of dismantlement and, now, mannequins, again complete and incomplete. One compartment full of legs, another of arms. The heads, which of course weren't needed, were thrown into a small skip in the corner, when they weren't kicked around the studio floor in raucous games of football, or adapted with special effects kits to look like gruesomely genuine body parts and left around the place as practical jokes: in a half-unzipped sports bag on the Tube, or thrown into people's laps or arms from moving cars.

I loved visiting the place. It meant a lot to me that Randall still wanted to share his works-in-progress with me; that I still had a use for him beyond the financial. When I gave a hint of this, he characteristically twisted it around the other way: 'I only asked you to look after my money so that I could be sure I had you close by, surely you know that, Vincent?' And, with a hand on my shoulder, his friendly-aggressive-ironical shake, 'I *need* you near me, Vincent. I never know what I think about anything till I've heard you ask me what it's supposed to mean.'

This was clearly a statement that struck him as particularly good. He saw me laugh, as much at his conceitedness as at the phrase itself, and grinned. 'Go on, then, Vincent. Write it down.'

And I got out my notebook and pen, and he repeated the words, leaning over me.

'I never know what I think about anything till I've heard you ask me what I mean by it.'

The notebook that I wrote this, and everything else, down in was a black Bruce Chatwin-esque number, embossed on the cover with my initials. It had been a birthday present from Randall in tribute to my habit of writing down things that he said, just as I clipped news articles and reviews from the papers and magazines about him, every inch the devoted parent. Obviously, Nasmith had a press team which was there to do that very job, and far more systematically than I ever could, but I kept it up, as best I could, for my own amusement. The notebook, though, was different. This was a job that no one else was doing, and it was clear, from fairly early on, that it would one day be a valuable resource. For him, it was a double treat – he got to have me write down what he said, and he got to rib me for doing it. He liked to sit there, on a slow day, and read through it, sometimes making corrections, adding in new possibilities, very occasionally scrubbing one out altogether. The whole thing wavered magically between the ironical and the genuine. It was like one of those holograms you get, or used to get, in cereal packets: tip it one way and you see one image, tip it the other and you see another. Both are *there*, printed on the little card, but it's impossible to hold them both in your perception at the same time. They are mutually exclusive, yet mutually indicative: each image seems to logically imply the other in a viciously compressed vicious circle.

At the risk of repeating myself – though this, I think, gets to the core of it – the irony seems like irony until you treat it as irony, at which point it starts to seem genuine. Then it seems genuine until you begin to treat it as such, at which point it becomes clear that it could only be ironical. The difficulty lies in the fact that the ironical version seems to encompass the genuine, whereas the genuine ignores the ironical.

The way it worked was this. He would say something – I particularly loved the way he did this when we were in company – and then give me a particular nod, on the quiet, or sort of on the quiet, sometimes no more than a pursing of the lips, or a concentration of the brow, and I would take out my book and write it down. Sometimes I would ask him to repeat it, and sometimes he would hold out his hand for the book, snapping his fingers, to check that I had got it down correctly. My books of Randallisms run to some two or three hundred entries. Ed Hitchcock begged me for them when he talked to me for his biography. He *begged*. But I refused. I think I knew, even then, that I'd want to try to write something about Randall, myself.

It was in Randall's Haggerston studio, then, that he worked on his telly-head people, the *Angry Puppets* that were shown first in Nagoya and then, in different configurations, in London, Germany and America. They were shop mannequins (reinforced with a steel skeleton) dressed in gender- and age-appropriate clothes, and their heads replaced with 14-inch colour televisions, though now he could afford plasma screens, rather than the bulkier cathode rays he'd previously relied on. These were linked by cables running down through their bodies to video recorders (this was, remarkably, before DVD) which played on them images of people's faces.

The power of the pieces settled chiefly on two things: firstly the arrangement of the mannequins, most famously a family of four sat slouched on a sofa, as if themselves watching television; and most infamously, two positioned as if having sex, the first, rather androgynous one, leaning half-bent over a table, trousers pooled around its ankles, the other as if entering him or her from behind, the whole organised so that, as far as possible, you couldn't actually tell if the things had genitalia or not.

The second factor was the images shown on the face-screens (none of the telly-heads ever had soundtracks). He ended up settling on a cast of four actors – who played a mum and dad and a son and daughter of roughly eight and twelve years. He filmed each of them at length, sat on chairs with their faces held gently between cushioned pads to keep them absolutely still, while they affected various emotions and attitudes – from the dully placid to the extreme, as if they were being tortured or (for the two adults) having sex. The footage was then edited and looped for each screen, the idea being that the mannequins started off with the correct faces for their size and clothing, but that they eventually started swapping around, and duplicating, so that (for the sofa family, for instance) dad's face appeared on daughter's body, and daughter's on mother's, and so on, or that dad or daughter appeared on two, three or all four of the screens. This was fine for the sofa family, of course, but caused untold – and quite predictable – controversy with regards to the fucking couple, which started off with mum and dad's faces on the correct bodies, but soon seemed to show dad fucking daughter, or mother fucking son, and eventually every conceivable combination of the four of them. No matter – or all the more matter – that the daughter's face, whether fucking or being fucked, never showed any expression appropriate to that situation, but instead yawned, frowned, beamed, laughed, chattered away or simply stared blankly at the camera. What Randall really wanted, but which the technology of the day wouldn't allow, was for each screen to cycle quite randomly through the different expressions. He had to settle for an individual hour-long looped video reel for each screen, which would then be started at a random moment.

Is it any wonder the show went down so well in Japan, land of such a chronically disturbed relationship to sex and the sexuality of youth? Japan, of course, would come to influence Randall in a far more decisive manner, in part through the guidance and influence of Justine, but that will come later.

But it would be a mistake to fetishize the studio as the place where, to use Randall's withering phrase, 'the magic happened'. The magic, most often, happened elsewhere.

Take the invention of Randall Yellow.

This work, like those in the very early days, began in the pub – although the pub was now London's ubiquitous Groucho Club, or the Colony, the setting for so many grim and grotesque anecdotes. Others have covered enough of these, with regards to Randall and those around him, that I feel able to pass in silence over most of it. It would be easy to say those stories have been exaggerated, or simply made up, but the fact is they probably aren't.

What I would say, though, is that most of the bad behaviour must be understood with reference to the creative tenor of the place and the time. By bad behaviour I mean: the rudeness to staff and other guests; the crowing and jeering and intellectual breast-beating and sing-songs; the nightly or near-nightly crescendo of drinking and drug-taking, almost as if everyone wanted to race to the end of the evening as quickly as humanly possible; the importuning of other, unfortunate celebrities. By the creative tenor I mean that while they were doing all these crazy things – Randall, and Andrew, and Tanya, and the others that crossed them or congregated around them, Tracey Emin and Keith Allen and Alex James and Jude Law and Ewan McGregor being only the most obvious ones – they were also conducting the closest thing the capital had at the time to an intellectual salon. They let their hair down, and more than their hair, but even as they were doing it, or perhaps right up until just before they began doing it, they were talking art, and talking film and theatre, and talking philosophy. Slurred philosophy is philosophy nonetheless. The same goes for hungover philosophy.

Among all this, the moment when Randall decided he needed to invent a colour does stick in the memory. It was in January of 1996. Kevin had just had his hugely successful debut exhibition with Larry Gagosian in New York, featuring his *Transatlantic Memory* pieces. This after winning the Turner Prize, the year before, having been shortlisted way back in 1993. Perhaps it was simple rivalry that made Randall sit up and say he was thinking of inventing a colour.

'No one's done it for ages,' he said. 'It's time someone came up with a new one.'

'And why do you think anyone would be interested in a new colour?' said Tanya.

Kevin was sitting back in his armchair, glowing with his American success. Randall might have been looking at him, or *not* looking at him, as he spoke, and though Kevin's response was no more airily dismissive than usual, it carried an accustomed weight.

'Whether anyone's interested or not isn't the point,' he said. 'There are no new colours.'

Malcolm Donner agreed. (He leaned forward and poked a finger; these days he did a lot of Kevin's leaning forward and finger-poking for him.)

'Right, it's not like it's Klein Blue or anything.'

'Well, Klein Blue wasn't exactly original, either,' Kevin continued, 'but in a world in which you can pop down to B&Q and get any colour you want mixed right in front of your eyes, the issue becomes academic. There are simply no dark, undiscovered corners, Randall, left for you to colonise. The palette is not exhausted, it's saturated.'

I spoke up then, perhaps speaking a little too obviously out of a need to support Randall. 'All things being equal, though, what colour would you go for?'

Randall clasped his hands and stared at the ceiling, humming. This wasn't meant to show that he was thinking, but rather the opposite, that the thinking had already been done, and he was merely waiting to give us the fruits of it. Then, when he had done as much pretend thinking as he thought he needed to, he brought his head down and picked up his glass and, just before he drank, said, 'Yellow.'

He drank, and we waited, then he wiped his mouth and said, 'Randall Yellow. That's got a good ring to it, don't you think? There's something shocking about it. Fluorescent vests and police tape. Wasps.'

'Hazardous chemical cylinders.'

'Sharps boxes in hospitals.'

'Precisely. The world holds yellow in reserve, for emergencies.'

'And this is an emergency, is it?' said Kevin. 'That you need a colour to attach your name to?'

'No, but I think I can get what I want out of yellow without doing any damage to its more practical applications. I'm talking about yellow in the art gallery.'

'So, you're, what – going to dip some naked models in yellow paint, and roll them along the wall?'

'I don't know *what* I'm going to do, to be fair, Andrew. The first thing to do is to get the colour right. Once I've done that then hopefully it should become fairly clear what to use it for.'

At first there were no entirely yellow works. Randall just started incorporating the colour somewhere in everything he did. *Sunshines* had it as one of their two colours, sometimes background, sometimes the smear. It gradually colonised the *Angry Puppets* mannequins, with here a jacket, there a pair of trousers.

'I think it's useful for people, when they're in a gallery, to be able to orient themselves. The yellow is intended to help them in this,' he wrote in the catalogue for 'Randall Yellow', his second show at Nasmith. 'It's like a flag, or a sign. It attracts attention and it identifies what it flags, all at the same time.'

'How very helpful of Randall to "flag up" his works in this way,' responded Brian Sewell in his review in the *Evening Standard*. 'It will save busy gallery-goers the bother of walking the length of a room to see if the vapid collection of mannequins with television screens for heads really is by him. Yes, they are. And no, it's not worth the walk.'

Yellow letterheads for our stationery. A yellow paint job for Jan de Vries's Bentley. A yellow three-piece suit by Ozwald Boateng that Randall wore to pretty much every opening in 1996 and 1997. Whether or not Randall Yellow was good art, it was certainly of the zeitgeist. The 1990s, after all, was the decade in which branding really came of age as an element of marketing. Advertising wasn't enough. Having a logo wasn't enough. Viral marketing was where it was at. Paying lots of money to hip young East End companies who made it look like you weren't spending anything on advertising, it was just *springing up*, irrepressible, a force of commercial nature. Hot on the heels of Randall Yellow came the launch of low-budget airline EasyJet, with its ubiquitous orange styling. Not that the one influenced the other, but that they were both of the moment.

There have been suggestions that Randall actually tried to copyright the colour, but that's absolutely not the case. (It's five parts Pantone 108C to three parts 3965C to one part industrial phosphorescent yellow, in case you're interested.) He *wanted* other people to use it. It's just that he wanted to stamp his mark on it, or stamp its mark on him, so whenever someone else used it, people would think of him first. So when *The Independent* printed its masthead and page furniture in it to mark Randall's Turner Prize win, that same year, and when the phone operator T-Mobile used it as the background to a series of adverts, and above all when Alexander McQueen sprayed Shalom Harlow with the colour in his 1998 Givenchy show, Randall was delighted.

Nasmith was less so. The fact was, though, the yellow work didn't sell particularly well. The show sold out, and was followed up by acclaimed shows in Utrecht, Copenhagen and Southampton, but it wasn't exactly followed by a flood of people clamouring for their own Randall Yellow work. In fact, *Sunshines* commissions started coming in with the request for any colour *except* yellow. It's not hard to see why. It was just too successful as a branding exercise – it concentrated everybody's ideas about him as an artist to a single element, but it simplified him, too. It turned him from a showman, a circus ringmaster, into a clown, a one-trick pony. Did Randall have in mind the events of The Great Day of Art, in 1998, from the get-go, two years before? I don't know, I would doubt it very much, but that's where Randall Yellow had its greatest moment, its apotheosis – where it made it biggest splash, so to speak. That's when it – and, in a way, he – went big, went over, went beyond Kevin, even, to some level of celebrity beyond that of a merely internationally successful artist, and left the rest of us behind.

UNTITLED (THE ARTIST'S STUDIO)

The room looked, undeniably, like it had stood untouched for years. Seven, eight years, whatever. The air was stale, carrying a faint antique sheen of paint, and heavy with dust. Dust speckled the air, and silted the floor, was scuffed and marked where shoes had disturbed it. It hung in grey strings between the strip lights. Somewhere, too, there was the smell of something still quietly desiccating, giving itself up mote by mote to the general atmosphere of the place.

Vincent blew his nose on a paper napkin from the coffee shop. He ran his eyes around the bare, whitewashed walls, the wide, thin single-glazed windows at front, the sheets of newspaper curling and yellowing on the floor. On them, and on the work benches along the long wall, were collections of tins and jars and tubes, all rammed with brushes, a confusion of angles. And everything – the handles of the brushes, the sides of the tins, the lids lying next to them – caked and scabbed with spills and drips of colour, darkened with age. Behind him, on the wall beside the doorway, there was a massive set of storage racks sticking out perpendicular. These, for the moment, he avoided.

Finally, near the windows, a pair of easels, each with a canvas set up on it, both paintings obviously unfinished, left in the middle of being worked on. The metal trolley holding the paints and brushes was right there beside them, the floor around it scattered with tissues and rags gone stiff as parchment.

139

It was one large room, probably knocked together from two smaller ones, with full-width windows looking out over the street, and a skylight at the back, together with a corridor heading off somewhere. Ceilings not particularly high, the top floor of the block, perhaps with access to the roof somewhere.

'Christ,' Vincent said, again. 'Bloody hell.' He was vaguely aware he was repeating himself.

Justine had gone over to one of the work tables and was leaning, arms crossed, with her backside against it. The table behind her was covered with a mess of books, magazines, paper. He looked at the easels, then at her. She gave a sort of shrug in response: that this time the permission was not needed, was not hers to give.

He stepped towards the two easels, but slowly, deliberately, putting on his glasses and scanning them as he approached, trying to make himself *see* them, in real time. Now he was here, in the studio itself, he had the certain feeling that he must grab every atom and quark of data in the room and fix it in his mind; that this was his job, to collect and store and process it.

The canvases were both laid out on the horizontal, maybe five foot by four. The one on the right was barely started, with nothing more than pencil marks showing the beginnings of what would have gone on to be bodies. The other, still only half-finished, was a close-up of someone, their head and hands, and what looked like another person's buttocks, there in outline only. The fur of dust where the canvas met the sill of the easel.

The face was half-familiar, but it wasn't until he stepped close enough to see the photo, thumb-tacked in the top corner of the canvas, that he recognised the subject. It was Sidney Vasquez, notorious art fair whore. In the photo, clipped out from a magazine, he was beaming inanely away in black tie at some function, caught just at the moment of leaning forward to drink from his flute of champagne. He must have just had time to twist his pre-sip physiognomy into this approximation of a camera-ready smile, but it was a silly pose all the same, and he must have hated it when he saw it, a month later in *Harpers*, or wherever.

And there he was in the painting ('Fucking hell,' said Vincent, quietly), the same foolish expression blown up to twenty, thirty times the size, the half-open mouth looming now not towards a flute of champagne, but towards a huge implied pair of raised arse-cheeks, these taken from the image fixed to the opposite top corner of the canvas, this one cut out from some hardcore magazine.

Vasquez had his tongue out, lolling disgracefully where it wasn't in the photo, and he had his index finger stuck into what would presumably have gone on to be somebody's arsehole or vagina, Vincent didn't care to think too closely about which. The finger, fully painted in, stopped abruptly, cut off, at the point where it disappeared from sight. The other hand clutched an invisible buttock, as if to pull it to one side. This other hand, too, was painted in. It surprised him to think of Randall working like this, taking one part of the picture nearly to completion before he started on the rest. It went against all his ideas, never particularly well developed if truth be told, of how you even worked in oils. But it spoke, he supposed, of extreme technical confidence, of working – if he understood it right – in something like *impasto* the way other people produced photorealist paintings. The way one colour was pressed into another, yellow into white, or white into brown, and then forced to combine, against their will, right there on the canvas. He leaned in, examining the landscape of the paint, its contours and accumulations, its little peaks and smeared glaciers. There was action enough on the surface.

'Fuck,' he said, again, and he turned to Justine, who'd come to stand by him. She had a coffee in each hand, and she passed one to Vincent. 'Is this really him? Really, truly? I mean, we can't show this, can we?'

He took a sip of his coffee, and wiped the froth from his upper lip. Justine drank from her cup, in turn, but didn't answer.

'Well,' he said at last. '*Can* we? Or can we?'

'Well, I guess we're saved the need of making a decision on this one, because it's not finished.'

It was as if she knew her answer wasn't good enough. A pinched flicker passed across her face, gone as quick as a camera shutter, then she went on. 'Come,' she said, passing behind him, brushing a hand briefly down the back of his jacket as she went.

He followed her to the wood-framed racks. She stood watching as she counted in from the left: one, two, three, then tugged at the fourth rack and brought it out a little way, sending specks of dust reeling in the air. She pushed aside the plastic sheet that hung down over the pictures.

'Hmm, no, not this one.'

She returned it to its place and slid out the next one to its fullest extension, its little metal wheel squealing and clupping as it ran over the floorboards.

There, once she'd flipped back the plastic sheet over the top of the frame, was a painting of a similar size to those on the easels. It was a reworked version of the one with Robert Rauschenberg and Carl, from the portfolio, but this time starring Rauschenberg, McKenna and Micaela Dysart, with two more people in attendance, one of them a man in a nurse's uniform, the other, possibly, Cindy Sherman. The background was fully finished, down to the pattern of the flock wallpaper and the clumsy folds of the curtains. The figures held halfway between a kind of verisimilitude and caricature, between Jenny Saville and Otto Dix.

Next to it was another painting. On it – clearly, cutely – was Jeff Koons, twice, giving himself what looked like the fuck of his life. One of him sat on what looked like a desk or dressing table, the other one of him leaning off the first one's cock, one leg on the floor, the other lifted up on the desk. Behind them, a window looking onto an apocalyptic sky, lava red.

'Well, that's what it is.'

'Isn't it just.'

142

'He, at least, you'd think, wouldn't sue. If these got shown. He wouldn't be able to, would he?'

'I don't know. I suppose not. Am I supposed to say something here about not being able to make it stand up in court?'

'Ha.'

He walked around to the other side of the rack. Here there was a slightly bigger painting, with Doug Veit – who had paid for the wolf *Superhero* outside the Galleria in Houston – and, bizarrely, Louise Bourgeois, busying themselves at each end of a befuddled-looking middle-aged man with close-cropped grey-blonde hair. The man was gripping a pair of David Hockney-style glasses in one hand, reaching behind himself with the other hand to palm Bourgeois' breast through her blouse. Vincent pointed at him, and looked at Justine: a question.

'Sami Blum. The Getty Trust.'

'Ri–ight.'

He hunkered down and looked at it.

'Justine, these paintings are fucking dynamite.'

He looked up at her, but she held her face still.

'No, they're not,' he said. 'They're not dynamite. They're plutonium. They're radioactive. They'd kill anyone who came near them.'

'We've come near them.'

'Then they'll kill us. And, look, just to be an idiot. They're definitely his? Absolutely, definitely?'

'Absolutely. Definitely.'

'And how do we know?'

'Because he signed them?'

'He *signed* them?'

She pointed, and there it was, a small black scar of paint collected in the bottom corner of the canvas.

'Christ,' he said, leaning so fast to look he tipped and had to steady himself on the rack, the wire biting his palm.

He let his finger dandle just over it. *IRT. 05.*

'I still don't believe it,' he said. 'I mean, he never signed anything.'

'Well, he signed these.'

He did, though, he thought. He did believe it. He believed it, completely, utterly, intimately. He believed another thing, too. He believed that all this, this room and everything in it, had been made with a purpose. The fact was, Randall wanted him here. It was a test, though what the test consisted of, and how he'd know when it was over, and whether he'd passed, was not something he felt confident he would ever be given to know.

He stood and tugged down the protective sheet, then pushed the frame back, and pulled out the next one, and then the next one. Not really looking at the paintings, just seeing that they were there, occasionally giving off a quiet expletive or exclamation. 'Marc Etieno. And Andrew Cheel. Fucking hell. He would *not* like that painting. Sorry. I should stop swearing.'

He looked round but Justine had gone to sit on a low, knackered-looking sofa towards the back of the room. She looked tired. He gestured at the corridor leading further back.

'Is it alright if I...?'

'Of course.'

The rest of the apartment consisted of a loo, a shower room, and a kitchen. Electric hob encrusted with carbonised remnants, a scattering of mugs and glasses on the surface, sun-faded juice cartons. The wrapper from a packet of biscuits, chewed and shredded as if to suggest it had been consumed by mice or rats. He opened and closed a few cupboards – mostly taken up with cardboard boxes of artist's supplies: Princeton, Blick, Atelier. The fridge when he opened it let out a stench rank enough to make him gag, but it, too, was not stocked for real life, just tomato sauce, milk and a few deli containers, the plastic clouded over and the lids forced upwards by some foul growth.

He went back out to the main studio room, and looked at the deep stainless steel sinks that had been put in at the corner: more dead, ruined brushes; bottles of white spirit and cleaner.

'What, should I just have a poke around?'

'Sure.'

'I mean, I won't touch anything. Or should we…'

'No. Go for it. I mean, this is really just to let you catch up.'

'Of course.'

Vincent made his way along the tables stretching along the left-hand wall. Those nearer the window carried all the paint, brush pots and other materials. Those at this end were given over to magazines, which piled, spilled and spread across them in various stages of evisceration, bristling with little bright-coloured stickers as place-markers. There was a more or less cleared space where Randall seemed to have worked on the images with a blade and rule, a mess of cut-out pages, with rectangles cut out of them. Images pinned to a cork board on the wall. The table, where it showed through, criss-crossed with blade cuts. At this end, mostly society and art mags: *Harpers & Queen*, *Tatler*, *ArtForum*. At that end, pornography, of the more hardcore variety: *Hustler*, *Private*, *X-Rated Action*.

He sifted the pile, sliding glossy paper against glossy paper, then gave a gruff laugh.

'Of course, we'll have to document all of this, you know, for the archives.'

'Yes, quite a collection, isn't it? He must have been the last man in New York actually buying printed pornography.'

'Ha.'

He moved down the table, to where there were a few stacks of books and art material catalogues. *Oil Painting Techniques*. *An Acrylics Primer*. *Color Mixing Recipes for Portraits*. *How to Paint Like an Old Master*. He picked them up and flicked through.

'You've seen these?'

'I've seen them.'

'It's unreal. He taught himself to *paint*. *Randall* taught himself to paint.'

'I know.'

'Holy shit. It's like… I don't know what it's like. It's incredible.'

'I know.'

He put down the books and looked around him. The dust, the plainness, the mess. This was where Randall, came, in secret – in *secret*? Did no one else *at all* know about this place? Where he came, and – what? Pulled on a beret and smock and painted, in oils and acrylic, like it was some ancient, ancestral vice?

He rubbed his neck and looked again at Justine. What he was going through, he thought, was only a version of what she'd already been through, was still going through. He went over and sat down next to her on the sofa, which dipped horribly when he landed. They sat there for a moment, the room laid out in front of them. He took off his glasses and pinched his nose. Long wooden boards, the windows at the end, like a cinema screen, the sense of abandonment, of a forgotten, fairy tale existence ready to shiver back to life at any moment.

A siren went past outside, followed by a clatter of wings.

'What,' he said, and stopped. He didn't know what to say. He'd thought they'd spend the morning looking at the pictures, looking and laughing together, and that the decision, of what to do with them, would gradually come into being, grow organically and uncomplicatedly between them.

'I can't imagine what it must be like for you,' he said. 'It's been, what, a week?'

'Something like that. Five days.'

'It's a mind fuck, basically.'

'Basically, yes.'

They were sat a span apart on the sofa, which sagged such that he had to hold himself slightly upright so as not to tip towards her.

'And you've not told Carl, or Tom?'

'I've told nobody.'

'Are they there in the paintings?'

'Carl, um, twice, I think. Tom a few times.'

'And Josh, you've not told him?'

'Nu-huh.'

She gave a sigh, and resettled herself so she was facing him.

'When I came here, the first time, it was easy enough to convince myself it wasn't him. I got a call from the landlord, that's how I found out about it. The lease was up, and did we still want it? Turns out he'd done it off the books, entirely. Ten years rent, in advance, in cash. The landlord had had to track Randall down by name – I mean, it was all done as Timkins, he had no idea who he was. I mean, my *first* thought, my original assumption when I found out, was that it was a fuck-pad, somewhere he'd set someone up, a pretty young assistant, or gallery dolly bird, I don't know.'

'Right.'

'I mean, that's what I was prepared for, when I came here. I stood there, right out there, five days ago, knocking on the door, expecting it to be opened by some no longer quite so young pretty thing. With, I don't know, a kid in the background, nine, ten, eleven years old, older.'

'Fuck.'

'Only of course there wasn't. Thank god.'

'Exactly.'

'There was just… this. Even then I thought it must be someone else, someone he'd set up. It was painting, I thought. Why *would* it be him? A protégée, then, I thought. But then it was so clearly abandoned. The dust everywhere, the state of the sinks. The fridge. I'd kind of glanced at the paintings, but not really looked at them. I was more looking at the newspapers and magazines, checking their dates. Were there any dated after he died?

'There can't have been anyone else involved,' she said. 'They'd have done something with the paintings, surely? Or come forward, made themselves known, whatever the situation.'

'Sure, of course.'

'And then it was silly things. A mug – god, disgusting – with this spongified mouldy crust on top, but it was one I recognised, from home. Books, you know, right down to the creases on the spine and the scuffed covers. An old Yankees t-shirt, over there' – she pointed to over by the easels – 'that looked like it had been used for cleaning brushes on, that I'd bought him.

'It was only after that, after I'd convinced myself that this was him, that he'd been here, and that probably no one else had been, too, that I started to look seriously at the paintings.' She laughed. 'And then, of course, it was obvious. It was him. All over. No one else could do this. I mean, anyone could *paint* it, they're good paintings...'

'They're *really* good.'

'But to do this, all these people, like this.'

'It's incredible.'

'It's unthinkable.'

She tailed off, shook her head.

'So there we are,' he said, when it seemed clear she had stopped for the time being. 'There we are, and I suppose we ought to start considering: what are we going to do?'

'Indeed.'

'No, it's a question, Justine. Straight out. I mean, what they are is obvious, but what we do with them is… less so. What do you think we should do?'

'I don't know.'

Three words, she dealt them out, like cards.

'But what are your, what *were* your first thoughts? Your gut instinct.'

She shook her head. 'Haven't got any. No first thoughts. No gut instinct.'

'But when you think, just as a thought experiment, when you think of those paintings on show, they'd be on Madison, or 21st – one, two, three along a wall.' He blocked it out with a sideways swipe of his hand, a gesture of Randall's, allocating real space to imaginary things. 'Or sold, they're sold, they're up in someone's townhouse, or beach house, penthouse. Next to a Prince, or a, I don't know, John Currin. If I put it like that, what are your thoughts?'

She shook her head. A sad smile and a lift of the shoulders.

'Right. Well, I'm glad to be such a help.'

He clapped his hands on his knees, and they laughed, both of them, thank god. He got up and went to the table, collected his coffee, tipped it back for the last, cold froth of it. What were they doing here? It was theirs to handle, to decide, to dispense with. They could ring Carl, let all hell break loose, let them all whirl out, like the evils of the world from Pandora's box. Or they could put them in deep storage. Bubble-wrap them in secret themselves and slot them into a discreet, climate-controlled art unit somewhere. Or they could just walk out, pay twenty more years' rent then drop the key down a drain in the street.

Or they could destroy them, erase them from the earth.

It was in their gift.

'Is there no indication...' he swivelled to face her. 'Is there no indication at all anywhere here, or back at the apartment, as to what he intended to do with them?'

'None. *God*, Vincent. This is why I called you up. If I knew what to do, I'd have done it. You're the only person I can think of who, well, who has no vested interest in this all.'

'Apart from the fact that I'm in some of them, doing I don't know what.'

She got up, coffee cup in hand, and went to put it back in its bag.

'Well, you and me both. But that's not the point.'

Vincent went to speak, but stopped himself. What he wanted to say, but couldn't bring himself to, was that that *was* the point. The point was to cause maximum embarrassment, maximum shame.

'Look, Vincent,' she said, sounding suddenly bright. 'When's your flight back?'

'Tomorrow. Late tomorrow.'

'And is there anything urgent you have to get back for?'

'Nothing at all.'

'So stay a few more days. Come out to the house in Amagansett. We can think it through there. Talk. You can come back here tomorrow. There's no rush.'

He nodded.

'Come back. Take all the time you need. But when we make the decision, it's got to be the right decision.'

'Okay,' he said.

'You'll stay?'

'Of course.'

'Good.' She picked up the coffee shop bag, seemingly ready to go. 'I'm glad.'

'Well, I'm glad you're glad. I'm glad to be – of help.'

'You are, Vincent. You are being of great help.' She grinned – again, he thought, as if she was responding to what he was thinking, rather than what he'd said. Then she put down the paper bag and clasped his arms, and shook him, gently, to and fro, a sort of arm's-length hug.

'Thank you for coming. I'm sorry it's such a *mind fuck*, as you so accurately put it. And look, as you're here. I wasn't going to go, but there's a fundraising thing at Moma this evening. I know they can be deadly dull, and all…'

He looked down at his outfit. 'I'm not sure I'm kitted out for fundraising dos at Moma.'

'Well, let's go and kit you out then.'

He averted his face, unable to suppress a smile.

'No, really. I don't get to buy Josh clothes anymore. It would be a treat.'

'If you put it like that.'

'I do. It'll be a gas. We'll go, to, I don't know, Barneys. Get some food somewhere. Okay?'

She picked up the bag, held it out for him to drop his cup into.

'And we can come back here tomorrow?' he said.

'I'm not trying to stop you from doing anything, Vincent. I just think we need to process it all, rather than just sitting stewing in the middle of it.'

He gestured at the paintings with his cup. 'You realise, of course, that we'll probably run into half this lot? At Moma, I mean.'

'Well, there is that. You think you can keep schtum?'

'I think it's more a case of keeping a straight face.'

He stood in the stairwell while she locked up. Feeling tired now, the day catching up with him. Clothes shopping. Dinner. Moma. The house in the Hamptons. This can work, he thought. We can make this work, and come out the other side in one piece. The right decision, at the right time. It's Randall's mess, a mess of his invention, and it's fallen to us to clean it up, or perhaps that was part of the plan, but the fact that it's *now* that we're doing it is entirely circumstantial, entirely random. No one else knows, just three people, one of whom is dead. He doesn't get to say what happens.

THE GREAT DAY OF ART

It's fair to say that Randall was not a political animal. When Tony Blair was swept to power in the 1997 general election on a tide of anti-Conservative and basically pro-shaking-things-up sentiment, he was as happy, or as energised, as anybody. He liked the (relative) youth, the (relative) modernity and the (unqualified) pragmatism of the New Labour movement. So when Randall got an invitation to a reception at the offices of the Culture Secretary and then, later that year, to Downing Street itself, he accepted happily. Kevin went along to the first, but turned down the second. Griff made it clear he wouldn't have gone to either. Which was, obviously, hilarious.

In terms of the Great Day of Art itself, that national jamboree that, along with the Great Day of Sport that followed it, served as a dry run for the disaster of the Millennium Dome, just eighteen months later, the big question was, for Randall and the others, whether to get involved. The risk, as laid out by Griff and various other people, was the simple one of selling out.

Tanya boiled down the 'against' position to the line: 'I just don't want anyone thinking I've had anyone's cock in my mouth, least of all Tony fucking Blair's.'

The words coming in her gruff squeak of a voice, squinting through the wisps of smoke from her roll-up cigarettes. Let's have her in dark blue jeans, with thick turn-ups, and walking boots, one foot up and resting sideways on the other knee, leg out an angle. Griff at her side, doggedly considering the floor.

She lets out the last of a lung-full of smoke, face angled politely away from the table, then reverts to Randall.

We're in the Devonshire, perhaps out of some sense of propriety, as if the issue is too important to be discussed at the Groucho or Soho House. As if somehow it concerns the collective soul of the group, and as such needs to be worked through somewhere with meaning, somewhere south of the river. There are twelve or thirteen of us, leaning in around a few of their rickety tables shoved together as best as circular tables can be. I've got my notebook on my lap, safely out of the way of spilled beer. The heading at the top of the page: 'GDA Summit'. It's three days before the deadline for applications to present a show under the general umbrella of the day.

'Tanya,' said Randall. 'Whatever you do, please don't worry about the ramifications for your career, or your soul or integrity or whatever, of having had Tony's cock in your mouth.'

Kevin nodded. 'Cock-in-mouth, I'm afraid, is pretty much a condition of existence.'

'Ha ha.'

Randall contined. 'No, for the people who really hate you – the people whose hatred is *important* – Tony's cock is of no consequence whatsoever. It might even add something. And this show is an unmissable opportunity, possibly our last, best opportunity, to get ourselves despised by the *people that count.*'

Kevin summed up. 'Basically, it's a no-brainer. We've got to do it, because of all the people out there who *assume* we wouldn't touch it with a barge pole.'

Someone, probably Andrew Selden, made another joke – that he was still talking about Tony Blair's cock – and Kevin raised an eyebrow and lifted his glass with an exaggerated suavity, at once avoiding responsibility for the joke and accepting credit for it. He grinned over at Randall, who laughed, and we all joined in, Randall drumming on the table with the flats of his hands to punctuate his hilarity, until the glasses and bottles clinked, until one of them tipped and spilt.

The fact is, this is the period, in the second half of the decade, when Randall was finding it harder and harder to keep it together. Actually, he was making no attempt to do so. It was if as he thrived on the splintering of his centres of control, using the cushion of alcohol to protect himself from the violence of his actions, hurtling after every random thought to its illogical conclusion. It felt like we, the people around him, were being used as agents or catalysts, like bumpers on a pinball machine, that he could use to propel him in any direction but where he was heading beforehand.

'It's like he wants to grab everyone he meets by the lapels and shake them,' is how Kevin put it. 'It gets tiring, but I think it's the only way he keeps his energy levels up.'

'By being frantic?'

'By being obnoxious.'

He got himself into fights. He got himself thrown out of numerous places. The Royal Academy (twice), the Groucho (more than twice), Brown's, the French House, Selfridge's, Wilton's Music Hall, the St Martin's Lane hotel (on its opening night, no less), a B&B in Hay-on-Wye, at one o'clock in the morning. Pubs, people's houses, his own studio. Kevin threw him out more than once that I can think of.

At first, the drinking and drugs were merely an annoyance. What was really galling was the way he relied on us to maintain his rate of dissipation. 'Come on, keep up' seems to be the terrible refrain of this time. Or, unscrewing and flinging away the lid from a bottle (of Laphroaig, of Absolut): 'Whoops, won't be needing *that* again.' Gradually he stopped trying to keep us on board. We were no fun anymore, or the effort of pretending that we were was.

It would have been difficult to get through 1995 and 1996 without seeing Randall's antics in the diary pages of the tabloids, and, increasingly, further forward than that. His squabble with

Guy Ritchie. The continued pissing in plant pots, now regularly photographed, and turned, occasionally, into eye-catching photo-spreads, and, on one occasion, into a night in the cells. His stumbling out of the kinds of Mayfair nightclubs we had always considered entirely anathema, and assumed we always would. The papers' ludicrous attempts to link him 'romantically' with various models and society hangers-on, and his even more ludicrous belief that he could play them at their own game. It's hard enough to outfox celebrity photographers and gossip page editors at the best of times, but when you're basically shitfaced, it's potentially fatal. Who knows what would have happened if Justine hadn't taken things in hand by marrying him.

Which is presumably the point at which I've got to admit that this memoir, if that's what it is, has been running, for a while now, if not from the beginning, on deceit, or at least denial. I've been soldiering on, turning in page after page, on the assumption – yours and mine – that what I was writing was a sober and objective account of Randall during those years, and of the world that flared and coalesced around him. A book in which I, the author, would be positioned on the margins, like the sad kid at the disco: observing, but never taking part.

Yet in one major aspect, I was there, caught right up in the dance.

That part was Justine. The woman I was in a relationship with for nearly five years, and who, when that relationship had ended, moved in with and then married Randall, and lived with him for another eleven years, until his death.

Which makes this part of the story painful for me to tell, and painful in part because of the wild notions that people might have about what happened. How did we manage this switcheroo, such that we went from being three friends, with me and Justine in a relationship, to three friends, with Randall and Justine the lovers, and then the married couple? Was it me that did the managing – by accepting my role as the chump, the cuckold that hangs around to suck up his own humiliation? At the risk of making this account more self-centred than I ever intended, I suppose the question had better be addressed.

And so.

Randall did not steal Justine from me.

Justine did not abandon me for Randall.

In the timeline of Justine's romantic life, for the avoidance of doubt, there is a clear gap of not less than six months between the end of our relationship, and the start of hers and Randall's.

The fact is that one thing ended, for various sad reasons that do not pertain directly to the narrative in hand, and, happily for all concerned, something else began. Which is not to say it was done without heartache, but that, at a certain point, I decided that it was up to me to choose how much heartache I wanted there to be.

I met Justine at the wedding of a work colleague, in the spring of 1992. She was a school friend of the bride, and we were sat together on a table at the wedding breakfast. It was a country house do in Berkshire, with maybe 300 guests: croquet on the lawn, boat rides on the lake, dancing in a tent. There were plenty of City types among the guests, which, like it or not, gives a certain flavour to any event. People not only ready to enjoy themselves, but fully intent on doing so.

If there was braying and boasting, I managed to avoid participating in it, if only because I had decided, very soon after shaking the hand of my neighbour at the table, and dipping my eyes to compliment her on her outfit, that I wanted very much to impress her. Justine Giovanni. Nearly as tall as me, five years older (it turned out), just as single, and clearly far outstripping me in poise, intelligence and all other relevant categories.

Her very first words to me were an invitation to set myself apart from the rest.

'Don't tell me you're some kind of investment banker, too.'

I replied that I was afraid I was.

'At least you don't *look* like one,' she said.

I made a little routine out of pretending to be offended, considering my suit, my shirt and tie, trying to work out what was wrong. That made her laugh. When Justine laughed, her hair danced, bouncing around her face as if it was saying, Look, look at those eyes. Every part of her was an invitation to consider, or reconsider, a different part of her. I was hooked.

She, it turned out, was something called a trend consultant, specialising in Japan and southeast Asia, especially Japanese contemporary culture. Manga and anime and the like, and *kawaii*, from the Japanese for 'cute'. As she put it: 'Hello Kitty, Miffy, Totoro, sad-eyed puppies with droopy ears, and cartoon schoolgirls wearing tartan skirts that show off their knickers.'

After the wedding breakfast I took her out in one of the dozen rowboats on hand, that crawled lazily across the lake, or rested on it, turning gently, like insects on a pond. I rowed out and we sat, drifting, and talked, enjoying this first moment of genuine privacy that was anything but private, being in full view of the guests on the shore. I have a photo of us, taken from land as we came back in. The green of the boat's hull, with its planks and cushions. Justine sat, in a pose caught halfway between gentility and sanctioned abandon, leaning back and propped on one arm to show off her dress, its oversized white-on-black polka dots shimmering like heat over the water, her other arm up to fix her hat, her chin raised to aim her dark glasses at the sun. Me, with my terrible haircut, sat crouched opposite her, gripping the oars, which rise at odd, kinked angles. My jacket off, I appear to be wearing a waistcoat.

We exchanged phone numbers and, over that summer, began to spend a lot of time together. My decision to keep the two parts of my life separate was made easier by the fact that Justine spent a lot of time in both Japan and the US. She knew that I had friends,

160

but I led her to believe they were dull City types, whose company it was no hardship for her to pass up on.

Eventually, though, as my and Justine's relationship solidified to that of boyfriend and girlfriend, with all the duties and responsibilities that entails, I had to come clean. She was put out that I had been holding something back, but that was easily swamped by her surprise and curiosity.

'You know *Randall*, the artist? What, you were at school together, or something?'

I said no. We had met a few years ago.

'So, you've been hanging out with Randall, those times?'

I said pretty much.

'Not hanging out in pole-dancing clubs with Barry?'

No.

'God, Vince. I don't know if I should be angry at you. Why have you been hiding him? Are you sure there's not some young woman artist there, in "his group"?'

I said there wasn't, and that it wasn't him I'd been hiding from her, it was her I'd been hiding from him.

Her laugh, its lift of the chin, the long pale throat.

'No, not like that. I don't mean he'd come on to you. Not as such.'

'No?'

I think that's true. It wasn't because I foresaw them going off together, or him muscling in on her, that I kept them apart. I was just jealous of them both – in the proper definition of the word: I wanted to keep each of them for myself. I enjoyed them both individually too much to risk diluting that pleasure by bringing them together. Maybe that's not true.

It's no great stretch for me to say that I honestly don't believe Randall would have thought of stealing her away from me. That's not what happened, after all, when I did introduce them. He was amused, just as she had been, by my coyness in bringing her forward, but he acted in an entirely generous way towards her, and us.

Romantically, Randall was a bit of a puzzle. He did have a couple of girlfriends during the first years I knew him – Evelyn Betts and another girl, called, I think, Judith – but these were low-key things. Out in the pub, for instance, you would have been hard-pushed to work out that Evelyn was attached to him, even if they were sitting right next to each other. If anything, he was less physically demonstrative towards her than he was to me, or Kevin, or even Tanya. He was a big toucher: not just hugs hello and goodbye, but arm around the shoulder, pinching your cheeks, slapping your bum, ruffling your hair, things like that. Really it was just an extension of his all-round physicality. While he talked, or you talked, he'd be rubbing his arms, scratching at his face, or his beard, putting his hands through his hair. He'd drum out a rhythm on his knees while sitting, roll his shoulders, clean his ears, pick his nose. He liked that playground thing of getting you in an arm lock and grinding his knuckles across your scalp.

Evelyn wasn't long on the scene once I arrived, back in the post-Goldsmiths days, and I remember Judith principally for her efforts to steal Randall away from us entirely, as if he was ever going to be solid boyfriend material. She kept trying to take him away for weekends in the country, or on a cheap flight to Paris or Barcelona. He went along, once. To the rest of us she presented a facade of glittering animosity, a lipsticked smile of adamantine hatred. We hated her right back. In the end Randall finished it.

'It was brilliant. She completely went off on one. Screeching at me like I'd done something unspeakable to her pony. I'd *used* her. I was shallow and unthinking and emotionally retarded. My art was a joke. I was like: Right you are love. Off you go now. I had to go and get her a glass of water. She'd lost her voice, she was shouting that much. Totally brilliant.'

It wasn't that Randall was totally sexless. It's just that he was a public person. He played out his intimate, emotional life in the world. He defined himself by who he was when he was with others. In my experience, what people want from sex, or perhaps from the intimacy that surrounds it, is a retreat from the world, a chance to be ridiculous and to be indulged. Well, Randall was ridiculous all day, every day. And he was indulged. What went on behind closed doors just wasn't a part of who he was.

He wanted, above all, to disassociate art and sex.

A Randallism: 'Perhaps the greatest achievement of conceptual art has been to render the idea of the artist and his muse/model/lover entirely obsolete.'

He went on (this from a 1999 interview in *Frieze Magazine*): 'Abstract expressionism tried to do it, but you've only got to look at all that paint jizzing about the place, all that quivering, knee-trembling, teetering-on-the-point-of-losing-control messiness. The canvas was the female body as much as any figurative nude, no question. Poor Jackson, you can just see him, down on all fours, trying desperately to make it up to Number 14 or whichever, telling it he does respect it, honestly, he just couldn't help himself.'

I know that he did have a relationship with Aya Inouye that, though vaguely defined, did stray into the physical. By which I mean that they slept together, from time to time, most likely most often during the time when they shared a studio, but it existed on a pragmatic, rather than a romantic basis. Perhaps it was just easier to fall into bed together at the end of a long hard day than to go out and get drunk. Perhaps they were just keeping warm.

You might say that Aya needed little from him, and that suited him fine. She was very self-sufficient in general, didn't talk much about her work, wasn't always angling for reassurance, like Gina, but also wasn't as massively self-confident about it, like Randall or Kevin. Her strange, cumbersome installations, those arrangements of everyday items, almost always in fours, never looked like they were going to set the world alight, yet now they sit in some of the most important collections.

Aya didn't really participate all that much in the public chatter that took up so much of the group's face time, but she attended, and she listened. She looked at Randall not so much with awe, as some did, or eagerness, or envy or animosity, but with a kind of quiet pride.

In fact she spoke very movingly at his funeral. She said that 'Randall pulled art out of the very air. It sprouted where he walked. When he was near, and it happened to rain, it rained art. His art cleared the air, it gave things back their smell. And when it rained, it poured down.'

She went on, 'Think of all the Randall canvases and sculptures around the world, the thousands of them, the pride of place they hold in galleries and museums and homes. They would mean nothing to him, I truly believe, unless they made people think, seeded a new rainfall of thought in them and around them.'

Needless to say, Randall and Justine got on famously – and why shouldn't they? After all, they had the perfect ice-breaker for their relationship: a shared hilarity at my idiocy. I seem to recall the occasion being a film somewhere: the BFI, perhaps. His little bow as I presented her, her sideways look at me, as they shook hands, as if trying to judge how much she would have to alter her already solidifying preconception of me, that I was so in with someone so... *in*. He ribbed me mercilessly in her presence, of course: it is the way of these things. The script writes itself. The deprecation, the jokes at my expense, the play of serious conversation between them as if over my head, all of it like a dry run for a best man's speech. (I would have loved Randall to be my best man. I think it was always my plan. I would have adored being humiliated by him in such a situation.)

She was immediately accepted into the circle and, for a few years we operated as a bona fide couple inside and outside of it, as it expanded, and climbed, becoming at once more distinct in the public consciousness and more disparate in ours. She came along to openings and outings, when she was in the country; she spent weekends with us; she stayed at Peploe: watching us, learning from us, fitting in. She slotted straight into the scheme of things at Peploe, right from the start.

Our first visit together was over a long weekend in the summer of 1993. She joined in the traditional activities of helping Hem in the garden, weeding and dead-heading, and of sitting captive in the drawing room while Matthew expounded on local history. She bonded with Kevin in the kitchen, which he liked to commandeer to produce a series of splendid dinners, the two of them laughing and gossiping together while I was sent out to drive round half the county in search of essential ingredients from far-flung delis and specialist retailers.

The nearest shop of any description was in a village by the name of Little-in-Sight. We loved that.

Justine had none of the awkwardness that I felt, even then, regarding my place in the group, no sense that she had to justify her presence. What the ease of her acceptance into the group showed me was how miraculous was the amalgamation of intellectual and artistic aims and straightforward *friendship* in Randall's circle. Perhaps it's the same for any scene, or salon, or movement in the history of the world. It's impossible to pick the two strands apart – whether everyone has the same values and aims with regards to the work, and the work in the world outside the group, because they're *all such good friends*, or whether they're friends precisely *because* they share those aims. It might almost be a matter of etiquette not to allude to the question at all; as the subsequent history of the circle shows (and, I suppose, that of every other scene or movement), once you begin to be able to see daylight between those different elements (personal friendship and artistic comradeship), you are a step away from the whole thing coming apart completely. We were still at the stage, in these mid-decade years, when we knew it couldn't last, but we couldn't yet see how it would end.

It was surely at Peploe that we were happiest – I mean, myself and Justine. I mean, we had our time together in London, our private life, like any couple. We had holidays, anniversaries, surprises. She showed me Japan. I showed her Spain and Italy. But it was at Peploe that I remember us best. Perhaps I was just happy to show her off, to have her alongside me. Perhaps I felt as if I still needed some kind of justification for my presence there, and she gave that.

There we are, around the fire, down on the foreshore. The fire doing its work.

'I like your friends,' Justine whispers in my ear, her arm around my back, a fleece jacket draped across her shoulders, all of us watching each other flicker in and out of visibility across the flames. Some sat on the trunks, some on the ground, leaning back against beloved or borrowed knees. Hands reaching up to rest on hands reaching down. Andrew Selden warbling away at his harmonica, his hand fluttering in spasms like a bird in a bird bath. Kevin and Griff having a poetry recital competition, to see who could come out with the longest ream of remembered verse. Griff was Wordsworth and Blake, Kevin was Shakespeare: 'My dog Crab' I remember, and 'I did dislike the cut of a certain courtier's beard' – stamping around the outside of the fire circle, crunching shingle under his boots in time to the words.

And there's Randall, not talking just now, but leaning in, preoccupied with a branch he is holding in the fire. He brings it out, watching to see how long it will keep aflame before the cool air douses it, then thrusts it back in the furnace. He looks up, glances across the void of the fire, and smiles, a quizzical, somehow reassuring smile. My friends. I still didn't know if the term applied.

Perhaps that's a lie.

However it seems that I am presenting myself, as some disciple or courtier, bearded or not, foolish or not, the fact is that I must have felt pretty confident, deep down, because three years later, or whatever it was, we were all back here, for a week at Easter, gathered just the same around the same fire, drinking and talking (saying the same things?) and smoking and thinking (the same thoughts) and joking (same jokes) and getting up and dancing, or throwing stones into the night-time river (same stones, same river). Only this time I was sat here, on this log, and Justine was sat over there, with Randall.

Now it was his fleece that was around her shoulders, his ear that her mouth was nuzzling up against, imparting secret whispered things, while what she was doing, just as much, was proclaiming, quite publicly, what everybody anyway already knew: that it was she and he that were a couple, not she and me. And when he and I looked at each other, that same smile was there, quizzical and hopeful and reassuring, only this time it was on my face.

Difficult to write this and guess how it will read. Such alteration, on the outside. Such continuity, inside. When I embraced Justine, at my arrival, or my leaving, or just at the end of the day, when they or I decided to call it a night, there was no less warmth, no less love than there had been before, when we were lovers. Similarly, when I hugged Randall, it was a hug that carried so much more meaning than before; it had trust, now, and acceptance, mixed with the love that was there before. That is what I gave to it, and took from it, at any rate.

That's what I mean about Peploe being a lodestone, or perhaps a touchstone. A place you return to year on year, that becomes a means of measuring your movement through life. The place remains the same (although of course it doesn't) while you change (although of course you don't).

So when I think of Peploe, I don't just think of Matthew and Hem, of their hospitality, and the willingness of Gina (and Clive, her brother) to open up her own private place of memories to us all. I don't think necessarily of the great feasts we had, of the trips – to the beach at Maenporth, or the Lizard, or playing grockels at Tate St Ives – or of the parties – Hem's seventieth birthday, her last, or the glorious fanfare of Millennium Eve, with the two bonfires, our private one down by the river, and the bigger, official one up near the house, on a piece of land cleared by us all of rhododendrons that autumn.

Justine and I were together for nearly five years, five busy years, socially and work-wise, for both of us. We never moved in together, but mostly bounced between our apartments, hers in the Barbican, mine on the Isle of Dogs. We always intended to buy somewhere together – when we started a family. Justine, thirty when I met her, already knew, from a previous relationship, that starting a family – having children – would not be easy. This was a project for her; it became a project for us.

The first time I think that she and Randall really had the chance to gel, without my nervy presence, was when he showed the *Puppets*, along with a selection of *Sunshines*, at the Shijobo Gallery in Nagoya. She was going to be in Japan at the same time, and I suggested that she offer to go along with him as a kind of cultural chaperone, as well as interpreter. (For all his outlandish confidence on home turf, Randall never adapted well to alien environments. It was a question of boundaries and protocols, I think. He needed to know what he was pushing against, and how far it could be pushed.)

They spent a week together, while he was preparing the show, and I feel confident that her presence there alongside him not only helped make the show the success it was, but also successfully introduced Randall, who had been so fearfully ignorant – so fearful indeed – of it, to Japanese culture as a whole. He was bowled over by it, by the clashing influences, the way that it seemed to be all surface, all affectless, connectless *now*, but yet which honoured a sense of tradition that made 'Old Europe' seem positively jejeune.

'Europeans and Americans write endlessly about postmodernism, with a misplaced pride, they like to think they embody it,' Randall wrote later, 'but you haven't truly experienced postmodernity until you've been to Harajuku District in Tokyo.'

And also, 'Punk was the last great – and fatal – disappointment of British culture: the revolutionary uprising that tripped over its own principles the moment it struggled to its toddler feet. But punk lives on in Japan. They honour it for what it was – a style, disassociated from any radical principle – and in doing so they honour the very principle that the original punks so wretchedly betrayed.'

And also, 'I love Japan for introducing me to Yukio Mishima, and to Takashi Murakami, and to Elvis Presley.'

The Nagoya show was a success, in local and immediate terms, but in a way it laid the foundation for much of the rest of Randall's career. 'The biggest surprise of all?' he wrote in the catalogue to accompany 2002's *SuperHeroes* show, 'That I've been making Japanese art all along.'

And, of course, the trip laid the foundations for Justine and Randall's own relationship. It was obvious, even from Randall's phone calls to me, and her emails, while he was out there, that they were getting on well, but I've no reason to doubt Justine when she told me, as she did when, later, she fell in love with Randall, that nothing happened when they were out there.

Our relationship – mine and Justine's – lasted another year or so, but it was increasingly strained. I applied myself to work. I didn't see Randall much, socially, but then I didn't feel particularly sociable. In any case he was going through a phase of intense practical application. Nineteen ninety-five was the year of the group show at Venice during the Biennale (not the official Pavilion show, but an accompaniment), with Kevin, Randall, Tanya, Griff, Sam and Fiona exhibiting, along with others: Andrew Selden, Georg Melba, Tacita Dean. Also, Randall was working without the help of Aya, for so many years his unpaid assistant, who had gone to take up an artistic residency in Buenos Aires and stayed. All this, and Kevin's continuing international success, drove Randall in a way I don't think he had ever been driven before. He was pushing himself hard, fuelled – as I've said – by drink and drugs, and ambition and success, and rivalry.

It was Justine who told me that she and Randall were in a relationship. It had been going on for a month or so, but was, immediately, very serious, very sincerely meant. Perhaps such a change is inevitable, when two people know each other so well, then suddenly tip into a whole other level of intimacy. This would have been in the summer of 1997, in the dizzy summer of Blairite optimism, just before it exploded, like an over-ripe fruit, into the hysteria of the death of Diana.

It was, naturally, an emotional conversation – she was worried how I would take it (though less worried than Randall, who, I realised, had been avoiding me for weeks). All the same, I gave them my blessing. How could I not? How could it be a surprise, or a shock, that the two people I most loved in the world, might love each other? It was, if anything, a validation of my individual loves for them. I wanted, more than anything, to see Justine happy, where I had been unable to make that happen. And I wanted to see Randall... what? More himself, a successful artist; but less himself, a parody of such. And if I had my doubts as to whether he could do the thing I wasn't able to (make her happy), then I had no doubts whatsoever that she could steady and support him. Any such doubts were proved wrong, in any case.

Justine and Randall married, quickly, in December of the same year, 1997, as if in celebration of his Turner Prize win. (It wasn't generally known at this stage that she was pregnant with Joshua.) Kevin was his best man. I think it would have been just too much, me doing that role. I think that was the right choice.

They bought a house together, a bigger house in Stoke Newington. Randall still had the Haggerston studio, but now he was spending as much time in Kent, churning out the now very professional-looking *Sunshines and Nightskies* and *Angry Puppets*. I visited him occasionally there, but it wasn't the same. He had twenty or thirty people working there, and naturally they had formed a close-knit group that, to a certain extent, replicated and replaced the original circle. The difference was in their lack of autonomy. Not that they were yes-men, and some of the key players were talented artists – Juan Bertrando and Sally Coute worked for him for a time – but in terms of their relationship to Randall, they were subservient in a way that we never had been.

What did keep Randall in London, and in the orbit of the original circle, however, was the Great Day of Art, and for that at least he was fully committed, if coming at things on a rather unhinged slant. The specific hope that was passed down from the Arts Council-backed steering group was that we would mount another show in the mould of 1995's 'General Release' in Venice, that really served as our formal introduction to the international art world, and the now celebrated 'Everywhere I Look', of 1990.

It would be a show that, although coming under the official umbrella, would showcase the independence and ambition of the rejuvenated British art scene, a vivid counterblast to stand between the new crop of student shows, the regional spotlights on all sorts of thoroughly worthwhile provincial and historical artists, and the major exhibitions lauding Turner, Hockney and – joke of jokes – Jack Vettriano. We were to be the anointed, internalised opposition, the establishment avant garde.

So it was back to the pub, and back to our good old arguing ways. The difference this time was that nobody truly had the interests of the group at heart, though of course nobody acknowledged this. Almost everybody felt they had a reputation to maintain, or protect. On the other hand they all agreed that the show was only worth doing if they could come up with something more than a standard group show, that had a spirit of its own. It had to have a point to it. And so it went, round and round in circles.

It was Randall who suggested having a show on a boat – 'a *party* boat!' – that could be docked for the duration of the show on the river, as a floating but fully-functioning gallery, but which would cast off as and when needed, for the opening and closing parties, to cruise us up and down the Thames. Randall was so fearsomely excited about his idea that in the end everyone just went along with it. Its sheer tackiness would protect them from accusations of selling out.

As for the work itself, Randall seemed to want to give out the idea that, as with the first group show, he was having trouble coming up with something good enough. On his curator's plan you could see space allocated for him, at the far end of the main gallery room, on the lower deck – which would have its windows blacked out, the upstairs room being left open to the view.

I suppose I must have pestered him to tell me, no doubt because I was jealous of his new *friends*, the Kent assistants. I asked Kevin and Tom Nasmith if they knew, but they both said they didn't.

'He just told me it was going to be memorable,' Nasmith told me afterwards. 'At that point, to be honest, I had rather given up on him developing as an artist at all. I thought shock-horror headlines were the best we were going to get.'

Eventually, Randall caved in, and invited me over to Haggerston.

'You're like a fucking child, Vincent,' he said. 'But this is tip-top secret. Not a word to anyone. Not Tom, not Kevin, not Justine.'

'Fine.'

'Seriously. You're either on the boat,' he said, 'or you're not on the boat.'

'Come on, Randall. Of course I'm on the boat. Everybody's on the boat.'

He folded his arms and opened his eyes wide, taking up a cheesy 'player' stance.

'Not that boat,' he said. 'The other boat.'

He went across the room to get a foolscap folder, which he emptied on to the table. He repeated the phrase as he sorted through the papers, enjoying the sound of the words – 'Not *that* boat, the *other* boat' – until he found what he was looking for.

It was a printout from a website showing a picture and details of a motor launch, a rigid inflatable with outboard motors and a steering console, the sort that coastguards used, and Greenpeace.

'So you're, what, going to arrive at the opening in a speedboat?'

'We're going to *board* the opening.'

'And do what?'

'Ha-hah!'

He ran over to a cupboard and produced from it a huge gun, a machine gun like an AK-47, but lighter, it seemed, more plastic. He turned and struck a pose.

'That's a paintball gun, right?'

'Uh-huh.'

He strode into the middle of the room where he took up another stance, gun at his hip, and sweeping it a juddering motion from side to side. 'Der-der-der-der-der,' he went, a child's imitation of gunfire.

'You're going to paintball your pictures?'

'That's more or less it, Vincent.' He cocked his head. 'You like?'

'It seems a little…'

'Shit?'

'Not that. It's just, have you ever done paintballing? They shoot tiny amounts of paint.' (I had, of course, been paintballing many times. It was just the sort of thing my City friends liked to do for stag do's and fortieth birthdays.)

'Oh, we'll think of something,' he said, pulling a further pose, gun cocked on his hip, barrel angled up towards the ceiling, like any cocky youth on his first day at terrorist camp.

In fact, Randall had tracked down a set of paintball enthusiasts who helped him out with specially adapted 'markers', as they called the guns, that were able to provide maximum coverage in the minimum time, using specifications that went way beyond what was allowed on registered paintball courses. They were just the kind of maniacs Randall loved. He fed off their obsessions, and yet was perfectly able to convince them that his attentions, as a genuine – and maverick – artist somehow helped validate those same obsessions.

He took me along to meet them in their HQ, a bunker (glorified shed) in a stretch of woodland outside Canterbury. They lounged around, these overgrown army cadets, on duffed-up sofas, in their paint-spattered fatigues, talking over each other with competing advice on compressed gas, Nerf rockets, reload rates and ball-jam avoidance, everyone's eyes glued to the shoot-em-up PlayStation game on the television in the corner, while Randall sat, as if on tenterhooks, hanging on their every word.

They invited us to take part in one of their idiotic play-battles, and Randall, naturally, accepted. I sat out in a chair on the flat roof of the 'bunker', watching them skulk through the undergrowth, ducking theatrically behind trees and concrete walls, and jogging unathletically across open ground, rattling off little pellets of paint in limp imitation of every war film they'd ever seen. Of course, they were all actually quite good at it, and Randall wasn't. Not that he minded; he enjoyed being hit, throwing himself eagerly, even balletically, to the ground again and again, each time with a preposterous grunt or wail or cry.

'Did you see me?' he asked, when they came back in. 'Did you see me do Robert Capa's *Falling Soldier*?' And when I said I hadn't he happily gave me a repeat performance: right arm out, holding his gun on the vertical, a slight turn away as he bent his knees and sat down with a bump on the ground.

In the end, I wasn't on the boat, or not on *that* boat. I was the inside man, on the *Marlow Duchess*, the rather squat three-floor boat we found for our venue. I was officially in charge of lights and music, though with my own set of instructions from Randall. On the day itself, after all the rigmarole of the official opening of 'A Bigger Splash', as the show was called, after the Hockney painting, and the various interviews and press meets and line-ups at sanctioned gatherings, we congregated at Chelsea Harbour. It was a warm late May evening. The day was judged to have been a success, there it was on the news, there was Trafalgar Square full of people: there were shots of school kids painting murals on their playground walls.

At 7pm we embarked: everyone, really, except Randall – and Justine, who was seven months pregnant, and had been put on bed rest by her doctors, who were worried about her preeclampsia developing into the full-blown condition. There was a certain amount of whispering about Randall – most people had worked out, or heard, that he was going to be doing some kind of performance, and were confused by his non-appearance – but equally there was a feeling about that, finally, the group had proved that it was bigger than Randall alone, that the quality of work in the show brought out exactly how marginal he was as an artist. There was a general sense that this might be the point at which he definitively showed himself up as a clown and nothing more, his great embarrassment.

If there was a star, it was Kevin, whose *Scalpeen III* was fitted to the front of the boat as a kind of figurehead. It was, and is, a tremendous piece, angled like the gnomon of a sundial and tapering to a vicious point, with a new precision and depth of reflection to its aluminium-coated silver. Then there were Aya's delicate barbed-wire balls, Tanya's fabric pillars, that might have looked cutesy if they weren't so overbearingly tall, so weirdly twisted about themselves: these were the things that people were talking about. Randall's three blank canvases, hung vertically, six foot by three foot each, didn't look ready to upstage anybody.

It helped that the entire show had been bought ahead of its opening, by a Stefan Grigorev, a young and obscenely moneyed Russian collector who wanted it as the centrepiece of his new gallery of contemporary art outside Moscow – the Russians were starting to make bigger and bigger inroads at this time, and Tom Nasmith did a sterling job in convincing the other dealers that this was a seriously beneficial move. Grigorev wanted the whole show or nothing, and Nasmith's argument was that the market was inescapably gravitating towards the east, and they would thank him for being part of the first wave out. Well, he was right, and he was wrong, and he lost a lot of friends that night, though he always insisted to me that he never regretted it.

While we circulated, drank and gossiped, Randall and his team of five, all assistants from his Kent studio, were boarding their launch at Greenwich. They were wearing protective overalls and gloves in Randall Yellow, together with full-face masks under their hoods. Each of them had a paintball gun modified to fire extra-large pellets, and a second, standard gun 'in case of problems'. Randall's main gun was a huge thing adapted by his Kentish military advisors that he called 'The Randallator', and he also had a grenade-launcher.

We had got just past Tower Bridge when the launch, coming upriver, turned and drew up alongside. The guests on the deck of the *Marlow Duchess* identified them easily – those yellow overalls – and word came downstairs that Randall was here. Some people went upstairs to watch them arrive, while others came down to get a good spot to watch whatever was going to happen. Corridors and stairways were a sudden jam of competing trajectories, colouring the heady atmosphere with a touch of latent chaos.

Randall and team boarded without trouble, the boat's crew having been forewarned that there would be a late arrival. With their bodies and faces completely covered – the masks had goggles for the eyes, sinister vents over the mouth and chin – they looked ridiculous and ominous at the same time. But the guns looked real enough, and the total silence with which the boarders responded to the greetings, cheers and catcalls of those on deck must have carried its own weight.

They walked in formation to the rear of the boat, where I was waiting to let them in through a crew-only entrance. They did look weird and scary. The strangest kind of scary, when you don't know exactly how scared to be.

I remember I said, 'Alright,' as I held open the door for them, but got no reply, not even a nod. Randall was identifiable only by the fact that he went first, that he was the one the others deferred to. I left them regrouping in the kitchen, just behind the main exhibition room, and went to man my controls. They came quietly through the swing doors, one of them remaining behind to lock and guard it. On Randall's nod I doused the lights – leaving a trio of spots focused on Randall's three canvasses, at the far end of the room – set a variable strobe going and pressed play on Randall's chosen soundtrack. This began with a very loud and dissonant drone backing, out of which emerged some cheesy cod-Elizabethan guitar picking. The opening section gave them roughly a minute to make their way through the crowd which, half-deafened and disorientated, easily and warily parted to let the five of them through. After some ominous tinkling cymbals, the guitars came in, bone-crunchingly loud (the song was 'Fight With Fire' by Metallica), then louder still, then, when the ludicrous vocals kicked in, they took up their guns and opened fire on the canvases at the end of the room.

Now, paintball guns are not that noisy, and even these adapted ones could not really be heard above the sound system, but still people put their hands to their ears, perhaps as a reflex. They bunched back, spreading themselves against the walls, as people do at these events. (I stood on a chair to get a better view. I remember waving across the room to Gina, who was filming on a camcorder.) What was impressive was the high-velocity impact of the pellets on the canvases, the way they sprang immediately to life, the paint thudding into the material, a lovely pattern of splatters springing up as if by magic, overlapping, spreading, moving some of them in dotted arcs, some of them horizontal lines from one canvas to the next, the collateral splats on the gaps between seeming to nail them as a piece to the wall. The barrels smoked with escaped gas. There might have been a smell, of the paint, but nothing reached me.

Now that the 'performance' had started, had defined itself, people relaxed, pressed forward, looking not at the act itself, but for the detail, for the angle they could use to tell the anecdote afterwards. They were leaning in to each other, shaking their heads with glee, trying out their put-downs and dismissals and qualified appreciations.

The actual 'painting' took less than a minute. It was messy, inaccurate, random. What actually ended up on the canvases, as Randall had it, was unimportant. This was just the entrée, the feint. The canvases were maybe two thirds covered in paint when he unslung his first gun and dropped it to the floor and kicked it away from him towards the paintings. He shouted an order to the team and swung his second gun, strapped across his back, round to his front. I made my last adjustment to the lighting – dousing the spots on the canvases and increasing the frequency of the strobe – and closed and locked the cupboard housing the controls. I mixed myself in with the crowd just as the two gunmen at either end of the line peeled off and went to place themselves in front of the twin exits, up onto deck, on either side of the canvases. The remaining three, Randall at their centre, turned and, yelling inaudibly under the music, opened fire on the crowd.

As opposed to the first, larger guns, these were standard paintball kit. They fired small pellets, but at over 20 rounds per second they caused instant mayhem. The crowd was trapped and disorientated; above all, it was a crowd. Bodies pressed and stumbled about me, the desire to get away from the assault overriding any sense of whether it was fear or anger that was driving it. Nobody likes being fired at from close range. Nobody likes getting paint all over their fancy clothes. The loud music and flashing lights and low ceiling didn't help. Anybody who tried to move towards the gunmen, or towards the doors, would have found that getting hit by paintballs does hurt. Having seen the impact of the powerful guns on the canvases, people wouldn't necessarily have worked out that these were feeble by comparison. Not that getting hit in the face, or worse, in the eyes, wouldn't have caused significant injuries, and of course none of them were wearing the protective gear you have to put on before anyone will let you anywhere near a paintball gun. Plenty of the women were in evening dress, arms and legs exposed.

They were able to keep the barrage up unopposed for more than a minute, largely because of the panic that, quite understandably, set in in the crowd. The people most likely to do something about it – the people who knew Randall, and didn't give a shit about him, or had a positive animus against him – were at the back; those at the front were the well-dressed dilettantes, keen to get a good vantage point for this bit of art fun. I saw Griff, caught in the flashing of the strobe, shoving his way through yellow-spattered and -speckled art world and society types, who were themselves pushing against him, to try to get out of range. Kevin, too, was making his way against the press of the crowd. They made it to the ragged front of the audience and together with three others started walking slowly towards the perpetrators. They moved as if into a gale, arms up to protect their faces. People were slipping on the paint now, and I helped up a woman who had gone to ground. She had paint on her dress and in her hair, the yellow glooped into the strands like vicious alien ectoplasm.

Somebody had found the switches for the main lights, and they blinked on to show people, still pushing helplessly away from the assault. The eye was drawn to each fresh burst of yellow – who was hit? who was hit? was I hit? People were sobbing and cowering. A man's voice, plummy and shrill, was repeating 'It's just paint! It's just paint!' over and over. Other people were yelling for Randall to stop, or for others to stop him.

The counterattack – Griff and two others – had covered half the distance between Randall and the crowd when Randall pulled round his third and final weapon, the short-barrelled grenade launcher. This gave the heroic vanguard pause, as well it might. Randall waved it in their direction, not firing, just to keep them back, then, as all four of his wing men provided covering fire, he turned to his left, took a step forward, and started taking carefully aimed shots at the other art works on display. The majority of the crowd was so far pushed back that he had a clear view of over half the works in the room.

One grenade at a time – splam splat, splam splat – into each painting visible and in range, each photograph, each sculpture. Backing away as he fired, unhurriedly adjusting his aim. He'd been training. The canvases jumped as they were hit. Sculptures toppled and fell. The glass of a framed photograph cracked. This was hardcore ammunition. The impact circles were massive, up to a foot in diameter. The yells of personal outrage took on a new, more urgent tenor, the movement towards Randall accelerated, but he was at one of the doors now, and gone.

With his departure, the sense of chaos in the room broke its bounds. People rushed, pushed, for the doors, to pursue, to escape. The retreating attackers had dumped their unused paintballs down the stairs from the top as they went, creating more slippage, more swearing, more mayhem. Watching Gina's recording of the event, you can see how in these instances it's the panic and crush that do for people, not the disaster itself. The video, frankly, looks like one of those edits of amateur footage you get on the net that show the wedding disco the moment after the floor gives way or the roof falls in.

Others, though, made for the artworks, their own, or others'. There was someone wiping at a canvas with their sleeve, only managing to smear the thick paint further across it. Most just moved apart, breathed, inspecting themselves, their level of damage and of those around them. There were laughs of disbelief and relief, the sharp barbed bark that convinces you you're alright after all.

I didn't follow the crowd up on deck. Partly, I think, because I was worried about what might happen up there – the fleeing boarders didn't have much of a start on their pursuers, and if they caught them there was a chance of a real set-to. I pictured fistfights against the gunwales, gritted teeth and grappling bodies, a struggle over the rope tying the outboard to the *Marlow Duchess* (is it still called a painter, or is that just in *Swallows and Amazons*?), someone pitching with a wail and a splash over the railing into the Thames.

In fact, the first of the pursuers did get there, just as the last of the attackers were reboarding their boat, and the casting off was something of a botched bundle, as you can see on the videos that exist of this moment, too. The yellow-suited clowns, hoods back and masks peeled off, pitching to the floor of their boat as it turns and accelerates away, laughing and hooting and firing off their last pellets of paint into the air.

Below-decks, the scene was one of, if not outright devastation, then continued, undiminished confusion and dismay. The strobe, still pulsing behind the main ceiling lights, gave the room a fluttering echo of panic. I was the one with the key to open up the controls and switch it off, but I hesitated to do so, partly because I was under instructions to let the moment continue, but also because I realised that doing so would identify myself as a collaborator, as part of the prank.

The pursuers having returned, deflated, the room turned into a running debate and deconstruction of Randall's prank, the discussion escalating, or regressing, pretty quickly, into bunched arguments around anyone who stood up for him. Others nursed their injuries. One thing I think Randall didn't quite factor in is that not everyone coming to these things is young. There were older people there, people whom a paintball to the torso would have caused considerable pain and anguish. A knot of the particularly offended formed itself around Tom Nasmith, who, to give him his due, was fully prepared to defend Randall. He shook his head, frowned, laughed, pursed his lips, folded his face moment by moment into an eloquent sequence of expressions: irony, deep seriousness, incredulity, mocking attentiveness, alert pedantry, devilish authority. People were pulling up their sleeves, showing their legs, displaying the nasty-looking welts that were already beginning to show.

If I dwell on this scene, the aftermath of the debacle, then I do so in part for Randall's sake. For him this, rather than the works themselves, or their creation, was the crux of the work. 'Conceptual art is a rhetorical art,' he said, afterwards. 'Its fruits are in the reaction it engenders. As a conceptual artwork, a tree falling unheard in a forest does indeed make no noise.'

He liked to compare what he did to the art of Japanese calligraphy – something he discovered through Justine. In that art form the artist empties their mind and creates in a simple, expressive gesture, without the possibility of editing or amendment. The mark of the ink on the paper is not valued in or for itself, but only as a trace of the pure, evanescent gesture. For Randall, conceptual art flipped this, so that the critical gesture came not before or at the moment of the work, but after it – and was not the artist's, but the viewer's. 'It's Hitzusendo in reverse,' he said. 'It's not that it comes from the empty mind, and the expression of the artist's self, but that it puts the viewer in touch with their own deepest essence. As art goes, it's as Zen as it gets. It's not about the artist at all.'

The paradox of this, of course, was that the artist would never know the true, felt, unmediated reaction of the viewer. Particularly so in this case, because the artist had fled.

A Randallism of my own invention: 'What we want, and can never have: the room after we have left it.'

A more melancholy take on the famous *ésprit de l'éscalier*: what our friends say when we have gone. The looks on their faces. The tenor of the silence we leave in our wake.

I pan through the lower deck room, then, of the *Marlow Duchess*, as across the battlefield the morning after the battle, and it is for him that I pick out the florid cheeks of the public gallery trustee, dabbing with a handkerchief at his dinner jacket, as at a toxic seam of seagull shit; the people with their phones to their ears, calling either the papers, their friends, or their lawyers; the others standing in a daze, trying to smile their way out of their shock; the gallery assistants picking up the few paint pellets left about the floor, shying them mischievously at each other.

I saw a crew member kneeling at the lighting cupboard, clearly unable to get inside, and made my way towards him, listening in to the conversations as I went. Some people wanted the boat turned around immediately, some demanded the river police be contacted, some wanted to continue the ride. This person was getting a migraine from the strobe. That one, at any rate, quite liked the music. This one weeping, that one wailing, our cat wringing her hands, and all the house in a great perplexity. It was, variously, a disgrace, a giggle, a trip, tired, a travesty, a terrible personal disappointment, a criminal act, possibly the best thing he'd ever done and an artistic suicide note writ large.

Tanya cut me off as I made it to the cupboard, the crew member now gone again. I'd seen her during the onslaught, laughing manically, twisting and turning under the fusillade, almost dancing, as if she was enjoying the hits as much as avoiding them. She had a dizzy drunk smile, the lights grabbing now at one side of her face, now at the other, showing where she'd smeared herself with the paint. She looked more than ever like some nymph or Nereid, dazed and ecstatic. She didn't seem to mind that her own works had taken a pelting.

'Good God, Vincent,' she said, leaning and yelling. 'Look at you, you're completely untouched.' She made as if to wipe me with her paint-covered hands, and I backed away. 'Funny, that.'

'How do you mean?' I said. 'I had no idea he was going to pull something like that.'

'Come on, Vincent. You were doing the music. I saw you.'

I knelt and unlocked the cupboard. Killed the strobe, turned down the music, to immediate shouts of relief. From the cupboard I retrieved the cardboard box with the printed sheets I was supposed to hand out, and lifted it onto the flat top. I'd seen an early version of the statement, a sort of mini-essay-cum-memento thanking people for their attendance at the 'Live action creation of three new Randall Yellow canvases'.

Tanya took a sheet from my hands, just giving me time to see that the wording had in fact been altered, and then Kevin was there, and suddenly the control desk was the centre of a scrum of attention, with people angrily reacting to the sheet, before I had had a chance to read it myself.

Kevin, in particular, took great pleasure in referring people to me, the slight nod coming down at me from atop his tall frame: 'That's the guy you want to talk to, Vincent Cartwright.'

Kevin was one of the few artists showing whose work remained unhit, though that was largely because the attackers had no time, in their mad scramble for the boat, to take aim at it properly. 'I tried,' Randall said later. 'But I missed. Thin target, shot taken over my shoulder, at speed. Kevin never forgave me for that. But it would have been a miracle if I'd got it.'

I had people round the side of the counter top now, grabbing at my sleeve, flapping the sheet under my eyes.

I shoved the box at Tanya, telling her to deal with it, and took one to read.

'A Bigger Splash, Remixed' it said.

Some of it I recognised: 'Art can be a messy business.' There was a neat little twisted disquisition on the action painters of the 50s. And, at the bottom: 'Please forward any dry cleaning bills to Tom Nasmith Gallery.'

The remixed works, it said, would remain on show for the remainder of the two-week run. Randall, together with some of the remixed artists, would take part in a live debate, as advertised, in the gallery, on Thursday 17 May. 'Good Art/Better Art: a discussion around themes of value in contemporary art.' Also as advertised would be the closing night party on Friday 18 May, a cruise this time upriver from Chelsea Harbour. Live music. No live art.

The 'remix' was Randall's grand idea, his attempt to sever himself once and for all from the scene he had grown up in and alongside, that had nurtured him and he had nurtured. The remix, the cover version, the mash-up, the doctored video: the development of so many art forms towards the synthetic, the radical irresponsible attitude to appropriated material – all of this Randall had either assimilated, or foreseen.

Contra Walter Benjamin, Randall was hung up on the idea of the aura of the artwork, the last, lost, forsaken shred of unique quintessence of individuality twinkling in the void. His twist was that aura came from viewing, serious viewing, and serious viewing was only guaranteed by ownership.

The work from the show, the work by his friends, that he 'remixed', or, if you want, trashed, or defiled, he already owned. Stefan Grigorev was a front. New to the art world, he had been easy to persuade that his participation in this prank would put him on the map. Which it did, to a degree: it put him on the map as contaminated land. It was a long time before anyone sold anything of worth to him again. He sued Randall for fraud and defamation of character, but by the time it came to court Randall was rich enough to be able to settle, and Tom, to his credit, worked hard to try to get him back in the game. The Grigorev Foundation Gallery is now a respected venue for international art, especially video and performance art. It owns work by Tanya, Gavin Turk, the Wilson twins, Gina, even, but nothing by Randall.

It was in response to this revelation of Randall's financial and artistic slight-of-hand that the mood on the boat changed. The party-poopers prevailed, and the *Marlow Duchess* turned, in sight of the Greenwich Peninsula, future site of the Millennium Dome, and dragged itself back upriver towards Chelsea.

The scrum around Tom Nasmith calmed itself, though there was still talk of further reparation, and even litigation. Nasmith responded by getting hold of a camera from someone and taking photos of anyone haranguing him about the ruination of their clothes, or evidence of bruising. He did this matter-of-factly, almost apologetically, pointing out that on-the-spot documentary evidence was the most sensible way of facilitating and organising claims, and soon enough there was an orderly queue of outraged punters, waiting patiently for their opportunity to pose, stoically upright with arms held out away from their sides, or turning demurely from the camera to show where they had taken their damage on the back or rump.

Randall laughed longer and harder at those photographs than at anything else I can recall from that time. The ruined clothes, *and* the welts where the balls had hit, like angry love bites – to give him his due, he laughed at them both. 'Real pain for my sham friends...' the obvious quote.

And he laughed at the people who wanted the entire cost of their outfit reimbursed, which Nasmith agreed to, paying out on receipt of the outfit in question, outfits that themselves went on show in due course, each encased in its own vitrine, like exhibits at the V&A. Randall even laughed when other, totally random people started putting their paint-ruined clothes on eBay, stopping only to call his lawyers if anyone suggested it was actually a Randall.

That evening he was uncontainable, overflowing with alcohol and synthetic energy, knocking over as many drinks as he managed to drink, throwing himself in and out of chairs, grabbing people and holding them, wrestling them, in hugs of hostile joy, re-creating time and again the ecstasy of firing on the 'happy campers', as he called them.

'The most basic Surrealist act consists in going down into the street, gun in hand, and firing it at random into the crowd.'

He told and retold – and took the first few telephone interview requests, but soon tired of it, and turned off his phone, chucking it ostentatiously over his shoulder, into the corner of the room, like the lid of that newly opened bottle of whisky or brandy – but more than that he asked and asked, wanting to hear everything, over and over again, interrupting our accounts, mine and Kevin's, for detail, repetition, confirmation,

'And then what? And then what? Who else? I didn't see. And what about Sarah Kent, was she there? And Burlis? Saatchi wasn't there was he? Who else, then? Yes, and what did they say? What about Tom?'

Two days later Justine went into hospital, and a week after that she was induced. She was adamant that she did not want a Caesarean section, despite medical advice. It was a difficult labour, as it had been a difficult pregnancy, with constant monitoring and medical support, because of Justine's age, and blood pressure, and multiple hospital admissions. The responsibility of it, I think, scared her. She had always known that pregnancy was going to be hard for her.

In fact it was that, as much as anything, that had ground our relationship down: the repeated failures, through various IVF cycles, for the magic to take hold – and the spectre of that failure repeating itself, over and over, into our shared future, on to the crack of doom. The thought of taking that gamble – and that makes it sound simple, easy, painless, when it was none of those things – of rolling those dice again and again, only to have them come up against us every time: this was a terrible thought, and it undid us.

A family had not been part of the deal in her relationship with Randall. I asked her precisely that, on that occasion, the previous year – I am repeating myself I think – when she invited me out to dinner specifically to tell me, before I heard it from anyone else, that they had fallen in love. Those were the words that she used. I asked her about children and she smiled and shook her head. She was past that, was the implication. She had accepted that motherhood was not something she was fated to see, not something she needed to beat herself up about.

But then a family appeared, or announced itself. I remember that evening at the Stoke Newington house when they – or she – gave me the news. January 1998. I'm backtracking again. Fuck it.

This was a time when I was not having very much to do with them. Randall had called me to invite me round for dinner, a sort of official private housewarming. He managed to put a particularly unpleasant homely spin on the thing, so that I felt embarrassed for my delight at having the two of them to myself in such a setting.

It pains me now to think of the look on Randall's face as I stood on the doorstep, with my bottle of wine and bunch of flowers. He was wearing a cardigan. He had a bottle of beer in his hand, a fair sign that he wasn't caning it, but was being responsible. There were tea lights lining the floor of the hallway, flickering off the wood. It was a lovely house, with steps with iron railings leading up to the front door, and the whole of the lower ground floor taken up with a splendid open plan kitchen and dining area.

'Vincent, old chum,' he said, by way of welcome. The way he stood aside, beckoning me in with a wave of the hand. It was almost as if in some way he was blaming me for turning his life into a middle-class cliché. That it was my fault he was married to Justine. The aroma, in that long narrow hallway, of good food cooking. My footfalls on the boards. The steps down into the kitchen, with its chrome and granite surfaces and Justine drying her hands on a tea towel as she turned, seeing me, clutching the big bunch of flowers before me.

I stopped, and held myself still, just long enough for the moment to expand, for me to see her eyes blink wet, and her mouth crack, and to see that the tears she was holding, there, as if in abeyance, were a response to the tears already coming to my eyes, and I knew I had to let her say it, that it wouldn't do to take even that away from her.

I felt like heaving the flowers into the air, like an idiot in an advert for who knows what, raining them down over us all, but I let them hang in front of me, and let her nod her head at me, and bite her lip, and she kept nodding her head, and I was probably nodding my head right back at her, then she opened her mouth to speak, and perhaps but I don't know if she even got half the sentence out before we had closed the space between us, and we were hugging and wailing away like babushkas. I had her in my arms, lifted up and spinning as best I could, both of us wringing out more and more of those ugly, throat-flaying sobs of happiness,

189

that seem to hurt so much for the face's muscles being pulled in too many different directions at once.

And then I let her down, and let her go, and there was Randall, leaning with what might have been intended to look like insouciance by the doorway.

'I say, chaps. Steady on,' he said.

And I said, as best I could, 'Fuck *you*, Randall,' and threw the half-crushed bouquet at him, adding in a moment of inspiration, 'You ridiculous cock-hungry peasant!' And I walked right over to him, and I hugged him too. It was a very particular hug, and I say that as someone who has been the recipient, over the years, of hundreds, if not thousands, of Randall hugs.

His hugs: it was as if his physicality was a way of keeping control of his personal space, of keeping people at arm's length by pulling them to you.

I lifted him off the floor and shook him, perhaps to see if I could squeeze some tears out of him. And I grunted my congratulations. 'Congratulations, you beautiful, lucky, glorious bastard.'

During the meal, and in fact for much of the pregnancy, Randall manifested a deliberate lack of interest towards the idea of fatherhood, a kind of blatantly offensive superciliousness. It may have upset Justine, I don't know. God knows it appalled me. No matter, I was happy enough for the three of us. Justine too – though, as I said, she was also scared. Scared, perhaps, a little of how fatherhood might affect Randall, but scared above all of having the thing dangled in front of her that she above all else wanted.

As it turned out, she was right to be scared. The baby came out blue, meaning it was oxygen-deprived, and soon after had a seizure. He was immediately taken to intensive care and Justine, who had suffered some internal bleeding, was sedated. The next day they were taken to another hospital, either because of a shortage of beds, or because of better specialist equipment at the other hospital, the exact reason was disputed, but whatever it was the transfer itself caused more aggravation to both patients.

All of this I found out only later. Randall rang me the morning after the nightmare night, but he just told me that it had happened, and that both were 'fine', the boy was called Joshua, everyone was really tired and he'd call me again soon. Of all the accusations that can be levied against my friend, this is the one that strikes hardest, and deepest, as far as I am concerned. When push came to shove, he didn't just reject compassion, he went out of his way to avoid it. And he did so when the compassion was directed not just at him alone, but at those close to him. He deprived *Justine* of my compassion, and Kevin's, and Gina's. It was nearly a week before I got to see them, a brief visit at the hospital. I sat with her for twenty minutes, then we went together, walking slowly to the lifts, to see Joshua, a floor down in the special care unit, lying in his incubator. We were there only ten minutes. There were other babies there so much sicker than he.

She was discharged soon after, they needed the bed, Joshua a week after that. A week spent travelling in every day, to sit in that hot, dry, awful place. They needed peace and quiet, Randall said, and nobody knew any better than to agree.

All of this coming out, in dribs and drabs, during the aftermath of the Great Day of Art.

The exasperation of the anti-Randall brigade, that he had been saved from the pasting they had in store for him, and by the kind of personal tragedy that defused or deflected any possible antagonism.

Griff and Tanya, splitting up soon after. Over Randall at the launch, or Randall and the debate that never was, or Randall and the sick baby, it wasn't clear what.

The show carried on for its three weeks, and was exactly the success Randall hoped for. A ludicrous attempt to get an injunction – I can't just now remember who by – to have the show halted came to nothing. The press, for or against, latched onto it as a genuinely dramatic twist to the otherwise by-the-numbers Government-sponsored parade that was the Great Day of Art.

Nor did it take long for Tom Nasmith's photos of the paint-hit visitors to make it into the art magazines, a visual index of their arrant uselessness. The photos were a marvel, the way they held themselves, arms held out stiffly, or turning to show a bespattered shoulder, their expressions perfectly mixing grievance and dignity and something like pleading.

People came in their thousands to see the boat, walking, most of the time, through pickets denouncing Randall even to get to the gangplank, Griff being foremost among the pickets. They came to see the splashes of paint still on the floor, the ruined artworks with their big yellow splotches. This time Nasmith had moved sharpish to make sure neither Tanya nor anyone else could repeat her trick of 'Everywhere I Look'. There was security on the boat, the full suit-and-earpiece model, to make sure no one walked off with the disputed works, or further defaced them.

Once mother and son had been discharged, the family relocated to a large country house in Throwley in Kent, not far from the Faversham studio. It was a surprise move. Not the last time Randall would up sticks and flee the scene of the crime. The move was supposedly partly to be closer to Justine's parents, partly to escape the press and grind of London – the simply huge number of people with an interest in them, of whatever kind: monetary, journalistic, gossipy, friendly, caring. It was simpler just to cut them – us – all out, than to try and discriminate between them, us.

The family retreated to the wilds of northern Kent – incredibly unfashionable at the time, though now you'd have to say, as in so much, he was ahead of the trend – and Randall retreated to his studio there. Nothing more was heard from him, artistically, for well over a year. I went out to visit a couple of times, practically forcing myself on them, it felt like, and though Justine was glad to see me, and to show off adorable, miraculous Joshua, there was a sense of isolation that I just couldn't cut through. She had been able to share her joy at becoming pregnant with me, because this was a joy we had rehearsed over and over, ourselves, but she was not able to share her joy at being a mother. The gift was too precious, and too dangerous. She spoke a little of how the experience of being at the mercy of medical intervention had dulled her pride, dulled her connection with Joshua. If not for science, and progress, and a thousand machines that bleep, she and he both would have died. 'I love him,' she said, 'but he's not mine, not entirely. He belongs to science, too.' Can I write this? Is it allowed? Can it go in?

Randall, on my visits, seemed to have shrugged himself further into a parody of distance. He wore a Barbour jacket and strode about the grounds of his house with an old walking stick with little metal badges running up its length. I don't know if it was his father's, or it came with the house, or he picked it up in a local charity shop.

It wasn't 'Vincent' any more, but always 'Old man' and 'Old chap', the tags delivered with a blunt thrust of nastiness. Likewise, Justine was 'the missus', and Joshua 'the little 'un'. He was no fun to be around. One time we got in his Land Rover, the two of us, to collect a curry from the Indian in a nearby village. We placed our order and went to wait in the pub on the corner and I watched as he downed his first pint in about five seconds, his non-drinking hand braced on the round table. We could just as easily have got the curry delivered, I realise now, writing this.

'Fuck me, that's better,' he said, and got up to get another.

'Don't fuss, Vincent,' he said, when he saw my face. 'I know these roads like the back of my hand. Anyway, you won't hit anything at this time of day except a pheasant, if you're lucky.' And he belched, covering his mouth with the back of his hand, and said, 'Did I say pheasant? I meant peasant.'

Even sadder, in a way, than visiting Randall and Justine was going to Peploe that New Year, with them absent. Andrew Selden had died, too, that year, and Hem the year before that, and those deaths and the birth of Joshua served as a kind of wake-up call for us all.

The circle, with its never-ending talk of plans and projects – of what everyone was *going* to do next – had been predicated, we now realised, it seemed, on the existence of an untroubled, endlessly extending future, in which all this work would get made, these plans come to fruition, and no one would ever die.

Randall and Justine weren't there, at Peploe, then, to see in 1999, but still they were the dead centre around which all talk morbidly turned. Randall was working, at least, people seemed to say, or to have heard. Joshua was in and out of hospital, but he was growing, gaining weight. Everything might turn out alright, and we made sure to remind each other of this fact as often as possible, but it was clear to us at least that this wasn't a fact that could be taken for granted.

UNTITLED (MOMA)

They arranged that Justine would pick him up from the studio the next day at two, giving him the morning in there by himself.

'Honestly,' she'd said. 'I don't need to be there. I don't want to be there. I just want you to have enough time to get your head around it.'

It was cold, on his own, though. He couldn't find the heating controls, and felt stupid ringing and asking. And, Vincent being Vincent, there was only so much looking and thinking he could do, sat with a coffee and a pastry and a take-out sandwich, to soak up the atmosphere, the implications, the possibilities, the ramifications. The silence of the place was oppressive. There wasn't a stereo, wasn't a radio, wasn't a television. There seemed to have been no purpose to this place but the painting. He put some music on his phone and left it on the table, but its tinny speakers made even Tom Waits sound like a fly caught against a window pane.

He started with the paintings, pulling out each large frame and giving himself ten minutes with it, and the paintings hung on it: sat on the chair; standing staring; looking and not looking; walking away, glancing back. He was trained in this, after all. This is what Randall had taught him to do, drip-fed it into him, year on year. Don't interrogate the painting, but wait it out. Give it time to betray its own first impression, to stutter and muddle its narrative. Stare it out. He gulped coffee, wished he'd brought more. There were too many paintings. He wished he could take them down from their storage racks and hang them on the walls, properly, but he was too scared to touch them. He wouldn't go out for more coffee.

He went to the windows and looked out. Went to the work tables, flicked open a few magazines. A bin bag stuffed under one of counters produced only paint-caked rags. The bins, carefully rifled, gave up no twinned Chinese take-out cartons, no empty panty liner or tampon boxes. He didn't know what he was looking for. No lipstick smears on the mugs and glasses in the kitchen sink. No sign of any other human being. No sign, even, really, of Randall, if you hadn't known it was him you were looking at.

He killed the music and used the phone to take photos instead. He'd have to come back with a proper camera at some point. General views, a half-hearted attempt at comprehensiveness, some individual shots of the paintings, with details on the faces, where necessary; close-ups of collections of jars of brushes, the mouldy coffee mugs, the discarded t-shirt. He knew Randall had been to the Francis Bacon studio in Dublin. Perhaps that's what this was all about. A fake palaeontology dig, with dinosaur bones carefully placed at the right depths.

He went back to the paintings, but with a notebook and pen. Again, this wasn't a proper catalogue he was making, just a list of the people in them, and their rudiments of their intercourse – who doing what to whom. He himself appeared three times, Justine five, Randall fifteen. There was no fully worked up version of the sketch of him and Justine, together, but the one of him and Randall was there, the two of them in a slightly different position, Randall more bent over, his hand reaching up and out and fixed around the neck of someone who might have been Matteus Voss. He went through them again, looking more carefully at the faces. It rankled him, distantly and, he knew, stupidly, that there wasn't one of him and Justine.

He ate his sandwich and carefully put the wrappings back in the paper bag. He washed his hands, then dried them on his trousers.

Using the filthy, corrugated towel – even if he'd wanted to – would have felt wrong, like contaminating the scene of a crime.

When he got the text from Justine to say she was parked outside, he was ready to go. But still it took him a few minutes to leave. There was nothing to check, but he checked everything nevertheless, like a burglar might check a house he'd turned over, before he slipped away. He didn't know when he might be back. He might never be back, he thought, as he took the stairs down.

Her car was a sleek, reasonably contemporary Range Rover. A good car for the Hamptons. A nonsense for this part of Manhattan. He slung his bag through to the back seat, then sat and strapped himself in, and fixed his gaze out of the side window.

She put the car in drive, and pulled out.

'Everything okay?' she said.

He nodded.

She seemed happy with this, with this lack of communication, happy to drive, in fact, and he relaxed, letting the various possible comments and statements and questions he had prepared all slip from his pre-speech brain, out the car window into the city streets.

She took them up the bank of the East River, through the tunnel, out onto the Expressway.

'We used to love this journey,' she said, a while later, when the traffic had calmed a little. 'Holidays, weekends, anything we could grab. Me and Josh in the back, Randall driving.'

Vincent said nothing.

'God he was a monster. Radio on full blast, and he'd be weaving across the road in time to the music, pumping the gas to the beat. Us lurching about, wailing and screeching. It was better than Coney Island.'

He gave a sort of grunt in response. It's true, Randall was a terrible driver.

He didn't want her to think he was being rude, that he was being deliberately off with her, or that she had done or said something to annoy him. But, like she said, this was about processing, about letting the thoughts order themselves, some settling, some evaporating. There was the jet lag, too, and last night.

They'd stayed at the museum longer than he'd thought they might, and he'd enjoyed himself, too, more than he'd expected. You forget how it works, that these are not necessarily socially oppressive occasions; they give you space to go slow and circulate and approach people, and be approached. Everybody is glad to see you, they want your company. That's why they're there. You fall in step. It's a conspiracy.

He'd felt nervous, going in on her arm, in his clearly fresh off the peg Ralph Lauren tux, her in a plain black long-sleeved dress that she'd likewise bought on their shopping trip, Helmut Lang, very elegant and just sexy enough, he thought.

There were a few people that remembered him, or pretended to do so, when prompted by Justine, plenty more that were happy to see her. It was clear that, as she'd said, she wasn't a regular at these events. That her presence was a boon of some sort. He was happy to hang back, let her make the running. He leaned to shake hands, repeat names, give little lying concoctions as to why he was in the city.

Randall of course was a constant. Vincent nodded and tilted his head to listen when people said what they felt they had to say about his friend: impossible to think he's gone, all those years, such a talent, such a character. As if their carefully delivered words might somehow fix Randall more securely in the firmament. When all they were doing, of course, was painting themselves further into the paintings, those who were there and those who weren't, making them seem more viciously indispensable than they'd seemed even in the studio.

Carl was there, and he'd barrelled through the crowd when he saw him, to clasp him around the shoulder, there in the middle of the floor. It's good to know, Vincent thought, that though the world moves on, you could step back onto the carousel, if the desire or need took you, and not be sent sprawling when you did.

'So, Vincent,' Carl had said, 'Good to see you. But, hey. What brings you to New York?'

Never less than sharp, Carl. The tanned grin, the polar bear crop, the twist in the eye like an eagle on its perch.

He'd spun some line about coming over to see an old work friend, and just dropping by to see Justine before heading back.

'Still,' Carl had said, gesturing to Justine. 'We should get together, the three of us. Have lunch, keep each other up to date on the gossip.'

'Is there much?' he'd said. 'Much gossip?'

It was the closest he'd come to giving it away.

'With Randall, there's always gossip, Vincent,' Carl had replied. 'You know that. It's what he was made of.'

Then they'd gone through to listen to Philip Glass's Third String Quartet. He'd enjoyed it, as much as it's enjoying that you do to these things. There was no getting hold of it now, though, the next day: the scratchy, tangled lines of the melodies were lost. They had not stuck.

'How about some music?' she said. They were half an hour in, now, well out of Manhattan, sliding down the grey tarmac, weaving around vans and cars in this buff, poised, purling car.

'Sure.'

'Hold the wheel for a sec.'

He put a hand on the wheel and she leaned down to open the storage compartment under her seat, coming up with a large, thick plastic-covered CD wallet.

'Christ. This thing has got a CD player?'

'Easy, tiger. This car is eight years old. It has been well looked after, is all.'

He opened the wallet on his lap, and started flipping through the pages, the discs in their textured see-through sleeves staring blankly back at him.

'Actually, no,' he said. 'I take that back. This is *incredible*. I haven't heard any of this stuff in *years*.'

'Better than Philip Glass?'

'Don't get me wrong. I love Philip Glass. Hey!' – he jabbed his finger at a disc – 'I gave you this. Remember?'

'Possibly.'

'I didn't give you *this* though. Do you realise some joker's slipped a Toby Turner album into your collection?'

'Ha ha. I stand by *everything* in there.'

He flicked on through the pages.

'And that particular album, you can't know how much it has meant to me, over the years.'

'If you say so.'

'Go on, then,' she said. 'What'll it be?'

'Give me a minute. I've just walked into the 1990s nostalgia sweetshop here. Primal Scream. 808 State. Here we go. Don't look.'

He slipped a disc out then fed it into the slot of the stereo.

A pause, road noise, then it began. First, a shuttling rhythm, a few repeating bars of breathy keyboard stutter. It had Justine nodding her head, he saw, even before the lisping hi-hat followed in, then the swagger of the bass line.

'Good *choice*.'

He faced forwards, letting the music fill the bubble of the car interior, the song constructing itself block by block, jaunty, insistent, propulsive. He leaned back in the leather of the seat and breathed deeply through his nose, then moved his head from side to side, as if experimenting with being back in his body, out of the studio. His hand rested on the padding of the passenger door, he half-hummed along with the song. When the melody came back in, in the form of a sweeping computerised cello, that somehow morphed into a parping, mock-serious horn sound, Justine joined in, nothing more than the most basic 'doo-doo-do-doo' backing vocals, but sung gamely enough. He tapped out the rhythm on the window, as much as an accompaniment to her as to the song itself.

The album moved on to the next song, with its tripping picked acoustic guitar intro and flute, or recorder, and the trees flicked past, giving him glimpses of the edges of towns and suburbs, chopped and shuttered like images in a zoetrope. A sign told him they were approaching somewhere called Hicksville. What would the citizens of Hicksville think of Randall's paintings? He could hardly imagine they'd care one way or the other that Randall had turned, in the end, to working in oils. They'd get something from the sheer offensiveness of them, to be sure, and even, perhaps, something of the satirical intent. But satire had a way of moving beyond the reach of the satirist. If Sherman Krantz bought the painting of himself sucking off Randall, while Randall simultaneously pleasured Golda Schapiro and Bob Q. Wright, and hung it in his Hollywood home, what would that do to the meaning of the painting? Who whom, then, Randall? What would you have to say to that? You'd shrug it off, but surely you'd feel it had failed, somehow.

He'd thought this, last night, in the museum, after the performance. He'd left Justine hobnobbing with her fellow philanthropists – she'd sent him off, more or less, telling him she didn't want him to see her brown-nosing and being brown-nosed in turn – and taken himself upstairs to the galleries. Strolling the rooms, glass in one hand, the other hand louche in his trouser pocket, he'd felt the old thrill of gallery-going: of choosing where to bestow your attention, on this acknowledged masterpiece, or that. The art hanging back, meekly, shivering in hopeless hope for the gift of your gaze. Slaves in the market square.

He strolled and looked, but really he was kidding himself. All along he was heading towards Moma's sole Randall, the strange late triple *Sunshines* that was among the last things he'd done. It had been hung, as per the wildly arrogant stipulation of its donation, opposite the museum's famous Matisse, the *Danse*, with its five pale pink humans dancing in a ring on a green hill. They were to be hung together for six months, very much contra the gallery's hanging scheme, but once the controversy had died down, it was found that the pairing had become popular, and it had stayed.

They had their own space at start of the fifth floor, a sort of anteroom before you went in to the galleries proper. There were fewer people this high up, and he had the landing to himself, except for one woman, small and trim-looking, in a clearly expensive denim jacket, with a colourful silk scarf tied around the collar. She'd been there when he came in, standing looking at the Randall. He stayed by the stairs, where he could take in both of the paintings, and her, looking at them.

It, the *Sunshines*, was a triple portrait, uniquely, so far as he knew, made up of three shit stains arranged side by side, the canvas near enough matching the Matisse in size. None of the previous *Sunshines* came close. For his colours Randall had taken the three colours from *Danse*: its luminous blue, the foresty green and the icky, flesh-stocking pink; the ground a deep harsh red. Also alone of its series, it wasn't named after its sitters, or sitter, but was just called *Dance (After Matisse)*. A daft, nonsensical title. It had never been made clear whose holograph was behind the forms.

A man appeared from the galleries and spoke to the woman. He got a glimpse of her face as she turned: a snick of a nose, cut over with a curve of hair. Mid-thirties, Middle Eastern, Iranian perhaps, and very pretty. They left the room, and he tugged himself off the wall to go over to the painting. Up close, it had the look of the one in the apartment, the original: worked over, by hand, with none of the glossy, machine-produced perfection that later ones had.

More than anything he wanted to reach out and touch it, like he'd touched *Mental Mickey* in the apartment. He wanted to *own* it. He wanted to own it, so that he could stand and stare at it all day, until it gave up its secrets. He thought about the new paintings, wondered how they'd sit on the wall alongside this, or his other works, in home and museums around the world. As always, there were antecedents, echoes, references. But there was nothing out there as horrific, as blatant as they were. People would sue, wouldn't they, surely? Unless it became a badge of pride to rise above it, suck it up, like politicians buying their spitting image puppets.

He thought, too, about Randall in Dubai, railing against just this thing: art in the museums; the nullifying, castrating effect of the white cube; the way it sapped the power of the work. The millions of pairs of eyes a year, untutored, uncaring, *unseeing*, that passed their gazes over the artwork in the museum, the three seconds it took them to suck the soul out of the work, as surely as a camera sucked out the soul of an Aborigine, squatting dark-eyed in the red dirt.

The CD ended, and he reached over to take it.

'What about that *Sunshines*, though?' he said to Justine.

'Moma's one. You saw it?'

'It's a weird one, isn't it?'

'Maybe.' She nodded at the CD in his hand. 'More like that, please.'

'Sure.'

'I don't know, Vincent. It was just that he was particularly keen on that Matisse, I guess. Or not even that one, really. What he really loved was the other one, the version he painted for his Russian patron, I don't know his name, and the one that went with it, *Music,* very eerie, of five people sat on a hillside, playing musical instruments and singing.'

'I know it.'

'You know what he said, that these two paintings were the absolute and unimproveable example of how art should be experienced. This was what he was banging on about when he was doing the *Superheroes*, sending these bloody great sculptures to sit there, plonk, in banks and hotels and in public plazas.'

'Art is for making or owning. Everything else is a subset of those, or is irrelevant.'

'Exactly. Anyway, this Russian guy had these two paintings hung opposite each other at the top of the stairs, in his Moscow palace or wherever. There they were, every day, when he walked downstairs at its start, and when he walked up them at its end.'

'I know. He tried that one on me, too. A daily encounter, in which the looker sets his or her interpretation, on that particular day, against the painting, which does not change.'

'Yes.'

'Which is the only way to truly test the work of art. The look, contingent, impermanent, against the work, unchanging, intractable. You get it right one day, but that victory will be as nothing tomorrow.'

He slipped the next CD into the slot in the dashboard.

'What's this, then?'

'Pop quiz. One point for the band, one point for the track, and one point for the film it was used in, that we saw.'

'Oh, good. You know how much I love pop quizzes.'

'The Lumière. There, that's your clue.'

He thumbed through a couple of tracks and then an airy mournful guitar chimed out of the speakers.

'Christ, here we go.'

'What?'

'Couldn't you find anything a little more cheerful?'

'Oh come on. This is good stuff. Guess the song, and you can have whatever you want. Toby Turner. Jive Bunny. Whatever.'

He watched for a reaction, but she chewed her lip, concentrating on the road.

I went as far as losing sleep, sang the singer. *I went as far as messing up my life.*

'So,' he said, a few lines in. 'Any guesses?'

'Please. Give me some credit.' She sang along with the repeated line, *When we sat lonely on the sand.* Flicked a quick glance at him, half smile, half sigh, that made his skin prickle with despair and desire. This was no way to behave. Things would happen, or they would not, but they would not necessarily happen here, now. The paintings were the paintings and Justine was Justine. To try and solve everything, all at once, risked fouling it all up. He pushed back in his seat, staring out through the windscreen. That was the problem with pop music. You fill it full of meaning, bean by bean, a bean of meaning dropped in with every listen, and you never know when the bag is going to split, spilling it all out over your lap.

When the song was finished, he ejected the disk, and put on some Underworld, which seemed to do the job. It shut them up, made her drive faster, more efficiently. It seemed they were making good time, moving up the island as the day greyed over, with cloud filtering in from the ocean, and it was a quarter to five when she pulled up to the gates. She zapped them open with a remote, while Vincent uncoiled himself from the corner of his seat, twisting his neck and shoulders.

'You've know I've never been here before?' he said.

'You weren't invited. No one was, really. This was where we came to get away from people like you.'

'Ha ha.'

'It's true.'

She put the car in drive and moved on up the track. Vincent held onto the strap hanging above his window as the car bounced this way and that on the dirt road. The low shrubs stretching off at each side, the desiccated trees. It levelled out, and they pulled up on the patch of sandy gravel by the side of the house. White clapboard, old but in good condition. Not a mansion like so many properties out here, but a retreat. Solid, dependable. The wide white dune lay ahead of them, spitting out thin blades of grass.

Justine put the car in neutral, and it settled on its chassis; she turned off the ignition, and it choked and died.

He watched as she leaned down and, pressing her head sideways against the steering wheel, unlaced her shoes, so close to him he could have reached out and stroked her hair. She smiled, and he wondered if she was smiling at her own contortions, or at something she could see in his face. She eased off her shoes and opened the door, sliding sideways over the seat.

'Come on, then,' she said, and she got out. She went round the front of the car and, not looking behind her, not looking for him at all, started the slow, slippy ascent of the dune, to where the sea, perhaps just audible through her open door, was waiting.

ANTI-CUTE

The news, then, that Randall had been selected to represent Britain at the 1999 Venice Biennale felt like a punch to the collective gut. It was the worst possible joke at the worst possible time. Many of the circle had been picked for the Best of British group show held alongside Leon Kossoff in 1995 – including an *Angry Puppets* tableau by Randall – but the show after that had been Rachel Whiteread, solo, and that had seemed eminently reasonable. It seemed like a step forward, a shaking off of a scene that already felt like it belonged to a historical moment. The artists from it, while still friends, most of them, and still retaining a practical and emotional comradeship, were fed up with being pigeonholed, and wanted their work to stand alone, on its own merits.

The fact of his selection seemed above all to be a sign of approval from on high for Randall's stunt on the Great Day of Art, which meant that it was equally a dismissal and rejection of everyone else, of those whose work had been attacked and appropriated.

'If he shows a single piece from the boat,' Griff told me, pushing me up against the wall at the White Cube gallery one night, 'I will kill him, I swear I will kill him. I'll drown him in a vat of his yellow fucking paint.' The threat was directed at me personally, his finger jabbing my Adam's apple.

Others were less aggressive. The general sense you got, from talking to them, was one of concern for the health of British art as a whole: if people out there thought that Randall was the best we had to offer, what would they think that said about everybody else?

When I rang him to offer my congratulations he thanked me, humorously, rather as if he was teasing me by pretending that I couldn't possibly be genuinely happy for him. When I asked him what he would be showing, though, he laughed openly – warmly – at the disingenuousness of my question.

'Oh, but Vincent, hadn't you heard? It's a big surprise. Nobody's allowed to see.'

'Well, yes, I did know that. I'm not completely out of touch.'

'So?'

'Yes, exactly. So. We've been here before, Randall, remember? You're not going to be tipping vats of yellow paint into the Grand Canal, are you?'

'Vincent, please. Give me some credit. This is *Venice*. I may be a cunt, but I'm not a fucking twat.'

'Fine. It's a secret,' I said.

'Not to you, Vincent. *You're* allowed to see it, of course you are. Good god, you of all people. You only need to ask.'

'Can I see it, then?' (Time was, I wouldn't even have had to ask.)

'No. Not yet. But you'll be first, Vincent. Promise.'

So it was tetchily, and with a measure of apprehension, that I drove, one spring day in 1999, out to Faversham. Come to the studio, he said, and he would meet me there. In fact, though I had been to the facility before, that had been three years previously. It had expanded since then, and tightened up: there were electric gates, security detail, and cameras everywhere.

There were thirty or so people there on the day I visited, including the office staff that worked in the converted farm house, but apparently that figure doubled as the deadline for the Biennale approached.

I sat in the entrance hall of the farm house, with its cold tiles and large, draughty doors, while a receptionist called Randall on a walkie-talkie. There was nothing showy or sophisticated about the place: no art, no flashy ranks of Mac computers, no branding, unless you counted the Randall yellow mug the receptionist drank her coffee out of.

Then Randall strode in, his legs making a swishing sound from the plastic overall he had on, the top half of it unzipped and tied by the arms around his waist. He had a beard coming, and his hair was longer, too, swept back in dirty grey-brown waves over his head, no longer frizzy, but just as hardcore as when I'd first known him. He grinned to see me, giving a low rumbling groan that rose in welcome until it became, as we embraced, a guttural roar that he coiled around my name, swallowing it whole and spitting it back out.

'Vincent! So glad you could come.'

It was like being in the presence, all of a sudden, of the Randall of old, immediate, uncomplicated and energised, with his cracked face, and fatty lips, and staring eyes, piercing you from behind their web of filigree veins. Is this it, I thought: has he regressed completely, sloughed off the skin of the brand-artist, the 'artrepreneur' behind Fugu and the Royal Opera House work and all the rest?

(If there was regression, it was temporary. By Venice, that summer, there he was again, shaven and shorn and slimmed down enough to slip into a shapely D&G suit, in the very thinnest of wools, and thinner black tie, standing one hand in trouser pocket outside the Palazzo Grassi for the benefit of the press, for all the world like a film star on the Croisette at Cannes.)

In Kent, though, we embraced, then he stood back and put both hands on my shoulders, holding himself at arm's length.

'It's been a long time,' he said.

I shrugged. 'It's been a *tough* time.'

'I'm sorry to hear that.'

And he clapped a hand on my shoulder, oblivious to his clear misunderstanding of my words.

'You've signed the official secrets act, I take it?'

I said I hadn't, that no one had given me anything to sign.

'I joke. But seriously, we've had journalists trying to get in, pretending to be delivery men, photocopier repairmen. One woman from the Sunday Times tried to pass herself off as a collector. Yeah, right. Like I'm going to fall for that.'

He gave a backwards jerk of the head, inviting me to follow him.

We went through the house to the back yard, which gave on to the converted and extended barn that housed the main studio. Dozens of cars and trucks parked along its outside wall. A guard buzzed open the door for us and in we went.

First we passed through a recreational area, with various people sitting around drinking coffee and eating crisps, then someone playing a video game on a huge TV screen while someone else lay stretched out on the sofa opposite, apparently asleep, and beyond that a man and a woman played ping-pong. Through a set of doors, the corridor opened out to the hangar-like main room, frosty with artificial light. Gantries, grills and lighting tracks obscured the ceiling. The floor, down a set of steps, was divided up into stalls running down either side, with a wide space left in the centre where there was parked the odd hydraulic lift, trolleys carrying sheets of Perspex. The radio was playing, mixing with the sound of conversation, laughter and back-chat, the steeply rising whine of a drill or saw. The palate-coating hum of heated plastic.

Randall walked quickly down the middle of all this, looking neither left nor right; nobody looking up to see him pass. I had time, going after him, to take in, in the stalls, work tables, men and women bending to their tasks, most dressed in overalls, a mixture of blue and white and Randall Yellow, as if that pointed to some kind of hierarchy. The objects of their attention were small, barely identifiable shapes, like toys being mended or dismembered. I thought of doctors bending to their surgery. A woman in goggles held the flame of an oxy-acetylene torch to what looked like a stretched, kneaded rugby ball, though with stubby protuberances of some kind, like vestigial limbs.

I caught up with him at the far door.

'Right,' he said, hand resting on a security keypad on the wall. He punched in the code, fingers jumping to their own private rhythm, and pushed open the door.

'Ready?' he said, and we went through.

I waited in the dark as the lights snapped on, tripping in sequence down the ceiling of a windowless, concreted space. The door behind us closed and made the air swirl with cold dust. What I saw, I first took for fish tanks, dozens of them shoved together in a row along the wall, four or five of them left out in the centre of the room, each on its individual stand. Then I recognised them for what they were: hospital incubators, for babies in intensive care, the twin circular holes cut in the long sides for access. In them were – not babies, but baby-sized objects. Scanning them, as I approached, I got a sense of colours, shapes. The first one, I can't remember what that one was; I was already past it, walking to the second one, which had two museum-style spots trained on it, the shape of the Perspex laying itself out in parallelograms on the ground on either side of it.

In it was a yellow baby, of a bright, not quite Randall Yellow yellow. It was certainly humanoid, but the limbs and face were instantly recognisable as being those of Pikachu, the main character of the Pokémon cartoon series. It was Pikachu, and it wasn't. Not so close as to be actionable, you'd have to say, but close enough to make the connection instantaneous and ineradicable.

It was lying on its back on a powder-blue blanket, fin-like arms and legs held in mid-pedal, like a dog at play, its face averted, the features caught halfway between cartoon opacity and human expression. Its normally rotund belly was shrunken, its ribs showing through, its mouth open. The paws remained paws, the feet toeless, the ears weakly trailing like empty socks – and here

215

was the lightning bolt tail, twisting out sideways from underneath, but otherwise it had the physique of a new-born. You would have to say, if pushed, that it was in pain, though whether caught in a momentary spasm by art, or frozen like that permanently, was less clear. It was Joshua. It was Joshua, in the hospital.

Aware of Randall stood close behind me, I forced myself to concentrate on the box. I crouched and put my face to the Perspex, positioning myself right in the creature's line of sight. The eyes, painted on, like the mouth, told me nothing. It was the posture, the concavity of the stomach that told you it was breathing in, that gave it its sense of despair, of horror even. I put a hand on the glass, almost as if I expected it to react to my gesture, to slowly blink and reach out a hand.

In the end I did stand. I did do that gallery thing of walking around the box, the piece, the work, as if seeing it from another angle would help.

A Randallism, one of my favourites: 'The second glance, in art, is always superfluous.'

Randall observing me, arms folded. I refused to look at him, to give him the satisfaction.

I spun on my heel and went to look at the other boxes, surveying them dispassionately, or what I hoped was close to it. The hare was one of them, the stuffed hare laid out in its side – so much longer, disconcertingly, than Joshua-Pikachu – dead or asleep, with the two extra pairs of legs protruding from its belly, arranged as if in flight, or a dream of flight. Another had one of the family of tumours, another the dead goldfishes lying in their inch of filtered water. Perhaps those were all the ones that were finished, at that stage. The other incubators lined up by the side were prepped but empty, ready for their occupiers.

It's true that some of the most disturbing pieces weren't there yet, for instance the delicately arranged circles of foetuses, or that squashed naked human body, folded to fit the tank like some piece of monstrous origami, the way the flesh pressed the walls, pale as a mushroom, and flattened, the blood squeezed from it, the black hairs held to the pane by a slick of moisture, as if the thing was alive and breathing, or actively decomposing; the way you had to get down on the floor and peer up to see if you could make out anything of the face, crammed between the knees. Those may have been the horror-show exhibits that made the headlines, and inspired the placards waved outside the British Pavilion, but none of them had the shock, for me, of that first one, the half-human crossbreed, crossed with, what is it anyway: a mouse? A rat?

I ended up back with Joshua-Pikachu, stood with him and his box between me and Randall, my hands flat on the top of it. I knew that, whatever I wanted him to say, to admit to or confess, I would have to drag out of him, syllable by syllable, and that, by the time I had done so, I would feel worse, more defiled by the process than he ever would.

We remained like that for a minute, maybe two minutes. I could vaguely hear the activity from next door. Eventually, perhaps rightly guessing that I wasn't going to give in, he spoke.

'Well, then, Vincent. Don't keep me in suspense.'

'It's horrible,' I said.

He nodded, his face down, as if chastened.

'It's fucking disgusting,' I said, 'is what it is.'

He moved, finally, coming up to the box and looking down at it.

'But it's good, though, right, Vincent? I mean, do you mean good fucking disgusting, or bad fucking disgusting?'

I waved my hand at the other incubators, trying to separate them off from the first one.

'Sure, they're fine. They're great, whatever.'

'You haven't seen the half of it, Vincent. There are some fucking doozies coming.' He gestured back towards the door. 'I just wanted you to see the finished ones first.'

'Well, there you go.'

I was holding myself back, hoping that I would somehow be able to register my disgust without having to speak it.

Of course, this was just the kind of compromised half-admission that he loved, that he would pounce on like a puppy dog on a spider.

'Come on, Vincent. This isn't any old thing. This is fucking Venice. If it's no good, I want to hear it.'

Was it good?

It made me want to laugh, with rage, to have him ask me that. It made me want to push him against the door frame and hit him, punch him in the arms and chest and stomach. Really punish him. What was he doing asking me if what he was doing was any good? I wondered what I was doing there at all, if he really wanted my opinion, or if I was still the chump, the doofus, the aesthetic crash test dummy.

Randall had a gag, back in the day, where I'd say something, about his work, something usually asinine, no doubt, and he'd repeat it, in a declamatory voice, making that gesture with his hand as if marking out a banner headline, a quote on a poster.

'"The best thing I've ever done" – Vincent Cartwright.'

'"A major step forward" – Vincent Cartwright.'

And if I make myself ridiculous, hemming and hawing over the 'goodness' of *Anti-Cute*, which went on to win the Golden Lion at Venice that year, and was bought by the Getty Foundation for a cool $1,000,000 shortly afterwards – and God knows what it would be worth now, or will be worth, when the tectonic plates of the international art world finally shift such that it comes on the market again – then so be it. I make myself ridiculous.

Of course it's good, of course it's great, a masterpiece; of course it's shocking and stunning and visceral and cerebral and demanding and revelatory and devastating and gob-smacking and mind-fucking and all and any other adjectives you care to throw at it – they'll stick, they always do – but back then, in a cold strip-lit room in a barn cum warehouse in deepest Kent, before the world saw it and acclaimed it, and it was just him and me and them in that room, all I wanted was for him to admit that he'd taken the twisted, cramped and suckered body of his baby boy and put him up there for the world to gawp at.

It's true that when you saw the installation as a whole, as it was seen in Venice, or as you can see it, today, in LA, this one incubator, with its occupant, became just one of many, of thirty-two to be exact, arranged in rows of eight by four. And it wasn't this one, this Joshua-Pikachu, that grabbed people's attention, perhaps because it was camouflaged by the presence of its near cousins, the mutant, half-human versions of Miffy and Hello Kitty and other anime characters, none of which seemed to me to have anything of Joshua in them. It was the tumours, and the foetuses, animal and human, arranged like candied fruit in a Parisian patisserie, and the squashed body, that repelled people; and it was the stuffed animals that amazed them, that were worked on by Trevor Dutton, the young British cinema prop maker: the blue tits and sparrows and bullfinches, some pierced with arrows, some with mobile phones protruding from their bodies, as if they themselves were nothing more than little feathered carrying pouches, some of them intact but massively overgrown, as big as small dogs.

And it's not like there wasn't some talk, among all the huge amount of critical coverage of the show, both in Venice and back in London, where it was shown before being flown to LA, that did touch on issues of parenthood, and Lynchian body horror. Parallels were made to the work of Jake and Dinos Chapman, and the German anatomist Gunther von Hagens, and Hieronymus Bosch. And it's not like nobody knew the sad facts of Joshua's birth, and the damage and danger done to him and to his mother, but of course they didn't mention it. And nor was it mentioned that nobody was mentioning it. And all of that – that wall of silence – I foresaw, that day, in Faversham, when I stood across from Randall

219

and challenged him to admit that he was putting his own life up on show.

I said as much to him, then.

'All I can say is, if I were you, I'd let Justine see this before the whole fucking world troops in take a look.'

'I'm not stopping her. She's got an open invitation, any time at all. But, d'you know what, Vincent, she's not that interested.'

'She would be, if she saw this.' And I jabbed my finger down on the glass.

'Oh, fuck off, Vincent,' he said back to me, and the way that he spoke to me, loudly, absolutely directly, across the travestied body of his son, was not a way he had ever spoken to me before. 'This is art. This is what I do.'

'This is your son, Randall. It's Joshua. No, don't shake your head at me' – for, finally, he was laughing at me, triumphant, his hands flung dismissively in the air, a true, noble, honest gesture; but the laugh, he couldn't restrain himself, was for the fact that he'd got me to say what he wanted me to say, for now that I'd said it, it was a piece of child's play to deny it – 'don't *do* that, Randall.'

'Do what? Vincent, this is not my son. It is an art work.'

'But, Randall, just imagine, for the fun of it, what it would be like if people had feelings? What then? How would they feel about being used like this? About their loved ones being used?'

'Nobody's using anyone. There's nothing there, Vincent. Calm down.'

And he came towards me, warm and magnanimous now that I had done the right thing and tipped myself into the ludicrous position of having taken something seriously. Now that I had shown my true colours and acted like a normal person, like a pleb, an oik, disgusted from Tunbridge Wells.

And he told me not to worry, that he had no intention of upsetting anybody, and he knew how much I cared for Justine, and he said how it was admirable that I stood up for what I thought was right and proper, and that I did so eloquently and passionately, and that passion was absent from so much talk of art, and that above all he respected my opinion, and my judgment, and he would think hard on what I had said, and all the time he was getting an arm around my shoulder, and moving me towards the door, and I didn't look back, the lights went off, and I didn't see any of those things again – I looked neither left nor right as we passed back through the workshop – until I saw them in Venice.

Perhaps that's what distressed me about Venice. That nobody noticed him, Joshua. They were too busy yelling slogans about the foetuses. I never talked to Justine about it, either, to my shame. That day, outside Faversham, I turned down the offer of lunch and got back in my car and drove back to London. Justine wasn't in Venice, and I didn't see her for a year or so afterwards, when she came up for the opening night of *Hedda Gabler* at the Royal Opera House, and even then we didn't have the chance to so much as exchange pleasantries. So I sat at the back of the press conferences in Venice, and watched, waiting for him to betray something, waiting for someone to ask the right question or provoke him as I'd been unable to provoke him, but it didn't come.

The year or so after Venice was the most difficult in the long years of our relationship. I hated seeing *Anti-Cute* being rolled out internationally. Single tanks, pairs, and larger configurations, twelve, fifteen, twenty. All manner of freaks and sideshow monstrosities, dreamt up by Randall and Trevor Dutton – though as far as I know, and I was able to watch the production line closely, thanks to my role on the board of Nasmith's gallery, nothing resembling Joshua-Pikachu was ever made again. He survives only in the original configuration, in Los Angeles. I've never been to see it.

It was the work that cemented Randall's reputation, that put him firmly on the international stage, that drove Nasmith to the brink of a nervous breakdown, that brought him fully to the attention of the New York market and induced Carl Greenwood to fly over to sign him up.

I watched as he stepped out from the gallery environment to, among other things, design the sets for *Hedda Gabler* and collaborate with Vivienne Westwood on a clothing line splattered with Randall Yellow paint, even appearing as a catwalk model in London Fashion Week, and then in adverts for Gap. You could now buy a Randall Yellow Alfa Romeo, and a do-it-yourself *Sunshines* kit in the Tate Gallery shop. You could eat at Fugu at two London venues, plus Edinburgh, Berlin, Barcelona, Bilbao, Miami, LA and New York.

Above all, it was clear that America was calling to Randall. It had always been, in a way. They spoke to each other. The country that had produced Warhol and Koons and Richard Prince was always going to find room for a talent like his, and a sensibility. He knew it, too.

No matter that he and London grew together, in a seemingly exponential but always proportionate relationship; no matter that the buyers grew with him, too; new, bigger (more 'serious') collectors coming into his orbit, swinging in from the further reaches of the money universe, as the smaller ones fell away. London was London, but for every Roman Abramovich who stuck around, bedding himself in with a Belgravia mansion, a Bacon triptych and a football club, there were a dozen Chinese or Middle Eastern buyers who simply turned up for the auctions – or not even that – and spirited their goodies away.

Tom Nasmith put it this way: 'If football teams were as moveable as paintings, they'd only be four teams left in the Premiership.'

London was growing, and it was good to be there while it was, but he was always going to come up against its limits.

The fact that, one day, London would be too small for Randall, meant that it was too small now.

And so, as advertised, they moved.

They went in fits and starts, beginning in early 2000, finding first the new studio in Brooklyn, then the loft apartment in Tribeca, the house on Long Island. I attended the big farewell party held at The Ivy in the autumn of 2000, and flew over for their New Year's bash. But they were, for me, sad affairs. They were moving faster away from me now, both in terms of Randall's career, and in terms of their relationship.

For a while, in terms of career, it was business as usual. Greenwood held a show in his West 24th Street gallery, with *Anti-Cute* tanks and *Sunshines and Nightskies*, then there was a second, bigger show in Japan, and one ground-breaking one in Moscow. He shifted his production of *Sunshines and Nightskies* to New York, and they flew off the printers 'faster than I could point people the way to the john'.

Then came 9/11, which affected Randall far more than I would have expected – or, indeed, for quite a while, believed. 'I've always loved America,' he said in an interview with *The Daily Telegraph* little more than a week after the events. 'But wounded America speaks to me in a way I can't ignore.'

'You feel you have something to offer America?' the journalist asked. 'You feel you can offer it something – help, or healing?'

'God, no,' came the reply. 'Or not exactly. Maybe. Maybe, I do think that, naïvely enough. Or maybe I just feel privileged to be near the hurt, you know. That thing about being part of one those generations that have never experienced war. And now never will. This is our war, if you know what I mean. And every war needs its war artist.'

The interview caused little stir, coming as it did in the maelstrom of liberal handwringing and symbol-wrangling that followed, but Randall's following statement, announcing his decision to embark on an international series of public sculptures in the name of world peace, most certainly did. Its grandstanding vocabulary, piling the semiotic atop the political, drew nothing but scorn from the British press.

'America is under symbolic attack,' he wrote. 'As such it is to artists that America must look for defence, and it is to America, as symbol of creative freedom against those that would abolish the very possibility of meaning, that all artists owe a duty of service.'

He was attacked, in the UK, for being reactionary, for being politically naïve, for mocking and demeaning the dead, for trampling them and using their tragedy, a country's tragedy, as a springboard for personal advancement. A letter to *Art Monthly* lambasting him was signed by five people who had shown in the original group show of 1990.

America, by contrast, welcomed the *Superheroes* sculptures with an eagerness that was something like desperation. By now it was now comprehensively caught up in the second Gulf War, and finding itself more and more isolated on the global political stage. Again, there was something in the response to these new works of Randall's that was, if not clutching at straws, then at least embattled. You could compare it to Bush's response to Blair's 'standing shoulder to shoulder' rhetoric. It soon became highly *patriotic* to own a Randall. He started turning up at gala dinners at Carnegie Hall, auctioning off works to raise funds for the Army Benevolent Fund, and pressing the flesh at the National Endowment for the Arts. It doesn't take much searching to find photos of him with Arnold Schwarzenegger, Dick Cheney, John Kerry, even Kofi Annan. He was, in Kevin's words, 'the Bono of the art world'.

For the first time, Randall actually had a vision of the art he wanted to create. It may seem incredible, but as this account has hopefully made clear most of his most celebrated works were created on the fly, a crazy idea that got trapped – as much by accident as by design – and fixed down, before it could escape. The *Superheroes* series, on the other hand, was meticulously planned, reverse-engineered to produce a particular emotional response.

And it was important to him to do them soon, for what use is solace if it comes too late? Most art that responded to 9/11 did so in a particular and rather limited way: firstly, apologetically, as if insisting above all on its uncertainty as to whether it even had the right to do so, so soon; and, secondly, as a commemoration of the dead or, more circumspectly, referring to the symbolism of the planes and the towers. What Randall was doing was different.

In the end, the difficulty of placing the sculptures, sight unseen, together with Greenwood's obvious commercial considerations, meant that Randall did do a show of gallery-sized *Superhero* pieces, in March 2003. It was, nevertheless, an unprecedented statement, a deliberate pushing of Randall's conceptual aesthetic – the aesthetic of the gesture – on to the wider stage. The pieces were massive, among the biggest Greenwood had ever exhibited, and so big that he had to split the show across both of his Chelsea properties. The great fibreglass figures didn't so much emerge as *protrude* from the walls as if entering the room by supernatural rather than physical force. Randall had considered having them bursting through in more realistic fashion, with plaster and broken bricks scattered on the floor beneath them, but he said he wanted them to be rhetorical sculptures, like the statues of generals on horseback you see around London, rather than narrative ones. They weren't 'sculptures of doing', they were 'sculptures of being'. Whichever they were, they loomed most impressively. They looked far heavier than they were, and the distance they projected into the room, cantilevered above the humble viewer, put you quite literally in their shade.

Randall on the *Superheroes*: 'I want it to feel like when you're near an airport, and a plane passes right over you, so low and so noisy you duck. That massive curved belly, like the belly of a whale, but longer, sleeker, gliding violently above you, and you feel as if you could reach up and touch it.'

Of the figures, those first half dozen, the most famous and immediately iconic was *Mental Mickey*, the yellow mouse that, all things considered, had as much of the 1980s cartoon character Mighty Mouse in it as it did Disney's Mickey. The closed fist at the end of an extended arm, the opposed leg raised at the knee, the face set in a determination that you would have to label as both grim and benign. The rescued baby wrapped in swaddling clothes clasped to its side spoke to America's sense of its own damaged humanity, the fact that the character was something as humble and harmless as a mouse, spoke to its sense of grievance, no matter how the country might be seen abroad. The more overtly aggressive and brutish figures – the *All American Bison*, the *Chrome Bionic Duck* – never achieved the same kind of exemplary power, although it is the duck, in its larger, fully chrome version, pushing out over the Chicago River below the Franklin Street Bridge, that has achieved the greatest public visibility.

So, his heroes were classical heroes, at a time when the wider culture seemed to want its heroes human, all too human: all those doomy, gloomy Batman and Spiderman comics and films with their tortured, morally conflicted heroes. Randall bundled up these references with, on the one hand, religious elements and, on the other, more deliberately infantile ones: Disney obviously, and not just the cheesy, chubby-cheeked look of its anthropomorphised menagerie, but the sleek-slabbed humans, too. And then there was the superflat look of Japanese manga characters, that Takashi Murakami, too, was putting into sculptural form just then.

This last, obviously, was the product of Justine's influence on Randall. She was still running her East–West consultancy, now with its headquarters in New York, though her management was somewhat semi-detached, and it was others who did most of the flying to and from Japan. I like to think of them, the young Nipponophiles she recruited, as her scouts, messengers returning from perilous missions who stepped nervously into her chamber to lay out before the latest dolls and charms, manga and DVDs, while Justine sat cross-legged behind her low persimmon-wood table, tea tray laid out before her, toddler Joshua on a cushion beside her; he stern and silent as a pasha, she noble and serene and indicating, with a soft, curt nod or shake of the head, her approval or disapproval of each offering.

Discussions over the first large-scale versions of the pieces were under way before the show opened, and production began soon after. There was First Bank America's version of the *Bison*, which you can still see in the atrium of their New York building; the Salt Lake City *Elk*; the Abu Dhabi *Leaping Horse*, now in the UAE Guggenheim.

The last time I saw Randall was at the Burj al Arab in Dubai, at the grand unveiling of the *Horse*, which was at that point the largest *Superheroes* sculpture, reaching – or descending – to thirty feet in height. It wasn't until the posthumous installation of *Iron-Clad Rectitude* in Philadelphia that it was outstripped.

Not that there was an unveiling as such. Things in a place like the Burj aren't unveiled: they have to be present, or not present; the idea of something being withheld from view is absolutely anathema. What you can't do is give people the impression that their experience today is less comprehensively, unimproveably luxurious than the experience that will be available tomorrow, when they have gone.

So it was already there when I arrived, hanging together with the Koons pink metal *Cheshire Cat* and the huge Murakami *Flower Matango* over the cascading water feature in the hotel's famously gargantuan atrium. It was my first time at the Burj and my feelings about it, and about Randall and the *Superheroes*, were confused and conflated, egging each other on to greater levels of disaffection. In short, I didn't like any of them.

I sat myself on the supremely hideous and supremely comfy bed in my suite, looking out through the balcony windows onto the endless blue of the sea, and tried to goad myself into going straight to the airport to catch the first flight home. I was angry with myself for coming, angry with Randall for making me come, angry that he could persuade me to do something I didn't want to, while I couldn't persuade myself not to.

'You'll love it,' he'd said, when he'd called to invite me to join him there. 'By which of course I mean you'll hate it.'

He wasn't talking just about the piece, but about the whole thing, the event, which was intended to mark the official unveiling of Frank Gehry's design for the Abu Dhabi Guggenheim, for which the *Horse*, Koons and Murakami were the first, founding and emblematic purchases.

Above all I was angry with Randall for the way that, when he could tell that I wasn't convinced, he let on that Justine and Joshua would be there too.

I was angry at being so easily played.

The unveiling of the design (that *could* be unveiled: it wasn't for the tourists) was preceded by a formal dinner in the hotel's ballroom. I was sat on a table between Gillian Wearing and Kurt Liebkind's cranky model girlfriend, with a jovially gossipy Liebkind – long a supporter of Randall – on the other side of her. Justine was directly across from me, Randall being on the top table, and Joshua up in their suite with his nanny, apparently barrelling around the rooms in a motorised toy car the organisers had laid on for him, causing all kinds of mayhem.

Justine, who didn't usually go in for finery on such occasions – she who proudly wore H&M to the Turner Prize dinner when he won – was wearing a heavy gold necklace and a flowing, floor length indigo-black velvet dress that she said had been given her by Stella McCartney, as a thank you for when Randall designed a show for her. We shared a grimace as we kissed each other in greeting. It was the kind of event we both despised, or affected to despise. But then most people affect to despise them, don't they? And I suppose we were only marginally less caught up in the carnival of the event than everyone else, analysing the seating plans, logging the presences and absences, trading gossip and rumour.

What everyone wanted, more even than seeing Gehry's model, was to know who among the people sat at the top table, alongside the Crown Prince's cultural representative and Thomas Krens from the Guggenheim, was going to be given the purse strings to the place, or at least be allowed to get a finger on them.

Randall was there, with Murakami and Koons, the artists spaced out among the suited Westerners, including Krens and Gehry, and the various robed and head-dressed sheikhs. These last were – to my mind – charlatans, plain and simple, who were buying their way into the art world, and the tourism world and the financial world, essentially by shoving the last of their oil and gas money into the middle of the table, like so many poker chips, knowing that no one, at that precise moment, had the wherewithal to call them on it.

Or perhaps they weren't charlatans. After all, they weren't pretending to be anything they weren't. Perhaps we were the charlatans: we were the ones pretending that *they* were charlatans. Greenwood was there, and Larry Gagosian, and Nicholas Serota, and François Pinault, and Amanda and Matthew from Frieze, and the Glimchers. Hell, if there were any people there among the 150 or so guests that I didn't recognise, or that you, dear reader, wouldn't have heard of, then frankly it's because they were simply too high up in the angelic orders for us to merit any knowledge of them, rather than the reverse.

Those on the top table did at least put on a show of respectability, talking soberly and seriously as they ate the exquisite food that was laid before us, that we were all too overexcited or self-obsessed to enjoy, beyond gushing to our neighbours how exquisite it was. But then they, the top-tablers, had no need to gossip and eavesdrop, like the rest of us, because they already knew the pertinent facts.

Randall seemed to be joining in with the general conversation, to be dipping his ear to listen to a comment from some sheikh or other, to lean forward to answer a question sent along the table from Krens, nodding vigorously in reply, giving delicate stabs and twirls of his fork to make a point.

'It looks like he's absolutely in his element,' I said to Justine, with what I hoped was a catch-all attitude of irony and amused conviction. She opened her eyes wide with surprise, then put down her cutlery and came around the table to crouch beside me.

'Vincent,' she said. 'He's a complete mess. He was up till all hours last night, ranting and raging. It was all I could do to stop him phoning you at god knows what time. He sent me a text just ten minutes ago that, well, I'll show it to you. We'd better catch him, after the meal, in case he does anything stupid.'

After the meal, though, and the speeches, it was impossible to get close to him, as people rose and pushed through to the reception suite to see the scale models of Gehry's museum in their display cases, and the CGI views and tours of it playing on various wall-hung screens.

When I found him he was at the centre of a group of the great and good, Serota, Greenwood and Gagosian included, holding forth on the aptness of opening a mega-gallery here, and lauding the Emirates as the new 'epicentre of the postmodern – its ground zero.' He winked at me, though, when I caught his eye, and he seemed fine. At any rate, I thought, if he started going dangerously off piste, Carl was on hand to ensure nothing too awful occurred.

I went instead to look at the models, in which the museum was shown both on its own and in the context of the emirate's 'Saadiyat Island Cultural District', to which it was a strange, dangly appendage. It was hard to get a good view, so intense was the crush of guests all oohing and aahing over its jumble-of-children's-building-blocks aesthetic, rather as the tourists oohed and aahed over the synchronised fountains upstairs.

Certainly, it was radical and eye-catching and like nothing on earth (apart from Gehry's various other radical, eye-catching, like nothing on earth buildings scattered across it), and it did what it so clearly needed to do – which was be distinctive enough to make people actually want to climb into the nearest plane and fly all the way from wherever they happened to be to this straight-from-the-box, just-add-water city thrown up on the edge of a thousand-mile desert.

A tap on the shoulder, and there he was. He eased in next to me, squeezed up against the side of a Perspex case. No embrace, no word of greeting. Somehow it seemed neither the time nor the place for an emotional reunion. We stood there, side by side, and in silence, while various people tried and failed to engage him in conversation, asking questions that were not answered, offering congratulations that were shrugged off, and judiciously witty comments that went unappreciated. The less he said, the better I felt, as if his indifference to them was a form of attention towards me.

'So, Vincent,' he said, at last. 'A penny for your thoughts.'

I paused, not wanting the spell to be broken, then spun out some line about it probably being one of those buildings that worked better as maquette than as real built thing.

'Isn't it just,' he said, bending his knees to see in past the reflections on the Perspex. He pointed, and I ducked, tight in the press of bodies, to follow his finger. 'If you look carefully you can see the figure of an artist, there, at the back of that triangular space, under that leaning cone thing, rotating ever so slowly on the end of a rope.'

He spoke quietly, but not so quietly that people didn't hear, and laugh.

He stood back up.

'I'm joking, of course. It's all been specially designed to prevent just such an occurrence. Anti-suicide paint. Artist-proof windows. Invisible futility fields all around the top of it to make you think it's just not worth throwing yourself off of it.'

More laughter. He puffed out his cheeks and boggled his eyes at me. 'You want to get some air?' he said. A jerk of the head, up and out. Then, raising his voice, emphasising the facetiousness of his words, 'It's specially imported from Switzerland, you know. This gorgeous little valley nestled under the eastern flank of the Matterhorn.' Then, as the titters expanded, moving out across the crowd, 'Oh why don't we all just fuck off?'

It took us an age just to get out of the room, slowed as we were at every step by more people wanting their own piece of his time. The hands extended, the cheeks offered and lips puckered, the friends and colleagues introduced. The idiots who just wanted to stand there and chat, shoot the breeze, as if they'd chanced to meet in the checkout queue at Tesco's.

Eventually we made it out, and up to the atrium, and Randall led me over to the gallery rail at the edge of the upper lobby, where it looked down, past the ziggurat of cascading fountains, flanked by the up and down escalators, to the hotel entrance.

Above our heads, the artworks. The horse, heaving itself down from under the first row of balconies, blue of skin and cataclysmic of hoof. Across the way, forming the other two points of a triangle, the *Cheshire Cat* and the *Flower Matango*.

Tourists milled, camcording. Taking in the art, if they took it in at all, merely as a constituent part of the greater spectacle. This strange Checkpoint Charlie where high-end tourism and genuine, exclusive ultra-luxury met, and stared uncomprehendingly at each other.

So, what do you think?' he said, with a jerk of the head up at the sculpture. It grimaced back, baring its mule teeth. 'At least Koons' cat has got the right idea. Or Takashi's flowers. Look at them. They're completely monged.'

I laughed. The expression on the metallic balloon cat's face did in fact seem entirely appropriate, at once oppressive and spaced-out, with a halfway psychotic shit-eating grin that seemed to say it fully accepted its position in this madhouse, seeing as it was stuck there with no possibility of escape. Randall's horse, by contrast, so proud and determined in countenance, channelling the history of its Persian ancestors into its Guernica-strength muscle and vicious manga curves, looked risibly out of place. And the *Flower Matango*? You would have to say it seemed blissfully unaware of anything at all, each flower beaming away from inside its own personal psychedelic oblivion.

'I've tried to get Koons to admit he hates it, but he won't give in,' Randall said. 'He's *got to*. Jeff, who wouldn't blink if you let off an irony bomb under his fucking bathtub. Surely he must bow before this great... phantasmagoria.' He turned, leaning on the railing, and looked around the atrium. 'Because it's him, isn't it? But bigger.' He gestured upwards, taking in the whole upended hangar of the place, an opera house outbid by a mosque outbid by a mall, and all of it so pristine as to make you want to at least get a dirty thumbprint on it somewhere.

'Talk about ushering in banality,' he said. 'You can't *usher* banality into this place, any more than you can usher a drop of water into the fucking Persian Gulf. I'll tell you what the problem with this place is.' And he swung his arm out over the colour-coded waterfalls. 'We've been subsumed.'

He stopped and took a drink from the glass of wine that I hadn't even seen he'd brought with him.

Also, we were no longer alone. People had apparently followed us up from downstairs, or perhaps they were already here, and were beginning again to move in, to congregate. It annoyed me, but he made no effort to dissuade them.

He said the word again, splitting it into its two halves. 'Sub. Sumed. We're all just baubles on the glitziest, flashiest Christmas tree ever constructed. And constructed by people for whom Christmas means precisely fuck-all. Christ, the whole place looks like it was designed by whoever designs those sofas you get advertised at Christmas. Remember those?'

He was babbling, pretty much, by this point, and, I could tell, well on the way to being drunk. You could drink in the Burj, but not like this, and he was soon approached by a member of staff asking him politely for his glass, which he gave him, politely, after having politely upended and drained it.

We moved on around the gallery, taking our gaggle of hangers-on along with us, past the sofas and a shamefaced grand piano, polished to a sheen to make a fetishist swoon. Randall took me by the arm and pulled me around to under the Koons, still talking. There was beginning to be an element of performance in this; he was talking to me, still, but he was talking louder, either uncaring that he could be overheard or positively intending to be so.

We watched the fountains again, pissing their time-coded hoops of water onto their squares of marble, and he continued to talk.

Being 'a bauble' was very much at the heart of his complaint. His point was that the three artists' work – his, Koons' and Murakami's – all to a greater or lesser extent played off received notions of high and low culture, of the place of kitsch in the academy. They worked by taking the glitz and glibness and shallowness of so much of contemporary life and setting it in the austere and hallowed halls of the museums they were exhibited in, where such things had no right to be. But put that same piece of kitsch somewhere like this, which was already kitsch embodied and multiplied and folded in on itself until it became a totalisation of humanity's desire for luxury, made visible, at the expense of taste, and the art straight away lost its effect, its resonance.

They had, he said, been rumbled.

It was a strange and yet deeply familiar spectacle. He was in a state that was almost beyond drunkenness. His voice increasing in volume, his gestures in grandiloquence. Half the time he responded to any comment or direct approach by grabbing whoever it was by the arm and telling them it was a disaster, a catastrophe, an arse-

236

fuck. The rest of the time he was saying he was over the moon, it was his 'apotheosis', brilliant, superb, 'a genius move'.

'But what about the museum?' someone asked. 'Surely you don't think the museum's going to look like this place, the exhibition space? Frank *Gehry*. I mean, come on?'

We were sitting on a pair of repugnant car-sized sofas. The gathering around us now numbered fifteen or twenty: dealers, gallerists, other people I didn't know. Maybe the odd artist or collector. Westerners, mostly. At one point I noticed that some of them had their phones out and were filming him – filming *us* – but when I tried to tell them to stop, Randall waved me down.

'Now then, the museum,' he said, and he steepled his fingers. 'Let me see. Well, the museum clearly isn't going to look like this. How could it? It will be, above all else, Guggenheimlich' – he put on a cod-German accent. 'Guggenheimlich, closely related to unheimlich. Antonym: Guggenmütlich. Lots of white, lots of walls, lots of space between those walls, lots of Swiss air specially imported and chilled to the ideal temperature for a perfect lack of interest in anything there. It will be the apogee of the white cube: the white cube cubed, the cube quadrupled.'

The irony of this. I can get down his words exactly, in this instance, because all I have to do is Google him and there it is: the video of our strange, improvised television chat show. Me as a befuddled Michael Parkinson, Randall as a sort of art world Peter Cook.

'The thing about this Guggenheim, Vincent, is that it is a monster, a will-less agency, like The Blob – you've seen the film? It *eats* art. It absorbs. It takes into itself any art work which you place within its field of influence. Put my sculpture in there, or anything, Koons' cat, a *Mont Saint Victoire*, a Leonardo, anything, and it disappears – pff!

'Or, it doesn't disappear, but it becomes invisible. It's on display, but you can't *see* it. Look at it, sensitively hung in this meticulously designed and controlled environment, and it's just not there. It's irradiated, wiped of meaning, like a videotape left next to an electromagnet. No art can survive that kind of megalomania. What's it going to be? Three hundred thousand square feet? A hundred and thirty thousand of exhibition space? That's no way to look at art.'

He sat back, a hand lying limply on the leather beside him.

'So what are you going to do, then?'

I wasn't me who asked it, but it was still to me that he looked.

'Well, that's the interesting question, isn't it? What I want to do… what I *want* to do is climb up there and get down that bloody great thing and march out of here with it under my arm.'

General laughter. No one but me got the reference, no one but me understood what it was he was saying.

How does an artist take back control of his work, once it's been given over to the market? You sell it, it's gone. That's the truth, as he saw it: that there's no such thing as a work of art as an autonomous entity, a Ding-an-Sich. When it's in the studio, it's still part of the artist. When it's in the gallery, it's a commodity, a boiling cauldron of hypothetical, as yet undifferentiated values, like that cat in that box. When it's hung on someone's wall, or in someone's museum, it becomes part of their collection, and takes its identity, to a greater or lesser extent, from theirs. Nowhere does it exist in its own right.

This is where it began. His grand plan to withdraw his works from big, public and publically-accessible collections. He showed me his list, the people he'd have to sweet-talk, or brow-beat, or blackmail. The response of the private owners – who needed Randall's work to be in the Gettys and Saatchis and Tates, to give their own any value.

Only two things you can do with a work of art: make it, and own it.

But what he hadn't realised until now is that the second trumps the first.

Public collections as the tyranny of democracy. Revenge of the meek. Not bomb the museums (Futurists) but liquidate them. Liberate the animals from the zoo. Moma. Funeral. Kevin. Justine. Obits. T's letter. Aya. Frieze. Serota. Turbine Hall farago. Amsterdam. Write something about the funeral. What F said. Fucking tom crock of shit blah blah gfucking blahhhhh

I'm sat at the big round pedestal table in the library at Peploe. It's early February 2014, and although it's only 11 o'clock in the morning it seems like it's getting dark already. I'm sat facing the French windows, which look on to a section of garden at the side of the house. The formal hedges are twiggy and unleaved. Wettest winter for decades, half the country flooded. Next to my computer are a coffee cup, a note pad and pen, and a stack of books. I am here at the invitation of Gina.

I haven't looked at this manuscript, such as it is, in years. Or thought about it, really. Or Randall. Even opening the file seems like a transgression. Although I'm still officially a trustee of the estate, I have very little to do with the running of it. For most decisions the say-so of two or three of the four of us is sufficient, and Justine and Carl are both in New York, so it's only natural that they take care of things. Everything seems to be running smoothly enough. Pieces are authenticated, or not. Frauds are taken to court. Maintenance, where needed, is organised and effected with due discretion. The work, when it comes to auction, sells well. Occasionally we buy back a piece, most usually a *Sunshines*, if there's a risk of it not reaching what we consider an acceptable price. Occasionally, even, to keep it out of less than ideal hands.

The house hasn't changed. That is a lie. The house is the same, except that it is not full of people talking, laughing, drinking, singing, dancing, shouting, falling over. Gina lives here alone

241

now – I'm tempted to say, with her ghosts, but why would they be just hers? Her parents died. Her brother and his family moved to Canada. Do people emigrate any more, or do they just move country, like they used to move house?

She has put me in the room I stayed in with Justine, when we were first here together, seventeen years ago. On purpose? I don't know. She has no children. This was her idea, the idea that I'd come down here and finish the book. 'You should do it,' she told me. 'You owe it to yourself.' As if the whole thing, right from the start, had been for my benefit.

I arrived last night, after a fucker of a journey, and already I want to leave.

Everything she says is said with a kind of watery-eyed tragic amusement. She's only four or five years older than me, but I don't think she's very well. If I look respectably grizzled, in a mid-to-late-middle-aged, edges-rubbed-off, taking-care-of-myself kind of way, she looks frazzled, as if she's been through electro-shock therapy. Frazzled, frayed and fucked. Her hair is sparse and un-*done*, like women of a certain age need their hair *done*. From the back, following her up the gallery stairs, I could see her scalp through it, like dry ground through grass in summer.

I haven't known anyone to so permanently have a cigarette on the go in years. The house reeks of it. It's a smell I'd forgotten – more than a smell, it feels like a physical assault on all five of the senses. Listen to me: we're all Californians now. The smell taints any stirrings of nostalgia that being here awakens in me. It makes me wonder if the house always smelled this bad. Perhaps that's the point she's trying to make, sucking up Silk Cut after Silk Cut: if it smelled this bad, back then, then how good can it all have been, really?

I look at the paintings on the walls – the ancestors and seascapes and morose dogs (the dogs, more than the people, look like they know their own mortality, know that their portraits will outlast them, live on to betray them) – and I think about the accretion of smoke particles. About the *patina*, and the job of restoration. About what would come off if you rolled a cotton bud across them.

How come I'm here is that we bumped into each other at a funeral. No one from back then, funnily enough, but the wife of one of my old friends from the bank, Jack Hambleton, who grew up in Porth Navas. We stood there in the cemetery, in the crisp, distant winter sun, embarrassed into proximity, and said how good it was to see each other. In a moment of foolishness I let slip to Gina that I'd been trying to write a book about Randall and us all, how I'd holed myself up in the villa for weeks at a time, even enrolled on a life writing course on a Greek island to try and force myself to finish it (that's when I wrote that section about this house, surely one of the bearable bits of writing in the whole godforsaken thing), but that I'd pretty much given up on it. The next day she phoned me and invited me down. Seeing the place again would be bound to stir up memories, she said, and we could talk, reminisce. And during the day – she said this sternly, almost flirtatiously – she would 'lock me in the library'.

But now the pages I've written, that I can bare to look at, look as stale as smoke-stained wallpaper.

I scroll through them on the computer, thinking of changes I could make, or should make, alterations, things I got wrong, or not quite right – and don't.

Writing fresh nonsense is less arduous than trying to actually deal with the nonsense I've written in the past.

Gina has laid out all kinds of books for me here in the library, and shoeboxes full of photographs. There are monographs, catalogues, collections of critical essays, special retrospective editions of contemporary art journals. Most of them I have, but those that I don't spark no curiosity or enthusiasm. I did leaf through a copy of the catalogue from 'Everywhere I Look'. It has taken on that smudged patina of – not age, but *existence*: the white is off-white, the corners of the cover burred, dulled from the dirt and sweat of human touch. It's as if, when an object – a book, or a painting – is brand new, it may look pristine, but that's just a chimera, a mirage. It's only once that newness has been rubbed off, has evaporated, been smashed and stamped into the mud, that the object shows its true self. Patina. Look at me, so out of practice I find a good word and I use it twice in two days.

Last night we sat up until the early hours, drinking and talking. It is clear that Gina is not well, is in the advanced stages of I don't know what – of alcoholism, certainly, but of something else, too. At a certain point in the evening all she could do was talk and drink and smoke. Everything else, even those actions ancillary to these three central goals – like getting up to get another drink, extracting another cigarette from the packet, lighting it, breathing, even – was a struggle.

What occurred to me, as we talked, is that she might have acted generously in inviting me down here, and laying out all the research material she has carefully amassed over the years, or allowed to accrete around her, but she regards my project to write about Randall as something of a joke.

'Have you got any regrets?' I asked her at one point, 'When you think back to that time.'

'*All* I *have* is regrets,' she answered, dragging herself upright – inching herself upright – in her chair. 'What *other* people call *memories*, I call regrets.'

(Transcribing her words, it seems like every second one needs to go into italics, which is surely as much to do with the effort it took for her to get them out, as with her wish to give them emphasis. A quick look in the library's OED confirms that there is no etymological link between *emphasis* and *emphysema*.)

The chair is the one I remember her father sitting in – what I think is called a wingback chair. Hem's chair, on the other hand, is nowhere to be seen: the slightly lower-seated one, with the elegant curved legs, that always looked rather as if it was crouching, tensed, in readiness to spring upwards and heave her into the air.

I said something in reply to her comment and she said, 'The chiselling *out* of *epi*-grams is an occupation re-*served* for those who *live* without *hope*.'

(I'll stop italicizing. It's clearly highly annoying.)

'To spend your time reliving the past, without the merciful anaesthetic of dementia, is a horrid thing.'

I asked, 'Do you mean your art, when you talk about what you regret?'

'Not especially. I'm not sure my artistic... emanations, deserve special treatment. Look, Vincent, I *remember* it all, clear as gin,' – and she lifted her glass to hold it before her face, so that my image of her distorted, ballooning sideways, as, presumably, hers did of me – 'but I can't *see* it as separate from now. I can't think of you or me or Randall or Justine, gallivanting around, without seeing how it all necessarily led back up the years to here and now. It may have seemed like fun, at the time, but that's just because we couldn't see the consequences. And, try as I might, I can't untangle the one from the other.'

She quoted a line of poetry at me: what I heard at first as Zeus's birds and the painted grape.

'Wait there,' she told me, and got to her feet and went out of the room, ignoring my offers of help. She was listing like a holed boat, and knocked against an occasional table on her way to the door. When she came back, quite a few minutes later, she had a book in her hand.

'The Metaphysical Poets,' she said, flipping the book to show me the cover. She made it back to her seat, set herself up with fag and glass, and found the page she wanted.

Here's what she read, from Abraham Cowley's poem 'Of Wit'. (The italics, this time, are Cowley's: I'm copying from the book, which she left with me when we went to bed):

> *London* that vents of false *Ware* so much store,
> In no *Ware* deceives us more.
> For men led by the *Colour*, and the *Shape*,
> Like *Zeuxes Birds* fly to the painted *Grape*;
> Some things do through our Judgement pass
> As through a *Multiplying Glass.*
> And sometimes, if the *Object* be too far,
> We take a *Falling Meteor* for a *Star.*

The satirical point of it was obvious, and remains so, this morning: Randall the meteor, vending his false wares; me, and people like me, with our multiplying glasses (telescopes), taking him for a star, a sun, when he was nothing of the sort.

Well, I said, I don't agree. Randall's place in the firmament is fixed. He took British conceptual art out of the corridors of Goldsmith's and onto the world stage. What Alexander McQueen did for fashion, he did for art. He was a serious artist.

She stopped me. It wasn't the meteor she was after; it was the grapes.

She explained the reference to me. Zeuxes, or Zeuxis, was a painter of Greek antiquity, who entered into a contest with his great rival, over which of them was the top dog. Zeuxes, for his part, painted a bunch of grapes of such miraculous verisimilitude that, when he pulled back the curtain covering the picture, the birds flew down from the sky to try and peck at them.

'That's all that Randall was doing, wasn't it?' she said, the book flopping closed in her other hand. 'He made things that looked *so much like art* that all the little birdies, Jan, and the Sheik of wherever, the bloody Akond of Swat, and that Yank who bought up all those *Anti-Cutes*, they all flew down and gobbled them up. Peck peck peck.'

And she put her head on its side, eyes narrowing as she drew on her cigarette.

I replied that it was certainly an interesting metaphor, but that, in any event, Zeuxes still won. I was pissed, and I didn't want to let that stand. The birds came, I said, and they pecked, didn't they? He was still the best painter.

But no. Apparently not. This next part took some time – some gin, some fags – to establish, in part because it wasn't in the poem, but the punch line of the actual story was that the other guy won. Zeuxes' rival, who was called Parrhasius, applauded the grapes, and then brought out his canvas, complete with curtain, for comparison. Parrhasius invited Zeuxes to draw back the curtain to see the painting, but when he tried to do so, Zeuxes discovered that the curtain *was* the painting. It was a painting of a curtain.

Zeuxes fooled the birdies, but Parrhasius fooled Zeuxes.

The looping, infinitely regressing, self-reflexing, paradoxical implications of this were, to say, the least, rather beyond us by this point last night. If Zeuxes is Randall, who was Parrhasius? Koons? Duchamp? She batted the question away. 'Pick who you want. Either way, there's no art there. It just looks like it. That's your precious friend.'

That's what gives me pause, this morning, as I leaf through the monographs in the library – the only place, after all, where I can be sure she'll leave me in peace. Is there any art in here, or does it just look like art? And is there a difference?

And the bitterest irony, as I look up and around myself, at the four walls covered floor to ceiling in books and books and books, is that the one person who could point me towards the ones that hold the arguments and references I'd need to even begin answering that question – and he'd do it, even if the arguments he produced for me were the ones that exploded him completely, in a final glorious puff of aesthetics – isn't here to do it.

Right then.

I have Gina to thank, for this at least.

I'm just back from taking a walk down to the beach. At Gina's suggestion. She couldn't come down with me, she said, she wouldn't get down, let alone back up, but I think she saw, at lunch, that I was on the point of making my apologies, and cutting and running.

You can't go without going down to the beach, she said.

So, after lunch, that's what I did.

Just the bare fact of the trees that I ran my hands over as I descended, the same trees that were there ten years ago, that preceded us all by decades, some of them, and will outlive us by that, or more, did something to loosen my mind, in its harness, or sharpen it. The trees, and the ferns and bushes and blades of grass.

Everything in the world runs on loops and cycles, but all at different rates. We are fooled by the persistence of the sun rising and setting, and of spring coming around again after winter, into linking our own lives to these cycles of recurrence. Carving your initials and that of your lover on a tree trunk gives you the momentary illusion that your love will last as long as that tree. When, of course, the tree, as it grows, distorts the letters until they are illegible. We will only truly be regenerated once we have give ourselves up completely to the soil, gifted our chemicals to the slow-grinding mills of the worms and bacteria.

The cold wet air of the riverside, the trees, and the pebbles on the beach. You can throw them out, but the sea shrugs, and rolls them back in on the next tide, or on a tide ten years from now, it neither knows nor cares.

I threw some stones into the river, skimming them like we used to do, until my fingers got cold.

Then I clambered back up the hill, and poured myself a coffee and came back here to open the boxes of photos.

Just holding them makes me feel as if we're all of us dead, not just him. There's even a couple of envelopes with the negatives in, long thin strips of shimmery dark film that you can hold up to the light to see us all, done up as evil clowns, posing ludicrously. How you would explain the process to someone today, I don't know. It must seem like something from the Middle Ages.

I've picked out and have in front of me some shots from Millennium Eve. There's one with Randall and Justine, Gina and Matthew, standing in the drawing room, holding drinks. Another shows what I suppose someone must have wanted to seem like a reunion: Randall and Justine, me, Kevin and Anton, Lee, Malcolm, Gina. The circle, or what was left of it, ten years on. You can just make out Matt, Tacita's partner, looking on, smirking at our oafish self-congratulation. Who else was there, that declined to take their place in the line up? It was a night characterised by awkward reintroductions, after all. I think Tanya must have been there. Aya was in South Africa, Griff in Berlin.

The photos don't speak to me. Nothing drifts up out of them. Nothing but our clothes and hair, that seem wrong, as your clothes and hair always do in photos, just that little bit out of date.

But being down there, sat on one of the tree-trunk benches, then moving to the next, then to the next, and getting nothing but a wet bum as my thanks.

It wasn't the first year since the death of Hem, but still I think Matthew wanted to make it more than just another New Year's party dominated by a gaggle of artists, 'snorting and cavorting' as Hem used to say, grooving chaotically away in the drawing room to purposefully bad music, before softly and suddenly vanishing away, minutes after midnight, to do it all again, with a better soundtrack, down by the river.

So he decided to frame our regular party inside a bigger, brighter one of his own design. Not that there weren't other parties to go to that night, and Peploe was out of the way, but he did it right: sent out the invitations early, impressed on people the idea that this was his big blow-out, to show that he had not succumbed to grief, a celebration of Hem's and his life together. And he was a man of some standing, a knight of the realm. Gina joked that we'd better enjoy the party, because it was probably costing her half of her inheritance.

I remember her dancing with her father, a delicate waltz, early in the evening – the dance he would have had at the wedding she never had – and being hugely moved by the amount of love and warmth towards them, or him, in the room. The thought that the two of them, the movement of their feet across the floor, were actually being impelled, driven, by the love in the room. Their dance was an expression of it, just as it, the love, was a reaction to it, the dance.

I was there, with a new partner, the first serious relationship I had had since Justine – or, to put it another way, the first person other than her that I'd taken to Peploe. It felt like a big moment, for me, although she wasn't as taken with my friends as Justine had been, and nor, really, was she that taken with me. No matter.

More importantly still, though, Randall was there, so soon after his triumph at Venice, with Justine, and Joshua, now eighteen months old and tottering around in a little hooded top like a pixie after his mother, crying to be picked up. He wouldn't be held by anyone other than Justine or Randall, and screeched when it was attempted. Justine, bless her, did try to give him to me. This strange, wonderful, improbable child. So robust, but fizzing with a kind of combustible danger, the way his limbs shivered with it, as if he might explode at any moment.

One of the photos in Gina's collection, taken by I don't know whom, shows me holding Joshua, and Justine standing next to us. Of course, Joshua is crying and reaching out for his mother, and of course there's a look of embarrassment and uncertainty on my face that marks me out as so obviously not a parent of anybody, least of all the child in my arms, but it's still, well, it's something.

Justine's happiness at seeing me, and her openness and warmth towards the woman I had brought with me, was accepted gladly, and honestly reciprocated. But then Justine was in a way more central to the event than Randall. She was a bridge between him and his former friends, many of whom now dismissed or resented him, for various and often muddled reasons, including the Great Day of Art debacle, and his genuine, unprecedented success, at Venice and after.

I remember how Randall glided into the room, sending Justine in ahead of him, as a kind of ambassador. People were always glad to see her, and their welcome, our welcome, was so genuine, that it would have been hard to completely snub Randall, when he sidled up, oh so humbly, to insert himself into our group. Fresh from Venice, from signing in the US with Carl, the world laid out before him. Grinning that shit-eating grin, knowing that half the people in the room would have been more than happy to lamp him. Myself including.

That's how it went, Randall hanging back while Justine approached people, dealt with and negotiated their delight and surprise and quick furtive scan of the room for her husband, and then talking, giving information, introducing Joshua, hitched up on her hip, face most often buried in her shoulder. And only then, once they had spoken for a minute or so, once a general aura of politeness had been established, gesturing to Randall to come over. A wiser, humbler Randall – if not ever quite an apologetic one.

And it helped that it was Millennium Eve. Nobody was going to start a fight on this night, of all nights. And Matthew's calming, cheering presence, inching from group to group, carer in tow, checking that everyone had a drink, that he knew who everyone was, that they were having a good time.

After the fireworks, as ordained, we loaded ourselves up with booze and hats and coats and made our way past the big bonfire, where we'd throw our millennial sacrifices, later – much later, as dawn was breaking – and we went, slipping and sliding, down through the trees to the river.

Kevin and Anton were already down there, supervising the fire, checking the pots of soup and mulled wine hanging over it, the jacket potatoes tucked away inside it.

More and more people came down, and the fire burned higher, and I remember an accordion, and dancing – of sorts. Silly, arms hooked through arms rounds around the fire. People bashing away at each other with sticks, like Morris men.

At moments, you could see Randall in quiet conversation with people, people who still had it in for him. Randall, head down, nodding earnestly, thoughtfully. Listening. Justine, watching him, watching for who else was there, waiting to speak to him. It was like people were lining up to let him prostrate himself before them. He was making things right, like someone about to start on a journey. Later, we talked, too. Sat on the corners of two of the trunk-benches. Justine snuggled up against him, the flames on the side of her face, my new partner snuggled up to me. The awful geometry of it, that felt wrong, even then. We didn't last much longer into the new year.

It was then that he told me he was going to America.

'Come with us,' he said.

'To America?' I replied, dumbly.

'Yes. It'll be dull without you, Vincent. I mean, I have to go. You see that, don't you?'

He stood and held out his hand and I put mine into it and he tugged, tugged me up, despite my resistance. 'Come on, Vincent,' he said, and pulled me to standing and tugged me down across the sand and silt and stones to the river. I resisted, laughing. We were so drunk, this may even have been how it actually happened.

'Come,' he was saying, flicking his head, cajoling, as if America was somewhere just across the water and over the brow of the next hill. 'Can't you see us?' And he stepped out on to these low flat rocks that stood out of the water near the beach. Stepping out on them like they were stepping stones, actually leading somewhere. He wobbled, held out his hands for balance, laughed. A foot went in, briefly, before he righted himself. I stood on the edge looking at him, his bad impression of a bad acrobat.

I had known him for ten years. Just ten years.

'The three of us,' he said. 'Together. The New World. Come on. It'll be just like old times.'

Justine and the woman I had brought with me were watching us, from their places by the fire, warily, each with their own desires, their own fears, their own reservations.

He, beckoning with both arms, wobbling on a stone that wouldn't lie flat. And he turned and threw out an arm, pointing, and sort of half-crooned, half-bellowed 'Go West', like in the song. 'There we are,' he said. 'Taking Manhattan. Flying down to Miami. Hopping across to LA. Lording it up on Martha's Vineyard. We'll be kings! Britain's finished. America's where it's at. America's calling.'

And then, with a last triumphant wave of the arm, almost as if it was intended – everything he did in his own life was almost as if intended – he overbalanced, and, windmilling his arms like the clown he was, he stepped down heavily into the shallows, then stumbled, went forward and onto his hands and knees, almost swimming in the night time water.

253

People hooted and clapped and it was, for a moment, almost as if the world was set back on its axis, and things were as they'd always been, and the way ahead was clear.

He got to his feet, making more comedy of his idiocy, shouting it out to the far shore, as if by embracing it he could transform the idiocy into heroism.

Justine insisted he go back to the house and change before he caught a chill, and he came stomping back to land, dripping and shivering already, his jacket hanging limp around him. He grabbed my arm as they came past.

'Come. Come,' he said, nodding up the slope, the pebbly beginnings of the path, the dark trees, the way unlit. 'Think about it, Vincent. For real.'

I allowed myself to be brought along.

'Seriously, what's keeping you here? Bring whatshername. And Justine wants you to come, too, don't you, darling?'

She turned to raise her eyebrows, her face dancing in the light from the fire. He was drunk. We were drunk. Ten years drunk.

'It's only fun if Vincent's there, isn't it?'

She gave a nod, and tugged at Randall, who tugged at me, and we started up the path, stumbling and tripping. I said I'd think about it. I think, for the rest of the night, and maybe even for a few days afterwards, I really believed it might happen, it might come true.

UNTITLED (ENSŌ)

She walked up the dune and the sea came into view, like a person standing up from a table. The water a flat grey, the beach the colour of weak tea. There was – or was there always? – a breeze, like a hand brushed down the side of the face, and the smell of, what? Salt on sand, the two grains sifting together. The days here with no breeze were just the breeze holding its breath, like a child in the bathtub, lying underwater, seeing how long she could last.

She wrinkled her nose and inhaled, deeply. The simmering awareness of a fresh air headache: the burden of freedom.

The beauty of the horizon, he always said, was that it wasn't ever perfectly flat. Follow it with your finger, he'd say, closing one eye and putting out a hand to point. It wobbles, like a Hodgkin. The only conceivable proof for the existence of God: that no straight lines exist in nature.

How like him, given this kind of place, given this kind of immense, unearned, inhuman peace, that he had to find something to *say* about it. He even wrote it down, in one of the notebooks he occasionally remembered to carry around with him, now that he longer had Vincent to do it for him. They always sound better when there's someone else to write them down, he'd said, and then he'd given her a look.

Right, like she was going to follow him around with a pad and pen.

She looked round for Vincent. He was standing by the car, bags in hand, looking up at her, giving her time. How polite he was. How careful. And how dangerous because of it. She felt certain that they were going to sleep together, now, at some point. It seemed inevitable. She had sensed it, or decided it, back in the studio, or before then, even: the morning she had woken up in the apartment, with the knowledge of him asleep in the next room, or the next but one. She'd seen the pair of them as if from above, lying in parallel: he on his side of the bed, the right side, if he still kept to it, and she on the left. All it would have taken, from that impossible perspective, would have been to lift him up and move him magically through the walls, to put him in her bed. Was that what was happening here? At the very least, she'd thought, she needed to get them out of New York, out of the apartment, to find out for sure.

'Come and look at the sea,' she called down to Vincent, and the breeze rose and dandled a strand of hair across her face, as if to mock her. She brushed it away.

He put down the bags and started walking up towards her, his shoes skidding and slipping on the sand.

'Vincent. Take your shoes off. You're on holiday now.'

He squinted up at her. 'Am I?'

'Yes, you are.'

He knelt and picked at his laces. His brown leather shoes, faithful as dogs.

'I didn't pack for the seaside either,' he said. 'Shall I roll my trousers up, too?'

He turned and threw the shoes, one then the other, to land and roll by the bags.

When he reached her, she took hold of his arm and stood them facing the beach and the ocean. She pictured them as they would look from the back, two wide vertical strokes, like fence posts, against the broad horizontal washes of the land and sea. She wound her hand further through the gap of his arm, then gave him, it, his arm, a squeeze. She felt a draught of gladness pass through her, like the coolness of a cloud passing in front of the sun, and the gladness was a response to the fact that she was able to communicate such things to him, and with such certainty of being understood. What she wanted to say – what she would have wanted to say – even as she perceived the outline of the thought in her mind, was that this was what she had missed since Randall's death: that there was no one to whom she could express her feelings in such an understated, *un*-stated manner. If she wanted someone to know how she felt, in her thrillingly packed and fulfilled life, surrounded as she was by people, all leaning, in some manner, towards her needs and desires, then she had to speak to do so. To say 'I want', or 'I need', or some obtuse inversion of them.

'If only I'd thought to bring my swimming trunks.'

She laughed. 'In March? You've got to be joking.' Saying it allowed her to tug again at his arm, a pretend admonishment, and then to disengage. She started along the ridge of the dune towards the corner of the deck. 'You'll bring the bags, won't you. Be a dear.'

'Yes, ma'am.'

Margaret had done her usual splendid job, stocking the fridge, putting out flowers, and cleaning just enough to make the place feel homely while still basically unlived in. She'd had to explain it to her, carefully, half a year into their arrangement, that they didn't want to arrive to a strict, hotel-room level of cleanliness. There had to be a certain sense of neglect about the place, so that you could fully enjoy the opening of the windows and doors, of airing the place yourself, liberating it. You expected to rinse a glass under the tap before drawing yourself a drink, even if you didn't quite want to see dust on it.

It wasn't a large place, compared with some of their neighbours': spacious rather than cavernous, deliberately short on guest bedrooms. Its purchase had, all along, been part of

259

the grand American plan, with its twin objectives of helping Randall's career step up to the next, truly international level, and of detaching him from the endless merry-go-round of partying and recovery that his life, even out of London, had become. This was a place for the three of them, for them to spend time together, as a family, and, in the evenings, a couple. To think and talk and replenish the reservoir of love that fed them, kept them whole and growing. And it had worked. Joshua loved coming here, and still did. In a way it was more his place now than hers, a venue for the kinds of hip, boisterous parties they had strictly avoided having before.

He'd made her laugh when he told her, in that gruff, resentful manner he used when he found himself being 'grown-up', that he'd ruled her gravel garden out of bounds to party guests. As if it was some kind of shrine to his father. The thought of his young man's sanctimoniousness in that regard nudged up against her memories of Randall in the garden, splashing his feet in the pond, or sat smoking a joint on the low stone bench, flicking the roach into the rings of gravel.

'Did I tell you I've invited Joshua up?' she asked Vincent, out on the deck with drinks, after they'd stowed their baggage in their rooms and she'd put something by Margaret in the oven.

'Yes,' he said, and paused. 'I mean, good. It will be good to see him.'

She knew full well that Joshua and Vincent's relationship was difficult, latticed with reticence and confusion, with mistimed gestures and deliberate and genuine misunderstandings, with gaps and sudden deep pits. At the funeral it had been Kevin and Anton who had looked to Joshua, all of ten, guiding and accompanying him, both in the dense choreography of the day itself and afterwards, more generally. Kevin had done the crucially important thing of taking the boy's grief and disorientation absolutely seriously, as the most serious part of the whole event.

It was Kevin who had made a point of seeing him whenever he was in town – which was more often than Vincent was, to be fair – of taking him to the movies and shows. It was him who sent the parcels that arrived out of nowhere, unattached to birthdays or other excuses, containing T-shirts and DVDs or whatever. The T-shirts were always the right size, whereas god knows even Randall couldn't be guaranteed to know how big Josh's feet were at any given time. The point of all of this being, so far as she understood it, that his father hadn't just been a famous artist, a celebrity, someone who was fair game for adulation or derision in the most public of spheres; he was also, Kevin seemed to suggest, an artist among artists, and this entailed a duty of care that, his father gone, devolved to him.

'Well,' she said. 'He's at a difficult stage.'

'A difficult stage, sure. Why not? It's just strange to think that in a couple of years he'll be as old as Randall was when I first met him.'

He stopped, and shifted his wine glass on the table.

She leaned to top it up from the bottle.

'You should watch some of his films,' she said.

As if that would help. Boys' art, she thought, is so often a plea for understanding that, the moment you reach out – to show you *do* understand – turns into an opportunity for evasion, slipping back behind another veil, another reference, another spoor of some other meaning. She thought of Josh's digital shorts, with their in-your-face insistence on his motor dysfunction, making of it an existential gambit, a challenge to the viewer. She knew why he made them – which wasn't the same as thinking them bad, or good. But she didn't doubt that they stood up to the scrutiny and approval they were already receiving, what with America's avowedly dynastic approach to the creative industries. Here, at least, being the son of Randall was no curse. She dreaded to think how people would take him, back in England.

'Sure,' Vincent said. 'I will. I'd be happy to. It's just, if he can't understand, just now, why his father so much as gave me the time of day, perhaps that will come. Perhaps one day he'll realise he needs someone dumb and philistine to use as a measure of his own brilliance. Or maybe not. Maybe it was Randall's particular genius to make friends with someone like me.'

'Someone like you. This is what your book is about?'

'It's not a *book*.'

'All this "I am not worthy" stuff. I'd still like to read it, you know. Honestly.'

'It's not for reading.'

'Why not? Just because of the paintings?'

He was looking out through the wooden railings towards the ocean, and she followed his gaze, seeing the water shimmering between the branches of the cedars and Virginia pines that grew on the dunes and shielded them from the joggers and walkers and, less often these days, occasional photographers.

Eventually he said, 'Don't they seem like a betrayal to you?' Then, when she didn't respond, 'I don't literally mean a betrayal. The sex stuff is just… It's more, who were we – who were *you* – to be kept in the dark about this stuff? The brilliance of it, the sheer fucking *technique*.' He was alert now, using a spoon to rap out a counter-rhythm to his words on the table. 'Aren't you *angry* about it? You must be, surely. Else, why were you so keen to be out of there?'

She spoke back quickly. 'Are *you* angry? Because, Vincent, that's who he was. That's what he did. The reason I wanted to get out of there was… well, it wasn't because of the work. It was because of the place. It was *thick* with him, Vincent. Everywhere I looked, bam! Randall, Randall, Randall.

'I've spent the last however many years carefully working him into the apartment, fixing him down. So he's there, all around, and for Josh too, but *safely*. Always where I expect him, never

262

jumping out to shout Boo! And to just stumble across that place, to walk into it, it was overwhelming. You remember how I used to get hay fever? Well it was like opening a door and walking into the middle of a field of grass and flowers, in the height of summer, multiplied a thousand times.'

Now he was looking at her, his spoon poised over the table.

'What he did in that studio is maddening, and as a trustee of the board I feel sick, to the stomach, at the thought of the choices and responsibilities it loads on me, but as his *widow*, the art is... pff!' A flick of her hand into the air, giving the gesture to the wind, to be carried away. 'In fact...'

'Yes?'

'Nothing. Your book, I don't know what you've written, but I can't see how these paintings have just invalidated it, just like that.'

She slowed her voice, spacing the words, giving them their measure: 'When two people have promised each other eternal friendship, it is rare for them to remain on good terms for ever.'

'Did he say that?'

'No.'

'A proverb then. A Japanese proverb.'

She bowed her head respectfully.

The temperature dropped, but she said she wanted to stay out on the terrace after they'd eaten. The darkness, after so long in New York, was like a balm. She sought out an old fisherman's jumper of Randall's for Vincent. The thick knotted pattern looked better wrapped across Vincent's chest than it had done on Randall. On him the design was too dainty. He didn't need anyone's help to look like your idea of a rugged trawlerman.

Vincent had actually gone round, setting out and lighting two dozen tea lights on the decking, in their little holders, and a few more in the paper shades hanging from wires around the side fences. He'd knelt with a cigarette lighter she'd had to search through three kitchen drawers to find, bending to the candles with the patience and concentration of a monk. She had humoured him by finding some shamisen music and setting it to play quietly. The glow of the concertina-ed shades, rose and pale yellow. Vincent shaking his hand, grinning, burned from using the lighter. A disposable model, translucent green, the one that Randall had used to spark up his joints.

To see him, now, put it down on the table, carelessly, unknowingly, was a lesson in something about time and the persistence of objects that she did not care to pursue. The muted clack of its putting down, the refraction of the liquid through the thick plastic. Its ignorance of who is doing the putting, the sparking, its absolute lack of interest.

They had finished the wine, and Vincent had now moved on to whisky, she to vodka. On the table next to the whisky, the vodka looked vapid, barely wet. The whisky glowed like varnish, it captured the flames of the lights hung around the terrace in its fist and crushed them to seeds and dancing filaments of brightness. No wonder they were so obsessed with the stuff in Japan. 'Unbelievable that it should not have been invented here,' said her friend Ikuo, who always asked her to bring him at least one bottle of something new with her when she visited. He liked to imagine some forgotten court official of the Heian period, dribbling it out in measured drops into a black lacquered bowl. Whisky had the earthy taste of the human soul, he said, with the look and intonation which indicated he was talking of something else entirely, something dark and unspeakable and approachable only obliquely.

Though perhaps you're right, Ikuo, she thought to herself, a while later, as she drank in the burnt note of the drink on Vincent's lips. Standing together next to the railing, their only point of contact their mouths. And, as on the dune that morning, she luxuriated in the sense that she was safe with him, that he would not kick anything over in the rush to get to where they both knew they would get to, eventually. It was the eventualness of it that pleased, and calmed, and reassured.

When they disengaged she found herself putting her hand up to the side of his face. She saw the way the pigment spots, that had once seemed like bitter freckles, had darkened and intensified, pinching in the skin around them. The eyebrows and the eyes. It was a good face. Time had strolled through it, run a gentle hand over it, not grabbed it and shaken it, like it had hers.

'I might have a whisky, now, after all,' she said.

'You might as well.'

He took two steps away from her, turned and picked his way through the scattered tea lights to the house. There was a wry doggedness about him now, compared to the Vincent of old, that somehow approached permanence. Where then he had wavered before so many things: business success, business failure, Randall's affection and approbation, the visceral–psychological assault course of assisted conception, now he seemed unfazeable. Still puppy-like in his eagerness, but settled, eased into himself.

When he had returned, and had poured out a drink for her, and she had taken it, she said what she had been rehearsing.

'Just before we go on, Vincent, I had best tell you that though that kiss gave me great pleasure...'

'Good.'

She took a sip from her glass.

'And it's a pleasure I would like to repeat...'

'Good.'

'At some point this evening there will be a line...'

'I know.'

'A line.'

'Absolutely.'

And by that time they were kissing again. She put her hand up to his head again and he reciprocated, as if he'd been waiting for her

265

permission, which she supposed she had in fact been withholding. His hand in her hair. She cut the kiss short.

'It's not that I don't want to go to bed with you' – and they laughed at each other, as well they might – 'but that I need a good night's sleep more. We can talk tomorrow. About this. About the paintings, and Randall, and everything. Don't you think?'

'Fuck Randall, is what I think,' said Vincent. And that was that.

Breakfast was a riot, a piece of ritual theatre they stumbled through, under-rehearsed, over-anxious, script in hand. It was, she thought, like the worst kind of date. Their solicitousness towards one other. The questions as to how they had slept. The distance they each maintained, circling each other in the kitchen and around the table, always somehow in each other's way, reaching for the same jug, pot, jar.

She had not slept well, but when she had tried to lie to him about this, he had brought her up on it.

'I heard you, walking about.'

'Sorry. Did I disturb you?'

'I was already disturbed, actually.'

'So neither of us got any sleep then?'

'There's irony for you.'

As if in punishment she put him in the downstairs media room with a vat of coffee and cued up some of Josh's films, on his site. They were largely mundane, self-regarding pieces, she knew, hovering halfway between art and indie cinema, no better than you would expect from any precocious middle-class New Yorker of that age, really. Their sole critical edge came from Josh's wayward handheld camerawork. 'The shaking frame' he called it, and the name seemed to have stuck. A permanent reminder of the physical presence of the camera in the digital age, and that it was the hand, not the eye, that filmed – he said, or said they said. A sentimental echo of Italian neorealism, she thought, but what did she know?

Vincent came out in under thirty minutes, having, presumably, either fast-forwarded through most of them, or just given up altogether. The face he pulled when she asked him what he thought of them gave the impression it was a struggle to come up with an opinion at all. His hand to the forehead, flicked away, as if to mime a thought that had been there, but that had gone.

Which was harsh. He wouldn't have been so dismissive of any of his friends' art, twenty years ago. And Randall used video himself, didn't he?

She was sitting in the sun lounge, reading a magazine.

'He can tell me what I'm supposed to think when he comes,' Vincent said.

She nodded, and continued reading.

He took a chair across the table from her, a hazy form in her peripheral vision. She carried on looking at the words and shapes on the page for another minute, taking nothing in, but unwilling to give in so easily. She turned a page with a snap, then looked up. He was tilted forward, arms on knees, staring at the table, his face tensed in a frown that, she knew, was supposed to have nothing whatsoever to do with Josh and his films. She closed the magazine and placed it on her lap.

'What I don't understand,' he said, after a moment, 'and apologies if this sounds like an accusation, is how you can not have known he was up to something.' He paused, as if to let her catch up with him. 'We were going to talk about this, right? That was why we came out here.'

She nodded.

'Fine, so. The smell of, I don't know, turps on him, or white spirit. It still smelled of paint in there. He must have come home reeking of it then. The sheer amount of time it must have taken him to make the paintings. I mean, there's no suggestion he was making them when you were back in the UK, is there?'

267

'He might have been, I suppose. It's unlikely.'

He had picked up some of the pebbles from the bowl on the table and was sorting through them. Grey, black, mottled or with stripes. They'd collected them, over the years, on day trips to the North Shore. He took up a handful of them and then tipped them to the other hand, pouring them in a brief clattering fall.

'Well, we were both busy people, Vincent. I don't have to tell you that.'

'Sure.'

The nature of his attention, the ocean-clouded mugginess of the day that came in over the trees and through the window, made it hard for her to be sure of how she was coming across.

'I said the other day about going there and thinking I was going to discover some lover he'd set up there. Well, I didn't just think that then. I thought that before, too,' she said. 'When he was alive I thought that. I mean, I think he probably was.'

'An affair,' he said. His face, angled up from his stooped posture, seemed as lidded as the sky. 'He was having an affair.' His hands still. The pebbles stopped.

She shrugged. 'Well, everything you said. The time away, and away from the Brooklyn studio, too. The cell switched off, the assistants not knowing where he was. The coming home showered and scrubbed. Not all the time, not every day or every week, but enough, and in bursts. Sometimes he said he'd been at the gym, but you couldn't believe him.'

'And you just...' His disbelief dredging a furrow in his voice, guttering it like a candle. 'I mean, didn't you say anything? What did you *think*?'

'Vincent, I didn't really think anything. Or, no. Don't be silly, of course I wasn't happy about it.' A seagull, passing by them along the skyline, let out a sardonic, throaty stream of *cark*s. 'I was not happy about it at all, Vincent, but, you know what? I didn't do anything.'

He came around the table to her, and sat himself down on the sofa, next to her. She had the sense, again, of them being situated somehow in parallel. He was alongside her, in a way that Randall rarely had been. He, Randall, was always tugging her forward, swinging her around ahead of him, always in movement, each one of them only ever still to pivot the other one onward. Perhaps that was what has changed, she thought. Whenever I thought of Vincent here, coming here, I thought of him *opposite* me, a challenge, something to be dealt with. Yet here we are, sat next to each other, facing the same way.

'This is Randall, Vincent,' she said, trying to speak evenly, hoping the words would come out as she meant. 'I don't have to tell you about him. I thought he was having an affair and, I didn't like it, and I didn't confront him about it, but I did accept it. For reasons that were small and dull and not necessarily expressible in simple, cogent terms. Our life, our home, Joshua, his happiness. His work, my work, our work together. Which was something, Vincent, that I wanted, more than anything. You know that. And of course there were other, bigger, sillier reasons, to do with who he was, his public image. Which, I know, is foolish, but still. It's a fact. And in any case, I had let it go before, so it made no sense to make something of it now. I felt like I risked exposing myself.'

'How do you mean, you'd let it go before?'

'I mean, if this was an affair he was having, which now it seems he wasn't – or, who knows, perhaps he was as well? It's not like the studio disproves anything – then it wasn't as if it would have been the first time. There was Aya, obviously, Maxine, I think, Gina.'

He said something she didn't get, and he stood, walked a few steps.

'Is that right?'

'It is.'

'What a *bastard*.'

'Vincent.'

269

'What a *bastard*. Is there *anyone* he didn't fuck?'

'*Vincent.*'

'And now he expects us to, I don't know.' He threw out his arm, angrily, hopelessly, gesturing at nothing. 'What does he expect us to *do* with this shit? Why should *we* have to make the decision, if he couldn't bring himself to do it himself, or wasn't able to? If we put them out there we'll fuck off a lot of people. *Fine*. But we'll make ourselves look ridiculous into the bargain. We will, right? We'll be a laughing stock. Unless we just put out the ones of other people, and trash the ones with us in. Which would make us exactly what kind of cunts?'

She held her silence, listened to him talk: it would be seismic, an earthquake. There was nothing like it that had happened in their lifetimes. It would be total devastation. Because there was no doubt about it: the pictures would blow everyone's sense of who he was, as an artist, sky-high. He mimed an explosion with his arms, puffing out his cheeks and goggling his eyes. The fallout, the dust clouds. The reverberations. The toxicity in the water table. She let the words wash over her: they would have to go into hiding. A convent. She'd have to take holy orders.

'Imagine what they'd say,' he said, now practically leaning over her. 'Imagine what Fried or someone like that would say, the language he'd have to reach for to describe the paint. The *method*, the application, the physicality of the paint, the way he's put it on, *screwed* it into the canvas, into what's already there. It's miraculous, isn't it?'

He crouched down in front of her, she heard his joints click, and smiled, but he missed the smile. He had her hands in his hands now. He was looking up at her, jigging her hands in time to his words.

'It's the best work he's ever done, isn't it?'

She sort of nodded.

'No one's done anything like it, have they?'

Again, the gesture adumbrated, barely sketched in.

'It would fuck them up, good and proper, if we put it out there. And I want to. I want to. But it would, don't you see, it would...'

His hands, holding hers, went on with their movements, silly motions like a girl jigging the reins of a pony, but the words had stopped, and the look on his face, when she looked at him, was one of, if you had to put a name to it, fear. Then, though it wasn't clear how it happened, or whose idea it was, his hands were holding her head, and his knees came down on her knees, hurting her, and he slipped to the ground and pulled her after him, half off the sofa, her mouth to his. A jarring, deliberately awkward kiss, with none of the delicacy of last night.

She tried to tell him to wait, to slow down, but the trying didn't reach as far as the telling, and she joined him in the kiss, as if that was the only way, now, to tell him.

He paused, tightening the grip of his hands in her hair, and he said, speaking the words so close that she felt the movement of his mouth on hers, and heard the honest terror in them, 'I would destroy every last one of those paintings, I'd build a bonfire and watch them burn, if it meant this, Justine.'

She pushed him away with her mouth. 'We can't do that,' she said, trying to look serious, and he nodded and said, 'I know,' but they were still kissing, and he had fallen over backwards onto the rug, one arm rested awkwardly on the glass table, with its bowls and its pebbles and its glass of water and its magazines and its pine cones, and she said, 'Get up, then,' and they got up, and when they were upright she pushed him backwards, her hands on his chest, guiding him, his hands locked about her wrists, like a game of trust, walking backwards, and he said, 'Now?' and she nodded, repeating his word, and steering him into her bedroom.

The fraughtness of their lovemaking, the unlikeliness of it, was as a provocation, the wilful amateurishness of it only making it more fraught, and she regretted it, even as they manoeuvred

271

emselves through it. She regretted their seriousness and their soberness and their lack of moment. But the moment had its own logic. This is passion, she told herself, as they removed the first, least complicated items of each other's clothes; this is passion and the consequence of passion. Passion in the daytime, as they quickly finished undressing, themselves, where it doesn't belong and so is so much more passionate. And if a kiss is a form of promise, she thought, then what is this, this polite, urgent, awkward fucking, is this a promise too?

She was aware of the play of negotiation and reciprocation in their love-making, even as they used those elements to try to obliterate or camouflage any sense of conscious design. Their turn-taking at grabbing and taking, at slowing and obstructing. Until that moment when she sensed him pull away, and watched him go, as if he was racing breathless up a hill whose summit she knew she would not reach. And perhaps out of delicacy, perhaps in order to concentrate on her own abstraction, she turned her head and looked out through the wide glass doors at the dark green and grey of the gravel garden. The circles and swirls seen slant in the gravel, and behind them the dark green backdrop of the Virginia pines, so eerie.

When he had come he lowered himself on to her and they lay like that for some time, and then he shifted sideways to lie next to her, on his back, breathing heavily. After a minute his breathing had slowed and softened, and she looked and saw that he was asleep, his eyelashes fluttering.

She lay looking at the ceiling. He on the right, she on the left.

After a while he woke from his doze and shifted himself up onto his elbows.

'What's that?' An almost peeved edge to his voice.

It was a scroll, by Deishū, hung on the wall opposite the bed, in an alcove they'd improvised between the wardrobe and the door to the shower room.

'It's Japanese calligraphy. A scroll.'

'It's a circle.'

'He bought it for me.'

'Like Randall's circles.'

'He bought it for me. It's called an ensō.'

He got off the low bed and walked naked over to look at it, then lifted a hand and traced the circle, the thick inked Zen swirl, giving a little twist at the end to disengage, there where the artist had let his brush tail off, leaving the merest hint of gap, making the shape both complete and incomplete.

'He told you about those, right?'

'Of course he did. This is eighteenth century. By Takahashi Deishū.'

'Should I have heard of him?'

'I wouldn't have thought so.'

'And this is a haiku?' Indicating the kanji next to it.

'Yes. By Kobayashi Issa. It means, *The world of dew. Yes, it is a world of dew, and yet. And yet.*'

She thought she might tell him more about the haiku, what it meant, the story behind it, but decided not to.

The way his hands hung slightly curled at his sides. She looked at him, looking. The old stone wall of his buttocks, his curved shoulders, the toned muscles of his arms and thighs, not a shred of self-consciousness. He gave a laugh that she found hard to interpret: dismissive, but dismissive of itself. And now his belly, hair-flecked like a dune with grass. The penis, innocuous, repentant, gone back whence it came.

'He made four thousand of them. Did you know that? Four thousand goes at a perfect circle.'

'This is different. These aren't supposed to be perfect. That's the point.'

'I know, but still. It's weird, don't you think?'

She thought, but didn't say: it's the imperfections you should cherish. She didn't want to give him that ammunition.

Later, though, they showered, and she said, almost unthinking, as she towelled his back, 'At least we know what we might be letting ourselves in for,' and at that he turned and took her face in the flats of his hands, and kissed her, most expressly and explicitly – in a way that seemed to carry a real intention. She closed her eyes and murmured her assent, thinking as she did so that, contrary to what she had thought earlier, it was quite possible to sleep with someone, to fuck them, by accident, with no promise attached, but that a kiss like this was always meant.

And then, when they were dressed, and she was sat at her dressing table drying her hair, he said he was going to make a fire, and something jumped inside her, an unpleasant jolt, and they looked at each other in the mirror.

'A fire,' she said.

'Yes.'

'To throw the paintings on?'

The severity of his expression was as if he knew he was being called, already, on the nonsense he had spoken in the heat of passion.

'If we had them here, now?' he said, talking to her reflection. 'Yes, I would. Right now, I'd throw them right on.'

'You don't really mean that, do you?'

'I don't know what I mean. There's too many thoughts jumbled up in my head to know which ones are real. But I'm going to build a fire, on the beach. I'm going to make myself a sandwich and go for a walk and collect firewood. It will be nice. We can sit out round it and pretend we're at Peploe. Watch the sun go down, have a beer. And it will give me something to do, building it. Otherwise, I'd just spend the rest of the day wanting to be in bed with you.' And he walked behind her, and lifted the hair from her neck and ran his hands through its length, combing it with his fingers. 'Which, even if that was how you wanted to spend the rest of the day, which I would by no means assume, would probably do me all kinds of physical damage.'

So while he went out, cockahoop, to gather firewood from up and down the beach, she went and sat out in her grey garden, and thought about meditating.

While she was sitting there, considering it, a scattering of tiny birds dropped by, like British sparrows, with speckled undersides, and she watched them fly hither and thither in the branches of the cedars and pines, almost as if they were getting blown about by the wind. She wondered when the hummingbirds would arrive. She was here so little, since he died, she had no sense of the seasons. It occurred to her that she could move out here, among her bowls and ink stones and prints and books. She could go back to the city when Josh wanted to use the house, or when something called her. She was sure she could be quite happy, living like that, for a time.

Then she thought about Vincent.

The hardest thing seemed to be working out exactly what had been said, and what hadn't, and what may have been implied by this. She thought of Ikuo, her friend in Kurashiki, the only other person since Randall that she had gone to bed with. And of how you might choose to interpret that fact, and the fact of the distance between them. And the fact that she more or less refused to see him in New York, only Japan. And she thought of how Joshua, when she had told him about Ikuo, last year, had seemed to accept the idea of such a person, but had then changed his mind about going with her on her trip to Osaka that summer. She reached up to the dwarf willow tree that grew by the bench, rising and falling like a fountain, and took and twisted a new leaf between her fingers.

The birds had gone from the garden. She considered it, now, the few trees and the grey rocks, scabbed with lichen where they should more properly have moss, and the rings radiating out from them in the gravel. She rolled and crushed the leaf in her hand, turning it to a sort of fleshy gunk, like the insides of a squashed bug. The garden, though beautiful, felt fraudulent, a *trompe l'oeil* that, if she took a wrong step, would be revealed for what it was, every rock, every plant, every tree a flimsy, two-dimensional cut-out. Who could be fooled by such a thing, she thought. She had come out here to meditate, but she wouldn't be able to meditate. She flicked the mess of leaf to the ground.

He returned at a quarter to five, happily exhausted. He was done, he said: 'A real Peploe fire. I wish the rest of them were here.'

She looked at him, collapsed there in a chair. She got a beer from the fridge and passed it to him.

'I do,' he said. 'I actually do. I was there, you know, last year, or, no, the year before, I think.'

'I know,' she said, but she didn't have the heart to tell him what more she knew: that Gina had phoned her, the very day he'd left, and asked her if she knew that Vincent was writing a book about them all.

'I was trying to write. Well, I'd given up, but somehow she convinced me to give it another shot. She'd pulled out all the stops, Gina. Piled up all these photos and books and stuff in the library for me to look at. It didn't work. I think I finally realised the project was too immense, or too wrongheaded. That the more I wrote, the less he was there.'

Then, as she busied herself putting quiche and potatoes and salad on plates, he went on. 'I don't know why I thought it would be a good idea for you to read it.' He laughed. 'In any case, all this... stuff has saved me an immense amount of effort.'

'How do you mean?'

'Well, it's all nonsense.'

She looked at him, passed a plate.

'Here, take this to the table.'
'But it *is*.'

She pulled on a scarf and a jacket and they went out and through the gravel garden, unlocked the beach gate and went between the banks of grass, she carrying a blanket, two cushions and two glasses, he a cooler with beer and, shoved under one arm, the bottle of whisky. They walked single file. He was in Randall's jumper again. They had not touched since the morning.

There was the sea again, seen before you saw the beach, far away and dark and deep. And there, as they crested the top of the dune, was the tide, a pale shimmer of movement beyond the fire, unlit, a small grey house of stacked wood. The sand was heavy, slow going, shifting out from under your feet in tiny, abrupt landslides, more so in the dark than by day.

The fire, when they got to it, was bigger than she expected, an irregular pyramid of bleached driftwood and darker branches from the cypresses and conifers. The pine that would crackle and spark. There were pale balls and twists of paper scrunched up and shoved deep into the gaps between the wood. One bigger log, that must have taken effort to shift, rolled into position for a seat.

Vincent knelt on the sheltered inland side of his fire and took out Randall's lighter, sparked it and touched it here and there to the paper, then scooted around to his right and repeated the exercise, until he had lit the fire at six, seven spots.

She laid out the blanket and sat down on it, her back against the log, enjoying the spectacle, him moving like that around the fire, like a boy. And she was glad when it seemed like the fire had taken, and he came and sat himself down, along from her. Close, but not too close. It had been good to get the sex out of the way, then, she thought.

'A Peploe fire,' she said, half a statement, half a question.

They watched it a while, then he said, 'A marker. That's how I always thought of the fires at Peploe. As punctuation. A way of measuring our lives.'

'The end of something, the start of something.'

'Maybe that. Yes.'

'You remember him, that Millennium Eve. His jacket. You put on, what did you put on?'

'My phone. My mobile phone. You put it in that book of poems.'

'Bashō. I'd forgotten that. How like you to remember.'

'Of course I remember.'

Over the next twenty minutes the fire grew, and diminished, at the same time, became concentrated, burrowed into itself, starting to throw out real heat. Vincent planted his beer in the sand between them, twisting it in, then reached over by his side and produced another piece of paper. He balled it in his hands and bent forward and threw it on to the fire.

She watched him, drinking her beer, as he repeated the process with another sheet, plucked from down beside him, where she couldn't see.

'What's that?'

'What's this? It's my book.'

Her laugh, a reflex, escaped her mouth even as she realised he was telling the truth. She unfolded her legs from beneath her and leaned, then lunged, to try to grab the sheet from his hand. The bottle stood between them toppled, sending its contents gulping out into the sand, so she had to pause to right it.

'What do you mean? You're not serious?'

They grappled for a moment, incompetently, the blanket rucking under them, he twisting away from her, to keep the sheet out of her grasp.

'Don't be stupid. Give me that.'

He shifted his grip and pushed her backwards by the wrists,

forcing her over and down onto the blanket with a grunt. It was a violent movement, deliberately careless, but it hurt her nonetheless, her wrist bent back to the limit, and she said, 'Ow.' His expression flickered with uncertainty, and she yielded, as much from a kind of compassion as from anything else. He had her arms pinioned either side of her head. She could feel the sand through the blanket. He lifted his leg so he was straddling her. The whole short sudden event seemed to her absolutely ludicrous, and impractical, and she waited to see if he would acknowledge this.

'I want to read it,' she said, aware as she said it of a childish taint to her voice. 'Why can't I read it?'

But his face was still tense, concentrating on his own sense of injury, and the words came out angry.

'Because it's shit.'

He pushed down on her wrists.

'Stop it.'

'It's shit and wrong.'

Another push.

'I said, stop it. You're hurting me.'

'Sorry.'

He released her and sat back, taking his weight off her. They were both breathing heavily. Rolling around on the blanket like teenagers, she thought, in accusation, and then thought that it was no less ludicrous than what they had done that morning in the bedroom.

But when he spoke he said, 'Because I thought I knew him and it turned out I didn't.'

She watched him, blankly, from where she lay, trying to follow the shuttling rhythm of his thoughts, flipping constantly between his two poles, Randall and her.

There was a breathed word that might have been another apology and he lifted himself off her. She sat up and sneezed, dusting sand from herself, shaking out her hair. When she looked again he was standing over the fire, bag in hand, then, as she watched, he upended the bag over it. The sheets fell with a great thump, smacking up sparks and sending a couple of rogue sheets blowing and flipping over the sand towards her. She grabbed them, looking to see if he would do anything to stop her. He didn't, and she brought them close to her face to read.

'"What was impressive",' she said, '"was the high-velocity impact of the pellets on the canvases, the way they sprang immediately to life, the paint thudding into the material, a lovely pattern of splatters springing up as if by magic."'

Vincent was crouching sideways, face towards the sea, as he poked the burning book with his stick, separating out the pages.

'Vincent. You're not seriously telling me that's your only copy.'

He settled back on his haunches, then toppled back onto the sand, half on purpose, making an 'ooph' sound.

'Of course not. God, I wish it was. This is a purely symbolic act.'

He stamped angrily down on another sheet that had lifted off the fire, pirouetted briefly in the air, then plummeted to earth.

'You can't destroy anything properly, these days.'

He waved his stick at the sky.

'It's all up there, somewhere. Everything's stored. Nothing's forgotten.'

He dragged the escaping sheet within reach, then picked it up and returned it to the fire.

She turned to the second sheet in her hand.

'"Somebody had found the switches for the main lights, and they blinked on to show people, still pushing helplessly away from the assault. The eye was drawn to each fresh burst of yellow – who was hit? who was hit? was I hit? People were sobbing and cowering. A man's voice, plummy and shrill, was repeating 'It's just paint! It's just paint!' over and over. Other people were yelling for Randall to stop, or for others to stop him."'

She laughed, and he looked at her, enquiring.

'The paintball show. This man. *It's just paint. It's just paint.*'

She caught his quick smile, the deep satisfaction that was beyond concealing.

'There's nothing wrong with this, Vincent. It's good. I mean, it's really well-written.'

'Thank you. But the well-written-ness of it is beside the point.'

'So help me out here. Are you angry with Randall because of the paintings, so you don't want to be his friend anymore, or are you angry at yourself because you were tricked?'

He lowered his head to knees.

A sound came from him, but if it was anything more than a mumbled groan, she wasn't able to say what it was.

She drank from her beer and watched him. Perhaps this was all a mistake. To become involved with someone who was still so caught up with the memory of someone else, her husband no less, was a sure-fire route to turmoil and regret. What he had said that morning, with regards to the paintings – though that was surely not what he meant – that they were free agents, and could do whatever they wanted, now seemed risible.

She walked down past the fire towards the sea, balling and throwing into the flames her two pages as she went.

The sight and sound of waves on the shoreline at night always seemed to her obscene, uncanny. The fact of their eternal, unceasing recurrence, during the day, was fine, but in the dark, when everyone was supposed to be asleep, it seemed demented, unreasonable, as if they were proof that the unconscious mind lived on after death. Your body was dead, but your thoughts kept right on coming, one behind the other, washing up on to an empty shore.

A shout from the house.

'Mum! Are you down there?'

She looked at Vincent, him looking at her, her surprise mingling with a gleeful kick of adrenalin: the ecstasy of being found out.

'I thought you said he wasn't coming till tomorrow.'

'He's not. He wasn't.' She shouted up towards the house.

'Hi, honey. Yes. We've made a fire. Come down.'

Josh's head and torso appeared over the top of the trees. He must have clambered up on the railings of the decking. An arm waved and she returned the greeting.

'We'll come down. Do you need anything from up here?'

She looked back at Vincent, who was using a branch to pivot bits of half-burned log from the outside of the fire into its centre. Even in his attempt to exorcise Randall, he was only ever copying him. The burning of the past, the raking of its ashes into the ground. We, Josh said. He would have needed someone to drive him up, unless he'd got the train and a cab. She wondered if this might be this new girlfriend, evident more in the gaps in what he would tell her, than in any direct account.

They appeared a few minutes later, two dark shapes in the dark. Together at the crest of the dune, they separated as they came down the beach, though the woman seemed to be aware of him as she walked, keeping carefully in range. She was short, in dark clothes, a sort of cropped biker's leather jacket and black skinny jeans. Justine couldn't see that well but there was nothing she recognised about her. Tightly packed and intense, quite striking, hair in an almost bob, with daggers of red cutting down to the edges of it in a couple of places – older than Josh. Mid-to-late twenties, at a guess.

'The ocean at night,' she was saying. 'This is just so evocative.'

A slightly whiny voice, with an unmistakable New York cadence, she fell silent as Josh wobbled to Justine, his unsteadiness accentuated by the sand, and half-fell into her, bracing himself on her arms. They kissed cheeks, knocking and nudging. His stubble was growing out into the closest he'd had to a beard. A silly flat cap on his head, like something a country gent would wear in England.

'Woah. Josh. Thanks for coming.'

'No problem.'

He righted himself, then took a step backwards and reached out an arm towards the woman.

'Mum, this is Gabriella.'

Gabriella stepped down the beach and put her hand out. 'Gaby, please.'

'Justine.'

'I'm very glad to meet you.'

'Likewise.'

Josh clapped his hands together. 'Good. Well, I'm glad that's done, then. What have we got here? Beer. Whisky. No s'mores then?' It was as if he'd upped his accent a notch. There was a bluffness about it, too, a bloke-iness that hardly boded well. 'Vincent. Good to see you, too, man.'

Vincent walked around the fire towards them, and he and Josh shook hands.

'How you doing, Josh. You're looking well. Gaby. I'm Vincent.'

Introductions done, the four of them arranged themselves on the log and the blanket, all facing the fire. Josh on the log, with Gaby in front of him on the ground, leaning her back against his legs.

She was a make-up artist, she said – but a good one, Josh added, listing the names of the magazines and shows she'd worked on, most of which meant nothing to her. Gaby talked animatedly away – about Marilyn Monroe, the photos of her on the beach at Amagansett, about Lou Reed dying while doing tai-chi and looking out at the trees – and Justine added in her small amount of knowledge on the subject. All of it utterly safe, gossip solidified to a kind of folklore.

'I've never been here before,' she said, 'but I mean it's lovely. It's easy to see why it's become what it is.'

Josh pretended not to know anything about any of it, and responded happily enough, making jokes, asking questions, deferring to his girlfriend as a kind of older sister, whose job it was to educate him in the cultural history of his second home.

Justine pictured the four of them, from above now, as she'd pictured her and Vincent, as a kind of schematic diagram: four black circles of varying dimensions, with dotted lines curving between them. The relationships, stated and unstated, the angles of influence and tension, the differing dynamics of each possible pairing. Justine imagined how she must seem to the younger woman, some ogreish mother-in-law, toxic with resentment and jealousy. Was Gaby, equally, worried at how she might seem to her: deficient, deviant, a cradle-snatcher?

They drank. Gabriella held onto her one beer, while Josh was already cracking his third. He was talking about his childhood memories of the place. The dog they'd had for a while, the kids he'd formed summer-long alliances with, the toys he'd buried in the sand. His fear of jellyfish.

Four notes, they made, it seemed to her, a strange intangible chord. She and Josh forming an octave perhaps. Vincent a seventh, desperately trying to resolve itself to her note. Or she was the base note and the others ascended variously from her. Gaby, wavering between them all, never still, creating fields of harmony and dissonance.

'Josh, darling,' she said, 'Gaby's finished her beer.'

'Sorry. Another beer, Gabs?'

'Actually, I'd prefer a glass of wine if you have one.' She looked at Justine.

But it was Vincent who replied.

'I'll fetch a bottle. I need to go to the loo anyway.'

He stood and dusted sand from himself. 'Anyone else need anything?'

'I'll come with you,' Gaby replied. 'I need to use the restroom too.'

Vincent held out his hand, and pulled her to standing.

Josh waited till they'd gone, then brought his beer bottle up to his mouth.

'So. You two. You having a nice time here?' he asked.

'Yes,' she said. She drew the word out, turning it half into a question.

'The perfect spot for a quiet, intimate weekend away from the hustle and bustle of the city. All those godawful *people*.'

'Exactly.'

'Those peeking, prying people. He was, what, just over here, was he, just passing through town?'

'No.'

'Thought he'd look you up for old time's sake.'

'No, actually.'

'Or has this been going on for a while, in secret, unbeknownst to me. Mummy rekindling her old flame.' He threw something, a scrap of twig or beer label at the fire. 'Poor Mr Ikuo.' A touch of parody in the voice, of offensiveness in the parody. 'He will be sad.'

He made a glum face, and looked sideways at her. She wasn't angry. Not yet. The rudeness was just a feint.

'He was here on trust business. Something we needed to discuss.'

'Oh?' He had produced a cigarette, hand-rolled, from a pocket, and it bobbed in his mouth, unlit. A joint, probably.

Part of her wanted to force the issue, to help him see her as an independent and autonomous person, as free now as he was, in his adulthood, but she recoiled from doing so. Something warned her that using Vincent to make this point had hazards of its own. Vincent was too blunt a tool with which to try to fine-tune her relationship with Josh.

'Nothing interesting,' she said to him.

He shrugged, then dipped his head to light the cigarette.

'So, more to the point. What do you think of Gabriella?'

Offering her the joint as he said it.

'This just weed?' she said.

'Sure.'

She got up and went to sit next to him on the log, and took the cigarette. She considered it, then took a small toke. She held in the smoke, hand on her sternum.

'She seems... nice,' she said, letting the words ride out on the back of the smoke.

'Nice? Christ, don't tell her that to her face, she'd be distraught.'

'Well, that's the thing about niceness, isn't it? Sometimes you need something to bring it out. Or set it off. A pinch of salt. Come on, Josh. I've only just met her. She seems cool.'

He laughed, one of his lopsided, yawing laughs, and she laughed, too, passing the joint back to him.

'She is. She's very cool. But seriously. You and Vincent. Are you two *going out*? Or whatever you want to call it.'

'It's early days, darling. I don't know what to say. It might happen.'

'Might *happen*? Please, spare me the details.'

'Well, Josh, it's already happened, since you ask.' He snuffed out smoke from his nostrils and laughed, a long, chest-pounding eye-watering cough of a laugh, and she grinned at his grimace. 'But it might go on happening, I don't know. I really don't know.'

She put an arm around him, felt the jitters and jumps of his body, felt how he relaxed, giving himself up to the embrace. They sat like that for a while, he with his chin on his knees, lifting himself only to smoke, she with one arm around him, the other pushing and pulling at his hair, arranging it around his ears, where it poked out from under his cap. She looked at the fire and wondered what Vincent had written about her in his book. She didn't – why would she? – want to know.

Then, when they heard the first sounds of the others coming back, he leaned himself back upright, and glanced at her quickly, an apologetic smile on his lips. They turned to watch them appear over the top of the dune, the two of them laughing at something. Vincent raised an arm, waving the wine bottle.

Josh shifted himself on the log, making a space between them, then said to her, quietly, while they were still out of earshot, and with a look of frank appeal on his face, 'Just not him, Mum. Not him.'

'Why forever not?' she said back, not hiding her hurt.

A jerk of the head. 'Look at him, Mum. He's a fucking douchebag.' His shoulders suddenly hunched with the effort, his mouth gaping, as he gagged on the words.

Then they were back, and the fire burned on, folding in on itself as it sank towards the sand, condensing its powers to a shimmering, hallucinatory centre. The beer and weed and now the wine that she drank some of dried her mouth and slid another harmonic and rhythmic layer in under her thoughts. Those four notes, that she had earlier imagined as a chord laid out on a piano keyboard, had unfurled into a rising melody on an acoustic guitar. La–da–da–da, la–da–da. She imagined herself playing it, her left hand holding down the pattern, the thumb and fingers of her other hand taking the same steps up the strings, over and over again.

She watched Gaby run her hand over her son's incipient beard, glad that she wasn't some simpering cute-as-pie girlie his own age, someone to fawn over him. She seemed to have the measure of his film work, too. 'He's got a good eye,' she'd said, when Vincent asked about it. 'Just so long as he doesn't settle for being the wonder kid with the shaky hand. There's plenty of people would settle for that, and being the son of Randall.' It was what she would have wanted to say herself.

The evening ended at around midnight. They gathered their stuff and made their way back up the slope, Gaby pressing herself

287

to Josh's side, seemingly hanging on his arm while, Justine saw, actually supporting his now rather watery steps. The older he got, or the more he grew, the more obvious it became, this knock-kneed, baby giraffe gait. She felt fiercely proud of him, keenly anxious that he didn't channel his frustrations into his art, for that was not how good art was made. And she wondered how she might tell him this – or if this Gaby might tell him for her.

The two of them disappeared along the corridor to Josh's room, leaving Justine and Vincent in the main lounge. She sensed him hang back, uncertain of the etiquette. It was amusing to have such minor sources of power, but she was too tired to exert it more fully. She took them to her room and they made love, again, with all the seriousness that a second time carries with it. There was a deliberate slowness on both their parts, with much shushing and caressing and, in his face, a certain sternness.

It lasted while it lasted, and when they were both done she found she had his head on her chest. His eyes were open, he was staring out at the garden, at where the garden would be if it could be seen. They could see each other's reflections in the glass doors.

'You're thinking about the paintings,' she said, and she brushed a little at the hairs of his eyebrows, smoothing them.

He talked, almost whispering, and she felt the movement of his jaw against her breasts. 'I thought when I came out here it would be easier, but it's not. There's something aggravating about it, I mean physically, like the feeling in your arms when you're trying to bring two identical magnets together. What I keep coming back to' – and she felt the words as much as heard them, the way they resonated through the cavities of her body – 'is that if we destroy them, no one will know. The world will carry on. My book, quietly erased. The paintings, gone. Do you remember Martin Creed? The whole world plus the work equals the whole world.'

'And Randall?'

'Randall. Do we owe him anything?' His eyes flicked up. 'Is that the wrong thing to say?'

'You seem to be saying that if he hadn't painted these paintings then he would deserve to have the world see them, but that having painted them somehow disqualifies him.'

'I'm not sure what he deserves. What about what we deserve? I even thought about them just now, when we were making love. How wrong is that? It's as if that was his plan.'

She said, 'That won't change, if we destroy them.'

'But if we show them, it will destroy *us*.'

She looked at his reflection, watching to see if he'd spotted the word he'd used. Was there suddenly an *us*? Not that her not knowing that there was would mean that there wasn't. She carried on with her stroking, looking down the bed to where the painted circle hung, with its poetry, its simple, single, endless, broken statement.

He was up before her in the morning. She found him on the sun deck, with no sun but only cold morning air. A coffee jug and two cups on the table in front of him. She poured herself a cup then took a chair. When she spoke she kept her voice low, aware of the presence of the others in the house, of not knowing how long they had to talk before they turned up.

'How about this. We don't destroy them. And we don't show them. We just put them in storage, in a lead-lined box in a bank vault somewhere, together with all the documentation, all the everything, and a little note that says, you know, don't open until after we're dead. How does that sound?'

'I know, I know,' he said. 'It's a good idea. And I've thought of it, too. But the thing is, I don't mind being a coward, but I don't want to be *thought of* as a coward. Destroying them is the cowardliest thing ever, but no one will ever know, so I can live with that.

But simply shunting them into the future, buying ourselves some time, so that we can have…' – and his words floundered – 'so that basically we can do what we want to now, while we're alive. Doing that would make us look ridiculous, because it will be obvious that we were ashamed.'

'But we'll be dead.'

'Doesn't matter. We'll still look pathetic. And petty. More to the point, we'll be killing the paintings as surely as if we pour petrol over them and set them alight. They only work so long as the people in them are alive. You, me, Tom, Carl, Jan. All the players and walk-on parts. That's their power. If there's no one around to slander, they're worthless.'

He looked at her, and said, 'What do you think?'

'I don't know what I think,' she answered, and they sat there, drinking their coffee and trying to think, while the day slowly unspooled.

'Morning.'

They turned, together, at the sound, and there he was, Joshua, stood in a dressing gown in the doorway. She wondered how long he'd been there, and decided it can't have been more than a minute or two.

'Morning, darling.'

'Hi there.' Vincent's efficient, pop-up smile.

'Any more coffee?' Josh said, scratching at his beard as he ambled over to them.

'You'll need a cup,' said Vincent, and he made to get up. 'Do you want me to get you one?'

Justine pushed hers across the table. 'Use mine. I've finished with it.'

Josh waited while Vincent poured him some into it, then said, before he even picked it up, 'I know, you know.'

'What?'

'I know about the studio, the paintings.'

'What do you mean?' she said.

'What?' This was Vincent, now, angry. 'What studio?'

The tone of his voice was itself a betrayal. She put a hand on the table. It was enough.

'The studio,' Josh said again. 'With the paintings.'

'Oh for fuck sake.' Vincent rattled the chair backwards across the wooden boards. He looked for a moment as if he wanted to hit Joshua, but he pushed his chair again and stepped away from the table.

Joshua looked at his mother, his face skipping and flicking with sly triumph.

'Well?' he said.

'Yes, alright. We've found a studio. But how did you know about it?'

'How did I know about it? I might ask the same of you.'

'For fuck sake. This is a fucking farce.'

'Vincent, please. Well, you might ask me, and I'd tell you, though it's not very interesting.'

'Well?'

'The lease ran out, and the landlord traced it back to us.'

'So you've been there?' He'd interrupted her, a small glimmer of anxiety.

'Yes, we've been there. But Joshua, how long have you known about it?'

'How long have I known about it? Oh, since about the day that Dad took me there.'

'He *took* you there?'

Josh looked at Vincent, mouth working away at itself. 'Yes, look. This is getting a bit tedious. How about I tell you all about what I know about the studio, and then you can tell me what you know.'

'Fine.'

'Or, even better, why don't I show you?'

Joshua refused to say any more until he had gone to get dressed. A straightforward gambit to rile Vincent. It was ten minutes before he re-emerged with Gaby, who looked rather bemused by the sudden acceleration of the day according to an unknown schedule.

'I don't mean to be rude, Josh,' Vincent said, when it became clear he meant to include her in this morning's activities, 'but I think this is really something we should be keeping to ourselves.'

Josh did a gawping double-take.

'You are joking, right? For a start you don't know what I'm going to show you. Secondly, this is a film that *I* made, with my father's permission. You can't decide who I show it to.'

'Who *have* you shown it to?'

'No one, as it happens. But it's my choice who I do.' He turned to Gaby. 'Come on.' And he led them down the stairs to the media room.

It was cool and dark in the room. Josh gestured at the sofas, telling them to sit, then went to the computer and started typing.

'Don't worry,' he said, while he waited for his log-in, wherever it was, to process. 'It's all perfectly secure.' Then, with an edge of seriousness to his voice, 'By the way, where *is* the studio?'

'Oh, roundabout,' said Vincent, acidly, cutting in.

'Alphabet City,' said Justine.

'You're not going to give me the address?'

'Not just now,' Vincent replied. 'Let's just see what it is you've got to show us.'

In the end she and Vincent sat on the ancient sofa. Josh perched on the wide flat arm next to his mother, holding the pair of remotes, Gaby sitting next to him on a big leather cube.

'Right, to set the scene, this was a day out. The date, which is recorded in the corner of the screen, is 18 July 2008.' Josh looked at them, giving them a moment to calculate for themselves the few months that separated it from Randall's death. 'A Daddy day out, with me filming it all, on a camcorder you'd given me for my tenth birthday. Unfortunately I didn't get to film the journey there, as the driver wouldn't let me use it in his cab.

'We started at Chelsea Piers. We had lunch, then we were going to go to the Police Museum.' Justine nodded; it was always one of his favourite places to visit. 'But then Dad changed his mind and gave the driver another address.' To Gaby: 'My childhood. It was a *treat* to go someplace in a yellow cab rather than in a chauffeured car. Anyway,' turning back to the others. 'I filmed about two hours' worth of stuff, just on that day, it's all unedited. This is about three-quarters of the way through.'

Then, 'Ready?' he said, a strange rising lilt to the word.

Justine felt how tense Vincent was, sitting beside her. She nodded.

Josh brought up a window on the computer screen, showing a street view, blurred, tilted and stilled. A yellow cab, a dark figure. Before she had time to analyse it, though, the image launched itself in time and sound on the television.

The wailing dive of a siren, a snatch of talk.

The street bright grey, Randall leaning in conversation with the cabbie, hands braced on the top of the door, words lost. The image jittering, in a way that was instantly recognisable.

Randall's hands drum out a beat on the metal of the roof, then he straightens and the car moves off, as if released.

It was the street alright, she recognised it.

'Ready?'

'Ha.' A curt laugh from Vincent, and she guessed at his meaning. The way that Josh had anticipated and copied exactly the intonation of his father's voice. It was Randall, delivering himself up in a single word. *Ready?* Anything, *anything* to get a rise out of life.

'Now Josh, like I said. This is top secret. Top. Secret. Not a word, to Mum, or anyone. It's just between you and me, and your little camera. Scout's Honour?'

Randall lifts his hand, formed into the three-fingered saluted, watching for the response. Satisfied, he nods, turns.

She looked over and saw that Gaby had shifted her stool nearer to Josh, and had her hand on his knee, with his hand on hers. Josh was fixed on the screen, mouth hanging open. His face was at once passive, given over entirely to the act of watching, and somehow strained, the mouth giving the occasional twitch.

The camera follows Randall up the alleyway to the door, the yard, retracing their steps from two days ago. But in the film it is the heat of summer. Randall in loose chinos and a grey Prada T-shirt. Then they are through the door and bouncing up the stairs, the camera jogging violently about as young Josh struggles to keep up. A pause at the top, then – 'Ta da!' – they are inside.

Randall takes a stride into the centre of the room, gives a foppish twirl of exhibition. 'Here we are. My gaff. Where I do my stuff.'

'Cool.'

Josh's voice, irrefutably her boy at ten, talking to her across the years and the involutions of the medium. She stole another sideways glance, but he was fixed on the screen.

The camera walks into the middle of the room and starts a slow panning turn of its own, leaving a stationary Randall to slide sideways to and then off the right-hand edge of the screen, smile on lips and hands on hips. The image runs over the back wall, with the chairs and lamp and sofa, then past where the corridor to the kitchen begins and on to the racks, guarding their secrets, then the door, then the big front windows, their leaded panes and long cluttered sills. It slows for the single picture stood on an easel – impossible to see what it is – and the pots and rags and general mess, and then the laden trestle tables.

'Josh,' she said.

He froze the picture.

'Did you go back again? Or is this the only time you went?'

'This is the only time.' Then, still holding the remote paused,

'The mad thing is, at the time I didn't think it was anything special. It was just somewhere he took me, a bit grubby, a bit pokey. The whole thing obviously meant far more to him than it did to me.'

'The only time, then.'

'The only time.'

She spoke softly: 'Did he *show* you the pictures?'

'We're getting to the pictures.'

And the frame slides on until it arrives back at its starting point, where Randall was, and should be, only he is gone. The camera waits, then, almost before you notice it, starts zooming in through the zone of his absence towards a coat stand placed incongruously in a corner, draped with jackets and an old-fashioned hat, a swatch of colour that might be a Hermes scarf. Then, still zooming in, it pans swiftly back to the right, towards the painting on its easel. It has just broached the edge of the canvas when Randall's voice comes from another room.

'You want something to drink?'

The image jerks away, throws itself wildly over a stretch of blank wall, then collects itself.

'You got a Coke?'

'Coming up.'

The camera walks over to the window and films out of it, its processor struggling to pick out objects in the dazzling wash of the sun, then turns for the re-entrance of Randall, can of drink in hand, and the image darkens, adjusts itself.

'Here you go. Look, put that down for a moment.'

Cut.

'There was a ping-pong table in it, a knackered old thing, and I thought, blimey, that's the life.' Randall is slouched at one end of the sofa, one leg hooked up on the other knee, looking sideways at the camera. Randall's slouch, his gut. The state of his hair. The image circles his face, then moves in on an ear, silently, hungrily, eating it up in pixels, until you can see the hairs tickling out of it. The continual and minute adjustment, like the movement of an insect. It leaves the ear and crawls across an acre of skin to the mouth – that moves, miraculously, in time to the words coming from it.

'We knocked about a bit. It was class. I'd love one here.'

'Why don't you get one, then?'

'Who'd I play with?'

'Me. I'd play with you.'

'Josh. Listen. Nobody comes here. Nobody's been here.'

A sudden movement on the sofa takes Randall out of the frame entirely, and the camera backs out of its zoom until he's caught once more. He's put his leg down and is sitting forward, turned towards the camera.

'Josh, you are the only person apart from me who has ever been in this room.'

'Why?'

'Because of the paintings I'm making here. They're… sensitive. You know about my work, right? The kinds of pictures and sculptures I make. I can't have anyone knowing about *these* paintings.'

Justine looked hard into the image, trying to read it, to gauge if there was any sense of awareness, in his eyes, or the lines around his mouth, of an audience beyond the camera. Is he talking to them, here, now, or is he just humouring a small boy with a video camera?

'Can I see them then?'

Randall shifts his gaze down the room to the painting on the easel and the camera follows. It's faint but you could see it's barely a quarter done.

'You want to see the paintings?'

'Uh-huh.'

'Okay, then. They're pretty rude, Josh, just to warn you.' But his tone is warm. Why would he have brought him here if not to show him the paintings? 'If Mummy knew I was showing you stuff like this she would be mad as hell.'

He gets to his feet and the camera follows, lurching up, and trying to disguise the lurch.

It melted her, almost, the bovine stupidity of the camera action, her son trying to use it as an eye, with a single focal point, swinging this way and that. He had, at least, improved in that.

Randall goes to the storage racks.

'Or perhaps we should treat this as part of your education,' he says. 'An addition to your birds and bees module. You've done all that at school, I take it?'

'Da-ad!'

'I mean, this is nothing I assume you haven't seen on the net.'

Randall looks at the camera, questioning, and the image lifts momentarily, riding the wave of a shrug.

'Right, then. What shall we have?' He compresses his face and gives a short bleak laugh, trails his hand along the ends of the racks, and says, 'No, no, definitely not.' Then he stops, tapping the wooden structure with a finger as he thinks. He gives a tug and trundles one out, about a third of the way along, stepping backwards to bring it into the room.

It has three canvases on it. The first is three people on a bed, the second a larger grouping in front of a window with thick red curtains – the one with Dennis van Rossen, Jasper Carson-Cooling and James Nyberg – and the third a weird one, of Richard Prince sitting on a bed by himself, looking sad. It's the first one the camera moves in on, though. It's the one of John Currin getting roundly worked over by two of his buxom women, satisfyingly well rendered.

'Oh my God.' Gabriella put her hand to her mouth, swallowing back a laugh that was half giggle, half shock. 'Sorry,' she said, and waved her hand in front of her face.

The painting grows, stretching itself to fill the rectangle of the frame, as the camera approaches. It becomes brighter, deeper, more intense.

'Actually, Josh. Probably best if you don't film these, if you don't mind.'

And the camera seems to linger, floating in the air, then cuts.

There was a momentary shift in the room, as the four of them adjusted themselves, but the film had already moved on.

Randall is stood at a table of paints, lifting and checking tubes and jars.

'That was...' – Gabriella gathered herself – 'quite something.'

'The artist at work,' says Randall, intoning deeply as for a documentary voiceover. 'Right, good. This should do.' He goes over to the barely started canvas – now she could see it was the one that will become the triple portrait of the Art Basel woman and the Hendersons – and he peers at it. He flicks at a speck of something caught on the surface with his forefinger. He has a ragged-edged piece of chipboard for a palette and a short stiff brush in his hand, then another, more pointy one, that he clamps between his teeth like a horse's bit.

He spreads some pink and some beige on to the palette and mixes them with the stockier brush, then swaps brushes and dots a tiny peck of it on the canvas, where the shoulder of Michael Henderson is spreading down towards his chest. He stands back and squints, bends back to his palette. The camera zooms in until the brush fills the screen, lifting and folding the two paints, bringing in some white, shifting ratios and tones. It works quickly and precisely, darting and waiting.

'Of course, real painters have assistants to do this shit for them.' The words come clumsily, the consonants obscured by the brush in his mouth. 'It's only Sunday painters who have to mix their own colours.' And back to the canvas. He gives a quick glance at the photos tacked in a row along the top of the heavy easel. The camera records them. Glossy mag shots of the festival director and the others, and three pictures clipped from porno mags.

'Who are they?'

'These guys?'

'The people in the photos, that you're painting.'

'Ha.' He pauses, umms. 'Just people, Josh.'

'Do you know them? Do they know you're painting them having sex together?'

'No, they don't.'

It's a response that seems to close down that line of enquiry. Randall steps back, and Josh moves in on his face.

Justine started, astonished, at the close-up as it hovers and holds: Randall, looking at a painting that he's in the process of making. It's the lines around the eyes, the constant, infinitesimal play of iris and pupil. All for these people, fucking on a bed. She could think of nothing he ever made, in his whole career, that he looked at with this degree of empathy and care. Junk model forts and moon buggies, slaved over with Josh at the kitchen table, yes; but not out there in the world, not professionally.

'How long does it take you to finish a painting?'

'A long time.'

'What sort of paints do you use?'

He laughs. 'What is this? You're, like, bloody Hans Namuth?'

'Who's Hans Naymouth?'

'Hans Namuth. He's the guy who made the film of the painter. Jackson Pollock. We saw it at Moma, remember? The guy dripping paint on the floor.'

'Yeah, I remember.'

Then he puts on a strangled voice, like a warmer Stephen Hawking. 'Sometimes I use a brush, but often prefer a stick. I thin the paint with Wild Turkey, I find it flows better from the stick.' A tumbling little laugh, at his own joke. He rubs an eyebrow and returns to the canvas. 'I also use sand, pebbles, glass broken up in the mouth or other foreign matter. Gold dust. Poker chips. Shattered remnants of my own ego. Technique is just a means of arriving at a statement. Or is the other way round? A statement is just a means of arriving at technique. Here.' He looks to Josh and gestures with the palette. 'You want to have a go?'

'Me?'

'This is unreal.' It was Gabriella that had spoken.

Vincent gave Justine a nudge, and nodded past her, across at Joshua. She looked, and saw it as much in his bearing as in his eyes, how they reflected the light from the screen. He wasn't crying, but he wasn't far off.

Then Gabriella noticed, and she reached up and brought his head down onto her shoulder. How easily it went, how placidly.

'Here we go,' says Randall.

They all turned back to the screen.

The image gives a vertiginous dive and slower rise that show the camera is changing hands, and suddenly there's Joshua on screen, from above. The top of his head.

Joshua, aged ten, looking up at his father. His hair long, draped in girlish bangs over his forehead. He's wearing a faded Spiderman T-shirt. His shoulders so thin, she thinks, his cheeks so apple-round. The nose a boy's nose, just beginning to descend. His head stuck just a little on one side, his mouth smeared into a smile.

'Oh my God.' This was Gabriella again, an exhalation that mixed delight and, Justine could tell, something like shock. Her fingers, in his hair, wrested his head from side to side. 'Look at you. You're so gorgeous.'

Josh was staring, fixed in his pose with an absolute determination. Justine looked up at the ceiling, blinked and widened her eyes, and looked back down.

Josh takes his place in front of the easel, uncertain, exchanging quick looks with his dad, who's giving him instruction and encouragement, his free hand darts out into the frame now and then, to point where to go.

All she could think, though, was that it wasn't her who had his head on her shoulder.

And a second, terrible thought, though it was only the crystallisation of what she already knew – that he was as lost to her, here in the room, aged eighteen, as he was on the screen, a child. There he is, her boy, putting tentative little dabs of colour on the canvas. It was like watching a baby take its first steps.

Young Josh groans in frustration, angry at his clumsy grip, at the sheer difficulty he has in making so delicate and precise an instrument do what he wants it to. She can see the quiver, see his attempt to master it.

'You're doing fine.'

'I *can't*.'

'You're doing great, Josh. Keep going. That's it. Now mix in a touch more of the white. No, no. Not so much. Don't worry. Yes, that's it. Now try that where it goes towards her neck. Just there. And a bit more. Good, good.'

Then comes an interruption. The trill of a cell-phone, instantly, stomach-grabbingly familiar. The camera drops to spin in space, presumably dangling by its strap from Randall's wrist, showing a blurred image of the floorboards, the corner of his shoe.

Over this abstract image, Randall's voice.

'Ha! It's your Mum. Look, hold this. And, Josh, shush, yeah?'

And then the camera is back with Josh and he has it on Randall, who puts the phone to his ear.

'Hello. Hiya, doll. Yes, we're having a great time.' He winks at the camera, and Justine put her hand to her mouth. Her other hand, the one that Vincent had, he gripped tighter. 'We're at the Police Museum. We were going to go and get a burger at the Parker. You want to come? Right, okay. Look, hang on a sec. I don't think I'm supposed to be talking right here. Josh, you wait here and look at these badges and stuff for minute.'

He waves a hand vaguely, imperiously in the vicinity of the easel, his eyebrows lifting in a dumbshow of conspiracy.

'Sure,' says Josh's voice.

'Wait. Say hi to your Mum.'

And Randall bends towards the camera. The phone, huge, disappears off-screen to the left, Randall's face invading and colonising the screen, a grotesque, unintentional close-up.

'Hi Mum.'

The voice comes distant and crackly.

'Hiya sweetie. You having a good time?'

What hit her, the thing she was able to compute, was the plain dumb foolishness, as always, of the sound of her voice. How silly and sing-song she sounded. That was something to cling to.

Her fingers had travelled up over her mouth so that they rested on her cheeks and nose, she was vaguely aware of the movement of her lips against her palm, saying words she could not hear.

'Yeah. Totally.'

'Good. See you later.'

'Later.'

'Love you.'

'Bye.'

Randall peels back. A grin of success, he puts his finger to his lips.

'Okay, I'll be two minutes,' he says, then, sternly: 'Don't move from that display case, yeah? Look at that motorcycle.' And he turns and walks away to the kitchen door. His words – the conversation he is having with her – diminish as he goes.

Hiya sweetie. The times she had said that to him, on the phone, and face to face.

'Josh,' she said, 'How can you not have showed me this?'

And she reached out to him, waving her hand for him to take, like an elderly person would, and he took it, his fingers holding and squeezing hers.

He was smiling and blinking, his face doing hiccups.

'Sorry, Mum.'

'Why didn't you *tell* me? About all of it.'

'I don't know. I tried, I suppose. Wait. There's not much more to go.'

And he slipped loose his hand and turned back to the screen. The camera is in rapid, chaotic movement, the image jerking and skidding as Josh trots across the room. Then there's his hand pulling, tugging at a frame, and out it comes.

Gabriella laughed. 'Good God. You little pervert, you.'

A brief glimpse of the triple portrait of Jeremy Dodd, Simone Klaus and Griff Dolis.

'Who's that?' A laugh. 'That's crazy. Doesn't he work at...'

'Wait. We're nearly done.'

And the camera scoots back around the pulled-out end of the rack to see the other side and there it is, the camera stops and lingers, catching its breath. There's a painting, but it's too close, out of focus. It's visible as blocks of colour only.

Josh moves back, giving the camera time to work out what it's looking at. It's big, huge. Double the size of the others, bigger. It's huge. An orgy. A roundelay of fucking and sucking and tugging and fingering.

You could hear his silence above their own. His breathing.

'Wait,' Justine said, and Josh paused the film.

She looked at the painting. She counted off Randall and herself and Tom and Jan de Vries and Gina Lopez, Cory Plouffe, Shannon Keene and Lisa Hanson, all serenely bundled and twisted and turning in a circle, like some obscene dance.

'Which painting is that?' she said to Vincent.

'I don't know.'

He got up and went towards the screen. 'Play it,' he said to Josh.

The camera steps back into motion as Josh begins to scan the canvas, starting in the top-left corner and moving methodically around it. She still couldn't work it out, though. There was simply no picture as big as this in the studio. She let herself be guided and instructed by the image. There's Randall, behind her, heaving away, grinning like a Christian, while he grapples behind him with de Vries's oversized dick, who's peering down at his protégé's performance with the look of someone being bounced at by a cute, annoying puppy. And her, gasping in what could just as well be pleasure as pain, but concentrating, too, on the progress of her hand up between the next pair of legs.

'Josh. Turn it off.'

This was Gabriella.

'That's enough, now. Give me that.'

'But I don't recognise that painting,' Justine said. 'It's not there, Vincent, is it?'

Gabriella and Josh were tussling over the remote now, whispering and muttering their argument.

'Give her the remote, Josh,' said Vincent.

'Fuck off, Vincent,' said Josh, looking at his hands, grinding the words out almost unthinkingly.

'Fine.' Vincent made for the computer, but just as he had his hand on the mouse Josh called out, almost yelping.

'Wait!'

He'd wrested the remote free from Gabriella and hefted it, held loose in his hand, his fingers outstretched, like a half-surrendered gun.

'Alright,' he said. 'Okay.'

Vincent looked at him.

Josh pointed the remote and pressed. The image froze.

'I said turn it off.'

'Josh.'

The image was on her and Randall, his cock half in her, half out, the dip and rise of her back to her shoulder and hair, her head thrown back. Even frozen and slightly blurred she saw the way the brush drew back across her cheek, through the paint, making it and the flesh one.

'What *is* that painting?' she said, again, but they all ignored her, Josh and Vincent madly fixed on each other.

'Look,' Josh said, waving his arm at the screen, shouting now. 'It's real. You can't make it just go away.'

Anyone looking at him who didn't know him would think he was drunk. The way his arm seemed to tip him close to over-balancing entirely. Gabriella looked ready to steady him if he went.

'I could click one button, and this would be out there. How long till it was in every in-tray in New York? You might have the paintings, you might know where they are, but I have evidence.' He was batting himself in the chest with the remote, his voice deeper and harsher than she had known it, running up against the limits of expressible feeling. Close again to tears. It wasn't anger that was doing this to him, she thought. It was something else. 'This is *proof*. And if I thought for one moment that you... In fact, yes. Perhaps now it's time that you told me what you were going to do with the paintings?'

He pointed the remote, now at Vincent, now at her.

She held his gaze. He thought the paintings were important, but they weren't. Which didn't mean they should be ignored, or destroyed, or anything-ed at all, but that they mustn't fool themselves, in the bust-up that was surely coming, that they were talking about art.

'Perhaps we should go upstairs. I could make some coffee.' Gabriella.

'Yeah, great. Let's go upstairs and drink some coffee. Every-thing'll be okay *then*.'

Gabriella went, head down, as if to spare herself the acerbity of his tone, and Vincent, at Justine's nod, followed her. She got up and went towards him, but he tossed the remote down at the sofa in a gesture that was half defiance and half disgust – it came that close to hitting her, she flinched – and moved around her towards the stairs.

Upstairs they were silent, the four of them turning, independently, between the kitchen and the lounge, all the time confirming themselves in this new configuration they seemed to have made. It must have looked to Josh like Gabriella had crossed over, that the three of them were a triangle set against him, or surrounding him.

That was certainly how he seemed to regard them, sat in the centre of the sofa, back to the view, his arms spread out along the cushions behind him. Head tipped high, chin jutting, a line of defence.

Gabriella put coffee on the low table in front of him, for which she got neither thanks nor acknowledgement. She positioned herself along from him on the sofa, but turned towards him. Justine too, would have liked to be able to walk over and sit next to him on the sofa, to break the pattern, but it didn't seem possible.

She took one of a pair of chairs across from them. Vincent was next to the kitchen counter. He seemed very intent on appearing serious.

By virtue of the way he ignored him, by the angle by which his gaze diverted from him, she could tell that, for Josh, this was primarily between himself and Vincent. Because of this, Justine made the first move.

'Josh,' she said, and his look was a picture of disaffection. 'Josh, above all, we have got be slow and sure and sensible about how we approach this. This stuff is extremely sensitive.'

'Wrong.'

'Josh. Let me finish.'

'No. Wrong. I don't what planet you people live on, but where I come from there was an artist called Randall. What he made was not "stuff", it was art. To be honest, we don't have the right to be sensible or slow or sensitive about any of this. That's not our job. Our job is to honour his memory, and to be grateful for what he gave us, and to share what we can.'

He leaned forward and picked at the bowl of pebbles on the table. He scooped up a handful and chucked them softly in hand, let the soft chatter of their fall play under his words.

'If you're embarrassed by what he painted, then bad luck. Embrace that embarrassment. It might conceivably make you a better person. Certainly, in a hundred years' time, when these paintings are still hanging in whatever passes for houses in whatever is left of this fucking world, and we're all, God willing, dust, then no one will think any the worse of you for your inclusion in them. In the grand scheme of things, to be a footnote in this particular story is more than any of us deserve.'

'Listen, Josh.'

'Ooh, Vincent. I'm all ears.'

'First off, no one is denying that these are great pictures.'

'Well, that's nice to hear. I know how much my father relied on your judgement in these things.'

'Joshua!'

Vincent went on, unfazed.

'They are truly astonishing, humbling pictures. But that doesn't mean we are bound to treat them in a particular way. There's any number of projects which *your father* followed through to quite surprising levels of completion, but which then, pfft!' – Vincent gave a conjuror's twist of the hand – 'were abandoned. There are, quite literally, warehouses *stuffed* with work that no one has ever seen, and most likely never will.'

He'd come away from the counter now, and sat himself on the arm of the chair next to her. A confident, casual pose, a boardroom feint. She watched Josh as he watched Vincent, passing the pebbles from hand to hand.

'This studio,' Vincent went on, and he gave an awed shake of the head. 'We've only just found it, only just started exploring it, and there's an awful lot of very careful sifting to be done, but there's no indication – and no indication in your film either, if we're honest – that he necessarily intended these pictures for exhibition. Yes, he was a joker, your father, and there's nothing he loved more than putting as many cats among as many pigeons as possible, but he also operated absolutely and entirely according to his own rules. If you try to approach according to normal precedent, you're going to come a cropper.'

Josh put up his hand. 'Vincent, I appreciate that you knew my father for many years...'

Vincent raised his voice. 'And that's not even taking into account the legal implication of the work...'

'But Vincent, if you think you *knew* my father, then you're *wrong*.' Vincent went to talk again but Josh shouted. 'Vincent, shut the *fuck* up.'

He took a pebble and flung it, so wildly that it went wide, hurtling over their heads.

Vincent ducked; they all ducked, even Gabriella.

Josh raised himself to his feet.

'You didn't know my father.'

Another pebble, going wide on the other side of him. It was impossible to tell if he was trying to hit him for real, or just scare him. She said his name, but he wasn't listening.

'You counted his money for him. You knew the inside of his bank account, his wallet, the state of his trouser pockets, but up here' – he knocked his balled fists either side of his head – 'you knew nothing about who he was. So I will not' – a pebble in the direction of Gabriella, who was up and moving towards him, another one thrown lengthways down the room so it hit the glass doors.

Vincent was up now, they all were, Vincent stepping towards him, Josh stepping sideways and back. The last pebbles left his hand in a fierce swipe that sent them skittering over the floor, over the kitchen counter, hitting glass, wood, metal, stone. One of them, finally, hit Vincent, who had his arm up to protect his face, in the chest.

'If you had an aesthetic cell in your body,' Josh was yelling. 'If you had an ounce of understanding or love for my father ...'

But Vincent had his hands on him, pinning his arms to his sides. They were all of them there, now, by the doors out to the deck, all of them shouting, their little configuration collapsed into this awful tangle. Justine was telling Vincent to let go of him, Vincent was saying things to Josh she couldn't, or wouldn't, hear, she only wanted them apart.

In the end it was Gabriella who got him outside, and Justine was left alone with Vincent.

He was livid, his face a strange mottling of red and grey. He threw his arm out at them outside, the action making him cough.

'How are we supposed to deal with this behaviour? It's like dealing with a ten-year-old child.'

'He *is* a child, Vincent, give or take.'

'What, so we're going to let him dictate what happens? We're going to let him ruin everything? This is a joke.'

She turned him from the window, bringing him back into the room.

'Vincent, come. Come. Think how long he's held onto this.'

'Exactly. He's happy keeping it to himself when it's his special secret, but now that other people are in on it he wants to blow the whole thing sky-high. It's pathetic.'

She listened to him talk, but really she was intent on Josh, through the window. He was leaning on the railing, bowed over it, his hands hidden by his body, blocking him off from the world. Gabriella was in a chair, sat sideways on to him, her hand up and rubbing the small of his back. She was talking, but he gave no sign of heeding her. He found physical exertion so tiring.

She was listening to Vincent, then, and watching Josh, but all the time she was thinking about Randall, in the video, leaning in to squint at the canvas, and talking to Josh, telling him where to put the paint. Holding out the phone to him. His voice. Her voice.

She turned to Vincent. 'I want what you want, Vincent, but we've just got to tread so carefully. Think about it from his point of view. The importance to him of all this.'

'Well, obviously.'

'And, really, we do need to go back to the studio, think about what it is we're dealing with. Take our time.'

'Take our time. Exactly.'

'Vincent, listen to me. I don't know *what* I think about the paintings. But if Randall wanted them shown, then we have to show them, now.' She gestured with her arm. 'Now' meant all of this: Josh, the film, Gabriella.

'We don't *know* what he wanted.'

'I know, but if. *If.* We can make it work, if it comes to that. If we take it step by step.' His look now was blank, an interrogation. It was her use of the word 'we'. He wanted her to repeat it, to empty it out, like you empty out a handbag for a security guard at the airport, to show what it contains. Her hand was on his arm and their eyes were locked and she was trying to make her look answer his question, to make it stand as surety for what she hoped was true belief. That they could make it work, whatever happened.

Then she caught a movement behind him. It was Gabriella, standing now, a signal for them to come out.

Justine slid open the door and stepped out. He was still facing out towards the trees and the ocean beyond, one hand thrust into the pocket of his hoodie. Gabriella's look said he was calm again.

The day was progressing, the grey cloud dissipated to let through a sort of glare. A breeze drifted across the decking, setting a lantern spinning on its wire.

Josh looked round at them. They were reconvened, sort of. Vincent leaned in the doorway, half in, half out, where Josh had stood earlier, a mere hour ago.

'Josh,' she said, and as she talked she chased after her own voice, trying to slip the leash of compassion around it, but the effort to make it convincing seemed to drain it of any truth. Her throat mangled everything that came through it. 'Josh, come here. We can sort this out.'

There was something that might have been a nod, might have been a shrug. She put her hand on his shoulder and noticed how, just before she did, Gabriella took hers from his other arm. She was fearful of shattering his trust, his belief in them all as people as real as himself.

They were embracing, but loosely. His one hand bunched in his pocket, the other laid flat around her waist. He patted her on the side, above her hip. A familiar gesture, that seemed almost one of commiseration, as if to apologise that this was the only intimacy left to them.

'It's just that fucker,' he said, nodding calmly across the decking at Vincent. 'I just can't stand the idea of him dictating what happens to my Dad.' He shrugged. 'Sorry.' The apology might have been aimed as much a Vincent as at her. And he disengaged himself from her, scraped out a chair and sat at the table. He took his hand out of his pocket. In it was his phone. He checked the screen, then put it on the table in front of him.

'He *trusted* him, Josh. That's why he wanted him as a *trustee*.'

'Not enough to tell him what he was doing, obviously.'

She sat down too. Vincent remained where he was.

'He didn't trust any of us enough for that,' she said.

'He trusted me.'

'Of course. He trusted you not to tell. That doesn't mean you alone get to decide what happens to them, Josh. We just need to take things slowly.'

311

'Take things slowly. It's funny. You all keep saying that.'

'These paintings, Josh. The thing to remember is that, at the moment, we are in control. The moment we put them out there, we lose control of them. The world will take over, and the world will not necessarily want what we want.'

Then a thrum and a trill. It was Josh's phone, drumming on the wooden slats of the table. But he didn't answer it. Instead, he stayed sitting in his chair and said, 'It's for you.'

Justine leaned forward and looked at the name on the display.

She picked it up and pressed answer.

'Carl,' she said.

'Oh. Justine. Hi. This is Joshua's phone, right? I just got this text.'

There was a sound and she looked round. A chair, that Vincent had just kicked over, spilling a plant pot and scattering tea lights, which rolled on their sides in weird little circles. He went in through the sliding door, spitting words and banging the glass with his hand as he went so it wobbled.

'Yes. This is his phone.'

'Is everything okay? He said there's something I've got to see. It's got to do with Randall, I take it?'

'Yes, Carl, it's to do with Randall.'

And she talked on, and her voice sounded more real to herself, disappearing into the clever little vortex of the phone, than at any other time over the last week. She took care not to look at Josh, or at Gabriella. She kept her voice sweetly neutral. She told the phone a day, and a time, and the address, and the clever phone told them to him, and then he was telling her something else, the phone was telling her something else, but she put it down on the table, still talking away, but tinnier now, more distant, and she slid it with a push towards Josh. He was talking to her, too, it seemed, but she ignored him and got up and walked into the house.

She called Vincent by his name. He didn't answer. He wasn't in the lounge, nor the kitchen. She called his name again and went through to the hall and along into the bedroom and out into the Japanese garden where, to judge by the gate standing open at the far end, he had just been. She took the round stones laid in sequence across the gravel, with its widening and intersecting patterns of rings, and past the flat silent pond to the gate and she went out through that and along the side of the house to the path down to the beach.

As she went past she glanced up through the section of slatted fence where you could see onto the decking, but it was empty. Josh and Gabriella must have gone inside too.

She breached the crest of the dune and there he was, walking past the remains of last night's fire. She walked faster, her feet slipping on the slope, feeling the sand creep in over the tops of her shallow slip-on shoes. She wanted to call his name again, but something prevented her.

He had stopped now, down at the water's edge, there where it laced the sand in wide shallow arcs, that looped on, without interruption, in each direction. And he stood, his hands by his sides, looking out towards the particular nothing that the ocean holds somewhere inside itself. She followed his gaze, as she passed the high water mark, walking now on sand that was firm and still half-wet, and the thought came back to her, like an echo, bouncing across the waves: that we made it here, together, to the far shore, we pilgrims. Not in the manner that any one of us would have suspected, but all the same.

'Hey,' she called, and again, 'Hey.'

He turned and they stood there, with only the wind between them, and the sound of the waves, that shushing sound they make, that is the sound of them depositing each tiny delivery of sand, and then the quiet scraping sound, as they claw back the next.

He rubbed at his eye and laughed, a dry, rueful, half-hollow laugh.

'What's so funny?' she said, although clearly nothing was funny.
He shrugged, as if in recognition of that fact.
And he said, 'What's so funny is that I've just worked it out.'
'What?'
'That big painting, the one in the video that you couldn't place.'
'Yes?'
'The one with everyone fucking everyone else, in a big circle.'
'Yes.'
'I've just realised where he put it.'

THE END

ACKNOWLEDGEMENTS

Thanks to all at UEA who read some or all of 'Randall' in its various stages, or talked it through, especially Giles Foden, Jake Huntley, Philip Langeskov, Priscilla Morris, Gavin McCrea, Seonaid Mackay, Anjali Joseph, Sam Byers. Also, Sam Riviere and Sophie Collins, and Imogen and Chris Lees, for their hospitality. To Dan Sturgis and Tom for insight and close reading, David Hayden for advice and encouragement. Neil Cole for audiovisuals. To my agent Andrew Gordon at David Higham Associates, and, at Galley Beggar, Sam Jordison, Eloise Millar and Henry Layte, ideal readers all. And to Sarah…